Praise for the books of *New York Times*
bestselling author

BEVERLY BARTON

"Beverly Barton writes with searing emotional
intensity that tugs at every heartstring."
—*New York Times* bestselling author Linda Howard

"Smart, sexy and scary as hell. Beverly Barton
just keeps getting better and better."
—*New York Times* bestselling author Lisa Jackson
on *The Fifth Victim*

"With its sultry Southern setting and well-drawn
characters, this richly textured tale ranks among
the best the genre has to offer."
—*Publishers Weekly* on *What She Doesn't Know*

"Hang on for another emotion-packed thriller."
—*RT Book Reviews* on *Worth Dying For*

"A riveting page-turner!"
—*The Best Reviews* on *On Her Guard*

Also available from
Beverly Barton
and HQN Books!

Witness
Dying for You
A Time to Die
Dangerous Deception
Worth Dying For

BEVERLY BARTON

'Til Death Do Us Part

Recycling programs
for this product may
not exist in your area.

ISBN-13: 978-0-373-77599-6

'TIL DEATH DO US PART

Copyright © 1996 by Harlequin Books S.A.

The publisher acknowledges the copyright holder of the individual works as follows:

BLACKWOOD'S WOMAN
Copyright © 1996 by Beverly Beaver

ROARKE'S WIFE
Copyright © 1997 by Beverly Beaver

CONTENTS

BLACKWOOD'S WOMAN

PROLOGUE

Trinidad, New Mexico
September 1925

WE MET IN our special place today and made love for the last time. Tomorrow Ernest, the boys and I will leave New Mexico and return to Virginia, and I will never see Benjamin Greymountain again. No, that isn't quite true, for I will see Benjamin through my precious memories until the day I die. We cannot be together, and yet we shall never truly be apart.

I had not experienced passion and real love until I met Benjamin. I would give my life to save his, but I cannot stay with him. I have given him my heart forever, but I cannot share my life with him.

He brought two rings with him. They are beautiful, intricately carved silver bands, each embedded with three small turquoise stones to represent the two of us and the child we can never have together. When he placed my ring upon my finger, I wept. He brushed away my tears and told me that he loved me. Then I placed his ring upon his finger and we pledged ourselves to each other for all eternity.

If only there weren't so many obstacles standing in the way of our happiness. No, I must not dwell on what could have been if our lives and the world around us were different. I must be thankful to have known such love, to have experienced such ecstasy.

For as long as I live—indeed, for as long as my soul exists—I shall love Benjamin Greymountain, and know that my love is returned in equal measure.

Joanna couldn't bear to read another word. She closed her great-grandmother's diary, tied the worn leather volume with the yellowed ribbon and laid the book inside her suitcase.

For the past six months, ever since she had returned to live in her parents' home and discovered the diary in Annabelle Beaumont's old trunk in the attic, Joanna had found solace in her ancestress's tragic love story.

In a world gone mad around her, Joanna had lost the ability to believe in love; and she could not imagine ever finding joy and passion in sex.

She had to admit that the months of therapy had helped, but nothing could ever erase the nightmarish memories of that fiendish face or the feel of those bruising hands. Even knowing that she and the three other women who'd bravely testified had put their attacker in prison for the rest of his life could never erase the past nor undo the pain. His punishment did not end their punishment. What he had done to them, and to others, had irrevocably changed their lives forever. Had changed Joanna's life forever....

Her fiancé had deserted her, her overprotective mother treated her as if she were dying, and she had resigned from her job at the museum, unable to cope with being around people every day. People who whispered behind her back.

But she knew she could not go on forever in this state of recovery. She was young and healthy, with the rest of her life ahead of her. And she had decided that she did not want to stay in Richmond where everyone knew what had happened to her, where her mother smothered her with attention, where she might run into her ex-fiancé and his new girlfriend. She'd made up her mind weeks ago, but had told her mother only today.

She, Joanna Beaumont, was moving to Trinidad, New Mexico, to find a new life, to paint the land and the people her great-grandmother had found so fascinating, and to dream of finding a man who would love her the way Benjamin Greymountain had loved Annabelle. A tender, sensitive and gentle man.

Joanna lifted from her suitcase a small leather pouch that had been tied to the diary she'd found in Annabelle's trunk. She loosened the drawstring, turned the pouch upside down and dumped the contents into her hand. She stared at the exquisitely lovely silver-and-turquoise ring, then picked it up and slipped it on the third finger of her right hand. It was a perfect fit.

CHAPTER ONE

No. ABSOLUTELY, POSITIVELY NO. Not now. Not today. Not on this lonely stretch of road. Not when it was ninety degrees in the shade.

Glancing at the red warning signal, Joanna Beaumont groaned. What could be wrong? Her Jeep Ranger was less than four years old and she had it serviced regularly. How dare it cause her a problem when she took such good care of it!

She wondered just how far she could drive with the warning light on before the vehicle quit. She was miles away from the ranch, even farther from Trinidad, and she'd left the reservation behind nearly two hours ago.

Clouds of white steam rose from beneath the Ranger's hood. Damn! That had to mean either the radiator was overheating or one of those stupid hoses had burst.

Admitting defeat, at least temporarily, Joanna pulled the Jeep to the side of the road, cut the engine and sat there fuming for several minutes. Well, no use just sitting. She popped the hood, opened the door, got out and marched around to the front of the Jeep. Water. She heard water dripping. No, she heard water pouring.

Billows of steam gushed from the engine. Joanna kicked the front bumper, then yelped when pain shot through her foot. If it had been a flat tire, she could have fixed it, but this was altogether different.

She gazed up at the midafternoon sun, blinding in its

intensity. Elena and Alex were in Santa Fe and wouldn't be home until late, so if she called the ranch, she'd have to ask Cliff Lansdell to help her. It wasn't that she disliked the ranch foreman, it was just that Cliff had a difficult time accepting the fact she wasn't interested in a relationship with him.

When the steam began to subside, Joanna leaned over cautiously and peeped beneath the hood. At first she couldn't see anything wrong, then she noticed a small tear in the radiator hose. Dammit! Well, she didn't have any choice. She'd just have to call Cliff and allow him to play her knight in shining armor.

Perspiration beaded on her forehead. Late springtime in northern New Mexico might be cooler than in the southern part of the state, but daytime temperatures could still rise to smoldering degrees in the month of May. When she'd first come to Trinidad, over four years ago, Joanna would have expected nothing but an arid desert region, had it not been for Annabelle Beaumont's descriptions of the mountains and trees and crystal-clear streams.

Slipping inside the Jeep, Joanna lifted her cellular phone and dialed the Blackwood ranch. The phone didn't ring. What now? Glancing at the phone's digital face, she saw that the battery was low. It was her own fault; she'd forgotten to charge the battery last night. How could she have been so stupid?

Now what was she going to do? Well, there was only one thing to do—start walking. It was a good ten miles to the ranch house, but if she was lucky, someone she knew would come along and give her a lift. Trinidad was a small town and she knew practically the whole population.

Locking the Jeep, Joanna swung her enormous leather purse, containing her 25-mm semiautomatic, over her shoulder and headed straight up the road. She hadn't gone

far when she thought she heard the sound of drums—
somewhere far away, just a distant rumble. Perhaps it was
thunder. Well, rain in New Mexico wasn't impossible.
Maybe an electrical storm was brewing. Glancing up, she
saw the sky was still clear. And blue, so incredibly blue.
Sparse, virgin-white fluffs of cloud floated overhead.

Lowering her eyes to protect them from the glare of
the sun, she saw a horse and a lone rider on a nearby flat-
topped hill toward the north. Blinking once, twice, she felt
certain the image was a mirage. But no. They were still
there. A big man astride a magnificent black-and-white
Appaloosa.

The sky at their backs, the afternoon sun coating them
with a coppery gold glow, man and horse resembled a
bronze statue. Joanna's heart pounded. Her palms grew
clammy. There was nothing to fear—not in Trinidad, not
from the fine people she knew and respected. Surely this
man was from the ranch, a hand she would recognize as
soon as he rode closer.

But he did not move, simply sat there high above her,
staring down at her. She waved at him. He didn't respond.

"Hey, there, are you from the Blackwood ranch?" she
called out as she walked off the road and began to climb
the hill. "My radiator hose sprung a leak."

The man didn't answer her, but he did direct his horse
into movement. She continued toward her potential res-
cuer; he rode slowly in her direction. Joanna swung her
purse across her chest, unzipped the top pouch and felt inside for her gun. She sighed when she felt the cool metal.
If this man turned out to be a stranger, he was a possible
threat. Joanna never took chances when it came to her
safety. Since surviving the brutal rape nearly five years ago,
she had purchased a small handgun and taken several self-
defense classes.

When the horse stopped a good twenty feet away, Joanna stared at the rider. She didn't recognize the man, had never seen him before in her life, and yet she had the oddest sensation that she somehow knew him. Her whole body trembled, but the quivering riot was contained within, showing only a slight tremor in her hands. She could not stop staring at the man even though the very sight of him created a sense of foreboding.

He was big, wide-shouldered, long-legged and narrow-hipped, and probably well over six feet tall. But it was not the perfection of his body that held Joanna spellbound; it was his gloriously rugged masculine face. Straight, jet-black hair that touched his collar at the back of his neck had blown down across his forehead, escaping his tan Stetson. Over his left eye he wore a black patch. He glared at her with his uncovered eye, the look unnerving her. Joanna swallowed, and tried to look away. She couldn't.

In one glance she took in his long, straight nose, his cleft chin, and the hard set of his full lips. Whoever he was, he was Native American, or at least part Native American. If he was Navajo, perhaps he would respond to their standard greeting.

"Yá' át' ééh," she said.

He merely glared at her even harder, and she instinctively knew he had understood her words.

In the four years she had lived in New Mexico, she had accomplished her goals of building a new life and establishing herself as an artist, but her romantic fantasy of finding a man like Annabelle's Benjamin Greymountain had remained an elusive dream. Until now.

Don't be ridiculous, she told herself. Stop acting like an idiot. She forced herself to look directly at the horse. Breathing in deeply, she took several tentative steps in the stranger's direction.

"Can you help me?" she asked. "My Jeep ran hot and I need to get to the Blackwood ranch."

He dismounted slowly, placing one booted foot and then the other on the ground. Joanna swallowed hard. He was a lot taller than six feet. Closer to six-four. And his eye wasn't brown as she'd thought; it was some light shade of amber and almost translucent in its paleness.

He stared at her, unsmiling, his brow wrinkled. He crossed his arms over his chest and inspected Joanna from head to toe. She slipped her hand inside her open purse, clutching her gun. Her instincts warned her that this man was dangerous, but somehow she didn't think he intended to do her any bodily harm.

"Look, I need to get to the Blackwood ranch. The main house is about ten miles from here," Joanna said.

He took a step toward her. Without thinking, she stepped backward. Realizing what she'd done, she stopped, tilted her chin and looked directly at him.

"Can you help me or not?" What was the matter with him? Was he deaf?

"I won't be heading back toward the Blackwood ranch for a while." His deep baritone voice had a gritty quality, a gravelly tone.

"Are you a new ranch hand?"

"No."

She wished he would quit inspecting her. She was beginning to feel like a bug under a microscope. "You realize you're on Blackwood property out here, don't you?"

Just a hint of a smile twitched his lips and then vanished completely, returning his mouth to its former frown. "If you're not in a hurry to get back to the house, you're welcome to come with me. Otherwise—" he glanced at the long, lonely stretch of road "—you'll have to walk."

Was he out of his mind? Did he think she'd go riding

off only God knew where, with a total stranger? "Can't you take me to the ranch and then come back and do whatever it is you were going to do?"

"Why should I change my plans?" Uncrossing his arms, he stroked the big Appaloosa stallion's neck.

"I suppose saying it would be the gentlemanly thing to do would have no meaning for you, would it?"

"None whatsoever," he said, turning his back to her.

"Well, what's it going to be? Are you riding with me or are you walking?"

She had every intention of telling him she would walk. Removing her hand from her purse, she turned around and faced the road. She glanced over her shoulder and saw him mounting his horse. The sun reflected off the silver ring on the third finger of his right hand. Since living in New Mexico she'd seen countless silver-and-turquoise rings, but none that was identical to the one she wore—Annabelle Beaumont's keepsake of love. The ring the stranger wore was an exact match. Was it possible that it was Benjamin Greymountain's ring? But how would this man have come into possession of the ring?

The stranger motioned the Appaloosa forward, coming straight toward Joanna. Slowing the horse to a standstill, he leaned his body to one side.

"Last chance." He held out his hand.

Joanna stared at his big hand, her vision focusing on the silver ring. Her heart hammered in her chest; the beating thundered in her ears. She looked up into his dark face—into that pale amber eye—and swayed toward him. She felt as if he was beckoning her.

"Who are you?" she asked, her heartbeat roaring in her ears like a hurricane wind.

"Who wants to know?" He stared at her, his gaze hard and intense.

"I'm Joanna Beaumont. I live on the Blackwood ranch."

Withdrawing his outstretched hand, he inspected her from head to toe, as if she were a prize piece of horse-flesh he was considering buying. Joanna stiffened her back, clenched her teeth and glared at him. Just who did he think he was? He's an arrogant, macho bastard, Joanna answered her own question.

"So, you're the Southern belle from Virginia who converted one of the old bunkhouses into a home."

He focused his attention on her face, then ran his gaze down her throat and to the V of her partially unbuttoned blouse. A wide trickle of sweat cascaded down her throat and between her breasts. She didn't like the way he was looking at her, and yet her body responded to his blatantly sexual appraisal. Her nipples tightened, jutting outward, and she knew he saw their hardened outlines pressing against her damp blouse.

"How do you know who I am?" If he didn't stop staring at her, she was going to scream.

"My sister has sung your praises to me on numerous occasions, Ms. Beaumont."

"Your sister? Elena?"

He nodded. The corners of his lips twitched as if he were going to smile. But he didn't. He just kept staring at her, the heat of his gaze unnerving her.

"Then you're—"

"J. T. Blackwood."

They stared at each other for endless moments, the hot sun beating down on them, an eerie quiet all around.

"If you're not in a big hurry to get back to the ranch, I'll give you a lift." J.T. broke the silence, damning himself for allowing this fiery redhead to arouse him. He had learned long ago that "ladies" fascinated by the "noble savage" were to be avoided at all costs. "When we get back to the ranch, I'll send someone to take care of your Jeep."

Joanna hesitated. She knew all about Elena's older half brother, the owner of the Blackwood ranch. And what Joanna knew about the man, she didn't like. He represented everything she disapproved of in a man. He was a big, rugged, untamed macho guy, a former Secret Service agent who was now a partner in a private security firm based in Atlanta, Georgia. And according to Elena, he had never had a truly serious and meaningful relationship in his life.

"Look, lady, are you riding with me or are you walking back to the ranch?"

He held out his hand to her again. She stared at the silver-and-turquoise ring on his finger. Benjamin Greymountain's ring.

She would be stupid if she walked ten miles when she could ride, wouldn't she? And it wasn't as if J. T. Blackwood was a stranger. She'd be perfectly safe with him. Besides, if he pulled any type of macho stunt, he just might not be safe with her.

She reached out to him; he grasped her arm, lifting her off her feet. He swept her up onto the horse, placing her in front of him and draping his arm around her waist. Joanna closed her eyes, willing her heart to quiet, questioning her own sanity. From what she'd heard, she didn't even like J. T. Blackwood. So why was she aroused by his very nearness?

J.T. guided the horse from a slow trot down the flat-topped hill and into a steady gallop across the road, then up into the wooded area at the very edge of the Blackwood property. Joanna glanced down at his muscular arm that held her close to him. She felt the hardness of his chest, felt the heat from his body and could not mistake the ridge in his jeans that pressed against her hip.

A sudden sense of panic swept through her. Had she lost her mind? Had the past taught her nothing?

"Where—where are you going?" she asked.

"To a small stream a little higher up the mountain here. It's a place I've thought about for years," he said. "I've been gone a long time. I just wanted to see if things were the way I remembered them."

She tried not to lean back against him, but the upward climb made sitting straight impossible. His arm tightened around her. She sucked in a loud breath. "You don't visit the ranch often, do you? I've been living in Trinidad for over four years, and we've never met."

"I come back about once a year," he said.

"It seems your yearly visits the past few years have coincided with my trips to Virginia to visit my mother."

"Yeah, well, I thought it best."

"What do you mean? Are you saying that you deliberately timed your visits for when I was away?"

"Yeah."

"But why? I don't understand."

"My sister's been trying to play matchmaker, wanting to throw the two of us together. Don't tell me you didn't know."

"No, I had no idea." Joanna tensed as he tightened his hold about her waist and the bulge in his jeans pressed harder against her. She tried to scoot away from him, but had no room to maneuver.

"Elena likes you a lot," he said. "I'm not sure why, but since she's determined to see me married off, she's been pitching you as a candidate ever since you two became friends."

"I assure you, Mr. Blackwood, that I had no idea Elena

was trying to— Well, I could have let her know I'm not the least bit interested. She's told me all about you, and you're not the type of man I want."

"Is that right?" He whispered the words against her ear, his warm breath fanning the loose tendrils that had escaped her ponytail.

She shivered, the motion completely involuntary. Her body ached with the start of a sweet longing that had lain dormant in her for a long time. For five years. No matter how many men she'd dated, and there had been quite a few—she had never felt any real desire—until now. And she didn't understand why; if and when she gave herself to a man, she would be the one in control. And a man like J. T. Blackwood would never relinquish his power to anyone, most certainly not a woman.

J.T. spread his big hand out across Joanna's waist, resting the tips of several fingers on her stomach. She drew in a sharp breath and squirmed against him. Why the hell didn't she sit still? J.T. thought. He was already so aroused he felt he was going to burst out of his jeans. She had to know how he was feeling. Was she taunting him?

He hated the effect Joanna had on him. He wasn't accustomed to such a strong, instant attraction, not since he'd been a teenager and got hard just smelling a girl's perfume.

And Joanna Beaumont was the last woman on earth he wanted to get all hot and bothered about. She was like the girl old John Thomas Blackwood had picked out for him to marry years ago. The girl who'd laughed in his face and told him bedding an Indian was fun and exciting, but marrying one was something she'd never do. Oh, yeah, he'd known his share of pretty, wealthy socialites over the years—women who couldn't get enough of him in bed, but were ashamed to introduce him to their friends.

As J.T. caressed her waist and stomach, Joanna told herself not to be afraid. If he tried anything, she'd shoot him. She laid her hand over his, halting his caress.

"How do you like living on the ranch?" he asked.

"I love it." His hand beneath hers felt hard and hot and tense.

"I wasn't in favor of your renovating the bunkhouse, but Elena insisted." J.T. threaded his fingers through hers, gripping her hand in his strong grasp.

"Did Elena tell you that we met a few months after I moved to Trinidad and in less than a year we became good friends?" He didn't respond; and he didn't release his hold on her hand. "I persuaded her to rent the unused bunkhouse to me. She said that once you'd seen what I did to it, you'd approve."

"I've seen it," he said. "It's very…Southwestern. You've obviously spent quite a bit of money on the place."

His breath was warm against the top of her head. Joanna hated the way this big, dark man made her feel. It had been such a long time since she'd felt anything close to sexual desire that she had a difficult time understanding her re-action to J. T. Blackwood. But she couldn't deny that she ached and throbbed with a need she thought had died the night Lenny Plott had raped her.

"I make a very good living with my paintings. Oil and watercolor. And my charcoal and ink drawings are in great demand." Joanna jerked on her hand, wanting desperately to free herself from his hold.

He released her hand, but kept his arm around her waist. "Yeah, I suppose you do. You're talented. I'll give you that. I've seen a couple of your paintings. The ones you gave Elena. You painted them on the Navajo reser-vation, didn't you?"

Joanna noticed they were moving higher into the mountains, the path becoming smooth near the ridge, the cottonwood trees more abundant. The sun had moved lower in the western sky. Somewhere in the distance she heard the sound of flowing water.

"You didn't grow up on the reservation, did you?" she asked and immediately felt his body tense. Had she said something wrong?

"You knew the minute you saw me, didn't you?" The words growled from his throat.

"Knew what?" she asked.

"Even before I told you I was Elena's half brother, you took one look at me and knew I wasn't a white man, that I wasn't a *bilagáana.* You even called out a Navajo greeting to me."

"Yes, of course, I knew. Considering the part of New Mexico we're in, I assumed you were Navajo, or at least part Navajo." Was that it? Did he resent his Native American heritage as much as Elena said he did? Did he dislike having his ancestry recognized? If so, he was certainly the exception to the rule. The Navajo she had met while living in New Mexico had all been fiercely proud of being one of the *Diné,* as they called themselves. "You should be proud of your Native American heritage."

"So polite," he said. "So politically correct. Not Indian or redskin or savage, but Native American." He clicked his tongue against the roof of his mouth. "Such a Southern lady."

"What gave me away?" She tried to sound teasing, hoping to defuse some of the tension radiating between them. "Couldn't have been my accent."

"What's the real reason a Southern belle like you is living in New Mexico, roughing it?"

She thought the sound he made might have been a begrudging chuckle, but it sounded more like a fractured grunt.

"I'm sure Elena told you that I came out here to paint. I'm fascinated by the land and by the people."

"So you're fascinated by the noble savage, huh? Do you have a particular fascination for half-breed Navajo men?"

"You're being insulting." Joanna resented the way he made her interest in the Navajo seem sordid and ugly. His comment tarnished her foolish dream of finding true love the way Annabelle Beaumont had done.

"For the record, I'm half Navajo and half Scotch-Irish." He eased his arm from her waist down to her belly, his hand pushing her backward, forcing her hips deeper into his arousal.

"Stop it!" She inadvertently squirmed against him as she maneuvered her purse in front of her where she could reach inside. "Take your hands off me. I knew Elena's big brother had a reputation for being a real stud with the ladies, but I didn't think he was the type to force himself on a woman."

"Are you kidding?" J.T.'s laughter was hard and cold. "I've never forced myself on a woman. They usually throw themselves at me."

Joanna jerked out the 25-mm. If this brute thought he could intimidate her, then he had another thought coming. No one controlled Joanna Beaumont except Joanna Beaumont!

J.T. saw the gun in her hand. Hellfire! What did she think she was going to do, shoot him? What was wrong with her, anyway? She'd made it abundantly clear she didn't like him, that his reputation had preceded him and she'd been put off by what Elena had told her about him. But he couldn't control his arousal any more than she seemed able to control her obvious desire for him. But if she thought he was going to force anything on her, she was crazy. He'd assumed she was as hot as he was.

The moment he'd seen her a few yards away from the stalled Jeep, J.T. had known the redhead had to be Elena's friend Joanna Beaumont. His half sister had been trying to pair him up with the Virginia debutante for the past three years. But the last thing J.T. wanted was to be part of some spoiled Southern belle's New Mexico adventure. She wouldn't be the first woman in his life to think a brief affair with a half-breed exciting.

But this trip home to the ranch was going to be a vacation. The first real vacation J.T. had had in the six years since he'd left the Secret Service and joined Sam Dundee's private security agency in Atlanta.

"Put your gun away, lady. I'm no threat to you. I like my women willing, believe me."

"Well, I'm not willing. Not now. Not ever." She clutched the gun tightly. "I want you to take me to the ranch house right this minute!"

"I told you when I offered you a ride that it would be a while before I went back that way." J.T. guided Washington closer to the stream.

"And I just told you to take me back to the ranch house right now. If you're smart, you'll do what I tell you to do. After all, I have a gun and you don't."

"Lady, is this any way to treat a man doing you a favor?"

"I don't consider your coming on to me as doing me a favor. I asked for help, not for you to...to—" she sought for the right word "—for you to proposition me."

He snorted. "I didn't proposition you. I just asked if half-breed men fascinated you."

"And you—you—" He had pulled her against him,

making her acutely aware of the fact that he was still very
aroused. His nearness created an unnerving sexual awareness in her—the first she had experienced since the rape.
And that desire frightened her. When this man, who wore
a silver-and-turquoise ring identical to hers, had swept
her off her feet and into his arms, her desire for him had
unsettled her equilibrium.

J.T. slowed Washington to a standstill, dropped the
reins and reached around the woman's body, grabbing her
hand. An angry woman with a gun was dangerous. Joanna
struggled against his superior strength, but in the end all
her fighting did was toss both of them off the Appaloosa
and onto the ground. She lost her .25 in the fall, the small
handgun clanking loudly as it hit a nearby boulder.

J.T. was thankful the damned thing hadn't fired. A stray
bullet could have killed either of them. Now Joanna pelted
her small fists against his chest, fighting him like a wild-
cat, and with absolutely no rhyme or reason to her hysterical battle. No, that wasn't exactly true, J.T. acknowledged.
He *was* a stranger. Despite the fact that he was Elena's
brother, Joanna really didn't know him. For some absurd
reason the woman assumed he was intent on ravaging her,
with or without her permission.

"I'm not going to hurt you," he said in as calm and
reasonable a voice as he could muster while the two of
them rolled around over the uneven terrain. "But you're
going to hurt yourself if you don't stop acting like this."

Joanna paid no heed to his warning. All she could think
about was the fact that she was lying on the ground, out
in the middle of nowhere, with a huge, hard man on top
of her.

J.T. grabbed one of her wrists, then managed to grip
the other, manacling them both in one of his hands. He
pressed his body against hers, cursing himself for being

aroused. Squirming beneath him, tossing her head from side to side as she jerked her shoulders in a vain effort to free herself, Joanna glared up at him and let out a blood-curdling scream.

In one swift move, J.T. stood, dragging the screaming redhead to her feet beside him. He released her immediately. Her breathing deep and ragged, she glowered at him, a pink flush staining her cheeks. Her eyes, such a dark green they appeared almost black in her anger, focused on him with rage as she balled her hands into fists.

J.T. lifted his arms above his head, high in the air, as a gesture of surrender. He hoped she would realize the error of her assumption and calm herself.

"What the hell happened to you?" he asked. "I apologize if anything I said insulted you or made you think I was going to attack you."

"It wasn't—" Joanna gulped for air "—just what you said. It was what you were doing."

"I didn't realize you hated the way I was touching you. I thought—"

"You had no right to touch me, to caress me, to press yourself against me like that!" She couldn't bring herself to look at him, to make eye contact.

"Lady, you didn't protest anything I did until I asked if you had a particular fascination for half-breeds. And then, you go crazy and brandish a gun in my face."

He was right. She had enjoyed his touch, had gloried in the feelings of desire he created within her, even though those strong emotions had also frightened her...frightened her enough to make her threaten him.

Had she overreacted? This wouldn't be the first time. For nearly a year after the rape, she hadn't been able to bear for a man to even shake her hand. But it had been well over three years since she'd allowed a man's nearness to scare her into acting like an idiot. Dear God, she had thought all the irrational fear was over, that she had truly put the past behind her, that she was in control. But J. T. Blackwood had shown her that she was still a rape survivor; a woman who could not trust any man.

"Maybe I did overreact," Joanna said, then immediately qualified her admission. "I'm not saying I did, just that I might have. I don't like your type. I never have and I never will. You think women are fair game, don't you? That all you have to do is show an interest and a woman will automatically succumb to you."

"Can you stand there and tell me that you weren't just as turned on as I was?"

Lifting her downcast eyes, she glared at him, wanting to scream, no, no, no, a thousand times no! But she knew it would be a lie. And he would know she was lying. J. T. Blackwood was a man of the world, a man who'd known a lot of women.

"Look, if it makes you feel any better, I'm not any happier about the situation than you are," he said. "I don't want to be attracted to you. You're not my type, either."

"That's good to know." Joanna couldn't seem to stop herself from glancing down at the zipper in his jeans. Feeling the burning sting of a blush warming her neck, she turned her head.

"A guy can't hide it very well when he's aroused," J.T. told her. "But you've got my word that while I'm at the ranch, I'll steer clear of you. We'll forget about what happened today. If we run into each other, we'll be cordial, but keep our distance. Agreed?"

"Agreed." She watched him walk over, reach down and pick up her gun. Holding her breath, she waited until he came over and handed it to her. "Thank you."

"Put it away, Ms. Beaumont. Guns should be used only by people who know how to use them."

"I know how to use my gun," she said.

"Fine. Just don't ever try to use it on me again."

"Don't ever make me think you're going to attack me."

"That's a promise."

"Fine," she said. "Will you take me back to the ranch, now?"

"Why not?" He grunted. "You've ruined any chance for me to enjoy this place. Whenever I come home, I always ride up here to this stream. It's been a favorite place of mine since I was a kid."

"I'm sorry I ruined your homecoming, Mr. Blackwood, but I didn't plan on our meeting the way we did."

"Call me J.T."

"I'd rather not, since it's obvious we aren't going to be friends."

"Or lovers."

Every nerve in Joanna's body quivered with awareness. "Or lovers," she repeated.

"Come on. Let's head back to the ranch."

She followed him to the big Appaloosa, waited for him to mount, then hesitated when he offered her his hand.

"You can sit behind me," he told her.

"All right." She mounted the horse, sitting behind him, relieved that she wouldn't have to endure the hard pressure of his body against her hips on the ride back to the ranch.

Within a few minutes, Joanna slipped her arms around J.T.'s waist in order to keep her balance as they rode down the side of the mountain. She found herself wanting to lay her head against his broad back and hug herself tightly to his big body.

What she felt was wrong, she thought; her overwhelming need for this man—this stranger. J. T. Blackwood might be wearing Benjamin Greymountain's ring, but he was not Joanna's dream lover. He couldn't be!

CHAPTER TWO

"NOT TONIGHT, ELENA. Please." Joanna clutched the portable telephone in her hand. "I'm tired from today's ordeal with my Jeep. I just want to take a nice long bath, look over the sketches I did at the reservation, and go to bed early."

"But this is J.T.'s first night home and I've planned a special dinner," Elena pleaded. "You don't have to stay long after we eat. But come over for a while. I was counting on your being here."

"I've already met your brother. Remember, he's the one who gave me a ride back to the ranch."

"I don't know what happened between you two, but whatever it was, I'm sure we can straighten it out tonight."

"I don't want to ruin your plans, but—"

"Then don't ruin my plans. Just come eat dinner and you can leave as soon as we smooth things over between you and J.T."

Joanna breathed a deep sigh. Stepping up on the raised floor of what had once been the back porch of the old bunkhouse and was now her huge bathroom, Joanna began unbuttoning her dirty blouse.

"There's nothing to smooth over between your brother and me. We understand each other perfectly." Joanna leaned over, turned on the faucets and watched the water flow into the big, pedestaled, cast-iron bathtub she'd found at an antique shop in Albuquerque. "Mr. Blackwood and

I have agreed that we don't like each other, that we aren't each other's type and that we have no intention of allowing you to play matchmaker."

"Just what did J.T. say to you?"

Joanna opened a bottle of scented bubble bath, sloshed a generous amount into the running water and set the container down on the unfinished, wide-plank floor.

"He told me that you'd been trying to get the two of us together for several years now and he has avoided coming to the ranch except when I was out of town."

"That no-account brother of mine!" Elena said. "He had no right to say something like that to—"

"Why on earth would you ever think your brother and I would be interested in each other? If I were looking for a man, I'd want someone more like your Alex. Gentle and kindhearted. A fellow artist. And someone who loves New Mexico the way I've come to love it."

"Oh, Jo, you need someone special in your life and so does J.T." Elena let out an exaggerated sigh. "All right, so I was wrong to hope you two were a perfect match. Come to dinner and I promise no more matchmaking."

"Not tonight." Joanna finished unbuttoning her blouse and dropped it to the floor, then unzipped her jeans.

"You've become my best friend," Elena said. "And J.T. is my only brother. Even if there can't be anything romantic between the two of you, I'd still like for you two to be friends. J.T.'s taking a real vacation and he's going to be staying a couple of weeks this time."

"If he's going to be here a couple of weeks, then there's no hurry in our getting to know each other, is there?"

"Isn't there anything I can say to get you to change your mind about dinner tonight?"

Tell me your brother isn't going to be there, Joanna

thought. "No, I'm afraid not. But…well, I'll come to dinner one night before Mr. Blackwood leaves. Okay?"

"Mr. Blackwood? He must have really made you angry today," Elena said. "Look, his bark is a lot worse than his bite. J.T.'s pretty cynical about life, and he's stubborn as a mule, but underneath, he's a good guy. After Mama died, he came to the reservation and brought me back to the ranch with him. He didn't have to do that."

"Look, Elena, I know how much you love your brother. That's fine and good, but just because you love him doesn't mean everyone else has to."

"Whew! He really pushed all your buttons, didn't he?"

"Drop it, okay? I'm not coming to dinner tonight and that's final." Joanna stepped out of her sandals, slid her jeans to her feet and kicked out of them.

"Okay. But—"

"We'll talk tomorrow. Bye." Joanna punched the off button on the telephone, tossed it on top of her discarded clothes and removed her underwear.

Standing naked in the middle of the stucco-walled bathroom, she stretched and gazed up at the slanted, split-log ceiling. She wanted to forget all about her disastrous encounter with J. T. Blackwood. She wanted to wash his scent off her hands and arms and face. She wanted to erase the image of him astride his Appaloosa stallion. And more than anything, she wanted to forget the way she'd felt when her body had been nestled intimately against his.

Joanna stepped into the warm, perfumed water, immersing her body beneath the layers of foaming bubbles. Reaching behind her, she lifted a gold washcloth from the black metal rack above the tub. She lathered the cloth with her moisturizing soap and scrubbed her face. After rinsing, she clutched the cloth in her hand and glanced

down at the silver-and-turquoise ring on her finger. The
ring Annabelle Beaumont's lover had made for her.

Where had J. T. Blackwood gotten the matching ring?
The one her great-grandmother had been certain Benjamin Greymountain wore till the day he died, as she had
worn hers. Had some member of Benjamin's family sold
the ring years ago? Perhaps they'd given it away. Or—was
it possible that J.T. was somehow related to Benjamin?

More than once, Joanna had been tempted to ask Elena
if she had ever heard of a Benjamin Greymountain or if
she knew how to trace his descendants. But despite her
close friendship with Elena, she hadn't been able to bring
herself to share the secret affair her great-grandmother
had written about—in great detail—in her diary. There
were times when Joanna herself felt like an intruder when
she read Annabelle's words. Somehow it hadn't seemed
right to tell anyone else about Annabelle and Benjamin's
scandalous love.

But tomorrow, she would ask Elena about J.T.'s ring
and explain her curiosity by saying she'd noted the similarity between his ring and her own. And she would ask
Elena to come to her home; that way she wouldn't have
to go up to the main house and run the risk of seeing J.T.
again.

THE SUN HUNG low in the sky, not quite prepared to set
and put an end to the day. Approaching twilight washed
an orange-gold translucence over the New Mexico landscape Joanna saw outside her windows.

After her long leisurely bath, she'd slipped into a
floor-length pink-and-lavender cotton gown. Barefoot,
she traipsed into the kitchen, opened the refrigerator and
retrieved a large pitcher of iced tea she'd made yesterday.
She poured herself a tall glass, added ice cubes and pulled

out one of the Windsor armchairs at her dining table. Before she could sit, she heard a forceful knock at her back door. Who could that be? Surely, not Elena.

Walking toward the back door, she peeked out the window over her sink, but couldn't see anyone. "Who's there?" she asked. She never opened her door without taking every precaution, even out here on the ranch where she knew everyone. Even now, there were times when she checked under her bed and inside her closets after returning from a trip.

"It's J. T. Blackwood," his voice thundered, deep, rough and gritty.

"What do you want?"

"A minute of your time."

"Go away." She did not want to see him again. Not now. Not ever. And she certainly didn't want him to see her in her simple cotton nightgown, her face scrubbed clean and her hair pinned atop her head in a disheveled mess.

"Joanna, open the door and talk to me." He waited for her reply and when she said nothing, he chuckled, a dark, tough laugh that rumbled from his chest. "If you don't talk to me, I won't be able to go back to the house and face Elena. She's convinced I was rude and hateful to you and said something that hurt your feelings. She sent me over here to apologize."

"I never told her that you were rude and hateful. I don't need an apology."

"Dammit, woman, open the door, allow me to apologize and then call my sister and tell her you've forgiven me. Otherwise my vacation will be completely ruined before it even starts."

Hesitantly, fearfully, Joanna opened the door. Just a narrow crack at first, but the moment she saw J.T.'s smirky grin, she flung the door wide open. She would not give him the satisfaction of knowing how nervous he made her.

"Come in." She swept her hand through the air in a cordial invitation.

Her heart fluttered and her stomach twisted into knots. He was raw, proud, masculine beauty. Every line of his face was hard, chiseled perfection.

He removed his tan Stetson and stepped forward; she stepped backward. He walked past her into her kitchen; she left the back door open.

He had showered and changed into clean faded jeans and a shirt of muted green-and-blue plaid. He smelled slightly of some manly-yet-expensive aftershave.

"Still rustic, but with every modern convenience," he said, glancing around. "Nice. Very nice."

"Thank you." Joanna felt undressed and vulnerable, wearing nothing but her nightgown, and J. T. Blackwood wasn't helping any by looking at her as if he found her greatly desirable. "Now, get the apology over with and then I'll call Elena."

"Aren't you worried about insects?" J.T. nodded toward the open door.

Joanna wanted to slam it shut, but instead, she closed it slowly. "The apology?"

"Right." He walked over to her, reached out and took her right hand in his.

She tried to pull out of his grasp, but he held tightly. "Please release my hand." She glanced down at their clasped hands and saw their twin rings, identical in every way except size.

"What are you so afraid of, lady?" He loosened his hold on her hand, allowing her to pull free.

"I'm not afraid of anything." She enunciated each word clearly and distinctly. "I'm just annoyed that you disturbed me. I like my solitude and I don't appreciate your bothering me."

"This little visit was Elena's idea," J.T. said.

"So you've already told me." Joanna swallowed, then looked her visitor square in the eye. "If you're going to apologize, then do it and leave."

"I'm sorry for whatever I said or did today that might have offended you. How's that? Was the apology good enough for you to tell Elena that you and I are friends now?"

"Friends? You expect me to tell Elena that we're friends?"

"She says that she's given up her plans to unite us romantically, but she still would like to see us become friends. So how about it? Tell Elena a little white lie and get us both off the hook."

J.T. watched the play of emotions on this lovely woman's face, her expression going from one of surprise and agitation to one of amusement. She smiled at him. His stomach tightened; his body hardened. Hell! This wasn't supposed to happen. Women's smiles didn't have this kind of effect on him. Not ever!

"Apology accepted," Joanna said. "I'll call Elena and tell her we're friends now."

"Thanks. It'll make my life a lot easier." J.T. allowed his gaze to follow the lines of her round, firm body, clearly silhouetted by the warm evening sunlight shining in the window and through the thin cotton material of her nightgown. Lord help him, he didn't think he'd ever seen a more beautiful sight. He grew painfully aroused just looking at her.

"Dammit," he muttered under his breath. That was all he needed—for her to notice his arousal. She'd never call Elena and set things straight. And if he couldn't pacify his sister, he'd just have to leave the ranch. In the twelve years since he'd gone to the reservation and brought Elena home with him, J.T. had grown to care for his half sister more than he'd ever thought he could care for anyone. He knew she meant well, trying to fix him up with Joanna. He couldn't make her understand that marriage and family life weren't for everyone.

"How long has Elena been trying to find you a girl-friend?" Joanna asked.

"Oh, she's not looking for a girlfriend," J.T. said. "She's looking for a wife."

"A wife? And she actually thought that I... I mean, she considered the possibility that you and I—"

"Despite being twenty-seven, Elena is still rather naive. She doesn't realize that there are a lot of women who cringe at the thought of being married to a half-breed like me."

"Mr. Blackwood, I didn't mean..." Joanna gazed into his good eye, that golden brown glittering eye, filled with anger and pain and—passion. "Your Navajo ancestry has nothing to do with why I dislike you." Indeed, his Navajo ancestry beckoned to Joanna, since it was another link, besides the silver-and-turquoise ring, that connected him to Benjamin Greymountain, and to the tender, gentle fantasy man she had dreamed of for over four years.

"I don't care what you meant or why you dislike me." He took several steps toward her.

Unmoving, she held her breath. Reaching out, he stroked her cheek. "You don't like me, but you want me. Oh, yeah, I've known your type before."

Without thinking about what she was doing, Joanna lifted her hand and laid it atop his while he caressed her cheek. "No, you haven't known my type before. You've never known anyone like me." She removed her hand.

He stared at her for a split second, uncertain whether he could believe her or not. Hell, it didn't matter. He wasn't going to allow Joanna Beaumont to get under his skin. While visiting the ranch, he'd find some way to avoid her or he'd cut short his vacation.

He grabbed her chin, tilting her face. "Call Elena and get me out of hot water, then I'll stay out of your way."

Joanna nodded. "I'll stay out of your way, too."

He made no reply, just turned, walked to the back door, opened it and left. Joanna stared at the open door for endless moments, then ran across the kitchen and slammed it shut. What right did a man like that have to wear Benjamin's ring? Benjamin, a man who'd been capable of the deepest, truest, most unselfish love? It was plain to see that J. T. Blackwood didn't know the first thing about love—real love, the kind Benjamin and Annabelle had shared.

AFTER HE'D SPENT several hours tossing and turning, J.T. gave up trying to get any sleep and got out of bed. His grandfather's bed. Old John Thomas Blackwood. The meanest, orneriest son of a bitch who'd ever lived. The man his father had named him for. The man who had forbidden his only son to marry a dirty Indian. The man who hadn't acknowledged J.T.'s existence until J.T.'s father had died and left the old reprobate without an heir. The man who'd come to the reservation when J.T. was five and taken him from his mother.

J.T., naked as the day he was born, threw open the double doors leading from his bedroom to the attached patio. The cool night air caressed his bronze skin. He ran his hand through his thick hair—hair he hadn't worn long since his first haircut at the age of five.

"Can't have you looking like one of those damned

savages," old John Thomas had said. "Bad enough you've got that woman's coloring. But from now on, boy, you're a Blackwood. And that means you're a cowboy, not an Indian."

And that was exactly what J.T. had become—a cowboy. He'd learned to rope and ride and herd cattle. Although there had never been any real love lost between him and his grandfather, he had come to love the ranch.

He supposed that was why—even though he couldn't live in New Mexico, couldn't face being torn between his two heritages—he always returned to the ranch. He loved this land, this wild, untamed wilderness, as much as the old man had loved it; as much as his Blackwood ancestors, who had fought and died to claim the countless acres that now comprised one of the largest ranches in northern New Mexico, had loved it.

And he loved the land as much as his mother's people did. The Navajo. A people he did not know, except through his half sister. A people and a heritage his grandfather had taught him to deny.

From the side patio, J.T. could see the back of the old bunkhouse. Joanna Beaumont's home. How long would it take for a society girl to tire of the West, to tire of painting the natives and return to Virginia where she belonged?

What had ever prompted a woman, whose mother was a Virginia senator and deceased father a renowned trial lawyer, to seek adventure in New Mexico? Had she fled from an unhappy love affair? Had she rebelled against her wealthy family? Elena had told him Joanna had come to Trinidad to paint, that she had chosen the town because her great-grandparents had once lived here for a whole summer while on an archaeological dig.

J.T. caught the glow of a light in his peripheral vision as he gazed out at the night, the land hushed and still. He focused his gaze on the light coming from a long, narrow window in the old bunkhouse. Joanna Beaumont stood in that window, looking up at the main house. What was she doing awake this time of night? Had she been as restless as he? As aroused and needy? Maybe she was thinking of him, and hating herself for wanting him, and yet was powerless to control that desire.

If he went to her now, would she accept him into her home? Into her bed? Into her body? J.T. shuddered with the force of his longing. Closing his eyes, he breathed deeply, drawing the fresh night air into his lungs. Opening his eyes, he took a last look at Joanna's silhouette in the window, then he closed the double doors, turned around and walked across the room.

He fell into the bed. Lying on top of the covers, he stared up at the dark ceiling. Only the faint moonlight illuminated his room.

He had to stop thinking about Joanna. He had to stop wanting her. He'd come home for a good, long vacation, the first in years. He wasn't going to allow some debutante to ruin his stay at the ranch. He would steer clear of her and she'd steer clear of him. And he'd make sure Elena didn't interfere.

JOANNA AND ELENA sat in cane-seated rockers on the front porch of the bunkhouse. Numerous potted geraniums lined the edge of the wooden porch and a trailing ivy vine sat nestled on a rough-hewn table between the two women. Elena downed the last drops of tea, then set the tall crystal glass on the table.

"So, are you going to tell me what happened between you and J.T. yesterday?" Elena asked.

Joanna smiled at her friend. She had met Elena and Alex at an art exhibit in Albuquerque. Alex was a sculptor, whose finest work was exquisite pieces of his beautiful young Navajo wife. The three had become instant friends and they had been thrilled to learn that Joanna had only recently moved to Trinidad.

"Come on, Jo. J.T. isn't talking." Elena crossed her arms over her chest and grunted in disgust. "Sometimes that brother of mine makes me so angry."

"I have a feeling that your brother makes a lot of people angry."

"I thought you two were friends now. That is what you said when you called last night and told me he had come by and apologized."

"We're on friendly terms," Joanna said. "I'm afraid we got off to a bad start when we met. We offended each other."

"How?"

"How?" Joanna stared at Elena, whose big brown eyes had widened with her question.

"Yes, how did you and J.T. offend each other?"

"Well...I misunderstood something he said and did. I thought he was... But he wasn't."

"He came on to you, huh?" Elena laughed, creating soft lines around her full lips. "J.T.'s pretty irresistible to the ladies, and he knows it. What did you do, slap his face?"

"No, I pulled my gun on him."

Elena's laughter filled the air. She doubled over in the rocker as she covered her mouth with her hand. "I love it. I absolutely love it. You pulled your gun on J. T. Blackwood, who is a private security agent, a former Secret Service agent and an ex-soldier. Good grief, Jo, I'd give a million dollars to have seen the look on his face."

"He was surprised." A hint of a smile played at the corners of Joanna's mouth.

"Okay, so he came on to you and you put him in his

place. That's how he offended you. How did you offend him? Did you tell him you didn't find him the least bit interesting and were totally immune to his masculine charms?"

"No. Not exactly." Joanna sipped on her tea, running her fingers up and down the side of the cold, sweating glass. "Despite the fact that I don't like Mr. Blackwood and am not interested in him, I can't say I'm completely immune to him."

"I knew it!" Elena slapped her hands together exuberantly. "You do find him irresistible, don't you?"

"Don't go jumping to conclusions. I just admit that he's very…well, he's very masculine. But I don't like his type, Elena, and I told him so."

"Hey, I can't believe J.T.'s ego is so fragile he couldn't take a rejection. Come on. Give. There has to be more to it than that."

"He said you wanted to find him a wife and I said I wasn't available. He took it the wrong way. He thought I was prejudiced, that I wasn't interested because he was part Navajo." Joanna looked down at her lap, uncertain she could face her friend. "I tried to explain, but he wouldn't listen. He said it didn't make any difference."

"That idiot! He's my brother and I love him dearly, but sometimes…" Elena laid her small hand on Joanna's shoulder. "J.T.'s all mixed up about a lot of things concerning his heritage. He's not really a white man and he's not really a Navajo. I think that's one of the reasons he left Trinidad and the ranch when he was eighteen and joined the army. No matter how hard his grandfather tried to erase everything Navajo from J.T.'s life and from his memories, that part of him still existed."

"Perhaps there's more to it than that." Joanna caught Elena's hand and squeezed. "Maybe some woman he loved broke his heart by refusing to marry him because he was part Native American."

"I can assure you that no one has ever broken J.T.'s heart. He's never been in love." Elena sighed. "I'm not sure J.T. knows how to love. His grandfather gave him everything money could buy, but he never gave him any love and warmth or genuine caring."

"He must have been a very sad, lonely little boy growing up with such a stern old man." Joanna did not want to think of J.T. as a child—an unloved, emotionally neglected little boy.

"Our childhoods were so different," Elena said. "I grew up on the reservation. My father farmed and raised a few sheep. We never had much money, but we were happy and I was loved by my parents. And I was taught a fierce pride in my Navajo heritage."

"And your brother grew up here, on his grandfather's ranch. Wealthy and unhappy."

"The only unhappiness in our lives, before my father died, was Mother's sadness in having lost her son."

"Elena?"

"Yes?"

"I noticed Mr. Bl—your brother wears a silver-and-turquoise ring. Do you know where he got that ring?"

"I wondered how long it would take you to ask about the ring," Elena said.

"You noticed, too, didn't you, that his ring is identical to mine?" Joanna held up her right hand; afternoon sunshine glinted off the ring's surface.

"The first time I met you, I saw your ring. I wondered about it, but didn't ask. I thought perhaps you'd bought it somewhere out here in New Mexico, and several times, after we became friends, I wanted to say something to you about the ring." Elena reached over and traced circles around the three turquoise stones adorning the ring. "I thought it was an odd coincidence. I've never seen another ring identical to the ones you and J.T. wear."

"Where did he get his ring?"

"Where did you get yours?" Elena asked. "Did you buy it after you came to New Mexico?"

"No. The ring has been in my family for years."

"Ah. I see. And J.T.'s ring has been in our family for years."

Joanna's wildly beating heart soared. J.T. was related to Benjamin Greymountain. Somehow she'd already known. But how was it possible that two men, related by blood, could be so very different?

"Whose ring does J.T. wear?" The moment she'd said his name, she wished she could call it back. Calling him J.T. seemed far too intimate. By referring to him as Mr. Blackwood, she could keep an emotional distance.

"When my mother grew very sick and we knew she was dying, J.T. came to the reservation to see her. I was fifteen and had never met my brother. But the moment I saw him, I knew him." Elena's eyes glazed with tears. "I hadn't seen the ring before that day, but my mother had kept it—saved it—for her son. The ring had belonged to her father and his father before him. Her grandfather was a silversmith."

"What was your mother's name before she married?" Joanna asked.

"Mary Greymountain from the Bitter Water clan."

"Greymountain?"

Elena nodded. "You have heard this name before… before you came to New Mexico?"

"Yes. My great-grandparents knew a Navajo silversmith named Benjamin Greymountain—"

"My great-grandfather!"

"Yes. Your great-grandfather—J.T.'s great-grandfather—made this ring." Joanna lifted her right hand with her left and stared at the silver-and-turquoise band. "This ring belonged to my great-grandmother."

"Ah. That's why you came to New Mexico, to Trinidad, to paint. You came in search of the ring's mate, didn't you? You knew Benjamin Greymountain had made an identical ring for himself. There was love between my great-grandfather and the woman he made the ring for. Isn't that true?"

"Yes. I have her diary. My great-grandmother. Annabelle Beaumont. She wore this ring until the day she died. I found it in a leather pouch when I found the diary."

"You wear Annabelle Beaumont's ring and J.T. wears Benjamin Greymountain's ring," Elena said. "It is a sign, is it not? I knew, somehow, when I saw your ring, that you were the woman for my brother."

"But I'm not, Elena," Joanna protested. "Your brother is cold and hard and cynical. He's filled with a rage that frightens me. I'm not the woman for him. I want—I need—a gentle, kind man. A man who wouldn't try to control me, to possess me, to exert power over me."

"J.T. needs a sweet, tender woman to teach him how to love." Elena smiled at Joanna. "You could be that woman, if you're brave enough to try to tame the devil."

"I'm not that brave."

Elena turned her head at the sound of horse hooves. Joanna looked up just as J.T. rode by on his big Appaloosa. He glanced at the two women, nodded and tipped his hat. For one brief moment, his golden brown eye met Joanna's green glare. Heat suffused her body. Tremors racked her stomach.

He rode on, not looking back. Joanna jumped up out of the rocker and walked inside her house. Elena glanced from her brother's retreating back to the open front door through which Joanna had disappeared.

CHAPTER THREE

J. T. BLACKWOOD had been home exactly one week when Elena finally persuaded Joanna to come to dinner. Joanna had known it was a mistake from the moment she'd agreed, but she also knew that Elena wouldn't leave her in peace until she accepted. Although she and J.T. had done everything possible to avoid each other, an occasional encounter had been unavoidable. And Elena, more convinced now than ever that Joanna was *the woman* for her brother, had taken every opportunity to throw the two of them together.

J.T. had shown up on the trail Joanna took for her morning horseback ride. They'd both gotten a good laugh over the fact that Elena had been the one to suggest the trail to J.T., saying he hadn't ridden over that part of the ranch in years. But J.T. had decided to finish his ride by taking another trail, and Joanna had been greatly relieved.

Elena had tried to turn a routine trip into town for groceries into a foursome luncheon date. When Joanna realized J.T. had been included in their plans, she'd apologized for changing her mind at the last minute and stayed at home. She'd driven into Trinidad by herself the following day to pick up her art supplies.

J.T. had only one more week of vacation. Surely she could survive another week. If she could live through tonight's dinner, all she had to do was continue avoiding the man. Maybe now would be a good time to take another trip. She'd been thinking about going back to the reservation to work. One of Elena's cousins, Joseph Ornelas, had promised to introduce her to the old shaman, James Bonito, who, people claimed, was a hundred and ten years old. She'd give anything to paint the man. She could leave tomorrow and stay away until J.T. had returned to Atlanta.

Tonight was the first time she and J.T. had agreed, beforehand, to see each other. Joanna berated herself for taking so long to get ready for a simple dinner with friends. She didn't want to admit that what J. T. Blackwood thought about her actually mattered to her. But it did.

Had Annabelle Beaumont worried so about her appearance when she had sneaked off for her clandestine meetings with Benjamin Greymountain? Had her heart drummed so fiercely? Had her nerves rioted in fear and anticipation?

What had it been like, Joanna wondered, to have Benjamin as a secret lover?

What would it be like to have J.T. as a lover?

Joanna shook her head, loosening her French twist. Damn, what a thought! She didn't want J.T. to be her lover. When she took a lover, he would be kind, understanding and tender. He would be the exact opposite of J. T. Blackwood. She wanted and needed a man who would allow her to set the pace, to be in control, to take charge. J.T. would possess her without loving her. He would take her with fury and passion, but without his heart ever being involved. He would always be the one with the power. Joanna could never allow a man to have power over her, to bend her to his will.

Busily she adjusted her hair, curling the loose tendrils about her face, softening the severity of the French twist. She checked her appearance in the mirror one last time, and approved of the image she saw reflected. She'd chosen to wear a thin chambray skirt with a ruffle around the ankle-length hem, and matched it with a simple short-sleeved white blouse. She picked up the silver-and-turquoise belt she'd bought from a Navajo silversmith and slipped it around her waist.

She took her time walking from the bunkhouse to the main house, humming to herself—something she'd done since childhood to shore up her courage. For the first time since she'd arrived in Trinidad, Joanna Beaumont regretted coming to New Mexico.

She had found a peace here she'd thought she would never know again, and she'd built a successful career doing something she loved. Her life had been content. Why hadn't J. T. Blackwood stayed in Atlanta for the rest of his life, or at least continued to avoid her as he'd done the past few years?

When Joanna neared the main house, a typical Spanish-style stucco with a red tile roof, she glanced up and saw J.T. standing on the wide porch.

Elena had told her that J.T. had gotten his coloring from their mother, but his size was pure Blackwood. Tall and rugged, every muscle well-developed to a whipcord leanness. This evening he had discarded his tan Stetson and had dressed in black jeans and a white shirt. A silver-and-turquoise jewel clasped his black bolo tie. His blue-black hair gleamed with a healthy vitality. Joanna visually traced the thin black band that held his eye patch in place.

"Cheer up, Jo, you're coming to dinner, not going to your own hanging," J.T. said.

She bristled at the use of his sister's nickname for her. No one except Elena had ever called her Jo. Somehow, on J.T.'s lips, it sounded far too intimate. But she wouldn't rise to the bait; she knew he'd called her Jo to see how she'd react.

"I feel like this is the condemned person's last meal and I'm that condemned person." She hesitated momentarily, then stepped onto the porch. "I am sorry that a week of your vacation has been ruined. Elena can't seem to let go of the notion you and I belong together. I know it's made your stay here at the ranch very unpleasant."

"You are so damned polite, Miss Beaumont." J.T. stood with one booted foot resting back flat against the wall. "Do you ever stop being a lady and act like a woman?"

Joanna clenched her teeth to keep herself from lashing out at J.T. Maybe he was right; maybe her good-manners-at-any-cost upbringing was so inbred that she could never escape it. But if her succumbing to him for a one-night stand would make her a woman in his eyes, then she didn't want to be a woman. Not his woman. Not ever.

"I don't think I acted much like a lady the first day we met." She tried to keep her voice even and calm, despite her anger. "If you recall, I pulled a gun on you."

"Oh, I'll never forget our first meeting. But even in pulling a gun on me, you were being a true lady. You were defending your honor, weren't you? That's what a lady would do. Or so I'm told."

Rushing out the front door, Elena glanced hurriedly from J.T. to Joanna. "Dinner will be delicious. Alex is barbecuing on the patio. Steaks this thick." She curved her thumb and index finger to indicate a good three inches. "Come on, you two."

Joanna helped Elena prepare the salads while J.T. assisted Alex with the barbecue. Within an hour the foursome settled around a black wrought-iron table in the right-hand corner of the patio located in the center of the stucco ranch house. The evening sun lay low on the western horizon. A soft, bluesy tune drifted from the CD player on the porch that surrounded the house on all four sides and opened onto the patio.

Joanna cut into her medium-rare steak, lifted a piece on her fork and brought the meat to her mouth. She glanced across the table at J.T. He was looking directly at her lips. Swallowing hard, she laid her fork down on her plate and lifted her mug of iced tea, all the while staring at J.T. He moved his gaze from her lips upward, encountering her hard stare. He smiled, an almost smile, just barely curving the corners of his mouth.

He picked up his mug of cold beer, silently saluted Joanna with it and took a deep, hearty swallow. She averted her gaze, turning to look at Elena, who was busy feeding Alex a bite of steak. The act of feeding her husband seemed terribly intimate and sexual. The two smiled at each other as if no one else existed. They were cocooned in their mutual fascination with each other—the skinny, bespectacled, blond sculptor and his lovely, exotic, brown-eyed wife.

Maybe that's what it's like to be in love, Joanna thought. So absorbed in your lover that you are oblivious to anyone else's presence.

Joanna lifted her fork again, but before she could bring it to her mouth, J.T. leaned over and slipped his own fork into her open mouth. Her body jerked. Her heart hammered. She glared at him. The piece of meat in her mouth felt huge and hot and heavy. Her first impulse was to spit it out—to spit it out in his face. Instead she began to chew slowly, keeping her gaze riveted on his.

"I take my steak rare," J.T. said. "I think this is medium-rare, don't you? Looks like we overcooked it a bit."

Joanna forced herself to swallow the chewed meat. "It's medium-rare. No taste of blood at all."

"Well, it's a good steak. I think I can finish it off." He cut another piece, then ate, following his first bite with many more.

By the time the others had finished their meal, Joanna had forced down several bites of her steak and a small portion of her salad. Finally Elena and Alex started a discussion about New Mexico's history, trying desperately to engage J.T. and Joanna in the conversation. The effort failed miserably. Joanna could find no pleasure in discussing Billy the Kid and John Chisum, and J.T. didn't seem to care anything about the fact that Lew Wallace, the author of *Ben Hur,* had once been the territorial governor.

"Come on, Alex, let's dance." Elena held out her hand to her husband, who quickly stood and lifted her into his arms.

J.T. and Joanna sat quietly at the table watching the couple slow dance in a sensual embrace.

"Every time I'm around those two I feel totally unnecessary," J.T. said. "It's been like this ever since they got married five years ago. You'd think they'd be sick of each other by now."

"They're in love," Joanna said.

"They're in heat." Grunting, J.T. shook his head. "I guess you don't know what that's like, do you?"

There was nothing she could do to stop the flush from spreading over her cheeks and down her throat. She'd been cursed with a redhead's pale complexion and a dusting of freckles across the bridge of her nose and over her cheekbones. When she blushed, it showed plainly.

"I've embarrassed you." He spoke the words in a tone of disbelief. "You can't be that naive. You're no teenager. You've got to be at least twenty-five or more. A woman your age is bound to have had several lovers."

"I'm twenty-nine." Joanna deliberately glanced away

from him and at the dancing couple. "And how many lovers I have or haven't had is none of your business."

Elena waved at Joanna. "Why don't you two take advantage of this fabulous music and that glorious sunset—" she nodded to the western sky, which was afire with orange-red flames "—and dance?"

J.T. held out his hand. "Come on, Jo, let's dance. It'll make Elena happy, and that's what this night is all about, isn't it? Pacifying my little sister so she'll leave us in peace for a while?"

Joanna hesitated, then stood, walked around the edge of the table and placed her hand in J.T.'s. His grasp was light and nonthreatening. Stepping into his arms, she followed him into the dance. He held her loosely, his grip around her waist barely discernible. She breathed a sigh of relief when she realized that he intended to keep a reasonable distance between them. She'd been so sure he would haul her close to his big body and force her to endure the feel of him, hard and powerful, against her own body.

If she'd been a bit taller or had worn heels, she might have been able to glance over his shoulder. As it was, she had to stare directly at his wide, muscular chest. He was so tall. Too tall. Too big. Too manly.

Even though J.T. did nothing offensive, Joanna felt trapped. She wasn't in control of this situation. He was. If he chose to pull her against him in an intimate fashion, she wouldn't be able to stop him.

Dammit, that wasn't true. All she had to do was tell him to release her and she could walk away. Admit it, she told herself. You aren't afraid of J. T. Blackwood; you're afraid of yourself!

"Are you always so stiff when a man holds you in his arms?" J.T. asked.

"Stop goading me," she told him. "You may find it amusing, but I don't."

"Sorry about that, Jo, but you leave yourself open to my teasing."

Just as she started to respond, the music ended. Joanna pulled away from J.T. He clasped her wrist, halting her escape. She turned abruptly and faced him.

"I'm tired. It's been a long day," she said. "I think I'll head on home."

"Oh, Jo, don't leave yet." Elena, her arm around Alex's waist, strolled over to Joanna and J.T.

"The night's still young," Alex said. "It's not dark yet. Hang around and we'll play a game of Rook."

"Not tonight." Joanna smiled at her friends, then glanced down at her wrist, still trapped in J.T.'s grasp. "Another time."

"Tomorrow night?" Elena suggested, her smile eager. "Come over for dinner again. Tonight was nice, wasn't it?"

"Not tomorrow night." Joanna wished Elena would just let her go home and stop trying so hard to push her into J.T.'s arms.

"The next night, then," Alex said. "I'll whip up some of my world-famous chili."

"I'm afraid dinner and cards will have to wait awhile. I'm leaving tomorrow afternoon to spend a week or so on the Navajo reservation." Joanna kept her phony smile in place—just barely. She felt J.T.'s hard, cold stare boring into her. She wanted to scream, to tell him, yes, a thousand times yes, he *was* the reason she had to escape.

"But why tomorrow?" Whining, Elena stuck out her bottom lip in a childish pout. "The reservation will be there a week from now. Please, wait."

"Leave her alone, Elena," J.T. said, then released his hold on Joanna's wrist. "She's made her plans."

"But she can go to the reservation anytime," Elena said. "You're only going to be here another week and—"

"I'll stop by tomorrow afternoon and say goodbye before I leave." Joanna's smile drooped. She sighed, bit her bottom lip, then reached out and hugged Elena. "Please, understand," she whispered.

Joanna hurried off the patio, onto the inner porch and through the house. When she reached the front porch, she stopped suddenly, her vision blurred by a fine mist of tears. She sucked in a deep breath of crisp, clean air.

She felt a big hand gently clutch her shoulder. Gasping, she turned quickly, bumping into J.T. and losing her balance. He grabbed her by both shoulders to steady her.

"Elena's all right," he said. "I promised her that I'd walk you home and try to persuade you to stay on at the ranch."

"Which you won't do, will you?"

He rubbed her shoulders with his big hands. "You're tight as a coiled spring, honey. What's wrong with you? You act like you're afraid of me."

"I told you once before that I'm not afraid of anything, most especially not you."

"Well, that's good to know, because I'm harmless. I'd never hurt you."

Joanna longed to believe him, to take him at his word, but she knew better than to trust a man like J. T. Blackwood. Any man, for that matter. Joanna hadn't trusted a man in five years. Not since a monster had sadistically raped her in her own apartment. Not since her devoted fiancé had walked off and left her to face the trial and months of therapy without his love and support.

"I'd never give you the chance to hurt me, Mr. Blackwood."

"I thought we were finally on a first-name basis. Remember, I'm J.T.—" he released one of her shoulders and tapped his chest with the tips of his fingers "—and you're Jo." He pointed to her.

"Please, don't call me Jo."

"Elena calls you Jo."

"I know, but that's different," Joanna said. "She's my good friend and you're…you're—"

"Not your friend?"

"No, not my friend."

"Then what am I?" He slipped his arm around her waist, urging her closer.

She couldn't seem to breathe. Her head spun. She clutched his arms, feeling firm muscles beneath her fingers.

They both heard a man clear his throat. J.T. glanced over Joanna's shoulder and saw Cliff Lansdell, his ranch foreman, standing in the yard. Turning Joanna around so that she stood at his side, J.T. kept his arm about her waist.

"What's wrong, Cliff?" J.T. asked.

"Sorry to bother you, J.T., but you told me to let you know when Queen Nefertiti was about to foal. I've called Dr. Gray."

"Thanks, Cliff. I'll come on out to the stables in a few minutes. After I walk Miss Beaumont home."

"That's not necessary," Joanna said at the same moment Cliff spoke.

"I'll be glad to walk Joanna home, if you're in a hurry to get out to the stables, J.T."

"I'll walk Jo home." J.T. said her name in a sultry way, tightening his hold around her waist.

Joanna had the oddest notion that J. T. Blackwood had just laid claim to her, that somehow he had warned Cliff that she was out of bounds to any other man.

"I'll see you over at the stables, then." Cliff's shoulders slumped. He glanced at Joanna. "Good night." He tipped his hat, turned and walked away.

"I can get home by myself." She snapped out the words, not caring how she sounded.

"Would you like to come to the stables with me and wait for the blessed event?" J.T. ran his fingers up and down the side of her waist.

Joanna sucked in her breath. "No. No, thank you."

"My Appaloosa, Washington, is the colt's sire and this will be Queen Nefertiti's first. It's a special occasion."

"Then you should go on. Don't waste time walking me home."

J.T. guided her off the porch and across the yard, not saying a word. When they reached her front door, she unlocked and opened it, then turned to him.

"Good night."

"Goodbye." He lifted his hand, touching her face with his fingertips; the caress was soft, hesitant and quickly over. "I'll be back in Atlanta when you return from the reservation, so it could be months, probably Christmas, before I come back to the ranch."

"Goodbye, then. I—I won't see you at Christmas. I plan to go back to Virginia and spend Christmas with my mother."

"If we're very careful, we should be able to avoid ever seeing each other again," he said.

She nodded agreement. They stared at each other for a brief moment before J.T. turned and walked away. Joanna took a deep breath, thankful that he hadn't kissed her, then went inside and locked the door behind her.

J.T. WALKED BY the old bunkhouse on his way back from the stables shortly after daybreak the following morning. He hadn't expected to see Joanna, dressed in jeans and an oversize shirt, sitting on her porch. He had thought—hell, he had hoped— he'd never see her again after last night. He couldn't quite put his finger on what it was, but there was something about Joanna Beaumont that sent up red warning signals inside his head. She meant trouble for him, and J.T. never let a woman cause him trouble.

"Good morning," she called out to him. "Is everything all right with Queen Nefertiti and her colt?"

J.T. walked over and placed his foot on the bottom step leading up to her front porch. "Mother and daughter are doing just fine. When I stopped by and told Washington he was the father of a beautiful filly, he acted as if he knew what I was talking about."

"Maybe he did." Joanna clutched a large, tan mug in her hands. "Sometimes I think animals are a lot smarter than we humans give them credit for being."

"Yeah, you're probably right." J.T. ran his right hand over his face, the overnight's growth of beard scratchy against his palm. "I need a shower and a shave and about ten hours of sleep." He eyed the mug she held. "But first I could use a cup of coffee."

She glanced into the pale brown liquid she'd been sipping on for the past few minutes, then looked down at J.T. "Come on up and have a seat. I'll go inside and get you a cup. How do you like it? Black?"

"Black, but with a little sugar. A teaspoonful will do."

"Okay. I'll be right back."

While she went inside to get his coffee, he walked up the steps and onto the porch, then slumped down in one of the cane-seated rockers. God, he was tired. But it was a good kind of tired. Here on the ranch he could work hard enough to physically exhaust himself, but he didn't have to face the stress and pressure of his job, which was far more exhausting—mentally as well as physically.

"This is high-octane stuff," Joanna said when she returned with his coffee. "If you're planning on going straight to bed, the caffeine could keep you awake."

He accepted the cup she offered, being careful not to touch her hand in the process. "I don't think anything will keep me from sleeping this morning."

Taking a swig of the coffee, he sighed. "Good. And just the right amount of sugar."

She sat down beside him in the other rocker and lifted her mug to her lips. She hadn't expected to see J.T. this morning. She'd had no idea he'd stayed at the stables all night. But there was no reason to panic, no reason to be rude to him. By noon today, she'd be packed and ready to leave, and when she returned next week, J.T. would be gone.

While she was away, she would have to come to terms with her foolish dream of finding real love and happiness in New Mexico. She had met the man who had inherited Benjamin's ring as she had inherited Annabelle's, and knowing J. T. Blackwood had opened her eyes to reality. There would be no fantasy lover come to life for her. There would be no happily-ever-after for a pair of present-day lovers, any more than there had been for the star-crossed lovers over seventy years ago.

"Do you always get up so early?" J.T. asked.

"What?"

"It's barely daylight and you're up, dressed, and have already fixed coffee," he said. "Is this your normal routine?"

"Not always. But sometimes I get up this early and

paint. There's nothing more glorious than a New Mexico sunrise, unless it's a New Mexico sunset."

"You're really in love with this country, aren't you? You've fallen under its enchanted spell like so many Easterners have done over the years."

"My great-grandmother fell in love…with New Mexico over seventy years ago, when she and her husband spent the summer here on an archaeological dig." Joanna finished her coffee, placed her empty mug on the table between the two rockers, then looked toward the east at the morning sky.

"Yeah, Elena told me the story, or what you told her." J.T. took another swig of coffee, then placed his half-full cup beside Joanna's. "Your great-grandmother was a married woman who had an affair with one of the natives, then left the guy and went back home to her safe, secure life in Virginia as the wife of a well-to-do college professor and renowned archaeologist."

Joanna's spine stiffened; she clutched the arms of the rocker. "There was a great deal more to their affair. They were truly in love. It broke her heart to leave him. She loved him as long as she lived." Joanna thrust her right hand in front of J.T.'s face. "She wore his ring until the day she died."

"If she loved him so damned much, why didn't she leave her husband and stay here in New Mexico with him?" Grabbing Joanna's hand, J.T. twisted the silver-and-turquoise ring around and around on her finger. "I'll tell you why. Because Benjamin Greymountain was good enough to take as a lover, but not good enough to marry. He wasn't good enough for her to give up everything and spend her life with him. That's not love, Jo, that's—"

Jerking her hand out his, she jumped to her feet. "What would you know about love? Listening to you talk about our great-grandparents in that way is a sacrilege. If you had read Annabelle's diary, you wouldn't say such things. You'd know how deeply she loved Benjamin, and how completely she trusted his love for her."

J.T. stood, grabbed Joanna and whipped her around to face him. "You're right. I don't know the first thing about love, but I know all about lust, all about how good it feels to scratch an itch that's driving you crazy." Lowering his head, he nuzzled the side of her face with his nose.

No, no! her mind screamed. She wasn't going to let him do this. She wasn't going to let him reduce the beautiful love Benjamin and Annabelle had shared into some meaningless sexual affair. And she wasn't going to let him prove his point by showing her that the two of them felt those same animalistic urges.

She struggled against his hold, a feeling of panic building inside her. J.T. clutched her waist, pulling her up against him. She gasped when she felt his arousal. "We could have what Benjamin and Annabelle had, if that's what you want. We could spend the next week making love night and day, and then I'll go back to Atlanta and you can write in your diary about how exciting it was, having an Indian lover."

"Let go of me." She glared at him, hating him. Hating him for making light of their great-grandparents' love. Hating him for stirring passion to life within her.

"You don't want the kind of affair your beloved ancestress had?" J.T. taunted her. "Are you saying you didn't come to Trinidad—" he yanked her hand up, entwined their fingers and pulled their hands between their faces so that they could see their matching rings "—with all kinds of romantic notions of a Navajo man fulfilling your sexual fantasies?"

"You don't know anything about me. About my dreams. Or my fantasies."

He lowered his head. She held tightly to his hand, trying to keep their clasped hands in front of her face. He pulled their hands down, leaned closer and brushed a light kiss across her lips. She stiffened.

"I know you want me—as much as I want you," he said.

She didn't fight him, made no protest when he kissed her. She had thought the kiss would be harsh and cruel and savage. But it wasn't. He took her lips with force, but it was a sweet, tender power that swept through her body like a strong but nondestructive wind.

She returned the kiss, opening her mouth, allowing his invasion. Tingling warmth spread from her breasts to the core of her femininity. When he cupped the back of her head with one hand and caressed her hip with the other, pushing her firmly against his hard sex, she slipped her arms up around his neck. She had never known anything like this raging hunger inside her, this overwhelming need to possess and be possessed.

Just when her knees weakened and she trembled with passion, J.T. pushed her away. He stood several inches from her, his breathing ragged, sweat beads dampening his forehead.

Reaching down, she gripped the arm of her rocker for support as she stared at him, not knowing what to say or do. She wanted to lash out at him, accuse him of something horrible, but she couldn't. She had been a willing participant, her need as wild as his.

"Go to the reservation, Jo. Paint your noble savages and your magnificent sunrises and sunsets. But find yourself another Indian to take as a lover. I'm not in the market for a summer fling with a bored debutante."

He glared at her. She stood ramrod straight, unmoving, her face an unemotional mask. When he turned and stomped down the steps, out into the yard and toward the main house, Joanna stayed on the porch, silent and still, until he disappeared from her view. Then she released the tight control she'd been determined to keep over her emotions. Tears filled her eyes. The unbearable pain in her chest burst free when she gulped in a deep breath of air and let out an agonized moan.

CHAPTER FOUR

JOANNA PLACED HER art supplies in the back of the Jeep, then lifted her small floral suitcase and her matching overnight bag. She'd packed light, taking two pairs of jeans, two blouses, a nightgown and several changes of underwear. She would stay with Elena's cousins, Kate and Ed Whitehorn, who had opened their home to her on several previous occasions. She had telephoned them this morning, apologizing for giving them such short notice, and found Kate delighted to have company.

Joanna glanced down at her watch as she stepped up on the porch. Eleven-twenty. She would double-check everything in the house, making sure no electrical appliances had been left on, then she'd fix herself a sandwich and eat lunch before running up to the main house to say goodbye to Elena. She prayed J.T. would still be asleep so she wouldn't have to see him again.

The telephone rang just as she entered the house. Leaving the front door open, she dashed across the living room. She picked it up on the fifth ring, just in time to keep her answering machine from being activated.

"Hello," Joanna said.

"Joanna?"

"Mother?"

"Yes, dear. How are you?" Helene Beaumont asked.

"I'm fine." It wasn't like her mother to call unexpectedly. Senator Helene Caldwell Beaumont was the most organized person Joanna had ever known. Her mother called twice a month, at nine-thirty on Sunday morning. "Is something wrong? Did Uncle Peter have another heart attack?"

"No, dear. Peter is just fine."

"Then what's wrong? Why are you calling?"

"I—I don't quite know how to tell you this, but—"

"For heaven's sake, Mother, will you just tell me? You're scaring me to death, acting this way." Her mother never stuttered, never hesitated, never postponed till tomorrow what could be accomplished today.

"That policeman, Lieutenant George, came to my office earlier today."

At the mention of Lieutenant George, every nerve in Joanna's body screamed, every muscle tightened. Milton George had been in charge of her rape case and all the other cases involving the serial rapist who had attacked a total of twelve women in the Richmond area before being arrested.

"What did Lieutenant George want?"

"I thought about flying out there to tell you, but—"

"Dammit, Mother, just tell me!"

"Lenny Plott has escaped from prison." Helene let out a long sigh.

"But that's not possible." Joanna couldn't believe the monster who had brutally attacked her was free and running around loose. "He's in a maximum-security prison. It would have been impossible for him to escape."

"I know what a shock this must be for you, dear, but I'm afraid it's true. Lenny Plott did escape. And—and I'm afraid there's more."

"More?"

"He escaped less than forty-eight hours ago and he's already found Melody Horton."

"What do mean he's 'already found' Melody?" Melody was the twenty-year-old college student who, along with Joanna and two other victims, had testified against their rapist and sent him away to prison for the rest of his natural life.

"She was kidnapped. A neighbor recognized the man she drove off with. She identified him from police photographs. It was Lenny Plott."

"Have the police found her?"

"Yes." Helene's voice was so low, Joanna could barely hear her.

"Is she...?"

"She was strangled to death," Helene said, her words spoken unquaveringly. "Lieutenant George wanted you and Claire and Libby to know that Plott is on the loose and has already killed.... Please, come home, dear. Your life is in danger. Come home and I'll hire a bodyguard for you."

"Lenny Plott has no idea where I am now," Joanna said. "He doesn't know I moved to New Mexico and he doesn't know where Claire and Libby are. I don't even know where Libby is."

"Lieutenant George is afraid Lenny will somehow find out where the three of you have moved. He thinks Lenny will hunt y'all down."

"How could this have happened? When Lenny Plott went to prison, our nightmare was supposed to have ended. I won't—I can't live in fear. Not again. Not ever again!"

Joanna would never forget those first few weeks after her rape when she lived in fear the man would return and rape her again. Even after Lenny Plott had been arrested, she hadn't felt safe. To this day, she knew there was always a possibility that it could happen again, but she had learned to face the fear and put it in its proper place. She was careful, always cautious of strangers and new acquaintances. She'd bought a gun and learned how to use it properly. She'd taken self-defense classes and had undergone months of therapy. No, by God, she would not allow Lenny Plott's escape to destroy the life she'd built here in Trinidad. She would not run scared.

"Joanna, are you still there, dear? Please, say something."

"I'm all right. I'm staying where I am. I'm safe here. I'll tell Elena about Lenny Plott. I should have told her a long time ago, but I wanted to pretend it had never happened. Out here, no one knows about the rape."

"But what if Lenny finds you?"

"He won't." Joanna tried to reassure her mother, but in the back of her mind, doubts swarmed like angry killer bees. "I'll tell Elena and she can explain to Alex. There are dozens of ranch hands around this place, macho guys who know how to use guns. And Trinidad is a small town. Everybody knows everybody. If a stranger were to show up, I'd hear about it."

"Lieutenant George is going to call you later today," Helene said. "He's promised to keep us updated. They... the police have a statewide manhunt under way. They're going to catch that monster and put him back in prison where he belongs."

"Yes, of course, they will. He probably won't get out of Richmond."

"I wish you'd come home."

"I'm safer here, and Trinidad is my home now."

"Call me every day, just to let me know—" Helene's voice cracked.

"Every day. I promise."

"I love you, Joanna. You know that, don't you?"

"Yes, Mother," Joanna said. "And I love you."

"Take care, dear. And let me know if there's anything I can do."

"I will, Mother. Goodbye."

"Goodbye."

Joanna hung up the phone slowly, then slumped down on the apricot-gold leather sofa. For just a minute she felt completely numb, as if her body and mind had frozen instantly. Then, just as quickly, the feeling returned. She shivered, suddenly cold. Her hands trembled. The quivering sensation spread up her arms, down her legs. A tight fist clutched her chest. She couldn't breathe.

Dear God, no, please, no. A sour taste, salty and hot, rose in her throat. Memories—horrendous memories—flashed through her mind. Memories she had buried so deep she thought they could never resurface. She had spent five long, difficult years recovering from that night, putting every thought of Lenny Plott and what he'd done to her out of her mind. Forgetting had been the most difficult thing she'd ever done, but she had forced herself to forget, had forced herself to go on with her life. She was too strong to allow what had happened to her defeat her.

Joanna broke out in a cold sweat. Her heart thundered at a frantic pace. Doubling over, she clutched her knees, drew them up against her body and rocked back and forth. Heavy, painful tears lodged in her throat.

"If you scream, I'll kill you." He had whispered the words in her ear as he held the sharp knife blade to her throat.

"No! Don't do this to yourself," Joanna cried.

Squeezing her eyes shut, she tried to capture her tears, to stop them from falling.

Piercing blue eyes glared down at her. Hard, bruising hands clutched her breasts. A bony knee thrust between her legs. The strong odor of stale whiskey breath covered her mouth. She tried to shove him away, tried to scream. The knife blade nicked her throat. Blood trickled down onto her chest.

Joanna's eyes flew open. She shook from head to toe as she kept rocking back and forth. "Stop this! Don't remember! Please, don't remember.... Don't—"

The loud pounding on the front door sounded muffled to Joanna's ears, overpowered by the sound of her own heartbeat. Her mind was so filled with pain, the pain of trying not to remember, that it took her a few minutes to realize that someone was knocking at her door.

"Jo? Hey, Jo. Are you about ready to leave?" Elena called out as she walked into the living room.

Elena. Her friend. Someone who cared about her. She mustn't let Elena find her like this. Move, dammit, move! Sit up straight. Stop crying.

"My God, Jo, what's wrong?" Elena rushed over to the sofa. Dropping to her knees, she grabbed Joanna by the shoulders. "What's happened? Are you sick?"

Joanna managed to shake her head, but when she tried to respond, she couldn't. "Are you hurt?" Elena asked.

Shaking her head again, Joanna opened her mouth and tried to speak. The sound was a squeaky gasp.

"Try to tell me what happened." Elena shook Joanna soundly. "Come on, talk to me, Jo. You're frightening me." Elena reached out and wiped the tears off Joanna's cheeks, then slipped her arms around her and hugged her.

Joanna gulped several times, then groaned. Her body relaxed. She eased her hands off her knees and slid her feet onto the floor. Elena held on tight, continuing to hug her.

"Five—five years ago, I was raped," Joanna whispered.

"Oh, Jo...Jo. I'm so sorry."

"I left Virginia and came out here to New Mexico to start a new life." Joanna hugged Elena, then pulled away from her. "I didn't want anyone out here to know. I should have told you, after we became such good friends, but by then I'd put what happened behind me. I worked so hard at trying to forget."

Elena rubbed Joanna's arms. "What happened today? Did you have some sort of flashback?"

"My mother called. It seems the man who raped me... Oh, God!" Joanna jumped up off the sofa and paced back and forth. "This can't be happening!"

"What can't be happening?" Elena asked, standing and following Joanna around the room in her frantic stroll.

"The man who raped me—Lenny Plott—was what the police refer to as a serial rapist. I was his eleventh victim. After he raped his twelfth victim, the police caught him."

"Then he's in prison, isn't he?" Elena swirled about in front of Joanna, forcing her to halt. "Isn't he?"

"I testified against him. Claire Andrews, Libby Felton, Melody Horton and I. We made sure he would never rape another woman."

"I know it took a lot of guts to do what you four did. But you did the right thing."

"Yes, we did the right thing," Joanna said. "And when our rapist was sentenced to life in prison, we all went on with our lives. Melody stayed on in Virginia and finished college. Claire moved back home to Missouri. Libby just left town. We never heard from her again."

"And you came to Trinidad."

"Elena, Lenny Plott escaped from prison."

"What?"

"He escaped about forty-eight hours ago." Joanna covered her mouth with her hands.

Elena grabbed Joanna's hands and pulled them away from her face. "What are you not telling me?"

"He kidnapped Melody Horton and murdered her. The day the judge sentenced him, he swore that somehow he'd get free and hunt us all down. He swore he'd kill us."

Elena put her arms around Joanna, hugging her fiercely. "You're safe here, on the ranch, with us. He doesn't know where you are. He can't find you here."

"But what if he does?" Joanna, her eyes dry and dazed, looked at her best friend. "I'm scared, Elena. I'm so scared."

Elena rubbed Joanna's back. "I know. I know. But everything's going to be all right. J.T. will know exactly how to handle this situation. He'll take care of—"

"J.T.? No, please, I don't want your brother to know about this."

"Don't be silly," Elena said. "J.T. knows more about protecting someone than anybody in the whole wide world. He was a Secret Service agent until he got shot in the head and blinded in one eye. For the past six years, he's been a partner in a private security agency."

"Mother wants me to come home. Back to Virginia. She's offered to hire a bodyguard for me. I'm sure, if I asked her, she'd hire someone and send him out here."

"But don't you see, there's no need to hire another bodyguard when we've got J.T. It's what he does for a living."

"No, Elena, I—"

"We're not going to argue about this. You're going to stay here on the ranch and live every day as normally as you possibly can. J.T. is an expert on private security. He'll know what to do to keep you safe."

"I can't tell J.T. that I was—"

"Don't sell my big brother short. He'll understand. You can count on him. Trust me, Jo. Please. And trust J.T."

Trust J.T.? How could she trust him? How could she trust any man?

"This agency in Atlanta," Joanna said, "are there other agents? Someone J.T. could send back here when he returns? Mother will pay for—"

"What do you mean when he returns! Once I tell him about your situation, he'll stay here and guard you himself."

"I wouldn't ask him to do that." She wasn't sure what she feared most, Lenny Plott finding out where she was or J. T. Blackwood agreeing to act as her bodyguard. If he found her, Plott could kill her. But if she allowed herself to become involved with J.T., he could completely destroy her emotionally.

J.T. DISMOUNTED, dropped the reins and spoke softly to Washington, who followed behind him while he walked along the bank of the stream—his favorite spot on the ranch, high in the hills, secluded and quiet, close to nature.

The rage inside him simmered. A hot fury that he barely controlled consumed him. Part of the anger he felt was directed at himself for being such a macho jerk, such a total idiot. He should have known there was more to Joanna Beaumont's skittish nature and wariness than just an instant dislike of him. His damn ego had gotten in the way of his usual keen perception. His ego and his male libido.

He wasn't sure he had ever wanted a woman the way he wanted Joanna.

J.T. pulled his rifle from its leather holster attached to the saddle and removed the cloth bag he'd hung over the saddle horn. He ordered Washington to stay, then began a

slow, steady climb up the mountainside. When he reached
the summit, he braced his rifle against the side of a huge
rock, then opened the cloth bag and removed a varied assortment of bottles and cans. He lined them up across the
top of the rock formation, then lifted his rifle and walked
backward, close to the edge of the summit. He aimed his
rifle and fired repeatedly, destroying the row of inanimate
objects he pretended were Lenny Plott. When he finished,
he stood there and stared up at the blue sky, the afternoon
sun blinding in its intensity.

"Joanna was raped five years ago." J.T. heard his
sister's voice. *"She testified against her rapist. He has
escaped from prison and already killed one of the women
who testified against him. He swore he'd hunt all four
women down and kill them."*

J.T. let out a bloodcurdling cry as savage and brutal as
the primitive emotions he felt.

*"I told her that she'd be safe here on the ranch. I
assured her that you'd know what to do to protect her."*

Protect Joanna. Yeah, he knew all about protecting
people. He'd spent most of his life acting as someone's
bodyguard. He had laid his life on the line every day he'd
been a member of the country's Secret Service.

After the army and college, he'd spent more than a year
undergoing exams, interviews and a complete investigation into his background before being hired in Washington. He had served time in field offices from Omaha to
New Orleans, which had taken him from tediously boring assignments to stakeouts of underworld counterfeit-
ing operations. He had guarded presidential candidates
more than once, and had even pulled White House detail
for several years.

His last assignment had nearly cost him his life—*had*

cost him the vision in his left eye. But it had gotten him the Medal of Valor and an early retirement.

For the past six years, he'd worked with Sam Dundee, a man who had become his best friend. Dundee's Private Security was one of the most respected and successful private security businesses in the country.

Oh, yeah, J. T. Blackwood was a security expert. Acting as a bodyguard was what he did best. There was only a couple of small problems associated with guarding Joanna Beaumont. The woman hated him, although he didn't much blame her. And he wanted her, but didn't have the vaguest idea what a woman who'd been brutally raped would need from a lover.

He'd be a fool to take this assignment. He was far too personally involved. Despite Elena's insistence that he take the job himself, J.T. wondered if it wouldn't be wise to bring in another man from the agency. Simon Roarke was available and Gabriel Hawk would be finishing up an assignment within a week.

But then, J.T. doubted an around-the-clock bodyguard was needed at this point. At least not a professional. There were enough hands on the Blackwood ranch to see that Joanna was kept under watch. If and when Lenny Plott discovered her whereabouts would be the time for a trained bodyguard to step in.

He had put off talking to Joanna long enough. He'd present her with several alternatives, assuring her he would guarantee she was safe on the ranch, then he'd let her decide what she wanted done.

J.T. climbed down the mountainside, returned his rifle to its sheath and mounted Washington. It had been a long time since he had dreaded anything as much as he dreaded facing Joanna, now that he knew what had happened to her five years ago. What if he said or did the wrong thing?

What if— Hell! What was the matter with him? When had he suddenly become the sensitive, emotional kind? He hadn't! Not now. Not ever. It was just that there was something about Joanna, something so gentle and tender and compelling, that he couldn't get her out of his head.

When he returned to the ranch, he turned Washington over to one of the stable hands instead of caring for the Appaloosa himself as he usually did. No point waiting any longer to confront Joanna.

He found her and Elena sitting on the front porch of the converted bunkhouse, both of them swaying back and forth in the rockers. Hesitating at the foot of the steps, he looked up at Elena.

"Where have you been?" his sister asked. "You rode off in a big hurry."

He glanced at Joanna; she stared down at her hands resting in her lap. Where was her fiery spirit? he wondered. Her face was too pale. She was too quiet. And she hadn't looked at him.

"I needed some time alone. To think."

"Lieutenant George called," Elena said. "The policeman from Virginia—"

"You've already told me who he is," J.T. said. "Did he have any updated information on Plott?"

Elena shook her head. "No. He pretty much just repeated what Mrs. Beaumont had told Joanna earlier when she called."

J.T. walked up the steps, stopping beside his sister. He placed his hand on her shoulder. "I need to talk to Joanna. Alone."

"Why alone?" Elena asked. "She needs me here. I don't want to leave her—"

"It's all right," Joanna said. "You go on home. I'll be fine. Really."

Elena stood, then pointed her finger in her brother's face. "Don't you dare be anything but gentle and understanding. Do you hear me?"

"I'll do my very best." But would his best be good enough? He might be able to manage understanding, at least up to a point. But he didn't know much about being gentle. There had been very little gentleness in his life and few occasions when he'd been called upon to show any tenderness. J.T. wasn't sure there was a gentle side to his nature.

Turning around, Elena bent over and hugged Joanna. "I'll do anything you need for me to do to help you through this." She squeezed J.T.'s arm as she passed him and walked down the steps and into the yard.

"Why don't we go inside," J.T. said. "It'll be more private."

"Why do we need privacy?" Still, Joanna stared down at her hands, avoiding making eye contact with him. "If I stay on the ranch, we won't be able to keep this a secret. Everyone will have to know."

"Fine." J.T. shrugged, then sat down in the rocker his sister had just vacated. "Do you or do you not want me to take charge of this situation?"

Joanna sighed. "Elena says that you're the very best at what you do—at being a bodyguard."

"I've spent years protecting people."

"I'll arrange with my mother to transfer whatever funds are necessary to cover your expenses." Joanna lifted her hands out of her lap and gripped the rocker's arms.

"I'll be here at the ranch another week anyway, so there'll be no charge." J.T. removed his Stetson, crossed his legs and perched his hat on his knee. "If you want me to stay on after my vacation, we can discuss my fee then."

"You'll stay on and take this assignment yourself?"

"If that's what you want." She looked so fragile, so vulnerable and helpless sitting there in the rocker, her small, delicate hands clutching the rocker's arms, her body wound as tight as a bowstring. "Or if you'd prefer, I can have one of the Dundee agency's best men fly out and take over the assignment."

"Elena wants you to be my bodyguard."

"What do you want, Jo?"

She raised her head, tilted her chin and stared him directly in the eye. "I want none of this to have happened. I want to go back five years and erase the past."

"Yeah, well…that's not possible, is it? All I can do is try to keep you safe now, in the present." J.T. wished he'd been around in the past to protect her. Scum like this Lenny Plott would never have touched Joanna, because if he had, J.T. would have personally annihilated him.

"Look, I'll be honest with you." Joanna released her death grip on the chair arms and stood, striding to the edge of the porch. She kept her back to J.T. "Before the—" she swallowed "—rape, I was fairly trusting and thought the world really was a wonderful place. My life had been almost perfect. I grew up as the only child of wealthy, successful parents, both of whom loved me. After I graduated from college, with a degree in art, I got a job at a small art museum in Richmond. I met and fell in love with an up-and-coming young lawyer in my father's law office and we became engaged. The only unhappy time in my life was when my father died of a heart attack about a year before…before the rape."

"What happened to your fiancé?" J.T. lifted his Stetson off his knee, stood and placed the hat on his head.

"I'm getting to that."

He walked up behind her, close, a hairbreadth away, but not touching. "Go on."

She tensed when she realized he was so close—so close she could feel the heat emanating from his big, powerful body. "The rape and what happened afterward changed me forever. Despite counseling, despite moving away and starting a new life out here in Trinidad, despite everything I've done to get over what happened to me, I've never been able to trust anyone easily again."

"I can understand how you might feel that way, at least for a while."

"Not just for a while." She wished he wasn't standing so close, wished she didn't have the almost-overwhelming urge to turn around and ask him to hold her in his arms. "After I was raped, my fiancé had a difficult time dealing with what had happened to me. When I needed him most—needed his love and support—he walked out on me."

"The bastard!" J.T. clasped her shoulders gently. Dear God, she was sprung so tight she was close to the breaking point. He was afraid that if she broke, she would fly into a million pieces. "You're better off without him, honey."

"Yes, I know." She wished J.T. hadn't touched her. Wished that his touch wasn't so firm and yet so gentle. Wished that his touch didn't make her want to lean back against his chest and have him surround her with his strong arms. "But Todd's desertion only made things worse for me. If I couldn't trust the man who had professed to love me, who had asked me to be his wife, who could I ever trust?"

"You can trust me, Jo." J.T. ran his big hands from her shoulders to her elbows and back up again, soothing her, his touch strong, gentle and nonthreatening. "Trust me with your life."

She shivered in his arms, the involuntary movement relieving some of the tension coiled so tightly inside her.

More than anything, she wanted to trust J.T., but she wasn't sure she could.

"I don't want you to have another bodyguard sent from Atlanta." She leaned backward, allowing her body to just barely touch his. "I want you to stay in Trinidad and...I want you to protect me, J.T." She took a deep breath, then let it out slowly. "I promise that I'll try to trust you."

J.T. lowered his head, bringing his lips close to her ear. "And I promise I'll do everything possible to earn your trust."

Closing her eyes, Joanna pressed her shoulders into his chest, tilting her head back to rest against him. "I'm scared. I'm very scared."

"I'll keep you safe," he vowed. "We'll stay here on the ranch and I'll make certain someone is with you at all times, until Plott is captured and sent back to prison."

"But what if—"

"If by some chance he finds out where you are and comes after you before he's caught, then I'll stay at your side night and day. And if he comes near you, I'll kill him."

"Oh, J.T., you can't imagine what it was like for me that night." Opening her eyes, she glanced over at his big hand caressing her arm. "And afterward...at the trial, when... when I had to tell all about what he'd done to me."

"Hush, honey. Don't talk about it. Don't remember." Dear God in heaven, he didn't think he could bear to hear any of the details. Knowing only the basic facts was enough to make him crazy. Learning that some sick pervert had forced himself on Joanna made J.T. want to hunt the bastard down and castrate him.

"It wasn't my fault. It wasn't! Maybe I should have fought harder. Maybe I should have just let him slit my throat with his knife." Tremors racked Joanna's body.

"Todd blamed me. He—he thought I could have prevented it, somehow. He couldn't even bear to look at me—afterward. That made me feel as dirty as I had right after the rape."

"Any man who truly loved a woman would never blame her," J.T. said. "What happened to you was Lenny Plott's fault. His and no one else's. I promise you that if it's necessary, I'll move heaven and earth to make sure he never hurts you again."

Breathing in the sweet, clean scent of Joanna, J.T. buried his face in her hair that hung loosely about her neck. He kissed her on the temple, then wrapped his arms around her and held her close against his chest. She didn't resist. They stood there on her porch for a long time, J.T.'s arms draped around her, cocooning her from the world. Protectively. Caringly. Possessively.

CHAPTER FIVE

JOANNA WASN'T SURE what had been the most difficult adjustment in the five days since her mother's phone call. Having to deal with painful memories and haunting fears she had thought were long since buried was a challenge she felt she was strong enough to handle. Losing a great deal of her privacy and freedom annoyed her greatly. She wasn't used to the ranch hands paying much attention to her, at least not since she'd first moved into the bunkhouse three years ago. Now, J.T. had a revolving shift of men keeping an eye on her. She certainly wasn't accustomed to someone knowing her whereabouts twenty-four hours a day. She'd been told she couldn't leave the ranch without an escort. She couldn't even go horseback riding on the ranch without one of the hands going with her. Elena and Alex had been wonderful—sympathetic, caring and understanding. The caring and understanding she appreciated; the sympathy she could do without. She felt sorry enough for herself without being weighed down by other people's pity.

She wasn't sure how she felt about J.T. knowing everything concerning her past. Relieved mostly, she guessed, but a little apprehensive, too. When he'd held her in his arms on the front porch and promised to keep her safe, he had said and done all the right things. Oddly enough, he'd been gentle and kind and supportive. She'd been so sure he would react the way her ex-fiancé had; that he would assume the worst about her. Todd certainly had. But J.T. wasn't Todd McAllister. The two men had absolutely nothing in common. Todd was a seventh-generation Southern gentleman; cultured, refined and, she realized now, an elitist snob. He would have been revolted by Annabelle and Benjamin's love affair. He never would have understood. Todd hadn't approved of "fornicating" outside one's own social circle.

Joanna laughed aloud. How could she have been in love with Todd? Pretty-boy Todd, with all his money and good breeding, had been shallow, conceited and selfish. She supposed she'd been drawn to him because they had seemed to have so much in common, her background being very similar to his. He was a fourth-generation lawyer, and her father had been one of the most respected lawyers in Virginia. Todd's uncle was a state senator and so was her mother. She and Todd had had numerous friends in common. In fact, that was how they'd met. A fraternity brother of Todd's had been dating Joanna's cousin, Diane.

Dammit! She hadn't thought much about Todd since she'd moved to New Mexico. After months of mourning his desertion five years ago, she had finally realized she was better off without him. Now, here she was, tormented not only by memories of her rapist, but by memories of her ex-fiancé's callous rejection.

Joanna jerked the piece of ninety-pound Saunders paper from the tray of water. Holding the piece by the edges, she shook off the surplus water and laid it on a drawing board, then dried her hands on her smock and stuck the edges of the paper down with strips of brown paper tape. Reaching into her pocket, she retrieved the thumbtacks and promptly stuck one in each taped end.

She needed to stretch several pieces and have them

ready for the three watercolors she had been commissioned to paint for a dealer in Santa Fe. Last week she had stretched the canvases for her two commissioned oil paintings, one of which already had a buyer.

She hadn't painted at all in the past few days. Instead, she'd busied herself with preparations for work, done some in-depth housecleaning, rewatched a dozen videocassettes—her favorite musicals from the thirties and forties—and read Annabelle Beaumont's diary through, from beginning to end.

When she had planned to visit the reservation to escape J.T., she had thought she could do enough sketches to foster some new ideas for the commissioned works. She wanted to try something different from her usual landscapes and portraits of the Navajo in typical settings. She had wanted to capture something of the Navajo spirit that had eluded her in her earlier work. No matter how diligently she tried, she couldn't seem to see past the surface, into the soul of New Mexico and the proud Navajo, the way her great-grandmother had done. But then, Annabelle had not focused her attention on a whole nation of people, but only on one man. A man she had loved as no other. It had been Benjamin Greymountain's spirit she had captured in her heart and then transformed the essence of her feelings into the words written in her diary.

But Joanna's trip to the reservation had been canceled. J.T. had said it was best to postpone any and all excursions for the time being. She knew he meant until Lenny Plott had been apprehended.

Slumping down in the overstuffed tan, green and apricot plaid chair, Joanna picked up her sketch pad from the hand-carved pine table to her right. In the early-dawn hours these past five mornings, when she'd been unable to sleep, she had told herself she should be painting, should be accomplishing something. Instead, she'd retreated to her sketch pad, using her charcoal pencils to fill page after page with hastily rendered images of J. T. Blackwood. In some sketches he wore his Stetson, in others his head was bare. Many were half-finished profiles, most from his right side, but several from the left, depicting his sinister-looking eye patch.

Flipping through the pad, she stopped and glared at the sketch she'd done this morning. This charcoal rendering was different from all the others. This was John Thomas Blackwood, rugged, hard, unsmiling. Neither white man nor Native American. Only primitive male.

She slapped the pad closed, then threw it on the floor at her feet. What ever had possessed her to fill half the sketch pad with drawings of J.T.? What would he think if he saw them? He might get the wrong idea and assume she—

No! She did not feel anything for J.T., except maybe gratitude. She was exceedingly thankful that he was in charge of keeping her safe; that if necessary, he would become her personal bodyguard. She prayed the necessity would never arise, that the authorities would arrest Lenny Plott and return him to prison before he was able to find her. Or Claire. Or Libby.

The second week of J.T.'s vacation would end soon, but he had promised to stay on at the ranch. Even though she had seen him only at a distance the past few days, she felt reassured by his presence. She knew that he was keeping close tabs on her and taking every precaution for her safety.

But there seemed to be no immediate danger. No one knew where Lenny Plott was. He could still be in Virginia. Or he could already be in New Mexico. Or he could have gone to Missouri to hunt down Claire Andrews. Or he could somehow have discovered Libby Felton's whereabouts. Only God knew what slimy rock that monster had crawled under.

No, there was no immediate danger from Lenny Plott, a man the authorities couldn't find. Joanna's only immediate danger came from her ridiculous thoughts of J. T. Blackwood. She was confused and overly emotional, her nerves strung to the breaking point. That's why I'm thinking the way I am, she decided. All right, so he'd been tender and understanding about the rape. And he had made a promise her heart wanted to believe he would keep— that he would protect her from all harm. Still, that was no reason for her to start thinking of him as some knight in shining armor, as a man equal to his great-grandfather, a man capable of fulfilling her romantic dreams.

The loud knock on the front door startled her. She jumped, then her body stiffened. Don't react this way, she told herself. She had to stop thinking every bump, every creak, every unexpected sound might be Lenny Plott. The man would hardly come to her door and knock, would he?

The knocking continued, then ceased abruptly. "Joanna? Are you all right?" J.T. called to her.

She opened her mouth to answer, but only a quivering squeak came out. Her mind issued orders, but her body didn't respond.

"Joanna!"

By the time she had convinced herself she could move, that her legs could actually hold her weight and walk across the living room, J.T. had used the spare key she'd given him to unlock her door. He stormed into her house, scanning the huge expanse of combined living and dining areas. She met him in the middle of the room. He glared at her, then reached out and grabbed her by the shoulders.

She knew he wanted to shake her, and realized how much control he was exerting to keep from doing just that.

"Why the hell didn't you answer me?" He squeezed her shoulders, then released her.

"I'm sorry. I—"

"Are you all right?"

"I'm okay. What do you want? Why did you stop by?"

"I came by to see if you'd like to take a ride with me," he said. "You haven't been off the ranch in five days. I thought maybe you'd enjoy an outing."

"Oh, I see. Was this Elena's idea? Did she tell you that I've been complaining about feeling hemmed in?"

J.T. grinned—a half smile, really, not showing any teeth. "She mentioned you were used to coming and going as you pleased, to taking off for hours at a time to sketch or paint."

Joanna nodded.

"Elena fixed a picnic basket," J.T. said. "Sandwiches. A thermos of iced tea. That sort of stuff." He glanced at Joanna, taking note of her appearance. "Have you been in your gown all day?"

"I'll go change." She whirled around, then saw her sketch pad on the floor. "Where are we going?" She walked by the plaid chair, stuck out her foot and kicked the pad under the chair.

"I thought you might want to go out past Trinidad to the old archaeological dig where your great-grandparents worked the summer they lived here."

Halting in the doorway to her bedroom, Joanna swung around and faced J.T. "What? I tried to get permission from the man who owns the land, to go out to the old site, but I could never get anywhere with him. He said he had enough trespassers traipsing around on his property, stealing artifacts and—"

"That old man was my grandfather's worst enemy. It seems Hezekiah Mahoney married the woman my grandfather had picked out for himself and John Thomas never forgave either of them. I think it pleased Hezekiah to see my grandfather taken down a peg or two when he had to claim a half-breed as his heir."

"Are you saying—"

"I'm saying Hezekiah and I have always understood each other." J.T. walked over and sat down in the plaid chair. "I've done him a few favors over the years, and he owes me one or two. He isn't unreasonable. He allows archaeologists and archaeology students to work out at the old dig."

"And he gave us permission to visit the site?"

"Yep. So hurry up and change clothes."

"Can we stay out there for the rest of the day?" she asked. "Do you have the time? I'd love to take a sketch pad and do some work while we're there. I need some fresh ideas for the paintings I've been commissioned to do."

"We can stay until the sun goes down, if that's what you want," J.T. said. "You can look the place over. We can eat Elena's lunch. And you can draw to your heart's content."

"Thanks, J.T."

He liked her smile. Real. Honest. Warm. "Jo, while we're out there, we need to talk. Okay?"

Her smile disappeared, and J.T. wished he'd waited to mention anything about their needing to talk. But he wanted to prepare her, get her ready for what he had to tell her. No matter what happened in the days and weeks ahead, he was not going to lie to her. Not about anything.

"Okay," she said, then hurried into her bedroom.

J.T. laid his Stetson on the hand-carved table to his

right. Leaning over, resting his elbows on his thighs, he let his hands dangle between his spread legs.

Today's excursion out to the old archaeological dig on Mahoney's ranch *had* been Elena's idea. She'd been after him for two days to call old Hezekiah and arrange to take Joanna on this special outing. After his talk with Lieutenant Milton George and his telephone calls—one to Sam Dundee, and another to an FBI friend, Dane Carmichael—J.T. had decided it might be easier for him to discuss hard, cold facts with Joanna while she was relaxed and enjoying herself.

In the five days since he'd accepted responsibility for her safekeeping, J.T. had taken precautions to keep Joanna Beaumont as safe as possible without actually placing a twenty-four-hour-a-day guard at her door. He had suggested she should move into the main house. After all, they had more than enough room. But she hadn't wanted to leave her own home. He supposed he understood how she felt. But if Plott did make a move, J.T. would have no choice but to insist she stay with him. Or—and he really didn't want to think about his other choice—he would have to move into the renovated bunkhouse with her.

He had lived in close confines with a beautiful woman more than once and been able to remain completely professional and emotionally uninvolved. But Joanna Beaumont was more than just a client. She was someone he desired. That could pose a major problem for him—wanting a woman he had sworn to protect. A woman who, by her own admission, didn't completely trust him.

Staring down at his booted feet, J.T. noticed the edge of some sort of book sticking out from underneath the chair. He reached down, pulled out the large notebook, and picked it up. Leaning back in the chair, he laid the sketch pad on his lap and opened it to the first page. The bottom dropped out of his stomach. He turned the page, then sucked in a deep breath and let it out. Hurriedly, he flipped through the pages, and on each, he saw himself. They were rough, obviously hastily sketched likenesses, but there was no mistaking Joanna's chosen subject. When he looked at the last sketch, about halfway through the pad, he closed his eyes, blotting out what he saw. In that one drawing, she had come too close to capturing the real J. T. Blackwood. A man at odds with himself. Hard. Cold. Cynical. A man torn between two cultures—the one his grandfather had forced him to accept, and the one the old man had taught him to be ashamed of and to completely reject.

J.T. closed the pad and slipped it back under the chair. He wished he'd never seen the damned thing. If Joanna was sketching him, over and over again, seeing past the facade he presented to the world and getting too close to the angry, disillusioned man inside him, that meant she had allowed all the romantic nonsense concerning their great-grandparents to make her think— Hell! He had to put a stop to this before it started. He wasn't averse to the idea of having an affair with Joanna, now that he realized she wasn't just another spoiled rich girl out for kicks. But no way did he want her to think of him as some dream lover who could fulfill all her fantasies.

It would be better for both of them if he set her straight today. He didn't know a damn thing about romance or happily-ever-after or making love to a woman who needed the utmost tenderness.

He wondered if there had been a man in her life, someone she had trusted enough to take into her bed, since the night Lenny Plott had raped her. What did it do to a woman to be brutalized that way, to lose all sense of power and control? What would I have done if I'd been her fiancé? J.T. asked himself. He knew he would have wanted to hunt Plott down and kill him with his bare hands. And he knew he never would have deserted Joanna. If she'd been his woman, he would have— But she hadn't been his woman, wasn't his woman now. And for both their sakes, he had to keep it that way.

"I DON'T KNOW how to thank you, J.T." Joanna spread her arms open wide as if somehow she could embrace the land and the sky, and perhaps even grasp the moment and hold on to it forever. "It still looks so much like Annabelle described it and yet so very different, too. They lived in tents right here on the site, and went into Trinidad for supplies."

"Your great-grandfather was the archaeologist. Why did he bring his wife along with him? This is some pretty rugged country, even now. It could hardly have been a suitable place for a Virginia society matron." J.T. lifted the thermos from the picnic basket he had placed beside him when he'd sat down atop the huge, oddly shaped rock formation.

Joanna looked down into the valley below. Such a wide-open space. Such an incredible view. Steep-walled canyons. Never-ending blue sky. And colors so sharp and vivid, they took her breath away.

"Annabelle was a lot more than a society matron. She was a site artist and photographer. She kept a detailed record of the artifacts her husband found, photographing or sketching every discovery. And, for your information, Ernest Beaumont wasn't just an archaeologist." She turned and smiled at J.T. "He was a world-renowned archaeologist, and he counted among his friends both Earl H. Morris and Alfred V. Kidder. He took part in Kidder's Pecos conference in 1927." Suddenly realizing she was babbling, Joanna hushed, shook her head and laughed. "I admit that, after reading Annabelle's diary, I found out everything I could about my great-grandparents."

"Did you discover the reason your great-grandmother committed adultery?" J.T. asked.

Her laughter died as quickly as it had been born. She sat down on the rock beside J.T. and watched while he poured iced tea into plastic cups. He handed her a cup. She accepted it, being careful to neither touch him nor look at him.

"Ernest Beaumont had been a contemporary of Annabelle's father, who had arranged the marriage for Annabelle, his only child, shortly before his death." Joanna sipped her tea. "She was eighteen when she married. Ernest was forty-two. She was a dutiful wife, who gave him two sons, and often accompanied him on his archaeological digs, working with him. They had a contented marriage, but not a passionate one."

"So Annabelle met Benjamin and saw her chance to put a little passion into her life." J.T. unwrapped a ham-and-cheese sandwich. "She had a summer affair with a wild savage, then returned to her safe, secure life in Virginia and wrote beautiful prose about her 'great love.'" J.T. grunted, his cynicism obvious in both his words and the cold expression on his face.

"She *did* love him. She never forgot him. Never loved anyone else."

"Yeah, sure. Look, Jo, if she'd really loved Benjamin, she'd have given up everything and stayed out here in New Mexico with him."

"How could she have done that? It wasn't as if all she had to do was pack her bags and leave her husband. She had two children. And it was Benjamin who told her she couldn't sacrifice her children for him. That if she did, someday she'd grow to hate him."

"Annabelle's diary sure has you hooked, doesn't it?" J.T. handed her a sandwich. "Elena packed chips and pickles. Want some?"

"No, thank you." She unwrapped the sliced sandwich, lifted one of the halves to her mouth and took a bite.

"Hey, there's no need for you to get upset with me or pout," J.T. said. "You and I disagree about our great-grandparents' affair. You think it was some grand passion, some eternal love, and that they're up in heaven now, reunited and happy. I, on the other hand, think they had the hots for each other, sneaked off together every chance they could, but when the summer ended, they went their separate ways without a bunch of mushy sentimental exchanges or broken hearts." Joanna chewed slowly, swallowed, and took another bite. She turned her back on J.T., not wanting to listen to him make light of their great-grandparents' tragic love affair. Obviously, the man didn't have a romantic, loving bone in his body.

J.T. grasped her shoulder. She jumped, then jerked around and faced him. "You don't know the first thing about love. Real love. The kind Annabelle and Benjamin shared."

"Let's drop the subject." He squeezed her shoulder. She glared at his hand. Immediately, he slipped his hand down her arm. His touch was light, but sensual. Joanna shivered. J.T. lifted his hand, clutched her chin and tilted her face. "Besides, we've got more important things to discuss than our ancestors."

Joanna held up her right hand in J.T.'s face. "You might not believe in mushy, sentimental exchanges or passionate, everlasting love, but Benjamin Greymountain did. He put his whole heart into crafting this ring." She grabbed

J.T.'s right hand, lifting it in hers. "And this one. These rings symbolized everything he felt. Everything he and Annabelle had shared."

J.T. glared at her. Her heart pounded, the beat drowning out every other sound. He grasped her by the back of the neck, sliding one hand under her long ponytail while gripping her waist with the other, and drawing her toward him.

"What do you want me to say, Jo?" He lowered his head, his lips so close to hers that he felt her breath on his mouth. "Okay. Maybe Annabelle and Benjamin were in love. How do I know? What the hell difference does it make? Just because you and I inherited their rings, doesn't mean there's some special bond between us."

Who was he trying so damned hard to convince—her or himself? He wanted to deny it, wanted to pretend it didn't exist. But it did. There *was* some sort of bond between him and Joanna. There had been since the moment they met. But it wasn't what she thought it was, wasn't what she wanted. It was plain, old-fashioned lust. And J.T. would bet his last dollar that lust had been the overriding emotion between Benjamin and Annabelle.

J.T. wanted to take Joanna. Here. Now. On this hard, hot rock in the middle of nowhere, with only the birds and the insects and the big blue sky as witnesses. And perhaps the ghosts of two long-dead lovers. Had his great-grandfather felt this way about Annabelle? Had his blood run hot every time he'd touched her?

J.T. took Joanna in his arms, kissing her as he had longed to kiss her since the day they met. A wild, hungry passion ruled his actions. He was neither gentle nor patient. When she did not respond, but sat in his arms, stiff and unyielding, he thrust his tongue into her mouth and cupped her hip with one hand while he held her head in place with the other.

He ended the kiss abruptly, resting his forehead against hers. His breathing was ragged and harsh. Taking her shoulders in his hands, he held her at arm's length. "I'm sorry, Jo. I didn't mean to be so rough. I'm not used to taking things easy or being gentle."

She looked directly at him. "You think I need to be handled with kid gloves, don't you? Because of the rape. You think I'm not normal anymore, that I can't react the way a normal woman would."

"I don't think any such thing." He rubbed her shoulders. "I just think my kiss might have been a little too brutal. You froze solid in my arms, honey."

"For your information, you aren't the first man who's kissed me since... I have dated. There have been other men. Is your ego so enormous you think all you had to do was kiss me and I'd fall at your feet, that you would be the only one who could sexually arouse me?"

"Did you respond to any of these men you dated?" His touch on her shoulders softened. "Did you have sex with any of them?"

"I—I don't think that's any of your business."

He ran one hand across her shoulder, then draped his big fingers around the side of her neck, caressing her with tenderness. "I made you a promise to protect you, to keep you safe. Now, I'm going to make you another promise. I promise that I'll never take your power and control away from you. That even if I possess you completely, it will be only because you've given me the right."

Joanna shivered. He was telling her that he wanted her, that he expected them to become lovers. Did she want him? Was she prepared to be his lover? "There hasn't been anyone since... My former fiancé and I—"

Releasing her, not touching her at all, J.T. lowered his head and kissed her again. This time his mouth moved over hers with soft, tender passion. When she made no protest, he deepened the kiss by slow degrees. Joanna slipped her arms around his neck, encouraging him, responding, hesitantly at first, but soon taking charge of the kiss. When she was breathless and trembling, she eased away from him and stood.

The bright afternoon sun coated her with warmth. She breathed deeply, then smiled at J.T. "You're a man of your word, aren't you, J. T. Blackwood?"

"I try to be," he said. "If I give a promise, I keep it."

She nodded, then turned away from him and looked back down over the wide expanse of northwestern New Mexico's rugged yet fiercely beautiful landscape. Did believing J.T. was a man of his word mean that she trusted him? She wanted to trust him—indeed, needed to trust him—and perhaps, on some level, she did. But not completely, and never with her heart.

"Before we left the ranch this morning, you said we needed to talk, and I know it wasn't about Annabelle and Benjamin," Joanna said.

He stood, walked over to her and drew her back up against his chest. She relaxed against him.

"I talked to Lieutenant George." Joanna tensed in his arms. "He has contacted Claire Andrews and Libby Felton."

"How did he find Libby?" Joanna asked.

"It wasn't difficult. She has a driver's license, a couple of credit cards. She files income taxes."

"Oh, I never thought about how easy it would be to find her. Where is she living now?"

"Texas," J.T. said.

"What else did Lieutenant George tell you?"

"Plott seems to have disappeared, and left no trace." J.T. hugged her to him. "And even if Plott has more trouble than the authorities had getting the information he needs on you and the other two women, it won't be impossible for him to get it."

"What are you saying? That if Plott wants to find us, he can?"

"I'm afraid so. I contacted an old friend of mine, Dane Carmichael. He's an FBI agent. You realize the Feds are already involved. They were called in when Melody Horton was kidnapped."

"And?"

"Hell, Jo. Why didn't you tell me Plott had millions of dollars at his disposal? The guy is some sort of Virginia blue blood whose name is really Leonard Mayfield Plott III, and he comes from the same kind of wealthy, aristocratic background you do."

"I know." She crossed her arms over J.T.'s where they wrapped around her. "But I don't see what his background has to do with—"

"A guy with that kind of money can pay to get any information he needs. God knows how much he paid out to engineer his escape from prison."

"He's going to find me, isn't he? And when he knows where I am, he'll come after me."

"Yeah, there's a good chance that sooner or later he'll come to Trinidad. But we'll be ready for him. I'll keep you safe."

They stood there, looking down at the canyon below them. Joanna thought she heard the sound of drums somewhere off in the distance, but when she saw a streak of lightning on the far horizon, followed by a low rumble of thunder, she realized she had imagined the drums—just as she had imagined them the first time she'd seen J.T.

At sunset, J.T. drove up to the ranch house and parked, then rounded the vehicle, lifted Joanna's sketch pad from her lap and assisted her.

"J.T.!" Elena ran out into the yard. "I was just going to call you on your cellular phone when Alex heard you drive up."

"What's wrong?" Joanna asked.

Alex stepped off the porch. Elena turned to him, her eyes pleading. Alex looked directly at J.T. "That Lieutenant George just phoned from Richmond. It seems Claire Andrews received a phone call from Lenny Plott this afternoon. He warned her that he was heading west, that he had business in Missouri and he'd be seeing her soon."

Joanna gasped, then covered her mouth with her clutched fist. J.T. put his arm around her and pulled her up against him.

"He's found out where Claire lives," Joanna said. "How long will it be before he finds me, too?"

CHAPTER SIX

His hand closed over her mouth, silencing her scream. He gazed down into her eyes and laughed when he saw the terror she could not hide.

"I promised I'd get out of prison and hunt you down, didn't I?" Lenny Plott's grin widened as he laid the knife across her throat. "I warned you that you'd be sorry if you testified against me. You and the other three."

She struggled to free herself, pushing up against him, but he pressed her down, trapping her with his body.

"You can't get away from me. There's no one here to save you." He removed his hand from her mouth, then kissed her hard, thrusting his tongue inside.

Joanna moaned. He slipped his hand under her gown, inching his way up her leg.

No, please, dear God. Not again. Not ever again! She prayed he would go ahead and kill her. She felt his fingers, painful and probing, and felt the knife at her throat.

Joanna's scream rent the night air. She jerked straight up in bed. Sweat coated her body, drenching her nightgown. Trembling from head to toe, she grasped the bottom sheet with both hands as she tried to slow her harsh, accelerated breathing. Reaching out a trembling hand, she switched on the bedside lamp.

A dream. Only a dream. But it had seemed so real. Too

real. Had it been a premonition? Was it inevitable that she faced Lenny Plott again?

With his 9-mm Glock pistol held firmly and ready to fire, J.T. flung open the bedroom door and quickly scanned the area for an intruder. When he saw none, he turned to Joanna.

"What happened?" Replacing his gun in the shoulder holster he was wearing, he walked toward the bed. "You scared the hell out of me."

"Where did you come from?" Sliding to the side of the bed, she slipped her legs off the edge.

"I decided to have the ranch hands take turns standing guard outside. Starting last night. I woke up early and came over to relieve Chuck Webb." J.T. sat down beside Joanna. "I hadn't been here more than ten minutes when I heard you screaming."

Joanna scooted away from J.T., not thinking rationally, only feeling vulnerable and insecure. "It was just a dream. A nightmare, really."

"Must have been some nightmare," J.T. said. "Want to tell me about it?" Joanna was acting skittish, like a spooked mare, he thought. If only she would let him, he'd take her in his arms and hold her, but he could see plainly that she didn't want to be touched. Not right now.

Joanna shook her head. "I'd like to forget it."

"Think you can go back to sleep?" he asked.

"No." She wondered if she'd ever sleep again without fearing the return of the nightmares. For months after the rape, in fact for nearly a year, she had seldom slept the whole night through. "What time is it?"

"It's about five o'clock. If you don't think you can go back to sleep, I'll fix us some coffee."

J.T. stood, but stopped abruptly before taking a step when he felt the tentative touch of Joanna's fingertips against his hand. He looked down at her hand reaching out for him. His chest tightened; his stomach knotted. Turning his hand upside down, he offered her his open palm. Damn, but he wanted to grab her, drag her into his arms and hold her close and safe. Instead he waited, holding his breath.

She laid her hand in his, threading her fingers through his fingers, clasping their hands together.

Nothing in his life had prepared him for the feelings that coursed through him at that precise moment. Desire softened by overwhelming tenderness. A fierce protectiveness that made him want to fight the world for her. And a primitive possessiveness that shouted, *This woman is mine!*

He could not bring himself to look at her, uncertain what he would see in her eyes, and afraid of what he might do.

Holding tightly to his hand, she eased off the bed and stood. "Thank you, for being here."

He lifted his downcast gaze, drinking in the sight of Joanna, all feminine beauty in her teal silk nightshirt. Her rich, dark red hair tumbled around her shoulders in a thick, fiery mass. She stared at him with earthy, moss green eyes.

He grew hard and heavy, the very sight of her arousing him painfully. "Joanna—"

"Let me put on my robe and I'll go fix our coffee." She released his hand, turned and picked up her matching teal silk robe from the corner chair. "I have some banana-nut muffins I made fresh yesterday."

The moment she pulled away from him, he felt bereft, as if he'd been robbed of the tentative closeness blossoming between them.

"Muffins and coffee sound good to me," he said, and followed her out of the bedroom.

She flipped on a lamp in the living room as they passed through, then turned on the fluorescent light in the kitchen. J.T. sat down in a Windsor chair at the table.

"Are you sure I can't help you?" he asked.

"Thanks, but I know where everything is and can do it quicker without any help."

He sat and watched her as she prepared the coffee and warmed the muffins. He couldn't keep his eyes off her. Damn! What was wrong with him? He hadn't been this horny in years. If he needed a woman, he could solve that problem easily enough. But that was it. He didn't want just any woman. He wanted Joanna Beaumont. And despite her denials and her brave show of strength, she was vulnerable and fragile and filled with distrust. There was a raging bull inside him, a rutting animal. But the object of his desire needed a patient, gentle and understanding lover. Hell, what a mess!

He traced the lines and shapes on the table cover, then noticed it was a woven cloth of Navajo design. He'd seen enough Navajo rugs and blankets and other items to recognize them. When he'd given Elena permission to redecorate the ranch house after she'd married Alex, she had used various Navajo items in almost every room.

Joanna placed two mugs of piping-hot coffee down on the table, then removed the huge muffins from the microwave and laid each on a separate plate. Placing a plate in front of J.T., she sat down opposite him. She tore her muffin in half, broke off a piece and popped it into her mouth. Chewing slowly, she swallowed, then washed the morsel down with a sip of coffee.

J.T. lifted his mug. The coffee smelled good. He always started his mornings with a pot of coffee. But this morning, he'd been too anxious to bother with it. His gut instincts had told him he should be near Joanna. Somehow he had known she was going to need him.

Holding the mug in both hands, he sipped the coffee. "Was your dream about Plott?"

She gazed down into the dark liquid in her mug. "Yes. He had found me and was—" Joanna looked at J.T. and drew in a deep breath when she saw him staring at her, an odd expression on his face. "He was raping me...before he killed me."

"No wonder you woke up screaming." J.T. laid his hand, palm up, on the table. "It's not going to happen, Jo. You're safe with me. Plott may find out where you are, but he'll have to go through me to get to you. And tougher bastards than Plott have found out it's not so easy to get through me."

Joanna glanced down at his outstretched hand. He was offering her comfort and support, the way he'd done in the bedroom. He wasn't grabbing, wasn't taking, wasn't forcing anything. He was just waiting for her to make the first move. She laid her hand in his. With gentle strength, he encompassed her hand with his.

She looked up at him and smiled. He returned the smile and squeezed her hand.

"I'm all right," she said. "I'll admit that I'm scared, but I'm dealing with it. I've had to deal with it before. For a long time after the rape, I had nightmares. I kept reliving what had happened over and over, and each time it got worse. That first year, even after I came out here to New Mexico, I seldom slept the whole night through."

"Yeah, I can understand," he said. "I had a few nightmares after this." He pointed to his black eye patch. "The bullet severed the optical nerve and screwed things up pretty bad inside my head. I was lucky I didn't die or wind up some sort of vegetable."

"The eye patch suits you. Makes you look roguish and a little dangerous."

"I am dangerous, Jo. You might do well to remember that."

"Are you trying to warn me about something?" she asked.

He squeezed her hand, released it and stood. Lifting his coffee mug, he took a swig of the warm, sweet liquid, then set the mug back down on the table. "You're a sentimental, romantic woman. You need something I can't give you. I don't want to wind up hurting you, but I could, if you let me."

He walked into the living room, propped his booted foot on the hearth and stared up at the portrait hanging above the fireplace. A beautiful woman with coppery-red hair, cut in a fashionable twenties bob, stared down at J.T. with compelling blue-green eyes.

"That's Annabelle Beaumont." Joanna walked into the living room. "I painted her portrait, using some old photographs to go by and from studying the portrait of her that was painted when she was sixteen. Her father had it done and it hangs in one of the guest bedrooms at Mother's house."

"I can see why Benjamin Greymountain wanted her," J.T. said. "She was a beautiful woman." Turning his head, he ran his gaze over Joanna's face. "As a matter of fact, you look a bit like her."

"Yes, I know. I resemble my father a great deal, and he was told he took after his grandmother."

J.T. wondered what she'd say if he told her that he looked a bit like Benjamin Greymountain, that although he'd never seen any photographs of his ancestor, and didn't even know if any existed, he had seen Benjamin's likeness. When his mother had given him the silver-and-turquoise ring, she had also given him a yellowed sketch, the edges of the paper frayed and the charcoal drawing somewhat faded. She had told him that the sketch went with the ring, that both had belonged to her grandfather, Benjamin Greymountain, a Navajo silversmith and a revered leader to his people.

J.T. paced around the living room, knowing he should leave before he said or did something he would regret, but he didn't want to desert Joanna. If he left, she'd know he was running from her. And where could he run? Outside to stand guard? He had the oddest notion that there was nowhere on earth he could run to get away from Joanna, to escape the way he felt about her.

He stopped at the easel set up before the row of windows looking out onto the front porch. Glancing down at the sketch, he caught his breath. Damn! Yesterday when he'd taken her to the site of the old archaeological dig, she'd spent a couple of hours sketching and several times he had caught her watching him. But he'd had no idea she was using him as subject matter.

Hell, he shouldn't be surprised. She'd already filled half a notebook with rough sketches of him. But this was not a rough sketch. This was a completed work. And there was something about the way he looked in the picture that greatly disturbed him. He couldn't quite put his finger on it, but there was something—something alien to him.

"I didn't mean for you to see that." She walked up beside him. "I suppose I should have asked your permission before drawing you."

He grabbed her wrist. She gasped. "Why would you have bothered to ask my permission to do another sketch, when you'd already filled a notebook with sketches of me?"

She jerked away, glaring at him, her mouth rounded in surprise. "How did you know? When did you see my sketches?"

"I found the pad yesterday while I was waiting for you to change clothes. It was sticking halfway under the chair I sat down in."

"Why didn't you say something then?"

"I didn't want to embarrass you."

"You didn't want—" Joanna laughed. "You're so damn egotistical, J. T. Blackwood. Those sketches aren't what you think. And neither is that one." She pointed at the completed sketch on her easel. "If you think I'm some lovesick fool—"

"I never said you were a lovesick fool. Just a sentimental, romantic fool. You've got it in your head that because your great-grandmother had an affair with a native, you're destined to do the same."

"I wish I'd never told anyone, least of all you, about Annabelle's diary!" Spinning around, she marched over to the easel, ripped off the sketch and threw it to the floor, then lifted her foot and stomped on the torn paper.

"There's no need for you to get violent. I didn't mean to upset you, only warn you not to build any romantic fantasies around me."

J.T. grinned, a stupid, smirky, macho grin, and Joanna wanted to slap that silly smile off his face. "For your information, I have five commissioned works to do, all with a Native American theme. I've built my career on creating unique oil and watercolor paintings as well as finely detailed sketches. But somehow I've never been able to truly capture the spirit of this land or the Navajo people. Using you as a subject has helped me focus on your ancestry. In a couple of sketches I've come so close to putting my emotions on paper, in delving deep enough inside myself to find the truth."

"What the hell are you talking about?"

"You might have been raised as a cowboy, J.T., but when I try to sketch you as a cowboy, I know something is missing. In this sketch—" she stomped her foot on the object under discussion "—I somehow captured the real you. A man who is both cowboy and Indian, and yet is truly neither."

He grabbed her, not heeding the warning voice inside his head, listening only to the primitive needs inside him and to the whispers of his heart. Pulling her up against him, he glared at her. "You see too much, Jo. You understand too much."

"I'm not afraid of you," she said, tilting her chin defiantly as she stared directly at him.

"You should be," he told her. "But heaven help me, I don't want you to be." Lowering his head, he took her mouth in a hot, bold kiss that quickly had her clinging to him.

The moment she responded, giving herself over to his ravenous attack, he gentled the kiss, then cupped her buttocks and drew her up against his arousal. He ached with the need to take her, to be inside her.

Lifting her in his arms, he gazed into her questioning eyes, then carried her over to the apricot leather sofa. He laid her down, untied her robe and spread it apart, revealing her silk nightshirt. Pulling the robe down her arms, he paused to kiss one and then the other shoulder. Joanna trembled.

"Easy, honey." He removed her robe and tossed it on the floor. Then he brought his body down on the wide sofa, placing his legs on either side of her. He braced himself by laying his hands flat on the cushion, one on each side of her head.

She raised her arm, reached out and caressed his face. "I'm not sure I can do this. There hasn't been... I don't—"

"Only as far as you want to go." J.T. kissed her forehead. "Trust me just a little, Jo. When you tell me to stop, I'll stop. It may kill me, but I'll stop. I promise. Just don't deny us some pleasure. I need this, and I think you do, too."

Nodding agreement, she tried to smile, but couldn't. Although she longed for J.T. to touch her intimately, to lead her along a passionate path to fulfillment, she wasn't sure that at some point she wouldn't freeze in his arms. And if she did, what would he do? Could she trust him to keep his promise?

He unbuttoned her nightshirt—slowly, kissing each inch of newly exposed flesh, painting a moist trail down her throat, between her breasts, over her stomach, then stopping just below her navel. He raised his head and looked at her. With the utmost gentleness, he spread apart her nightshirt, exposing her naked body completely.

"Joanna." He had never seen anything as beautiful as the woman who lay beneath him, all slender curves and creamy flesh.

He ached with wanting, his need urgent and painful. Patience, he told himself. Patience!

He slid over onto his side, lifting her as he turned. She gasped, grabbing him, holding on to his shoulders as he placed her on top of him. Raising her body up, she stared down at him. He slipped his hand beneath her nightshirt to caress her buttocks. Joanna sighed and closed her eyes, savoring the sensations his touch aroused in her.

Capturing her nipple with his teeth, J.T. tugged playfully. Joanna moaned, then shivered. He licked and suckled one breast, then moved hurriedly to give the other equal attention. And just when she thought she could bear no more of the torturous pleasure, he stopped and kissed her throat. Lifting his arms, he slipped the fingers of his right hand through those of his left and placed his hands behind his head.

"J.T.?" With labored breathing, she spoke his name in a harsh whisper.

"I've been doing all the work," he said. "It's your turn."

"My turn?" What did he mean? What did he expect her to do?

"Undo my shirt."

"Oh." She obeyed his command instantly, her nervous fingers working quickly to unsnap his shirt. Sliding her hands beneath the chambray material, she spread his shirt back, revealing his chest the way he had revealed hers. She sucked in a deep breath. Dear God, *he* was the beautiful one. All sleek, hard muscle and hot bronze flesh. Lowering her head she licked one tiny, pebble-hard nipple, then kissed it. He groaned. She repeated the process on the other nipple.

He reached around and grabbed the back of her head in one hand, threading his fingers through her hair. She dotted kisses all over his chest, moving steadily downward until her mouth reached his belt buckle.

Grasping her shoulders, he pulled her upward until her breasts scraped over his chest. He took her mouth, thrusting his tongue inside. Her breathing quickened and she responded with a fervor that astonished her.

He drew away from her, and whispered against her lips, "Would you like to unbuckle my belt, honey?"

Nodding her head, she smiled, then sat up on top of him, resting her hips on his legs. She clutched her hands into fists, trying to stop the trembling. Taking her hands into his, he lowered them slowly to his belt. He helped her undo the heavy silver-and-turquoise belt buckle, then released her hands and waited for her to make the next move. She touched the zipper tab, then jerked her hand away.

"I—I can't," she said.

"Then don't," he told her. "It's your call, Jo."

Clasping the zipper tab between her thumb and index finger, she eased the zipper down and laid her hand over his throbbing sex. Only his thin cotton briefs separated her hand from his naked flesh. J.T. groaned deep in his throat. Heaven help him, he was about to lose it. She had no idea what she was doing to him, what torment she was putting him through.

Cupping her hips, he pressed her downward, positioning the apex of her thighs directly on his arousal. He pushed upward gently, allowing her to become accustomed to the feel of him. Her whole body trembled, then instinctively undulated against him.

He couldn't take much more. Her innocent explorations were driving him crazy. "I want you, Jo. I want to make love to you." He kissed her hard, hot and hungrily.

She quivered beneath his touch, responding fervently, but when he eased his fingers inside her warm, damp body, she tensed. Bracing her hands on his shoulders, she pulled away from him.

"I can't. Please. I can't." Tears filled her eyes. She knew she had disappointed him, that he was on the verge of losing control.

He shoved her up, lifting himself into a sitting position at the same time. Settling her in his lap, he put his arms around her and hugged her close to him. "It's all right, honey." He nuzzled her neck with his nose and kissed the side of her face. He pulled her nightshirt together, then buttoned the three middle buttons, just enough to hold the material in place.

"I'm sorry." She choked back the tears.

"You have nothing to be sorry about," he said, holding her with a gentle protectiveness. "What we gave each other was enough for now. We both needed some loving. When you're ready for more, you'll let me know."

"Oh, J.T." Covering her mouth with her fist, she took several deep breaths and gulped down her sobs.

He sat on the sofa and held her in his arms while she cried. He ached unbearably. He had never wanted a woman the way he wanted Joanna. But he didn't want to hurt her, in fact, he would do anything to make sure she was never hurt again, especially not by him.

Was this the way Benjamin Greymountain had felt about Annabelle? Had he wanted her with a desperate, all-consuming passion? If so, J.T. understood why his great-grandfather had taken another man's wife. What he didn't understand was how Benjamin could ever have let her go.

ELENA GREGORY SQUIRMED on the stool where she sat perched, her waist-length black hair swaying softly with her movements. "I need a break, Jo. I'm sore from sitting in one position for so long."

Sighing, Joanna laid her brush aside. Elena had a difficult time sitting still for longer than fifteen minutes at a time. Joanna was beginning to wonder if she'd be able to complete Elena's portrait in time for Alex's birthday.

"Okay, we'll take a break. I could use some iced tea." Joanna wiped her hands on her jeans and walked around the easel. Glancing down at her watch, she realized it was after one o'clock. "Hey, we might as well take a lunch break. I didn't know it was so late."

"There's no need for me to go back up to the house

for lunch," Elena said. "Alex started on a new sculpture yesterday, and you know how he is when he starts a new project. I'll be lucky if he comes out of his studio for dinner."

"Then stay and have lunch with me. We can fix sandwiches."

"I'll help you." Elena glanced down at her clothes. "Maybe you'd better get me an apron. I didn't bring a change and I don't want to get anything on my outfit."

Elena had chosen an ankle-length gathered skirt and a long-sleeved blouse made of the same red cotton material—simple in design, but a striking contrast to her dark coloring. She wore an abundance of silver-and-turquoise jewelry; several rings and bracelets as well as dangling earrings. She had chosen a squash-blossom necklace with *naja* pendant because it had been crafted by Benjamin Greymountain and given to Elena by her mother.

Elena followed Joanna into the kitchen. She took the bread and baked chicken breasts out of the refrigerator while Joanna set the table.

"How are things going between you and J.T.?" Elena asked.

"Things are fine." Joanna tossed Elena a large tan apron trimmed in ecru crocheted lace. "I feel much safer knowing he's handling the security around me. I guess you saw Tim Rawlins outside when you came in, didn't you?"

"Yes. J.T. told Alex and me last night that he planned to put a man on guard duty around the clock." Elena sliced the cold chicken into strips and prepared their sandwiches. "J.T. took over guard duty bright and early this morning, didn't he?"

Joanna dropped the bag of potato chips on the table. "Yes. Fairly early." She cast her gaze downward, not wanting to face Elena, who was sure to suspect something if she could see Joanna's eyes.

"He was in an odd mood when he came back up to the house for breakfast." Elena returned to the refrigerator for ice, then filled their glasses. "He was just about as talkative as you are now when I asked him about it."

"About what?" Joanna asked.

Elena poured the tea into their glasses and brought them to the table. "Something must have happened between you and J.T. to make you both so secretive."

Joanna forced a quick laugh. "Just because you've had this plan to get your brother and me together for several years, doesn't mean J.T. and I have any intention of going along with your plans."

"Something did happen! I knew it. Confess. Did he kiss you?"

Someone knocked on the front door. Joanna jumped and Elena gasped. Both women turned around and faced the living room.

"Boy, we're as nervous as a couple of cats in a room full of rocking chairs," Elena said. "I'll go see who it is."

"No, you finish getting lunch ready and I'll go to the door."

Joanna crossed the room, opened the front door and sighed with relief when she saw Cliff Lansdell standing on her front porch.

"Afternoon." Cliff removed his hat. "I just wanted to stop by and see how you're doing. I hope I'm not intruding."

"Not at all, Cliff." Joanna stepped back to allow him entrance. "Come on in. Elena and I were just about to have lunch. Would you care to join us?"

"Done had mine, but thanks."

Joanna had liked Cliff since they'd first met, but

despite his rugged good looks and gentlemanly manners, she had called a halt to their budding relationship after half-a-dozen dates. Cliff's feelings for her had been much deeper and far more sexual than hers had been for him.

"How about a glass of tea?" Elena called out from the kitchen.

"Don't go to any trouble, Elena. I can't stay long. I just dropped by to say…well, to let you know, Joanna, that I—" he transferred his hat from one hand to the other and then back again "—I'll do anything I can to help J.T. keep you safe and not let that Plott fellow get anywhere near you."

Joanna reached out, laid her hand over Cliff's and gave it an affectionate squeeze. "Thank you. I appreciate your concern and—"

The telephone rang. Joanna tensed. Dammit, she had to stop this! Every time someone knocked at the door or the telephone rang or she heard an unusual sound, she overreacted.

"Want me to get it?" Elena asked.

Joanna nodded. Cliff placed his hand on her shoulder. She glanced at him and felt somewhat comforted by his friendly, caring smile.

"Hello," Elena answered the telephone. "Oh, hi there, Mrs. Beaumont. Yes, Joanna's right here." Elena held out the phone.

Hesitantly, Joanna walked over and took the phone out of Elena's hand. "Hello, Mother. How are you?"

"How am I?" Helene asked. "I'm worried sick about you, that's how I am."

"I'm perfectly all right," Joanna said. "There's no need for you to worry."

"My dearest girl, how can you say that? I know Lenny Plott has already discovered where Claire Andrews lives and has called and threatened her. It's only a matter of time until he finds out where Libby Felton is and where you are."

"I realize that's a possibility, Mother, but we can't be certain."

"Of course, we can be certain." Helene sighed. "Lenny didn't become a pauper when he went to jail. His family has millions, and that idiot mother of his will make sure he can put his hands on however much money he needs. Money can always buy information, Joanna. You know that as well as I do."

"I'm well guarded here at the ranch. J.T. has posted ranch hands outside my house day and night."

"A wise decision on Mr. Blackwood's part, I'm sure, but I'd feel much better if you came home to Virginia. Mr. Blackwood could escort you home, if you'd like, or I could send a bodyguard to get you. We'll hire around-the-clock guards here. Please, Joanna, come home."

"Mother, I am home." Joanna bit her bottom lip, then rolled her eyes heavenward. "I plan to spend the rest of my life here in New Mexico. I'm not ever going to move back to Virginia."

"But surely, someday—"

"Not now. Not ever."

"You'll change your mind," Helene said. "When you decide to marry and have children, you'll come back to Virginia to find a suitable husband."

"What makes you think I couldn't find a suitable husband out here in New Mexico?"

"Joanna, there isn't anything going on between you and this Blackwood man, is there?"

Joanna gripped the telephone with white-knuckled strength. "Why would you ask such a question?"

Joanna noticed Elena staring at her, questioning her

silently with her eyes. She glanced over at Cliff, who seemed equally puzzled.

"I know how totally enamored you were with that diary of your great-grandmother's. I told myself when you decided to move all the way to New Mexico that it was a temporary move. You needed to get away from…after the…after what happened to you. I understood. And I even went along with your romantic notions about Annabelle Beaumont and that illicit love affair she had with some Indian. But I never thought you'd stay out there or that you'd actually become involved with…well, with one of those people."

"One of those people? Native Americans? Is that what you mean, Mother?"

"I've had that Blackwood fellow thoroughly checked out," Helene said.

"You did what? How dare you!"

"When it comes to your safety, I'd dare almost anything. Besides, the man seems to be the very best at what he does and the firm in which he's a partner is considered one of the top private security firms in the nation."

"Then you have no reason to worry about me or want me to come back to Virginia, do you?"

"You didn't answer my question about you and Mr. Blackwood. Have you become personally involved with him? I know that he is Benjamin Greymountain's great-grandson."

"My God, Mother, when you said you had J.T. thoroughly checked out, you weren't kidding. You must have spent quite a bundle on private investigators." Joanna glanced back and forth between Elena and Cliff, and wished she wasn't having this conversation in front of an audience. Especially not Elena.

"If you won't come home to Virginia, I'm coming out there," Helene said.

"No, Mother, don't do that!"

"I'll fly out tomorrow and see if I can't talk sense to you, face-to-face. At a time like this, you should be at home."

"What are you so worried about, Mother?" Turning her back toward Elena and Cliff, Joanna lowered her voice. "What has you the most upset, the fact that Lenny Plott might find me and try to kill me, or that I might fall in love with J. T. Blackwood and ask him to marry me?"

"You're being irrational. There's no point in our discussing this anymore. You can expect me tomorrow."

"No, Mother, don't come out—" The dial tone hummed in Joanna's ear.

Cliff Lansdell walked across the room and placed his hand on Joanna's back. When she turned toward him, he slipped his arm around her shoulders. She rested against him, glad to have someone to lean on.

"I take it that we can expect a visit from Senator Helene Beaumont," Elena said.

Joanna nodded her head. "She'll be here sometime tomorrow."

"Are you all right, Joanna?" Cliff asked.

Slipping her arm around his waist, she hugged him. "I'll be fine as soon as I cool off and calm down. I love my mother dearly, but she has always tried to run my life."

Elena untied the apron she wore, folded it and laid it on the back of the sofa. "You never told me your mother was a bigot."

Joanna laughed. "She certainly doesn't consider herself one, but she is. She's horrified at the idea I might—"

"Who's horrified at what?" J. T. Blackwood stood in the arched opening leading into the kitchen.

They hadn't heard him enter the house. All three of them turned and stared at the intruder.

"You left your back door unlocked," J.T. said. "From now on, make sure it's locked." He walked into the living room. His eyes focused on Cliff Lansdell's arm draped across Joanna's shoulder. "What's going on here? Who were you talking about being horrified at something you might do?"

"My mother just called," Joanna told him.

"Mrs. Beaumont is worried about Joanna's safety," Cliff said.

"She's horrified at the thought Joanna might be hurt." Elena didn't look at her brother when she spoke.

"Are you worried about your safety?" J.T. walked up behind Joanna and glared at Cliff.

Cliff removed his arm from Joanna's shoulder and took a step away from her. Joanna watched the silent exchange between J.T. and Cliff, and couldn't help feeling a bit sorry for Cliff. At that moment, she realized few men would have the courage to stand up to J.T. and confront him. There was something powerfully intimidating about J. T. Blackwood; something other men obviously sensed instinctively. Cliff was a big guy, rugged and strong. She had seen him riding and roping and issuing orders in his duties as ranch foreman, but he hadn't dared make a stand against J.T.

"Guess I'd better be going," Cliff said. "If you need me for anything—"

"She won't need you," J.T. interrupted.

Cliff nodded, then made a hasty retreat out the front door.

"That show of machismo wasn't necessary." Joanna whirled around to face J.T. She placed her hands on her hips and glared at him.

"She's got you there, big brother," Elena said. "All Cliff was doing was giving her a little comfort."

"If you two will excuse me, I'm going into the bedroom for some privacy." Joanna patted Elena on the arm when she walked past her. "I'll call Mother back and see if I can persuade her not to fly out here tomorrow."

The moment they were alone, Elena turned to J.T. "You didn't hide your feelings very well."

"What the hell are you talking about?"

"I'm talking about your proprietary attitude toward Joanna. If you could have seen the look on your face. I thought for a few minutes you were going to rip Cliff's arm off."

"You're talking nonsense."

"Am I?" Elena smiled. "I don't think so. Cliff got the message. Everyone in this room got the message, including Joanna."

"What message?" J.T. asked.

"You've staked a claim on Jo and were sending out No Trespassing signals, loud and clear."

"You're reading too much into what happened."

"Look, Joanna doesn't need you acting like some macho jerk right now. She just had a rather unpleasant conversation with her mother. Senator Beaumont wants Jo to come home to Virginia, and she wants to hire another bodyguard. She's afraid her daughter might be getting a little too personally involved with the wrong sort of man."

"The wrong sort...you mean me?"

Elena shook her head. "Joanna really let her mother have it. She disagrees with the way her mother thinks. Joanna isn't like that."

"Senator Beaumont doesn't want her daughter to become seriously involved with a half-breed. That's it, isn't it? Well, the woman has nothing to worry about. Whatever happens between Joanna and me won't be serious. Her mother doesn't have to worry about her marrying—"

"I couldn't get through to Mother." Joanna stood across the living room, staring at J.T., her face pale, her eyes glazed with a fine mist of tears.

Damn, he hadn't meant for her to overhear his conversation with Elena. Joanna looked as if he'd slapped her. He had hurt her with his careless words. Why hadn't he been more cautious? The last thing in the world he wanted to do was cause Joanna any more pain.

"Jo, we need to talk," J.T. said.

"No, we don't need to talk." Joanna glanced at Elena. "I'd like to be alone for a while. Please."

"I'm not going to leave like this, not until we've talked." J.T. took a tentative step toward Joanna.

Elena grabbed him by the arm. "Call me later, okay?" she asked Joanna, then tugged on her brother's arm. "We're leaving now," she told him.

J.T. hesitated, but when he saw the anger and pain etched on Joanna's face, he turned around and walked out of the house with Elena.

Joanna went back into her bedroom, sat down on the edge of the bed and covered her face with her hands. The tears were trapped inside her, choking her, restricting her breathing.

Whatever happens between Joanna and me won't be serious. Won't be serious. Won't be serious.

She'd been a fool to think that just because J.T. wanted to make love to her, he might actually care about her. Maybe her mother had been right all along. Hoping to find the kind of love Annabelle Beaumont had found with Benjamin Greymountain was a fool's fantasy.

Joanna twisted her great-grandmother's ring around

and around on her finger. Sometimes she wished she'd never found the old diary and the leather pouch containing the ring. Maybe it would have been better if she'd never come to New Mexico, searching for a new life and dreaming of finding true love.

One thing was certain—J. T. Blackwood most definitely wasn't the man Benjamin Greymountain had been. But then, maybe she wasn't half the woman Annabelle had been.

CHAPTER SEVEN

J.T. NODDED AT Tim Rawlins when he stepped up on
Joanna's front porch. Standing at the door, he hesitated
before knocking. He'd given Joanna a couple of hours to
be by herself and calm down, but he'd waited as long as
he could. His patience had run out.

He hadn't meant for her to overhear his conversation
with Elena. He could have kicked himself when he'd seen
the look of hurt and disillusionment in her eyes. But who
knows, he told himself, maybe it's better this way. At least
now, she knew exactly where they stood. He wanted
Joanna, wanted her in the worst way a man could want a
woman. But if she was expecting love and "forever after,"
she had the wrong guy. *Love* wasn't a word that existed in
his vocabulary. And there was no such thing as "forever
after." He lived his life a day at a time.

Joanna opened the door, took one look at J.T. and
started to close the door in his face. He stuck his foot
over the threshold and grabbed the edge of the door.

"May I come in?" he asked.

She glared at his hand, then down at his foot. "Doesn't
look like I can stop you." She stared directly at him.

"I'd like to come in and talk to you, but I won't crash
my way in if you say no."

"Come in." Turning her back on him, her spine stiff as
a board, she marched into the living room.

J.T. followed her over to the easel supporting Elena's portrait. "You're capturing my sister's earthy beauty."

"We didn't get a chance to do much work today," Joanna said. "I need only a couple more sittings to be able to finish it. Elena wants it for Alex's birthday present."

"Well, it'll certainly be something he'll treasure."

"I hope so."

J.T. stared at the unfinished portrait. "Elena looks a lot like my mother. The way I remember her from my early childhood. When I saw her again after so many years, she was dying and had aged terribly."

"You and Elena resemble each other some, enough to recognize the fact you're brother and sister." Joanna covered the portrait.

"Elena was fifteen before I ever met her, before I even knew I had a half sister. One of my mother's relatives called and told me my mother was dying." J.T. strolled around the living room, surveying the changes Joanna had made in the old bunkhouse. She'd turned a ramshackle old building into a warm, comfortable home.

J.T. glanced at the portrait of Annabelle Beaumont hanging over the mantel, and wondered if he should show Joanna the picture he had of Benjamin. His gut instincts told him that Annabelle had been the artist who had drawn his great-grandfather's likeness in a stark, totally male black-and-white sketch. Suddenly J.T. noticed a small fire burning in the fireplace.

"It's too hot a day for a fire," he said.

"I needed to burn some trash." She sat down on the leather sofa. "Is there a reason you came over here to see me?"

J.T. took a closer look at the "trash" she had decided to burn. A tight knot formed in his throat when he recognized the notebook she had half-filled with sketches of him. Dammit! She must hate him. And he didn't want her to hate him. All he wanted was for her to accept this thing between them for what it was. Lust. Good old plain lust. Nothing less, but nothing more.

"Maybe you should go back to Virginia the way your mother wants you to," he said.

Snapping her head around, she frowned at him. "Why?"

"Why? Well, you'd be better off without my being involved in the case. I think it's pretty obvious that things aren't going to work out between us. Our expectations are different."

"Oh, I see. So, you're saying that if I return to Virginia and get a different bodyguard, I won't wind up making a total fool of myself over you."

"Dammit, Jo, that's not what I said." J.T. slumped down in the overstuffed plaid chair across from the sofa. "If you go back to Virginia, neither one of us will wind up making fools of ourselves. I want something from you that you're not willing to give, and you want something from me that isn't in me to give. It's as simple as that."

"Nothing's ever that simple."

"If you want to go home to Virginia, I'll call Simon Roarke and have him fly out here tomorrow and go back to Virginia with you whenever you're ready to go."

"Who's Simon Roarke?"

"He's been an agent with Dundee's Private Security for several years. He's top-notch. You'd be safe with him." J.T. grinned, but there was no mirth in his smile. "Besides, your mother might approve of him. He's pure Scotch-Irish all the way back to Adam. Not a drop of impure blood in him that I know of. But his folks were poor Southern farmers. Think that will disqualify him?"

"It might disqualify him as husband material," Joanna

said, "but I think Mother would approve of him being my bodyguard."

"Then I'll call him and have him catch the first flight—"

"There's no need to call Mr. Roarke. I'm not going anywhere. I'm staying right here in Trinidad, New Mexico, on the Blackwood ranch, and I'm holding you to your promise to stick around as long as I need protection." She smiled, just barely turning up the corners of her mouth. Her green eyes glistened with triumph.

"Your mother isn't going to be happy."

"I really don't care. I'm just sorry that you and Elena and Alex will have to endure her visit. She's a charming Southern lady on the surface, but beneath that Virginia-belle facade, beats the heart of a born politician. She's not above saying or doing whatever she thinks is necessary to get her own way."

"And that includes taking potshots at me."

"I'm not worried about you." Joanna stood. "Your hide is pretty tough. I'm worried about Elena. She's very protective of you, and she'll jump to your defense if Mother casts aspersions on your ethnic heritage." Joanna walked toward the front door. "I think we've discussed everything we needed to, don't you?"

J.T. stood. "Here's your hat. What's your hurry?" he said jokingly. "One question before you kick me out."

Shrugging, she nodded agreement. "All right. One question. Then you'll leave."

He glanced at the notebook, now almost totally consumed by the blaze in the fireplace. "Why did you burn the sketch pad?"

Every muscle in Joanna's body tensed; her nerves jangled like a zillion tiny bells. She couldn't bear the way J.T. was looking at her, as if accusing her of something sinful. How could she possibly answer him without lying? His thoughtless remark that nothing serious would ever happen between them had cut her to the quick. She didn't want to admit to him how much he had hurt her. But he already knew. The burning sketch pad was all the evidence he needed to know the depth of her anger.

"I understand exactly where we stand," she said. "We are not our great-grandparents. There is no grand love affair in our future. You don't want a serious relationship with me, and I don't want any type of relationship with you, other than in a strictly business capacity."

"You're a hard woman, Joanna Beaumont. You want all or nothing, don't you?"

"I'm afraid so."

"I'll keep a guard posted outside around the clock, and I'll check in with you from time to time." He walked over to her, hesitated momentarily; then, when she didn't respond to his gesture, he opened the front door and stepped out on the porch.

Just as she started to close the door, the telephone rang. She rushed across the room, grabbed the receiver and said hello. J.T. stood in the doorway and waited.

"Hello," she said again.

"Hello, Joanna."

"Who is this?"

"Don't you recognize my voice, baby doll?"

"No—no, I don't." But she did. She would never forget that cultured Southern drawl, that soft, effeminate voice or the "baby doll" endearment.

"I've already talked to Claire and Libby. I told each of them that I'd be paying them a little visit anytime now. I didn't want you to find out about all the attention I'm giving them and get jealous."

J.T. stepped back inside and closed the door behind him

slowly. He watched Joanna. Her face paled. She clutched the telephone fiercely.

Joanna glanced over at J.T. He mouthed the words, "Who is it? Plott?"

She nodded her head. J.T. cursed softly under his breath.

"What's the matter, baby doll?" Lenny Plott asked. "Surely you're not surprised to hear from me. After all, you knew it would be only a matter of time before I'd look up all my old friends. I suppose Lieutenant George told you what happened to poor little Melody."

"You strangled her."

"Is that all he told you?" Lenny Plott laughed—that shrill, diabolical laugh Joanna would never forget. "You know what else I did to her before I strangled her, don't you, Joanna?"

There was no way Joanna could keep Plott on the phone long enough to run a trace. From everything he'd found out about Leonard Plott III, J.T. knew the man might be deranged, but he wasn't a fool.

"I'll be seeing you," Lenny said. "But you don't know when. You don't have any idea who I'm coming after next. Will I go to Missouri or Texas or New Mexico? Who knows, maybe I'll throw darts at a map."

"If you come after me, you'll be sorry," Joanna said. "I'll kill you before I'll ever let you touch me again."

"So brave, aren't you, darling girl? Well, just remember this, you won't recognize me when you see me. I've changed my appearance. I doubt my own mother would recognize me."

The line went dead. Joanna replaced the telephone receiver. J.T. grabbed her by the shoulders.

"What did he say?"

"He said he had changed his appearance enough that

I wouldn't recognize him, and that he knows where all three of us—Claire, Libby and I—are. We don't know which one of us he'll come after next."

"Look, Jo, he just told you that to try to frighten you even more than you already are. Our boy Lenny sounds like the type who likes to play head games."

"Phone Lieutenant George and let him know about this call," Joanna said.

"I'll phone from the main house." He rubbed his hands up and down her arms, soothing her. "Will you be all right here by yourself until I get back?"

"Tim Rawlins is still outside. And I have my gun." She pulled away from J.T. "There's no need for you to come back over here."

"You're wrong about that, honey. Plott knows exactly where you are now. I'm moving in here with you. It's time for me to start acting as your private, around-the-clock bodyguard."

"No!" She backed away from J.T. "That's not necessary."

"This isn't up for discussion. We're not taking a vote. From now until Lenny Plott is arrested, I'm not leaving your side. Do you understand?"

Reluctantly, she nodded her head. Dear God, how had her life come to this? Lenny Plott had escaped from prison and was threatening her life. And J. T. Blackwood, a man she both desired and despised, was moving in with her.

JOANNA STARED AT the shaving kit sitting on the left side of the vanity in her bathroom. She had never shared a bathroom with a man. Even when she'd been engaged to Todd, they hadn't lived together. Having J.T. sleeping in the room next to hers, the two of them together twenty-four hours a day, seemed far too intimate. She might not like the idea, but she wasn't going to ask J.T. to leave. In the sea of fear and uncertainty her life had become, J.T. was her lifeline—the one person standing between her and a deadly enemy.

Dragging her gaze away from the leather kit, Joanna picked up the jar of cleansing cream, unscrewed the lid and delved her fingers into the solution. Smearing the cream on her face, she glanced in the mirror. Her green eyes stared back at her, mocking her, telling her she was a fool. Although her body longed for J.T. and her romantic heart cried out for his love, she knew they were all wrong for each other. She was a permanent type of woman; he was a temporary kind of guy. She believed in love; he didn't. And to complicate matters further, she could not bring herself to fully trust J.T. She didn't doubt his sincerity when he promised to protect her from Lenny Plott, but she didn't dare trust him with her love. Of course, it didn't really matter. He didn't want her love. All he wanted was her body.

She wiped off the face cream, washed her hands and lifted her silk robe from the wooden wall peg. She had thought about going to bed early, but had decided she would not stay in her room to avoid J.T. She had work to do, a life to live, an orderly routine to her days. She'd go crazy if she couldn't maintain some semblance of normalcy in her life. She'd just have to get used to J.T.'s presence.

Before leaving the sanctuary of her bathroom, she glanced back at the shaving kit.

She found J.T. standing in front of the fireplace in the living room, gazing up at Annabelle Beaumont's portrait. Joanna sucked in her breath. The sight of him, partially disrobed, left her breathless. He had removed his boots and socks, leaving his big feet bare. His unbuttoned shirt hung loosely about his hips. In that one brief moment before he turned and looked at her, Joanna saw a glimpse of what she thought might be the real J. T. Blackwood. Pensive, brooding and yet somehow vulnerable. And in desperate need of love.

"I have something to show you," he said. "Something you can have, if you want it." He reached down in the plaid chair, picked up a large yellowed, frayed piece of paper and held it out to her.

"What is it?" she asked, noticing that it seemed to be a sketch of some sort.

"Here. Take a look."

He handed it to her. Holding the sketch by the edges, she gasped when she saw the strikingly bold features of a handsome Navajo man. Obviously the drawing had been done years ago. Over seventy years ago?

"This is Benjamin Greymountain, isn't it?" Joanna had always wondered what he'd looked like, if he'd truly been as handsome as Annabelle had thought. He had been.

"Yep. That's him."

"Where did you get—"

"My mother. When I went to see her, shortly before she died…" Pausing for a split second, he swallowed hard. His jaw tightened, then relaxed. "She gave me her grandfather's ring and this sketch of him. She told me the ring and picture went together."

"You know Annabelle sketched this," Joanna said. "She couldn't keep it, couldn't take it back to Virginia with her and look at it day after day."

"What makes you think that? More than likely, she knew she'd have no use for it once she left New Mexico. She probably wanted to put her summer affair behind her."

"That's where you're wrong." Joanna stared down at Benjamin's image. There was the hint of a resemblance between J.T. and his ancestor; a similarity in the eyes, in the cheekbones, in the full lips. "I knew that Annabelle had done several sketches of Benjamin. She wrote about them in her diary. She gave him one—" Joanna glanced down at the treasured portrait in her hands "—this one, as a keepsake, and she destroyed the others before she returned to Virginia. She said it was best if the only picture she had of him was the one forever etched on her heart."

J.T. swore under his breath. Snapping her head around, Joanna glared at him. She carried the sketch over to her work desk in front of the row of windows overlooking the porch. Reverently, she laid the image of Benjamin Greymountain down on top of the desk.

"From what you just told me, I'd say your great-grandmother was quite a romantic." J.T. hooked his thumbs under the waistband of his jeans and laid his palms flat on his hips. "She must have had a really miserable marriage to have spent so much time idealizing some summer affair she'd once had."

"I found the diary in an old trunk in my parents' attic," Joanna said. "I looked for things to occupy my mind after... Well, needless to say, I was intrigued by my great-grandmother's tragic love affair. Believe me, J.T., what she shared with Benjamin was far more than just some summer affair."

"I don't see what was so damned tragic about it." J.T. padded softly across the wooden floor, easing up behind Joanna.

She knew he was hovering over her, only inches away. And he was waiting for her to turn on him, to denounce his insensitivity. Keeping her back to him, she glided her fingertips around the edge of the sketch.

"If you're right, and they weren't deeply in love, then there was no tragedy. But if I'm right, just imagine how they felt—how you'd feel if you'd gotten to spend only a couple of precious months with the one true love of your life."

J.T. couldn't imagine. He'd never been in love, didn't believe in the nonsense and wished Joanna didn't. If she were less of a romantic, their relationship would have a better chance. If only she could admit that wanting each other was enough, without clouding the issue with sentimentality.

"Let's agree to disagree," J.T. said, wanting more than anything to ease her into his arms, untie her robe and slip it off her shoulders. She had such pretty shoulders. Soft, pale skin, with a light dusting of freckles just like the freckles that dotted her cheeks and the bridge of her nose.

"If you read the diary, you might change your mind." Joanna felt his warm breath on her head. If she turned, would he take her in his arms? She pivoted slowly, facing him. "Would you like to read Annabelle's diary?"

"No, I wouldn't. And you'd be better off if you locked the thing in a drawer and forgot about it." He touched her then. Hesitantly. Tenderly. Reaching down, he lifted her hands into his. "I want you. You want me. There's nothing wrong with that. As a matter of fact, I think it would be wrong if we denied ourselves the pleasure we can give each other."

J.T. held their clasped hands between their bodies. When Joanna glanced down, all she saw was their matching rings, the old silver gleaming faintly in the lamplight. She was tempted. Dear God, how she was tempted. But when their affair ended, what would she have left? Memories, some inner voice told her. But her memories would be tarnished, not golden the way Annabelle's had been. Love made all the difference. It had to Annabelle. It did to Joanna.

"Would you consider making a bargain with me?" Joanna asked, wondering if she'd lost her mind even considering the proposition she was about to make.

"What sort of bargain?" Lifting her hands to his lips, he kissed each fingertip.

Joanna shivered. "You're interested in an affair. Nothing serious. Nothing permanent. You'd just like for us to become sexual partners while you're acting as my bodyguard, then when your services are no longer required, we both go our separate ways. No regrets or recriminations on either side."

"What are you getting at?"

"I'm willing to consider what you want, to give us both a chance to see exactly what there is or isn't between us." Joanna already knew. She'd gone and done the unforgivable. She was falling in love with J.T. How stupid could she get? She wanted tenderness, understanding, patience, and a man interested in a lifetime commitment. J.T. offered nothing she wanted—nothing except himself. And *he* was what she wanted most of all. Even if he could be a part of her life for only a few weeks.

Cocking his head to one side, J.T. grinned. "What's the catch, honey?"

"I want you to read Annabelle's diary," Joanna said.

"You want me to do what?" He released her hands, dropping them quickly, as if her touch had burned him.

"You read Annabelle's diary, one entry at a time, and I'll give you the chance to persuade me to become your lover."

"You're serious." He laughed, the sound deep and hearty. "By God, you are serious."

"Is my asking price too high?"

"Go get that damned diary!" He pulled her into his

arms, lowered his head and whispered against her lips, "I'd read a hundred diaries for the chance you're offering me."

She shoved him away gently, then took a step backward, her hip bumping into the easel holding Elena's portrait. She grabbed the easel, steadying it.

"Not tonight. Too much has happened today. Discovering that Lenny Plott knows where I am. Having you move in with me. And knowing Mother will arrive tomorrow and start issuing orders." Joanna groaned. "Tell me, J.T., am I making a deal with the devil? I really don't trust my own feelings. And I don't trust you at all. At least not when it comes to—" she'd been about to say *love* "—our having a physical relationship."

"You handle things with your mother and I'll take care of Lenny Plott. You trust me to keep you safe, don't you?"

"I want to trust you completely," she said. "I know you seem to be a man of your word, a man who keeps his promises, but I... Well, I don't know if I'll ever be able to completely trust a man again. Not after the rape. Not after Todd's desertion."

"I'd like to be the man who teaches you to trust again," J.T. told her. "And I'm not the devil, honey. I'm just a man. A man who's going to keep you safe. And that is a promise."

And I'd like to be the woman who teaches you how to love, Joanna thought, but said, "Promise me something else, J.T."

"What?"

"Promise me that, no matter what happens, you'll try to open up your heart and your mind to your mother's people. Elena told me that you know practically nothing about the Navajo."

"What is it with you? You want me to read Annabelle's

diary. You want me to get in touch with my Native American roots. You want to change me, Jo. I swear, a person would think you don't like the man I am now."

"I'm not sure I do like you," Joanna admitted. "At least, not the J. T. Blackwood you present to the world. I want to get to know the man inside you, the real J. T. Blackwood."

"Don't kid yourself. The real J. T. Blackwood is who you see right here in front of you."

"What I see when I look at you is only the physical, and I like that just fine. What I want to get to know is the spirit, and that's the part of you that you keep hidden from everyone. Even from yourself, I think."

"I'll read Annabelle's damned diary." J.T. marched across the living room, his bare feet slamming against the wooden floor. When he reached the hallway, he stopped and turned around. "And if it'll make you happy, I'll let Elena give me 'Navajo lessons.'" J.T. grunted. "But I'm warning you that reading some old diary filled with a lot of mush and learning more about my mother's people won't change me."

"Maybe. Maybe not," Joanna said. But in her heart she hoped that while J.T. was putting his life on the line to protect her, she could help him discover the man he really was beneath all the bitter cynicism—a man capable of giving and receiving love.

CHAPTER EIGHT

We have been in Trinidad a week now. Ernest is quite pleased to be here, although the heat seems to bother him terribly. Yesterday's find, though not of prehistoric origin, was enough to pacify him. He and his assistant, Horace Grisham, discovered several items of Spanish origin—iron, copper, glass and porcelain. Ernest says that finding these items at this site is a result of the Pueblo Indians having taken refuge here with the Navajo after the revolt against the Spanish in the late seventeenth century.

The boys are doing well, running and laughing and playing as boys their age will do. They're quite a handful at eight and twelve. But they are the joy of my life, my beautiful sons.

We met a most interesting man today. He is a Navajo silversmith, and without a doubt the most handsome man I've ever seen. He came riding into our camp on his big Appaloosa stallion. I must say that horse and rider were a spectacular sight.

His name is Benjamin Greymountain, and his father is a member of their tribal council. Although he wore white man's clothing, his black hair, which he had tied back off his face with a bandana, hung to well below his shoul-

*ders. He is young—I suspect, a good ten years
younger than I.*

*I feel extremely foolish admitting this, even
to myself, but the first moment I saw Benjamin
Greymountain, I thought I heard drums beating somewhere off in the distance, and when
he looked at me, the most extraordinary feelings spread through me. I am a bit afraid of
those feelings. I must, of course, control them.*

*Benjamin's father sent him to our camp to
offer his services as a guide, if any of our party
should wish to take excursions about the countryside. It seems there are some Indians here
who hate the archaeologists who are poking
and digging about in their heritage, and the
senior Mr. Greymountain hopes that he can
prevent any unpleasantness between his people
and ours.*

*I cannot help wondering how I will handle
seeing this young man every day for the next
two and a half months. I am a married woman
of thirty-four, with children. I must remember
who I am. But the memory of those black eyes
staring at me, devouring me, almost, makes
me think that Benjamin experienced the same
jolting emotions that I did.*

"JOANNA'S MOTHER IS here," Elena called from the hallway.
"Aren't you coming out to meet her?"

J.T. closed Annabelle Beaumont's diary. An odd, queasy
feeling hit him in the pit of his stomach. No wonder Joanna had become so engrossed in her great-grandmother's
diary. The woman certainly had a captivating way of ex-
pressing herself. And it was apparent that she had been
sexually attracted to Benjamin Greymountain from the

first moment she saw him and had been determined to fight those feelings.

Placing her hands on each side of the door frame, Elena leaned into J.T.'s study and gave him a hard look. "Well, are you coming or not? I'd think you'd want to make a good impression on Joanna's mother."

"I'll be there in a minute. Go on without me. By the time Alex escorts the senator into the house, I'll be there."

"Joanna could use a little moral support," Elena said. "She's waiting in the living room, pacing the floor. She really didn't want Mrs. Beaumont to come out here. When Joanna lived in Virginia, her mother tried to run her life. From what Joanna's told me, the woman is a first-class manipulator."

"Has Mrs. Beaumont ever visited Joanna before?" J.T. asked.

"No, not once since she moved to New Mexico. Joanna goes back to Virginia two or three times every year." Dropping her hands from the door frame, Elena stepped into J.T.'s private domain—the study that had once belonged to old John Thomas. J.T. had changed it very little, adding only the modern conveniences of a computer and a fax machine. "But Joanna's life has never been threatened before. I believe Mrs. Beaumont loves Joanna and is genuinely concerned."

"I'm sure she is." J.T. sat down on the edge of the huge oak desk. "But she must know Joanna wouldn't be any safer back in Richmond than she is here in Trinidad. At least, not any safer from Lenny Plott."

"What are you not saying, big brother?"

"I don't know what Mrs. Beaumont suspects is going on between Joanna and me, but whatever it is, she doesn't like it. My guess is the senator's visit to New Mexico has more to do with my presence in her daughter's life than with Lenny Plott's escape from prison."

"Just what *is* going on between you and Joanna? You're my only brother and she's my best friend. You already know I'd like nothing better than to see you two get together, but... You seem to mix like oil and water."

"If you're so interested in Joanna's relationship with me, why haven't you asked her?"

"I have asked her," Elena admitted. "She said you were her bodyguard, and when I asked if there wasn't more to it, she said to ask you."

Hearty laughter rumbled from J.T. Elena's eyes widened; her mouth fell open.

"Joanna and I aren't lovers. Not yet, if that's what you're asking, nosy little sister." J.T. stood straight and tall, the remnants of a smile still on his face.

"Don't you dare hurt her." Elena slipped her arm through her brother's. "She's very special, you know."

"Yeah, I'm beginning to see just how special."

J.T. led Elena out of his study and down the hall, pausing when they heard voices coming from the foyer.

"I'm almost as nervous as Joanna," Elena said. "I want Mrs. Beaumont to like us. I've planned a wonderful dinner, in the dining room, for this evening."

"Come on, then, let's go meet the queen bee." J.T. hoped, for Elena's sake, that Mrs. Beaumont proved his suspicions wrong and didn't show herself to be the "just-slightly prejudiced" person she was.

When they entered the living room, they found Alex preparing Mrs. Beaumont a drink, while mother and daughter seated themselves on the sofa. Joanna glanced up, a tentative, strained smile on her face.

"Please, come and meet Mother."

Joanna stood and held out her hand to Elena, who

rushed across the room. Helene Beaumont looked directly at J.T., who waited in the arched doorway. She sat up just a bit straighter, squaring her shoulders. When she turned her head to greet Elena, her chin-length, salt-and-pepper hair flared outward. Impeccably dressed in a neat little red designer suit, she looked every inch the wealthy, successful woman she was.

"Mother, this is Elena." Joanna clasped her best friend's hand.

Helene lifted her hand, offering it to Elena, who accepted the older woman's firm handshake. "I'm simply delighted to meet you, my dear. Joanna just raves about you and your Alex. You can't know how pleased I was when she finally made some friends out here in this wilderness. In all honesty, I didn't think she'd end up staying out here permanently. Joanna's always been a city girl, you know."

"Well, we've pretty much turned her into a country girl," Elena said, her smile warm and genuine. "We're glad she decided to make Trinidad her home. Like Alex, she's found this land an inspiration for her work."

"My, yes," Helene said. "I'm so proud of my little girl's success. Of course, with talent like hers, she would have been a success anywhere."

J.T. glanced down the hallway when he heard the back door open and then slam shut. Before he could go check on things, Alex called out to him.

"That's just Willie bringing in Mrs. Beaumont's luggage," Alex said.

"Did you tell Willie where to put her things?" Elena asked.

"I'm staying here?" Helene turned to Joanna. "I thought you'd told me you had two bedrooms in your house."

"You'll be very comfortable here with us, Mrs. Beaumont," Elena told their guest. "We have tons of room and if you'd like breakfast in bed, all you need to do is ask."

"Why aren't I staying with you?" Helene tilted her sharp little chin upward, glaring at her daughter.

"Well, Mother, you see, it wouldn't be convenient. There just isn't enough room right now."

"I'm afraid I don't understand. I took time away from my work to come out here to be with you, Joanna." Helene glanced up, smiling at Elena and then at Alex. "As much as I appreciate the Gregorys' offer to stay here, I'd much prefer staying with you."

"Mother, that's impossible. If you stay with me, you'd have to sleep on the sofa."

"Why would I have to sleep on the sofa?"

J.T. strolled into the room. "You wouldn't, if you have no objections to my sharing Joanna's bed."

Joanna sucked in a deep breath. Elena gasped. Alex covered his mouth to hide a chuckle.

"J.T. is staying in the second bedroom at my house," Joanna said. "He moved in last night, after I received a telephone call from Lenny Plott. J.T. is going to be with me twenty-four hours a day until Plott is back behind bars."

"I see." Helene glowered at J.T., then quickly centered all her attention on her daughter. "If Plott knows where you are, if he's found you here in New Mexico where you thought you might be safe, there's no reason for you to refuse to come home with me."

"Let's discuss this later. Please." Joanna knew she would have to stand her ground with her mother or she'd be run down like a steamroller. Helene Beaumont liked things her own way, and she was happiest when she controlled the lives of everyone around her.

"Very well," Helene said. "Perhaps, you'll stay long enough to show me to my room."

"Here you are." Alex handed Helene the vodka collins she had requested.

"Thank you, Alex." She sipped her drink, then smiled with approval. "Perfect, simply perfect."

"Mother, I'll be staying here until after dinner," Joanna said. "Elena is preparing something special, just for you."

"How delightful." Helene's campaign smile returned in full force, brightening her dull gray eyes and softening her sharp features. She took another sip of her drink, then stood. "I'm dreadfully tired after my plane ride. Why don't you show me to my room, dear, and then stay and we'll have a little talk while I rest?"

Joanna grimaced, dreading the upcoming confrontation with her mother. The only time she had ever won a battle with the formidable Senator Beaumont was when she had decided to move to New Mexico four years ago.

"Dinner will be at six," Elena said. "So there's plenty of time for a nap, if you'd like."

Helene blessed everyone in the room with her gracious smile, even J.T. Slipping her arm through Joanna's, she held the vodka collins in her other hand. "I'm looking forward to dinner. We'll see you around six, then."

Joanna gave Elena a pleading look, asking for her friend's understanding. Helene tugged on Joanna's arm, the action so subtle, no one else noticed.

"I'll be with Mother for a while," Joanna told J.T. as they walked past him. "I won't leave the house."

"I'll be close by." J.T. looked directly at Joanna, avoiding eye contact with her mother.

The minute the Beaumont ladies were out of earshot, Alex blew out a huffing breath. "Well, well, isn't she something! I can see why Joanna doesn't want to go back to Virginia."

"You're being unkind," Elena said.

"Unkind, my rear end." J.T. crossed his arms over his chest. "Instead of giving Joanna her complete support and understanding, Mrs. Beaumont is here to create problems. It's obvious she doesn't give a damn what Joanna wants, and she certainly doesn't like me."

The corners of Elena's mouth twitched. "You deliberately baited her with that comment about sharing Joanna's bed."

"I'm wealthy. I'm successful. I'm highly trained to protect her daughter. What could the woman possibly have against me?"

The partially formed smile on Elena's face vanished. "You're half Navajo. You think that's the reason she doesn't like you, that she's prejudiced because of your Navajo blood."

"If the shoe fits," Alex said, as he slipped his arm around his wife's shoulders. "Kind of makes you wish you hadn't planned such a special dinner for her tonight, doesn't it?"

"Well, no matter what, she's Joanna's mother and I'm going to be nice to her for Joanna's sake." Elena cuddled against Alex.

"Let me know when that special dinner is ready," J.T. said. "I'll be in my study."

HELENE TIED THE belt around her silk dressing gown, then sat on the edge of the bed and held open her arms to her daughter. "Come give me a hug."

Joanna obeyed. She adored her mother—her beautiful, brilliant mother—but sometimes she didn't like her very much. Helene had been the "perfect" wife and mother, always doing what she thought best. But there had been times when Joanna had wondered how much of that "perfection" had been an expression of love and how much had been just for show. What the world thought of Helene meant a great deal to her and she had spent her life presenting herself and her family in the very best light.

Helene hugged Joanna, released her and patted the bed beside her. "Sit with me for a while and let's talk the way we used to when you lived at home."

Sighing, Joanna acquiesced to her mother's request and sat down on her right. "I can save us a lot of arguing back and forth. There's no need for us to have a talk. I'm not returning with you to Virginia. I'm staying here in New Mexico. This is my home now."

"But Plott knows where you are."

"Lenny Plott will find me wherever I am and we both know it. With his kind of money, he can buy whatever information he needs to track us down. I doubt there's a place on earth we can hide that he couldn't eventually find us."

"What are you saying?" Reaching down, Helene covered Joanna's hand with hers.

"Sooner or later, I may have to come face-to-face with Lenny Plott, and if that happens, J.T. will be there with me. I won't feel safe anywhere without J.T."

"The man's just a bodyguard, dear. I can hire half-a-dozen bodyguards for you, if having them around will make you feel safe."

"I don't want just any bodyguard. I want J.T."

"What's going on between you and that man?" Helene released Joanna's hand. "Somehow he has convinced you that he's the only person who can protect you."

Joanna stood, walked across the bedroom and looked out the window at the far distant horizon. "That's what this is all about, isn't it, Mother? This little trip isn't about keeping me safe, about protecting me from Lenny Plott. It's about getting me away from J. T. Blackwood. That's it, isn't it?"

"I'm not blind," Helene said. "I can see plainly why any woman would be attracted to him, but don't you realize how wrong he is for you?"

"Just what are you so afraid of?"

"I'd think you'd be the one to be afraid." Helene laid her open palms flat on each side of her hips, pressing down against the bed. "To my knowledge, you haven't been with a man since the night that monster brutalized you. Do you honestly think J. T. Blackwood is the kind of man you need as your first lover? I've had his background checked out. Putting aside the fact that he was illegitimate and his mother was a Navajo, the man has spent his life in one brutal business or another. First the marines, then years as a Secret Service agent and for the past six years, he's been a private security agent. The man is practically a hired killer. Just how gentle and kind and patient do you think a man like that will be in the bedroom?"

"My love life is none of your business." Joanna kept her back turned on her mother. "I know you love me and you want what you think is best for me. Maybe you really do believe I need a more gentle lover, but let's be honest, shall we? You're far more concerned that I might marry J.T. Then how on earth would you ever explain it to your friends? Oh, it might be all right to speak out for and even vote for racial equality, to have friends and associates who aren't pure WASPs, but you don't want your daughter marrying outside the inner circle, do you?"

Knotting her hands into fists, Helene jumped up from the bed. "It's that ridiculous diary of your great-grandmother's, isn't it? Someone should have burned that thing long ago. To think that woman actually filled a book with details of her illicit love affair with some wild savage."

"We aren't going to agree on this." Joanna turned

slowly, took a deep breath and faced her mother. "You are not in charge of my life now. I am. I choose where I live. Not you. And I decide who I love, and who I marry."

"Has he asked you to marry him?"

"No, Mother, he hasn't, but that doesn't mean I won't ask him, one of these days."

"I don't know what's happened to you since you left Richmond. You were always such a sweet, easygoing child. You made all the right choices. You had a wonderful fiancé, a good job, a bright future."

"I did everything you wanted me to do," Joanna said. "You made all my decisions for me. You planned my life. But you didn't plan on Lenny Plott beating me half to death and raping me, did you?"

"I would give anything if I could change what happened." Tears misted Helene's eyes.

Joanna walked over, wrapped her arms around her mother and hugged her. "I know you would. But what happened can't be changed. I'm a different person now. I'm stronger. I can never go back to being your sweet little girl."

"I want only what's best for you." Pulling back from Joanna, Helene cupped her daughter's face in her hands. "I truly believe J. T. Blackwood is the wrong man for you."

"Let me make that decision," Joanna said. "If I get hurt, I'll have no one to blame but myself."

JOANNA HAD THOUGHT dinner would never end. She had forgotten what it felt like to watch her mother preside over a gathering, commanding all the attention, issuing orders and playing the Southern belle to the hilt. She only hoped that while she and Elena cleared the table and straightened the kitchen, her mother wouldn't say or do something unforgivable.

Joanna stacked plates in the dishwasher while Elena hand-washed the pots and pans.

"I think your mother enjoyed dinner." Elena placed a copper pot in the drainage rack. "She said she loved the spicy chicken and she raved about the homemade ice cream."

"No one could find fault with your cooking," Joanna said. "If anyone ruined your dinner party, I did. Or perhaps J.T. He didn't say ten words the whole time."

"He thinks your mother doesn't like him."

"She doesn't know him, she just thinks she does." Joanna placed the dirty glasses in the top rack of the dishwasher. "But I'm beginning to think that I really don't know J.T., either. He acts like he's two different men. Every time we get a little closer to understanding each other, he withdraws and we wind up in an argument."

"J.T. *is* two different men," Elena said. "Maybe even three different men. One part of him is the man John Thomas Blackwood made him, while another part of him is Navajo, and then I think another third of him is the man he longs to be, a man at peace with the other two-thirds of himself."

"I suppose there's more than one person inside all of us, isn't there?" Joanna filled the detergent dispenser, closed the door and turned on the dishwasher. "There's still a part of me that's the proper young lady my mother raised me to be and part of me is the independent, confident woman I've become since moving to Trinidad. But there's also a dark, frightened part of me. That's the part Lenny Plott and Todd created nearly five years ago. No matter how hard I try, I can't completely let go of that fear and anger and distrust."

"I can only imagine what it must have been like for you, but you must know that even when Lenny Plott is arrested and put back in prison, you'll never be free from him until you can destroy that dark part of you he created."

Joanna dried her hands, then tossed the towel to Elena. "I thought I had destroyed most of it, until he escaped and forced me to face the past, to face the truth about myself. I have so much love to give the right man, but I can't trust enough to completely give my heart and my body to anyone."

Elena laid the towel on the countertop, put her arm around Joanna's waist and gave her a hug. "Let's join the others and see if your mother and J.T. have drawn swords yet."

Joanna laughed, but the sound was hollow. When they reached the end of the hallway, Joanna heard her mother's voice. Jerking Elena back against the wall, she held a finger over her lips, silently asking Elena not to speak.

"Joanna has always been a very sensitive girl," Helene said. "She hated confrontations of any kind. She always cried whenever she overheard her father and me arguing. Not that we argued very often."

"I'm sure Joanna's sensitivity is a great asset to her in her work," Alex said. "Most of us artists have sensitive souls. We seem to feel things more deeply. I suppose we have to be able to do that in order to put a part of our souls into our work."

"No doubt." Helene cleared her throat. "But I'm afraid that, in some people, sensitivity makes them rather weak and vulnerable, and thus easily hurt."

Joanna clenched her teeth tightly. What was her mother doing? There was always a method to her madness, a scheme behind the most innocent-sounding conversations. Elena squeezed Joanna's hand.

"Surely you're not talking about Jo." J.T.'s voice sounded deeper, darker and rougher than usual.

"I'm afraid I am," Helene said. "She was always fragile and sensitive and a bit naive. Then, after Lenny Plott attacked her, she went completely to pieces. It took months of therapy before she'd go out of the house in broad daylight without someone with her."

"Isn't a reaction like that fairly normal?" Alex asked. "I'm sure different women react differently after living through such an experience."

"Jo isn't weak," J.T. said. "She's one of the strongest people I've ever met. It's obvious to me that you don't know the woman your daughter has become."

"You're quite wrong about that, Mr. Blackwood. I know my daughter far better than you. She's still just as fragile and sensitive and vulnerable as she was before she left Virginia four years ago, and I worry that she's going to be hurt and terribly disappointed if she continues living in this dreamworld she's created for herself."

"I'm afraid I don't understand," Alex said. "Joanna is a very sensible woman. She—"

"You're referring to her interest in Annabelle Beaumont's diary." J.T. grunted. "And my connection to Benjamin Greymountain."

"Joanna needs the right kind of man. Someone as sensitive and gentle as she is. Another artist, perhaps. Someone who can offer her a safe, contented life." Helene's sweet Southern drawl sharpened into a louder, rather sour tone. "I thought that sooner or later she'd experiment with having a brief affair with some Indian and then she'd see the foolishness of having built some ludicrous fantasy around her great-grandmother's illicit love affair."

Joanna ripped away from Elena and flew into the living room. "Go home, Mother! Go back to running the state of Virginia and leave me alone."

Helene's face lost all color. She held out a hand to her daughter. "Joanna, my dear, I didn't mean for you to hear.

I'm so sorry. I simply thought it best for Mr. Blackwood to understand."

"To understand what, Mother? That I'm some weak, helpless, fragile little girl who lives in a fantasy world? That's what you just told him, wasn't it?"

"Don't upset yourself this way." Helene took a tentative step toward Joanna. "I'm only trying to protect you from being hurt."

Joanna backed away from her mother. "In your own subtle way, you were trying to warn J.T. to stay away from me because I'm so fragile that if he dares to touch me, I'll break."

"Joanna, dear, let's not turn this into an ugly scene," Helene pleaded.

Hysterical laughter rose from Joanna's throat, tearing holes in the tension-filled atmosphere. "No, we wouldn't want to do that, would we? Whatever would people think? Wasn't that your greatest concern after Lenny Plott raped me? Oh, you were heartbroken for me and hovered over me, smothering me with attention, but I knew. Damn you, I knew! You were so ashamed. Ashamed that your daughter had let herself become front-page news in a serial rapist's trial. Ashamed to have to face your friends. Ashamed that I wasn't strong enough to cope without therapy!"

Joanna turned and ran from the room, into the hallway and out the front door. Elena called after her.

J.T. looked directly at Helene Beaumont with his one good eye. "Call tonight and make reservations for the first flight to Richmond tomorrow. Alex will have one of the hands drive you to Santa Fe."

Without a backward glance, J.T. exited the living room, walked down the hall and entered his study. He flipped on the overhead switch, bathing the room in light. Quickly he picked up Annabelle's diary, shoved it into his pocket and rushed down the hall and out the front door. He saw Joanna several feet away, standing in the middle of the yard, her arms wrapped around her middle.

"Joanna," he called out to her.

"Go away!" Spinning around on trembling legs, Joanna faced him. "Leave me alone."

"I can't leave you alone, Jo. I'm your bodyguard. Remember?"

"Oh, that's right. I hired you to protect me from Lenny Plott because I'm so weak and frightened and fragile and sensitive and—"

"Stop talking nonsense." J.T. walked down the steps and into the yard. "Your mother doesn't know who the hell you are. She's the one living in a fantasy world, a world where she can control you."

"She did control me. All my life. And I let her."

"She doesn't control you now. You make your own decisions. Right?"

"You know what the funny thing is, J.T.?" She watched, unmoving, while he walked toward her. "As different as you and Helene Beaumont are, you do agree on one thing."

"What's that?" he asked, halting a couple of feet away from her.

"You both think Annabelle Beaumont was a foolish adulteress and the great love she and Benjamin shared was nothing more than a lonely, unhappy matron's fantasy."

"I've just started reading the diary," J.T. said. "I'm not sure what I believe. Not anymore."

"Don't you dare try to pacify me with lies, John Thomas Blackwood. Don't pretend something you don't believe."

"Nobody calls me John Thomas. I'm J.T. John Thomas was my grandfather."

"Sensitive, are we?" she taunted.

J.T. grabbed her and held her by the arms, keeping a good foot of space between their bodies. "Yeah, honey, I'm sensitive about some things. Everybody is. And it's all right for you to be sensitive." Still holding her arm with one hand, he grasped the back of her neck with the other. His touch was strong, yet gentle. "Your sensitivity is one of the things I like about you."

"Don't you dare be nice to me out of pity!"

"Pity has nothing to do with the way I feel about you."

His kiss, like his touch, was strong yet gentle. Her momentary resistance disappeared as quickly as smoke in the wind. By the time his tongue entered her mouth she eagerly accepted him, responding with a desperate hunger.

He ended the powerful kiss, but pulled her into his arms and pressed her face against his chest. "I want to make love to you, but I don't want you to agree as an act of revenge against your mother."

"If and when I agree to make love with you, it will be for only one reason," she said. "Because I want you."

"Why don't we go to the bunkhouse? I'll fix us both a drink and you can tell me more about Annabelle and Benjamin."

"You're willing to do anything to cheer me up, aren't you?" she said teasingly.

J.T. let out a deep breath, pleased to see her smile. "Just about anything."

"All right, why don't we go home to the bunkhouse? You can fix us both a drink, then you can tell me about what it was like in the Secret Service, and I'll tell you something you want to know about me."

"What's wrong, Jo, are you afraid if we talk about our great-grandparents, we might find ourselves following in their footsteps and—"

She laid her index finger over his lips. "Shh."

J.T. kissed her forehead. "I read Annabelle's first entry in the diary. The day she met Benjamin."

Pulling out of J.T.'s arms, Joanna backed away from him. "The day we met, when I first saw you sitting astride Washington, I thought I heard drums." Joanna turned and ran across the yard and toward the bunkhouse.

J.T. raced after her, catching her on the front porch. Grabbing her, he slowly turned her around. "You're hell on a man's nerves. Why did you have to go and tell me something like that?"

"What difference does it make?" she asked. "You don't believe I heard drums any more than you believe Annabelle heard them."

"I told you that I don't know what I believe. Not now."

"Come on, let's go inside and talk. You tell me about the Secret Service and I'll tell you about—"

"You tell me about your art. About when you first realized you wanted to be an artist and how you could draw better than anyone else in kindergarten."

She slipped her hand into his. "Thanks, J.T."

"For what?"

"For not paying any attention to my mother. For not letting her run you off."

"Nothing and no one is running me off. I made you a promise, and it's a promise I intend to keep. You can't get rid of me, honey. I'm sticking to you like glue."

Hand in hand, they entered the bunkhouse—a woman who, more than anything, wanted to be able to trust this man; and a man who, for the first time in his life, wondered what it would be like to truly love a woman...this woman.

CHAPTER NINE

JOANNA AWOKE WITH A start. At first, she had no idea what had awakened her and then she vaguely remembered hearing the front door open. Was J.T. awake? Had he gone outside? She got out of bed, slipped into her thin silk robe and walked into the living room. The floor lamp behind the plaid chair was on, and an open book lay, spine up, across the overstuffed armrest. Undoubtedly, J.T. had been unable to sleep and had been reading. She glanced over at the front door, which stood open, with only the screen door closed. The shadowy outline of J.T.'s broad shoulders caught Joanna's eye. He stood on the edge of the porch, staring out into the dark night sky.

When Joanna neared the plaid chair, she realized the book perched on the armrest was Annabelle's diary. Had J.T. been reading another entry? Joanna picked up the diary, turned it over and glanced down at the open page.

I know I should feel great shame for having committed such an unpardonable sin. But I feel no shame, only an overwhelming joy. How could loving someone the way I love Benjamin be wrong? I knew we would consummate our love today. He took me to a cave in the mountains, high above the world, quiet and secluded. I was far more nervous with Benjamin than I had been on my wedding night nearly sixteen years ago. He sensed my unease, my doubts, my fears, and he soothed me with sweet words that I did not understand because he spoke them in his own language. But my heart knew their meaning.

When we came together, it was as if we had both been waiting a lifetime for the moment. Benjamin seemed to know me better than I knew myself. Sheer instinct seemed to guide him, telling him what I wanted, what I needed. The love we shared, I have never shared with another, and know in my heart I can share only with him. Benjamin. My Benjamin. My tender, passionate lover, who taught me the meaning of ecstasy.

Tears gathered in Joanna's eyes. She closed the diary and hugged it to her breast. Had J.T. read a third of the diary tonight, or had he skipped through parts of it, coming to this account of the first time Annabelle and Benjamin made love?

Joanna padded across the room, her bare feet quiet on the wooden floor. She opened the screen door, stepped outside and let the door slam shut behind her. J.T. didn't flinch. He had known she was there; he had probably heard her stirring about inside.

"Did I wake you?" he asked, keeping his back to her.

"I'm not sure," she said. "I think I might have heard the front door open, but I wasn't sleeping soundly anyway."

The moonlight combined with the glow from the lone lamp in the living room, creating a muted illumination that cast everything into soft shadows. J.T. wore nothing except a pair of faded jeans. His broad, muscular back looked like polished leather. Joanna barely controlled the urge to reach out and touch him. She wanted this man, wanted him in a way she had never wanted anyone or anything. He stirred needs in her that were new and powerful and frightening in their intensity. Yet, as much as she wanted J.T., she was afraid of the very virility and masculine power that attracted her to him.

"If I weren't working, I'd go somewhere and get riproaring drunk." J.T. gripped the banister that bordered the front porch. "I never had any idea it was possible to want a woman as much as I want you."

Joanna went hot all over; a flush of excitement and pure feminine exhilaration spread through her body. She reached out and touched his shoulder. He flinched. She withdrew her hand.

"You read some more of Annabelle's diary, didn't you?" Joanna's voice sounded strange to her own ears, its quality low and earthy and undeniably sensual.

"Yeah, I read a couple of entries after the first one, then I just flipped through the pages."

"You read about the first time they made love." Joanna laid her hand on his bare back. Dear God, how she longed to wrap her arms around him, to cuddle up against him and hug him close to her.

He whipped around, knocking her hand off his back in the process. "I wish I'd never made that bargain with you. I wish I'd never read a word in that damn diary."

Joanna's heart roared in her ears. She swayed slightly. J.T. grabbed her by the elbows, steadying her. She looked up at him, and suddenly the whole world condensed into this time, this space, this one man.

"It's painful, isn't it?" Joanna realized that Annabelle's words had touched J.T.'s heart. "Reading about how she felt, how much she loved him and how hopeless their love was, always makes me cry. And of course, they'd both realized, from the very beginning, that they had no future together."

J.T. knew what Joanna wanted him to say. She wanted him to admit he'd been wrong and she'd been right about their great-grandparents' summer love affair.

After reading her diary, it had become obvious to J.T. that Annabelle Beaumont had been deeply in love with Benjamin Greymountain, and that it had broken her heart knowing they couldn't spend the rest of their lives together.

How had Benjamin felt? What pain had he suffered? J.T. wondered. Unlike Annabelle, whose emotions lived on in her words, Benjamin's thoughts and feelings had died with him. Had he suffered the way she had? Had he lived out his life yearning for a love that could never truly be his, except in his memories? And how had he felt having an affair with a woman, knowing he had nothing to offer her? He'd been a poor Navajo silversmith and she a wealthy Virginia socialite. How many nights had Benjamin stared up at the stars and raged against heaven?

"Would you do what Annabelle did?" he asked, drawing Joanna into his arms. "Would you risk everything for a brief affair with a man who could offer you nothing more than heaven in his arms?"

"Yes." She slipped her arms around his waist and laid her head on his chest. Silently she added, "If I loved him, I would risk everything."

"I promise that I won't hurt you. Not now or ever," J.T. vowed. "I want you, Jo. I want to lift you into my arms and carry you to bed and make slow, sweet love to you all night long."

"I want that, too, but—"

"You take charge, honey. You tell me what to do. Every step of the way. I won't do anything without your orders."

He was promising her what she wanted to hear, assuring her that she would be in control of the situation. But could she trust him? J.T. looked like a man on the edge, a man ready to explode. He might promise her anything right now to gain her acceptance, but what would he do in the throes of passion?

"I'm not sure. I want you, too, J.T. I want you till I ache with the wanting. But I'm afraid."

"Trust me to be true to my word."

Lifting her head, she stared up at him. "You're so big and strong and…if I asked you to stop and you didn't, I'd be powerless."

"If you ask me to stop, I'll stop. I promise."

Closing her eyes against the sight of him, against the temptation of his pure masculine beauty, she took a deep breath and choked back her tears. Reaching into the depths of her soul she sought and found courage—Annabelle Beaumont's kind of courage; the courage to risk loving a man who could promise her nothing more than the moment.

"Hell, Jo, take your gun to bed with us if that'll make you feel safer!"

Tears escaped from her eyes, trickled down her cheeks and into her mouth. She smiled at J.T. "You want me so much you'd risk getting shot?"

If she refused him, he'd die. But if she accepted him, making love to her slowly and tenderly would kill him by degrees. He wanted her wild and furious this first time, wanted her passion to equal his. But if he acted on his instincts, he'd scare the hell out of her. "Yeah, I want you that much."

"Then take me to bed," she told him.

He thanked God that she hadn't denied him, and at the same time prayed for the strength to be the lover Joanna needed, to be man enough to relinquish the power to her and allow her to make love to him. It was the only way, and he knew it. Yet every primitive, masculine instinct in him cried out for him to take her, possess her, dominate her and make her yield to him.

He swept her up in his arms, swung open the screen door and carried her into the living room, then closed and locked the front door. Joanna kept her arm draped around his neck as he carried her down the hall and into her bedroom. After laying her down, he stood by her bed and waited.

"I'm not sure what to tell you to do next," she admitted. "I haven't done this sort of thing before and I... J.T., what do I do?"

"What do you want to do?"

"I want to touch you."

His already aroused body stiffened painfully. He sat down on the edge of the bed. "How's this?"

She scooted over toward him, wrapped her arms around his waist and laid her cheek on his back. "You're hot." She ran her fingers up and down, over his stomach and chest.

J.T. sucked in his breath. Her hands stilled on his chest. He laid his hands over hers gently. "It's all right. You didn't do anything wrong. I love having your hands all over me."

"Would you...would you lie down and let me look at you?"

Slipping out of her arms, he rolled over and lay down flat on his back, then raised his arms and crossed them behind his head. "How's this?"

Joanna edged backward, easing her knees up in front of her and hugging her arms around her legs. "You're a beautiful man, J.T. The most beautiful man I've ever seen."

He grinned. She smiled. And the bottom dropped out of his stomach. "And I'm all yours," he told her. "Putty in your hands. Yours to command."

"I guess I'm just a bit overwhelmed with all this power."

She surveyed him from the top of his head to the tips of his bare feet, taking inventory of every inch of his big, hard body. He lay there watching her watch him. His arms bulged with muscles. She reached out and ran her fingertips over one arm from elbow to armpit, then slid her nails down his side and over across his broad, sleek chest. When she touched one tight little nipple, he made a sound, and Joanna knew he was trying to stifle a groan.

She wondered if his body ached the way hers did; if he throbbed with desire, wanting her the way she wanted him.

She couldn't mistake the evidence inside his jeans— the truth about the way he felt. His body revealed his need for her. "Would you take off your jeans?" she asked.

"Why don't you help me take them off?" He took her hand, brought it over to the snap on his jeans and placed it directly over his zipper.

Her hand trembled. She'd never touched a man this way. Shaking like a leaf, she unsnapped his jeans and undid the zipper, then jerked her hand away.

He lifted himself up off the bed, tugged his jeans down his legs and tossed them on the floor. Joanna watched his every move, becoming more and more fascinated by the sheer masculine glory of J.T.'s body.

"I suppose I should take something off, shouldn't I?"

"Only if you want to, honey." J.T. wasn't sure he had the strength to resist his need to take this woman. But, God in heaven, he had to resist. He had to be strong for

Joanna. He had to give her all the power; otherwise, she'd be lost to him forever.

Joanna removed her thin silk robe. She sucked in several deep breaths, then dropped the robe on the floor and edged her way closer to J.T. Sliding close to his side, she eased one leg up over his and rested her elbow on the bed as she leaned over and kissed his chest. She explored his body, touching, kissing, licking him from forehead to feet.

J.T. could imagine no torture more unbearable. He called upon every divine force in the universe to help him.

Suddenly his prayers were answered when Joanna said, "Touch me, J.T. Please, touch me."

Touch her? Where? How? What he wanted to do to her would be too much too soon. Slow and easy, Blackwood, he told himself. Don't do anything to frighten her, to take away her sense of complete control.

He lifted her up and on top of him, showing her how to straddle him the way she did a horse. He sat her down directly on top of his arousal, allowing her to feel his throbbing hardness through the thin cotton of his briefs.

"Oh," she gasped. Her body clenched and unclenched with pulsating need. She braced herself by placing her hands on his shoulders.

J.T. bucked up against her once. She gasped again. Still clinging to his shoulders, she clenched his hips with her knees.

"Do you like that?" he asked, and circled her waist with both hands, urging her to lean forward.

"I'm tingling all over," she said. "Tingling and aching and—"

Her breath caught in her throat when she felt his hands spreading out from her waist, slowly covering her buttocks. He caressed her through the silk gown, the feel of his big hands gentle yet sensual.

"I'd like to kiss you," he said. "Would that be all right?"

"Yes. Please."

Every muscle in his body strained, every nerve roared like a wounded beast. Take her! Take her now! his body ordered him. Be patient. Wait. Make sure she's ready, his mind told him. While his body and mind fought, his heart won the battle. He brought her downward, inch by inch, until she lay atop the full length of his body. She lowered her head and touched her lips to his.

She played with his lips, licking, nibbling, and then finally enticing him to open his mouth and allow her tongue entrance. Once she had initiated the dance, he fell into step, thrusting and tasting, becoming a full participant in the wild fandango their kiss became.

J.T. eased her gown up her hips, one tiny piece of material at a time. When he slipped his hands beneath the silk and stroked her bare buttocks, Joanna moaned into his mouth and shivered violently.

He ended the kiss. They both gulped in air. She cuddled up against him like a sleek, purring kitten. He wrapped his arms around her.

"I want to kiss your breasts and your belly and taste the sweetness of your body," he said. "Will you let me do that?"

With her head still resting on his chest, she nodded, then whispered her agreement. Gently shoving her upward until she straddled him again, he gripped the hem of her gown, which rested about her hips.

"May I take this off?" he asked.

"My gown? Yes. It's all right. Take it off."

He pulled her gown up over her head, tossed it on the floor on top of his jeans and then rolled her over onto her back. While he anointed her face with dozens of sweet kisses, he ran his hands over her breasts, cupping them, lifting them, caressing their roundness.

Her nipples beaded into hard buds. Her breasts felt heavy and achy. "J.T.?"

"It's all right, honey. I know what you want." While he suckled one breast, he stroked the other between his thumb and forefinger.

Joanna's lower body lifted off the bed, the movement completely instinctive. "Oh, J.T., please, do something. I'm aching so."

He rose over her and looked down at her face, her beautiful face, flushed and damp with passion. His gaze traveled over her breasts, round and full, the nipples tight with desire.

Lowering his head, he kissed her belly. She moaned. He painted a moist trail downward until his lips encountered the fiery red triangle between her legs. "Let me touch you…here." He nuzzled her with his nose.

"Yes. Please."

J.T. cupped her softly, petting her, then slipped his fingers inside the hot, wet folds of her body. She quivered uncontrollably for a few seconds, then closed her thighs, capturing his hand.

"Easy, Jo. Easy, sweet darling."

She relaxed her legs and allowed him to part them slowly. After he'd settled himself between her legs, his lips sought and found the secret heart of her. When he kissed her there, she cried out. When his tongue worked tirelessly against her, she clutched his shoulders and wept as her body tightened and released, tightened and released, until she was wound so tight, she was wild with need. With one final stroke, he sent her over the edge, then lifted himself upward to take her cries of completion into his mouth.

She shuddered as spasms of earth-shattering ecstasy

claimed her body. Taking her in his arms, J.T. rolled them over, positioning her on top of him. He had to take her— take her now—or he'd die on the spot.

"I want you, Jo. I want you so much."

"Yes. Please. Now," she cried, as the remnants of her release echoed through her body.

J.T. lifted Joanna and brought her down onto him, thrusting inside her. She gasped several times, then whimpered softly.

"Are you all right?" he asked, praying he hadn't hurt her.

"Yes. Oh, yes."

Nothing he'd ever experienced had prepared him for the feel of being inside Joanna, of becoming her lover. She was hot and wet and tight. So very tight. Her body sheathed him like a glove. A perfect fit.

"Take charge, honey," he said. "Do whatever you want to do to me."

"I want to make love to you, J.T., but I'm not sure I know how. I've never... I mean, there wasn't anyone before—"

"You and your fiancé never made love?" Was it possible? he wondered. Had she been a virgin when Lenny Plott raped her?

"No. Todd and I didn't make love. I wanted to wait."

"Then I'm the first," J.T. said.

"You would be, if...if I hadn't been—"

"I'm your first," he told her, moving out and then back in, claiming her as his own. "No other man has ever been your lover."

She wept, tears of joy and of sorrow. Tears that washed away any residue of shame she'd felt. Tears that proclaimed her gratitude. He might not realize the truth himself, but Joanna knew, in her heart of hearts, that J.T. was the other half of her, her life's partner, her soul mate.

"Making love is so easy," he said, "when you want each other the way we do."

"I do want you, J.T. I want you so desperately."

"Then take me, honey. Ride me…hard and fast. Give us both what we want…what we need."

Pure, primitive feminine instinct took over, guiding her into a mating ritual as old as time. She moved, slowly, tentatively, uncertain of herself and of him at first. But as the momentum inside her body gradually built, she gave herself over to the passion, to the basic animal urges she didn't want to control. J.T. stroked and petted her hips and buttocks. He suckled at her breasts, moving from one to the other, paying equal homage. And he whispered sweet, dark, erotic words of praise, and in the moment of fulfillment, he cried out to her, *"Ayói óosh'ni,"* the words strange to his own ears, the language the Navajo tongue of his childhood.

She whispered his name over and over, telling him that she loved him, as release claimed her only seconds after he fell headlong into completion.

He held her in his arms, atop his sweat-dampened body. She cuddled to him, not wanting to move, wishing they could stay this way forever. Happy, fulfilled, complete, and safe from the outside world.

He spread a line of kisses along her cheek and jaw, then reached down, pulled up the sheet and covered them.

"Shouldn't I move?" she asked. "I can't stay on top of you all night. I'm too heavy."

"I don't want you to move," he said, stroking her hip. "Go to sleep right where you are, honey."

Sighing, she relaxed on top of him, then kissed his

chest. "What did you say to me when…just as you…you know… those strange words? Were they Navajo?"

"I don't speak *Saad*." He kissed the top of her head resting on his chest. "Or at least I haven't since I was a little boy. I don't have any idea what I said. It must have been something I remembered from my childhood."

"Something very wonderful?" she asked.

"If I said it to you, then it had to be something wonderful."

"Thank you, J.T. Thank you for making this so good for me—so special."

"Don't thank me, Jo. I should be thanking you. Do you know how honored I feel knowing I'm your first lover?"

"But that's why… Don't you understand?" She cuddled into him as if she were trying to bore her way inside him, seeking shelter and safety in the harbor of his big, strong body. "Todd wanted to be the first. He wanted a virgin bride."

"I told you, honey, the man was a bastard. And a stupid one, at that." J.T. wrapped her tightly in his arms, cocooning her in his warmth and strength, protecting her in the safe haven of his embrace. "What Lenny Plott did to you had nothing to do with making love. In every way that matters, you were still a virgin until tonight."

"Do you really believe that?" She could not stop the tears, could not keep herself from clinging to J.T., could not keep her heart from bursting with the joy of loving such a special man.

J.T. took her chin in his hand, lifted her face and kissed the tip of her nose. "The way I see it, you gave your virginity to me tonight. I'm your only lover. There's never been another man. Only me."

"Yes. Only you." Only you, J.T. For now and always. My only lover. My only love.

JOANNA AWOKE SHORTLY after dawn in J.T.'s arms and found him watching her. They made love again, lingering over every touch, drawing out every sighed expression. He was as tender, as gentle and as passionate the second time as he'd been the first, and their fulfillment had been even more complete. Joanna had never dreamed loving someone could be so good. Now, she truly understood how Annabelle had felt about Benjamin.

When she roused from sleep the second time, she was alone in bed. She called out to J.T. He answered her from the kitchen, telling her to stay put. She waited patiently for his return. Within minutes he entered the bedroom. Joanna's heart filled with warmth at the sight of him standing there wearing nothing but his briefs and carrying a tray of food. He set the tray at the foot of the bed, then eased himself down beside her.

"Breakfast is served." He dragged the tray up the bed and lifted it on top of their laps. "I whip up a mean batch of scrambled eggs, if I do say so myself."

Joanna inspected the tray, taking note of the white rose lying on her napkin. "You picked one of Elena's prized roses! She'll kill you."

"How's she going to know one's missing?" J.T. shrugged, then picked up a glass of orange juice and handed it to Joanna.

She took a sip. Her eyes widened. "This is fresh-squeezed. I don't believe it. You're a man of many talents."

"Oh, honey, you've just seen a few of my many talents." He slipped his hand under her gown and up the inside of her leg.

"Behave yourself." Joanna swatted at his hand. "We can't play around all day. Mother will be up soon and if I don't confront her up at the main house, she'll be down here trying to move in with me."

J.T. removed his hand from beneath her gown. "I've been trying to forget that your mother is still here." Lifting his mug to his lips, he took a hearty swallow of sweet, black coffee. "Jo?"

"Uh-hmm?" She finished off her orange juice.

"Last night I told your mother to make reservations to fly home to Virginia today."

"I'll bet she loved being ordered to get out of Dodge," Joanna said. "She's probably ready for a showdown this morning."

"I can deal with your mother by myself, if you'd rather not see her again."

"Don't do that." Joanna placed her hand on J.T.'s shoulder. "Don't start trying to fight all my battles, especially not the ones with my mother. I'm not the fragile, helpless creature she made me out to be, even if last night I—"

"You were no fragile, helpless creature last night," he said. "You were a woman filled with powerful emotions who took charge of our lovemaking." Covering her hand with his, he lifted it and brought it to his lips. "You are brave and strong and so very beautiful. You're everything a woman should be. Don't hold it against me because I'm an old-fashioned, macho kind of guy. I can't help wanting to protect you. And not just from Lenny Plott, but from anything or anyone who could hurt you."

She cupped the side of his face with her hand, leaned over and kissed him. "I won't hold it against you, if you're willing to accept the fact that I need to be the one to make my decisions, to be in control of my life, as much as possible."

"I understand." He returned her kiss. The tray on their laps slid off the side of the bed, hitting the floor with a resounding crash.

They looked down at their scrambled eggs and toast

scattered across the handwoven rug and wooden floor, then they both laughed. He wrapped his arms around her and pulled her down in the bed, devouring her with kisses. She rubbed her body against his, moaning as ripples of pleasure radiated through her.

The loud pounding on the front door ended their passion before it went any further. They sat up straight in the bed.

"Who the hell?" J.T. grumbled as he got out of bed, picked up his jeans and struggled to get into them as he crossed the room. "If that's your mother, I'll strangle her."

Joanna glanced at the bedside clock. "It can't be Mother. It's only seven o'clock. She's never up and dressed this early unless there's an emergency."

By the time he'd made his way to the front door, J.T. had managed to zip and button his jeans, but his chest and feet were still bare.

"Whoever it is, go away," J.T. said through the closed door. "Everything is fine here."

"J.T.?" a man's voice said, the tone husky, the accent Southern. "Come on. Open up. We need to talk."

J.T. unlocked the door, swung it open and stared into the face of his old FBI friend, Dane Carmichael. "What the hell are you doing here?"

"I've got news on Plott," Dane said. "Bad news."

"Come on in." J.T. held open the door.

Dane walked in, glanced around the living room and then down the hall. "Where's Ms. Beaumont?"

"She isn't up yet," J.T. said. "What's this about Plott? And why didn't you just call me?" J.T.'s gut instincts told him that Dane Carmichael wouldn't be here unless the Bureau had sent him.

"We're going to be sending a man out here to New Mexico and another one to Texas."

"Why?" J.T. asked. "And why just New Mexico and Texas? One of Plott's victims lives in Missouri."

"We've already got people in Missouri," Dane said. "Claire Andrews has disappeared."

"What?" Joanna stood in the hallway, one hand clutching the lapels of her robe where they crossed over her chest, her other hand knotted into a tight fist at her side.

"Jo, honey." J.T. rushed over to her, put his arm around her and guided her into the living room.

"What happened to Claire?" Joanna asked. "Has Lenny Plott kidnapped her?"

J.T. held Joanna close to his side, supporting her trembling body with his strength.

"Ms. Beaumont, I'm Agent Carmichael, with the Federal Bureau of Investigation. And I'm afraid we don't know for sure what happened to Ms. Andrews," Dane said. "Her boyfriend called us when she didn't come home from work yesterday. Claire worked at a local grocery store. Everyone in town knows her, and yet no one has any idea how she simply disappeared when so many people were supposedly looking out for her."

"He found her and kidnapped her and—" Joanna's breathing became fast and frantic "—raped her and killed her. That's what he said he'd do to her...to all of us."

J.T. pulled Joanna into his arms. She buried her face in his chest. He ran one hand up and down her back, soothing her, while he held her hip with the other.

"We're going to put a man in the vicinity. I'm here now doing preliminary planning," Dane said. "I know you don't need help guarding Ms. Beaumont. Our man will be here to do a job—to apprehend Plott—while your job is defending Ms. Beaumont. If we're lucky, we'll catch Plott before he gets anywhere near the ranch."

"Send one of your best men," J.T. said. "I'll consider it a personal favor."

"I'm sending Landers, Hal Landers. You don't know him. He's a fairly new agent, but he's fast become one of our best."

With her arms still wrapped around J.T., Joanna turned her face and looked at Dane Carmichael. "How will your agent recognize Lenny Plott if he's changed his appearance? He could come into town, even come out here to the ranch, and no one would know who he was."

"Landers will be working with the local authorities to keep an eye on any strangers coming into Trinidad," Dane told her. "He'll get settled in town, then he'll stop by the ranch and introduce himself. If you need him before he makes contact, just give me a call."

"Agent Carmichael?" Joanna called out to him.

"Yes, ma'am?"

"Please let me know as soon as you find Claire. No matter what."

"Yes, ma'am, I'll give J.T. a call."

"Thank you," she said. "J.T., why don't you see Agent Carmichael to the door?"

"I'll see myself out," Dane said.

The minute they were alone, J.T. lifted Joanna into his arms, sat down in the plaid chair by the fireplace and held her in his lap. Cuddling in his arms, she rested her head on his shoulder.

"Claire's dead," Joanna said. "I know she's dead."

"Maybe not, honey."

"He's going to come after Libby and me. But which one of us is going to be next?"

"If he comes after you—"

"*When* he comes after me," Joanna corrected J.T.

"When he comes after you, he'll have to face me." J.T. took her chin in his hand and looked directly at her. "I told you before, nobody's going to get to you without going through me first, and so far, nobody's ever gone through me."

She tried to smile, but could manage only a faint curve of her lips. She closed her eyes and sighed. He kissed her closed eyelids, then drew her into his arms, holding her, soothing her, reassuring her.

Why had life played such a cruel joke on her, bringing J.T. into her life at the same time Lenny Plott escaped from prison? She'd spent the past four years in New Mexico, dreaming of and searching for a love of her own to equal the one her great-grandmother had found. Now, when there was a chance of that dream coming true, her life was in danger. And the one person who stood between her and certain death was the man she loved.

CHAPTER TEN

"PLEASE TRY NOT to worry about me too much." Joanna kissed her mother on the cheek. "J.T. will do everything possible to keep me safe. And now that there'll be FBI agents in Trinidad keeping a lookout for Lenny Plott, it should be only a matter of time before they arrest him."

Helene hugged Joanna, then released her. Holding Joanna's hands in hers, she smiled. "I can't stay. As much as I would like to be here with you, I have too many obligations back in Richmond. And since you refuse to come home with me, then—"

Joanna squeezed her mother's hands. "There's absolutely nothing you could do if you stayed here. As a matter of fact, we're probably better off with a couple of thousand miles between us. If we were together, we'd only end up arguing. You were too accustomed to running my life when I lived in Richmond, and since moving to Trinidad, I've become used to making all my own decisions."

"I still think you're making a mistake getting involved with J. T. Blackwood," Helene whispered, then glanced over her shoulder at J.T., who stood on the ranch-house porch, watching and waiting for her departure.

"If having an affair with J.T. is a mistake, then it's my mistake, Mother."

"I don't want to see you hurt again. I simply couldn't bear—"

"You'd better get going." Joanna tugged on her mother's arm. "Alex and Elena are waiting in the Jeep."

"They're very nice people," Helene said. "I'm glad you have them as friends. But friends can never take the place of family. Remember that."

"If y'all don't get started right now, Mother, you'll miss your plane," Joanna said.

"I wish you could at least ride into Santa Fe with us."

Joanna opened the Jeep door and assisted her mother inside, then leaned over and kissed her again. "I'll call you often to let you know I'm all right." Joanna closed the door.

Helene waved goodbye as Alex drove away; Joanna watched the departing vehicle until all she saw was a trail of dust.

J.T. put his arm around Joanna's shoulders. "It would be nice if we all had perfect parents."

"I wonder if anyone does?"

"Probably not," J.T. said. "After all, parents are only human beings, with faults and weaknesses. I used to blame my parents for all my problems, for all my unhappiness. But that was when I was a boy. When I grew up, I realized that they were just a couple of kids who fell in love and were too young to overcome all the obstacles in their path. Mainly old John Thomas."

"I'm not sure my parents were ever in love. I think their marriage was more or less a merger of two old Virginia families."

"Marriages have been based on far less."

"Why have you never married, J.T.?" She slipped her arm around his waist.

"I decided a long time ago that I wasn't the marrying kind, honey. I'm a hardheaded, cynical son of a bitch, who doesn't like to compromise. I'd make a lousy husband."

"Have you ever been in love?"

"Nope."

"I thought I was in love with Todd, but I came to realize that what Todd and I had was a lot like what Mother and Daddy had. We were compatible, came from the same social circle and probably would have had a fairly contented life together. At least for a while. Until the day came when I discovered that I needed more in a relationship."

"I suppose that's what happened to Annabelle," J.T. said. "After sixteen years of marriage, she decided she wanted some passion in her life."

"You've changed your mind about Annabelle and Benjamin, haven't you?" Joanna nudged J.T. in the ribs. "Come on. Admit it. You know there was more to their relationship than a summer affair."

"I concede that there might have been more going on." He gave Joanna's arm a gentle yank, guiding her into motion. "Come on. You need to go change into something comfortable for riding."

"We're going riding?" she asked. "Now?"

"It's a beautiful day. Not hellfire hot. Alex and Elena graciously volunteered to take care of your mother for us, so that gives us the day to ourselves."

"What if Agent Landers tries to contact you?" Joanna asked.

"I'll take my cellular phone. I'm sure Dane gave Landers all the numbers where I can be reached. Now quit making excuses and go get changed." J.T. shoved her across the yard. She glared at him, then laughed.

"Where are we going?"

"I thought we'd ride back out to the old archaeological dig, and after that, I have a surprise for you."

What J.T. wanted more than anything was to get her mind off the fact that Claire Andrews had been kidnapped and no one had any idea where she was. Sure, the odds were that Plott had her, and she was probably dead. But they'd face that reality if and when they found Claire's body. He was sorry for Melody Horton and Claire Andrews. He hoped the Feds caught up with Plott before he got to Libby Felton, if Libby was next on his list. But his main concern was Joanna—keeping her safe and sane, until Plott was back behind bars.

"Why don't you go get our horses ready while I change," Joanna said. "I won't be long."

"We've got all day. No need to rush." J.T. followed her up the steps to the bunkhouse porch.

She stopped dead still, turned slowly and looked at him. "You *are* going to stick to me like glue, aren't you?"

"I'm not going to take any chances where your safety is concerned. Consider us temporarily joined at the hip."

She nodded, turned and went inside, with J.T. directly behind her. He waited patiently for her to change into boots, jeans and a cotton shirt. When she came out of the bedroom carrying her hat, J.T. took it from her and set it on her head.

"You look like a real cowgirl now, honey." He kissed her, quick and hard, yet nondemandingly.

She loved the way he smiled when he looked at her, as if he found the sight of her delightful. She and J.T. were lovers now and that should mean they were relaxed around each other. But Joanna found herself trying to second-guess his thoughts and actions. What exactly had their making love meant to him? Was she more important to him than the other women he'd had sex with over the years? Or was she nothing more than his latest affair?

She watched him while he prepared Washington and a spirited mare named Playtime. He checked his rifle before attaching the scabbard to the saddle. He packed his Glock in the saddlebags, along with a couple of flashlights, a flask of water and his cellular phone. Then he tied down a folded blanket.

"Flashlights and a blanket," Joanna said. "I'm getting curious about this surprise of yours."

"Don't start asking questions. Just wait and see."

They rode off Blackwood property and onto Hezekiah Mahoney's. Within an hour they had reached the eastern section of Mahoney's ranch, where the old dig was located near the foothills of the mountain. Although Joanna had painted the vibrant colors of this land time and time again, the breathtaking beauty of the red sandstone canyons, the mushroom-shaped cliffs and the golden cottonwood trees that grew along the arroyos would always make her want to put brush to canvas.

Giving their horses a rest, they walked, hand in hand, over the old archaeological site. The earth had long since given up most of her buried treasures here, leaving only a random find for the occasional student whom eighty-four-year-old Hezekiah allowed on his property.

Joanna tried to imagine what her great-grandfather's campsite would have looked like. Closing her eyes she could almost smell the cook fires burning. Could almost hear the sound of Annabelle's young sons, one her own grandfather, laughing while they played. Could almost see a young Navajo silversmith gazing down from his Appaloosa stallion at the woman who was to become the one true love of his life.

"Hey, wake up." J.T. nudged her. "Where were you? Off in some dream?"

"Just trying to picture what this place must have looked like in 1925, the summer my great-grandparents worked here."

"Fantasizing about Annabelle and Benjamin's first meeting?" J.T. asked.

"Yes, that, of course," she admitted. "But wondering how my great-grandfather could have been so blind. His wife was having an affair right under his nose and he didn't suspect a thing."

"Maybe he did," J.T. said. "Maybe he just chose to keep his mouth shut and pretend nothing was happening."

"But how…why?"

"He must have known she wasn't in love with him, since her father had arranged their marriage." J.T. took Joanna's hand in his while they traipsed around the old site. "He was a lot older than she was, and my guess is they weren't sexually compatible. Ernest Beaumont would have been pretty sure his wife would never give up her sons, and that's exactly what she'd have had to do if she'd left him."

"So, you're saying you think my great-grandfather simply stood by and endured Annabelle's affair, knowing in the end, she'd return to Virginia with him."

"Think about it. It makes sense."

Joanna kicked the dirt under her feet, stirring up some ancient dust. "Can you imagine the intense emotions, the high level of tension? I'm surprised we can't still feel it in the air around us."

"I think you're feeling some of it right now, aren't you, Jo?" He whirled her around and into his arms. "It's all right to get a bit caught up in our ancestors' lives. For the time being, it's good for you to have other things to think about. But keep in mind that these were their lives, not ours. You're not Annabelle and I'm not Benjamin."

"Yes, I know. I'm not a married woman with two children. You're not a poor Navajo youth. The obstacles that kept Annabelle and Benjamin apart don't exist for us.

Where their affair was doomed from the start, ours isn't. We're free to do whatever we want with our lives."

J.T. stared at her, his gaze softening. He caressed her cheek. "What I want right now is to show you my surprise."

He didn't want to think too deeply about his feelings for Joanna. She was a woman who deserved far more than he could ever give her. She needed more than his passion, more than the momentary pleasure they found in each other's arms.

"What's the surprise? Where is it?"

J.T. thought she looked like a little girl, bright-eyed, rosy-cheeked and almost giddy at the prospect of being given a secret present. He hoped she wouldn't be disappointed. He didn't think she would be. But often reality dulled beside the brilliance of fantasy.

"It's about a three-mile ride from here. Up the side of the mountain."

J.T. led her to their horses and helped her mount, then guided them up the mountainside. With the jagged peaks high above, the yellow pine and white oak trees kissing the royal-blue sky and an almost-holy solitude surrounding them, he dismounted, lifted her off Playtime and held her in his arms. She clung to him, her heartbeat thundering in her ears.

Sliding her slowly down his body, he caressed her. Releasing her, he turned and undid one saddlebag and retrieved two flashlights. He handed one to her. "Come with me."

She removed her hat and hung it on the saddle horn. Then she followed him to the mouth of a cave, partially hidden from view by an outcropping of scrubby bushes.

"Take a look," he said, moving aside to allow her entrance.

Switching on her flashlight, she aimed the beam into the cave and took a tentative step inside. She sucked in a deep breath. J.T. turned on his flashlight and doubled the illumination inside the cave as he urged her to venture farther.

Together they explored the small cavern. Able to walk upright less than twelve feet inside, they stopped when the sandstone ceiling had gradually lowered from a good eight feet to less than five. From there, the cave decreased to a crawl space.

"Is this what I think it is?" Joanna asked.

"I believe so," J.T. said.

"How did you know about this place?"

"I discovered this cave when I was about eleven. I used to ride all over, exploring. I knew someone had used this place as a refuge of some sort, but not until I read part of Annabelle's diary did I put two and two together."

Joanna ran the flashlight's beam over the floor, where an animal skin of some sort still lay. Had Annabelle and Benjamin made love, their bodies entwined, on that fur rug? A shimmering glow of light reflected off the shattered pieces of a kerosene lamp, the bottom portion broken into only two pieces.

"I found this cave when Cliff and I were out riding," J.T. said. "His father was ranch foreman and he and I grew up together. We're the ones who accidentally broke that lamp."

"This is Annabelle and Benjamin's special place." Joanna's mouth felt dry, her throat tight. She bit down on her bottom lip. Her nerves zinged with excitement.

"Yeah, I think it probably was." J.T. placed his hand in the small of her back. "It would have been fairly close to camp and yet far enough away to have been private. And you've got to admit, the place is pretty isolated."

"The way she wrote about their special place in her diary, I pictured it cosy and warm and inviting." Joanna continued visually exploring the cave, waving her flashlight back and forth in slow motion.

"In reality it's a dark hole in the side of the mountain. Hard, rugged and very unromantic."

"But it was their special place." Joanna glanced down at the ratty old fur rug. "The only place on earth they could truly be together, where they could be lovers."

"Kind of sad, isn't it? But remember, things looked a lot different seventy years ago. The fur rug was undoubtedly new and clean, not rotted with age. And the kerosene lamp probably cast warm shadows on the wall." He set his flashlight on its base, allowing the light to shine straight up and create pale shadows.

Joanna set her flashlight down beside his, increasing the muted glow and doubling the sense of cosy warmth. "From what Annabelle wrote, the happiest moments of her life were spent here, because she was with the man she loved."

"There's something I want to show you. I think it'll pretty well confirm that this was our great-grandparents' trysting place." J.T. turned her to face him. "You stay right here. It's in my saddlebag."

When he started to walk away, she grabbed his arm. "What is it?"

"Just let me get it and show it to you."

She nodded agreement and waited in the cave for his return. The eerie silence crept up her spine. She shivered. Somewhere off in the distance she heard the sound of drums. She listened, thinking she was imagining the rhythmic beat.

No, the sound was real, even if it existed only in her heart, as surely as it had existed in Annabelle's heart long ago. A magical drumbeat, summoning lovers together, speaking without words of a love that was meant to be.

"Here it is." J.T. came back into the cave, a blanket over his arm and a tattered book in his hands. "I found this ragged old book in the cave when I was up here exploring by myself one day. I was always collecting stuff, taking it home and adding it to my treasure trove. But it's not so much the book itself I wanted to show you, but something pressed between the pages."

He held the book out to Joanna. Her hands trembled as she reached out for it. The binding had been broken and numerous pages had fallen out, probably years ago. She opened the book to the first page. J.T. spread the blanket on the ground, lifted one of the flashlights and slid his hand under Joanna's elbow.

"Come on, honey, sit down."

He eased her down on the blanket, then sat beside her and held the flashlight on the thin volume of verse. "Go ahead and read it."

The inscription read, "To Benjamin. Forever and only yours, A."

"It's a stupid book of poetry," J.T. said. "Why an eleven-year-old boy ever kept such a thing, I'll never know. I suppose at that age, I considered it some sort of treasure. I stuck it in a bottom desk drawer in my room, where I kept a lot of the junk I collected."

"Christina Rossetti's poems," Joanna said. "This book must have belonged to Annabelle. There're references to Christina Rossetti's poems in her diary. One in particular."

"Look about halfway into the book," J.T. told her, then watched as she carefully turned the brittle, yellowed pages.

There, lying atop the poem entitled "Echo," was a four-inch braid of hair—strands of jet-black hair and fiery-red hair blended together and tied with a faded yellow ribbon. Joanna gasped. Moisture stung her eyes. She swallowed her tears.

Closing the book with reverence, she laid it beside her on the blanket, then looked at J.T. "You think it's all a bunch of stupid, sentimental hogwash, don't you? You can't understand why they would have cut strands of their hair and braided them together as a keepsake for Benjamin, can you? Or why she would have given him a book of poems by her favorite poet?"

"Hey, seventy years ago, people were different than they are today. Maybe everybody was more romantic." J.T. rubbed his hand up and down Joanna's back. "I think we both know Annabelle Beaumont had a romantic streak in her a mile wide. So if Benjamin really loved her, then he would have catered to her romantic nature, don't you think?"

"Well, I'll say one thing for you, J. T. Blackwood, you certainly know how to get a woman's mind off her troubles." She tried to smile, but the effort failed. Instead, she caressed his cheek with her fingertips. "That's why you chose today to show me this cave and the book with the hair braid. You wanted me to forget about Claire's disappearance and Lenny Plott's threats."

"Obviously it didn't work."

"Yes, it did. I'd much rather think about and talk about our great-grandparents than about living in fear of what Lenny Plott will do next."

"I thought you'd like to keep the book," J.T. said. "I figured it'd mean a lot more to you than it ever could to me."

"Thank you." She caressed his cheek again. He covered her hand with his, trapping it against his face.

"What are the odds that you and I would ever meet, let alone become lovers?" he asked.

"You don't believe in destiny, but I do. You and I were destined to meet and become lovers, just as Benjamin and Annabelle were."

"Now, Jo, don't start comparing us to—"

"I'm not! I know very well that you and I aren't our great-grandparents, and we aren't destined to relive their tragic love affair. We're very different people than our ancestors were, and our affair is different from theirs." She pulled her hand from his.

"I'm glad you see it that way. I don't want you to think just because I showed you this cave and gave you that book—" he pointed to the volume of poetry "—I'm buying into any of this romantic nonsense. I'll go so far as to admit that I believe Annabelle and Benjamin probably cared deeply for each other, but I think this tragic, eternal love between them is something your great-grandmother concocted in her fantasies. Benjamin had to have gone on with his life and married someone else and spent his life with her. After all, he did have a child—my mother's father."

"You don't know anything about your family history, do you? Your grandfather Blackwood really did cut all your ties to the Navajo, didn't he?"

"Yeah, you're right. I don't know anything about my mother's family, but I don't see what my ignorance concerning my Navajo heritage has to do with—"

"Benjamin Greymountain was a young widower with a four-year-old son when he met Annabelle. His wife had died in childbirth, and he never remarried. When I asked Elena about Benjamin, she told me that her mother said he died of tuberculosis at the age of thirty-eight."

J.T. grunted, then blew out a huffing breath. "I give up.

Benjamin went to his grave pining for Annabelle, and she loved him and no other as long as she lived. Now, are you satisfied?"

Joanna grinned. "You don't really believe it. You're just saying that to pacify me." Lifting her arms, she circled his neck. "In your own gruff, moody way, you're very sweet, you know."

"I've been called a lot of things, honey, but never sweet. There's no reason for you to read more into what I say and do than—"

"I know. I know. You can't give me anything, aren't offering me anything, except your protection and a temporary love affair."

She realized that he had no idea he was catering to her romantic nature. Just as, perhaps, Benjamin had catered to Annabelle's romantic nature. When a man cared deeply for a woman, he made concessions. Was that what J.T. was doing? Did his feelings for her run far deeper than he wanted to admit? She could only guess at J.T.'s true feelings. It was possible, even probable, that he didn't know himself. Long ago, as a young boy, he had sealed off his emotions, protecting himself from being hurt. He had been stolen from the only love he'd known—his mother's. And he'd been raised by a bitter old man who obviously hadn't known the first thing about love; only about controlling and possessing.

"Exactly what did you have in mind when you brought me up here to this cave?" Joanna leaned closer, hugging J.T., pressing her breasts against his chest. "Considering how intrigued I am by Annabelle and Benjamin, you might have thought I'd want to make love here, in their special place."

Clearing his throat, J.T. shuffled his hips on the blanket. "I don't want you to think I brought you up here with the intention of—"

Joanna covered his lips with her index finger. "Why did you bring along a blanket?"

"Now, Jo, you're doing exactly what I told you not to do. You're reading something into my actions that—"

She silenced him with a tongue-thrusting demanding kiss, then toppled him down on the blanket, knocking off his Stetson. Covering his body with hers, she ended the kiss and smiled at him.

"If I promise not to misinterpret your actions and start thinking there's something magical happening between us the way it did between our great-grandparents, will you make love to me here…in this cave…now?"

J.T. cupped her buttocks in his big hands, lifting and positioning her so that her softness settled directly over his hardness. "Honey, I'll make love to you…anywhere… anytime."

She had dreamed of this moment, but she didn't dare tell J.T. Since the first time she'd read her great-grandmother's diary, she had fantasized about meeting her own passionate lover, here, in this special place where Annabelle and Benjamin had consummated their love. Perhaps she was just a foolish romantic, a woman for whom reality had become cruel and bitter. But Annabelle had been a romantic fortunate enough to find a lover who had fulfilled her fantasies.

Joanna kissed J.T.'s leather-brown neck, then laid her head on his shoulder as she draped her body over his. "I'm glad I waited for you. It wouldn't have been the same with anyone else. It wouldn't have been so absolutely right."

He rolled her over onto her back, leaned down and unbuttoned her shirt. She shivered when his fingers touched her bare skin. "Are you sure this is what you want?"

"Yes, I'm very sure." Reaching up, she unsnapped his shirt and stretched her hands out over his chest. When he sucked in his breath, she smiled. "You make me want to learn all there is to know about making love. You make me want to trust you completely, to give myself over to you and believe you'd never hurt me."

He undid the front opening of her bra, lifted her just a fraction off the blanket and removed her shirt and bra. He gazed down at her breasts—round, full and tempting. Covering them with his hands, he slid one leg between her thighs. Lifting his knee, he massaged her intimately.

"I want you to trust me completely," he said. "To know that what happens between us now is a mutual loving. We both give and we both take." Clasping her hand in his, he carried it to his belt buckle. "I take you. You take me. And when you lose control, I lose control."

With a precision of familiarity, as if they had undressed each other numerous times, Joanna and J.T. divested themselves of their clothing. When they lay naked, side by side on the blanket, J.T. took her in his arms and turned her to face him. "Will I frighten you if I'm not gentle this time?"

He fondled her, testing her readiness. She clung to him, her answer a gasping sigh against his lips. "No, you don't have to worry. I don't feel very gentle myself. Not here. Not now." Not when the passion within her had been ignited by the chance to fulfill a dream, to capture for herself some small portion of the magic Annabelle had known.

His kiss devoured her, as hers did him. He rolled her on her back and cupped her behind, lifting her. She clutched his back, biting into his flesh with her fingernails, bucking up to meet him. Wrapping her legs around his hips, she issued him an invitation into the sheathing warmth of her body. He thrust into her forcefully. Moaning with pleasure, she kneaded his tight buttocks.

Heat poured into her body as if a searing liquid fire had entered her bloodstream. Her breasts ached, her nipples beaded into tight buds. As he moved in and out of her, his hard chest grazed her sensitive nipples, the sensation shooting pinpricks of pain and pleasure to the very core of her femininity.

Her breathing quickened. She gasped for air as the tumult within her built, stronger and stronger with each powerful stab. What he gave her was too much, and yet at the same time, not nearly enough. She wanted him to end this torment, but she wanted the loving to go on forever.

He increased the depth and pace of his lunges. Erotic words, spoken harshly and urgently, told her of his needs and intentions. Joanna trembled as the first warning signs of fulfillment rippled through her.

J.T. didn't know if he could hold on much longer; the tight clutching of her body brought him to the very edge. The moment he felt her shatter into paroxysms of release, he hammered into her repeatedly, his own release coming hard and fast. He cried out, the sound one of a triumphant male animal. Pure masculine completion controlled his body.

His jackhammer thrusts created anew the climactic spasms within her. Her moans of pleasure grew louder and louder. In the final moments, he uttered Navajo words to her, words neither of them understood. *"Ayóí óosh'ni."* But in her secret heart of hearts, Joanna believed she knew what J.T. had said to her, even if he did not. His words were Benjamin Greymountain's words—his proclamation of love to Annabelle.

J.T. wrapped his arms around Joanna, their bodies resting spoon-fashion. He lay there, holding her, listening to the soft, sweet sound of her breathing as she slept peacefully, sated and safe. Somehow he'd allowed this beautiful, loving woman to get under his skin, to get past the protective armor he'd kept securely around his emotions. He was a fool for getting personally involved with her, but heaven help him, he had never wanted or needed a woman so much.

He had promised her that he'd never hurt her, but he had lied. He had lied as much to himself as he had to her. Oh, he'd never hurt her physically, but he knew that sooner or later he'd break her heart. And for a woman like Joanna, his precious romantic Joanna, breaking her heart would be far more devastating.

She believed in things he didn't, and wanted more from him than he had to give. He almost wished he could be the man she wanted. But he couldn't. She wanted him to be the reincarnation of Benjamin Greymountain; to come to her with a Navajo soul, to love her with a mindless passion. Joanna wanted the two of them to capture the spirit of their ancestors and bring to life the love Annabelle and Benjamin had taken to their graves.

When Joanna awoke, they made love again. Sweet, slow love, each learning the other's body by touch and taste and sight. The burning sun melted into the late-afternoon sky, splaying the earth with golden light. They dressed unhurriedly, taking time to savor their last moments alone in this special place. Joanna clasped Annabelle's book of poetry to her breast. A shadowy sense of sadness settled on her heart. Would this be the only day she and J.T. would make love here? Was there no future for them?

J.T. helped her mount Playtime, then took the book from her and put it in her saddlebag. "Time to go back to the ranch. Elena and Alex should be home by now, even if Elena did a lot of shopping while they were in Santa Fe."

Joanna nodded. Yes, it was time to go back to the ranch, back to reality, back to the threat on her life.

JOANNA AND J.T. returned Washington and Playtime to the stables, taking time to give their horses a rubdown themselves, instead of handing them over to a stable hand.

"After we shower, how about my grilling steaks tonight?" J.T. said. "We can call Alex and Elena and see if they want to join us."

"Sounds like a great idea." She tiptoed her fingers up J.T.'s arm. "Especially the part about taking a shower."

"Are you suggesting we shower together?" He slipped his arm around her waist and drew her to his side.

"I've never taken a shower with anybody. It would be another new experience for me."

J.T. eased his hand down, spreading it out over her behind. "I'm glad I'm the one who's getting to share all these new experiences with you."

Joanna unlocked the front door and walked into her house, with J.T. following her, his hand still on her rear end. She gasped when she saw the state of her living room. She rushed inside, then stopped dead still. J.T. cursed.

"The place is a total wreck," she said. "What could have— Oh, my God, no!"

J.T. came up behind her, draped his arm around her middle and rested his chin against her temple. "Take it easy, honey."

"The room's been ransacked," she said.

Sofa and chair cushions lay haphazardly about the floor. Lamps had been shattered and pictures ripped from the walls. Someone had done a thorough job of plundering, turning neatness and order into total disarray. Pull-

ing away from J.T., Joanna crossed the room to the easel
that held Elena's portrait.

"Dammit!" she cried when she saw the defaced painting. "He destroyed Elena's picture."

J.T. read the message that had been written in red paint
across the surface of his sister's portrait. "I'll be back."
He gripped Joanna by the shoulders, then closed his eyes
for a moment, a burning black rage searing him.

"He's been here." Joanna trembled in J.T.'s arms. "He's
been inside my home. How did this happen? Why didn't
someone see him and stop him?"

"I don't know." J.T. tightened his hold on her, silently
cursing Lenny Plott, damning his soul to everlasting hell.
The man was a slippery, slimy, conniving polecat. Somehow he had slid past Dane Carmichael and Hal Landers
when he'd come through Trinidad. But what if he hadn't
come through Trinidad? It was possible that he'd gone
southwest, then north and had doubled back in the opposite direction.

J.T. knew from having read reports on him that Leonard
Plott III was a sick, evil man, but he was nobody's fool. In
his own way, the man was a genius, having raped dozens
of women and eluded the police in Virginia for several
years. If his last rape victim's boyfriend hadn't returned
home unexpectedly, Plott might never have been caught.

Not only was Plott smart, he was rich. And with his
kind of money, he could buy just about anything he
needed—even certain people's help and other people's
silence.

Leonard Plott was a dangerous animal. Sooner or
later, someone was going to have to bring him down. J.T.
wanted to be the one to do it.

"It's not safe here, is it?" Joanna turned in J.T.'s arms.

He hugged her fiercely. "I'm not safe anywhere from that monster."

"You're safe with me," J.T. told her. "Right this minute, you're safe. Here. In my arms. And I'm going to keep you safe."

"What are we going to do? He'll be back. He won't stop until he's—"

"Don't say it, honey. Don't even think it. If you don't feel safe here on the ranch, we'll find another place."

"Someplace where he can't find me?" Joanna asked. "Dear God, J.T., I don't think such a place exists."

CHAPTER ELEVEN

"WE'RE GOING TO catch this guy," Dane Carmichael said. "It's only a matter of time."

"Time isn't on our side." J.T. glanced across the room at his old FBI friend and Special Agent Landers, the two men seated side by side on the leather sofa in J.T.'s study. "Plott has already kidnapped and killed one woman, and possibly a second. And today, he came onto my ranch, right under our noses, and ransacked Joanna's home. No one saw him. Not one person on this ranch had any idea an intruder was anywhere around. That should tell us all something about Plott, shouldn't it?"

"It tells me what I've known all along. That we're dealing with a highly intelligent and very dangerous criminal." Uncrossing his legs, Dane eased to the edge of the sofa. "His access to an unlimited amount of money makes our job more difficult and his revenge scheme easier for him to achieve."

J.T. cut his gaze toward Joanna, who sat in the swivel chair behind his desk. He had asked her to let him speak privately with Carmichael and Landers, but she'd insisted on being present. He understood her need to be involved with the investigation; after all, it was her life on the line. She was one of Plott's prey, possibly his next intended victim. She looked up at J.T. and nodded, silently telling him that she was all right.

"It doesn't help that Plott has somehow changed his

appearance," Agent Landers said. "He didn't have time to get any kind of plastic surgery done, so whatever changes he's made have to be superficial. Dyed his hair, maybe. Possibly got contacts. There's no way to know."

"We've been running checks in Richmond, passing out Plott's photograph to see if anyone anywhere recognizes him. We're desperate for a lead of some sort." Dane stretched his long lean frame up and off the sofa. "But a man with Plott's money can pay people off, get whatever help he needs and make sure nobody talks."

"His mother insists she hasn't seen him or talked to him," Landers said. "But Lieutenant George has told us that the old woman would do anything to protect her son."

"Has the FBI sent more agents to Texas to protect Libby?" Joanna asked. "I know that she can't afford private security any more than Claire could have."

"We're taking every precaution where Ms. Felton is concerned," Dane assured Joanna. "In Shelby, where Ms. Felton lives, we've brought the local authorities in on the case, just as we're doing here in Trinidad."

"You understand that resources and manpower are limited, Ms. Beaumont," Landers said. "We're doing all that we can. And I can assure you that we're going to get Lenny Plott."

"Before or after he kills all four of the women who testified against him?" Although she quivered inside, Joanna's voice was strong and steady.

J.T. noticed that her tight little fists rested in her lap. Lifting himself up from where he'd had his hip propped against the edge of the desk, J.T. walked around behind the desk and gripped the back of the swivel chair.

"I'm taking Joanna away," J.T. said. "First thing in the morning, we're leaving the ranch."

"There's no need to do that, Mr. Blackwood." Agent

Landers jumped up off the sofa. "Dane's bringing in more agents, and we've got the local police department and county sheriff's office to back us up."

"Where do you think you can take her where she'll be safer than she is here?" Dane asked.

J.T. glanced at Dane, then over at Landers. "To the Navajo reservation. My sister is making arrangements with members of our mother's family. Elena and Alex will know how to reach us."

"See here, Blackwood, are you saying you plan to take Ms. Beaumont to some sort of hideaway on the Indian reservation?" Landers asked. "I don't recommend this move, and if you insist on—"

"I insist." J.T. glared at Landers.

Landers's face reddened. He cleared his throat. "In that case, I'll have to insist on our knowing your exact whereabouts. Perhaps you can have your sister draw a map and give us telephone numbers where we can locate you."

"Dane has my cellular phone number," J.T. said. "And the tribal police will know our whereabouts."

"I don't understand your reasoning." Landers marched across the room, stopping in front of the huge oak desk. "You've got the FBI here, as well as local authorities as a backup, and you're taking Ms. Beaumont out in the middle of nowhere and expect the tribal police to protect her."

"You've said too much," Dane told his subordinate.

Snapping his head around, Landers glowered at Dane, who was watching J.T. Landers looked at J.T., then swallowed hard. "I didn't mean—"

"I'll protect Ms. Beaumont," J.T. said. "I expect the FBI to do their job and find Lenny Plott."

Landers wisely kept his mouth shut when Dane Carmichael asked J.T. to walk them outside. Dane said goodbye to Joanna, then motioned for Landers to follow him into the hallway.

J.T. slipped his hands down the back of the chair, grasped Joanna's shoulders and squeezed. "I'll be back in a few minutes and we'll talk to Elena and Alex."

She laid both of her hands atop his, patting him reassuringly. "Try not to kill Agent Landers before he leaves the ranch."

J.T. chuckled. "It'll be an effort to keep from strangling him, but I'll do my best."

Joanna watched J.T. follow the FBI agents. Leaning over, she rested her elbows on the desk, then lowered her chin, cupping it in her hands.

In such a short period of time, her whole life had changed. She had found peace and contentment in Trinidad, and her career as an artist had excelled beyond her wildest dreams. And after waiting for so many years to find a special man to love, J. T. Blackwood had ridden his Appaloosa stallion into her life.

But as he had done once before, Lenny Plott threatened to destroy her happiness.

"Are you all right?" Elena's question interrupted Joanna's thoughts.

Joanna gasped, then looked up to see Elena standing in the doorway. "I'm fine. Come on in. J.T. will be right back. He's seeing the FBI agents to their car."

Elena nodded, then walked across the room and lifted herself up on the desk. Dangling her legs off the side, she faced Joanna. "I just got off the phone with my cousin Kate and she's going to go out tonight and tidy up Mama's house. No one has lived there since she died, but Kate and Ed keep an eye on the place and Kate airs it out and cleans it a couple of times a year."

"I remember you telling me about your home on the

reservation," Joanna said. "I had planned to have Kate take me out there to see it the next time I visited her."

"Now, you'll be living there with J.T." Elena bent over, leaning closer to Joanna. "He's been back to the reservation only three times since he was a child. Once when Mama was dying, and again a few days later for her funeral. Then the last time, to get me and bring me back to the ranch."

"Maybe our stay in your mother's home will help J.T. as much as taking refuge there might keep me safe from Lenny Plott." Joanna clasped Elena's hands. "I'm in love with your brother, you know. I didn't mean for it to happen, but it did. He hasn't made me any promises—other than to guard and protect me."

"J.T.'s afraid to love anyone," Elena said. "I know he cares about me, but...well, I think maybe Mama was the only person he ever loved. You know, when he was a little boy. After he was taken from the reservation, he was told Mama had given him away because she didn't want him anymore. That cruel grandfather of his taught him to hate Mama and everything Navajo. Old John Thomas Blackwood saw to it that J.T. grew up hard and cold and cynical, just like him."

"I think J.T. needs to come to terms with his mixed heritage." Releasing Elena's hands, Joanna rose from the chair and walked over to the window, looking out at her converted bunkhouse. "If only he would allow himself to be the man he is. Half white. Half Navajo."

"He told me once that the reason he didn't stay in New Mexico is because out here he isn't either. Not white and not Native American. He doesn't feel accepted by either people, doesn't feel a part of either world. But in the marines and then in the Secret Service, he was just J. T.

Blackwood. A soldier. An agent. His past didn't matter. He had a job to do and he did it."

"But he has no personal life. No real home, despite having inherited this ranch from his grandfather," Joanna said. "And although, as you say, he cares about you, he won't let himself be part of a family."

"You've gotten to know J.T. very well in a short period of time, haven't you?" Elena smiled. "I knew you and J.T. would be good for each other, if I ever got you together."

"I don't know about that. Sometimes I think maybe J.T. and I are very bad for each other. I've fallen in love with him and I trust him with my life, but... Well, there's still a part of me that doesn't completely trust anyone. I love J.T., but I don't trust him with that love. He can't make a commitment to me, can't promise me a future. And I don't trust what there is between us enough to believe we have a chance together."

"Be patient with him. Try to have faith in his ability to change." Elena walked over and placed her hand on Joanna's shoulder. "If you can learn to trust him and trust what you feel for him completely, then maybe he can learn how to love you."

"Maybe I'm the wrong woman for him." Joanna stepped away from Elena. Stretching her shoulders, she clasped the back of her neck with both hands and tilted her head. She took a deep breath, relaxed and dropped her arms to her sides. "After what happened to me...the rape...maybe I'll never be enough woman for a man like J.T. He's so...so..."

"All man," Elena said. "Yeah, my big brother is primitive macho masculinity personified, isn't he? But I'll tell you what I think. I think that if J.T. can't love you, he can't love anybody."

"Where's J.T.?" Alex walked into the study.

"Seeing the FBI men off," Elena told him. "Did you tell Benito that J.T. wants to take Washington and Playtime with him when he leaves in the morning?"

"Yes, I told Benito. He'll have them in a trailer and have it hitched to J.T.'s Jeep by eight in the morning," Alex said. "J.T.'s already told me that he wants to get an early start."

"I'll have to go back over to my house to pack." Joanna dreaded walking into her living room again, although she knew J.T. had asked Benito's wife, Rita, who worked as a part-time maid for Elena, to clean and straighten the mess Lenny Plott had created. "I want to take some supplies and try to do some work while I'm gone. We have no idea how long we'll be away. It could be days or even weeks."

"There's an old hogan close to Mama's house," Elena said. "My great-grandparents lived there. You might want to do some sketches."

"Are you saying this hogan belonged to Benjamin Greymountain?" Joanna asked.

Elena nodded. "While you have J.T. on the reservation, see if you can get him to open himself up to our heritage and become acquainted with our relatives. You know our mother's family far better than J.T. does."

"I'll try," Joanna said.

Returning to his study, J.T. found Alex and Elena with Joanna. Taking Joanna to the reservation had been Elena's idea, but after giving it some thought, J.T. had agreed with her. There was no way to predict what Lenny Plott's next move would be or when he would act. One thing for sure, he knew exactly where Joanna lived and how to get to her. Taking her away was the wisest move. Of course, even on the reservation, hidden away from the world, there was no guarantee that Plott wouldn't figure out a way to find her.

If and when Plott showed up, J.T. would handle him. A part of J.T.—that primeval, protective, possessive male part of him—actually looked forward to a confrontation with Plott. Although J.T. had killed before, in the line of duty, he took no pleasure in it. But if he had to kill Plott, he would, and have no regrets.

"Well, did you get in touch with your cousins?" J.T. asked Elena as he walked into the study.

"*Our* cousins," Elena corrected him. "And they have names. Kate and Ed Whitehorn. Kate's mother and our mother were sisters."

"Fine. Did you get in touch with this Kate and make arrangements for me?"

"Yes, I did. She'll clean up Mama's house and have it ready by the time you and Joanna get there tomorrow," Elena said. "I explained the situation to her and—"

"How much did you tell her?" J.T. asked.

"Everything! We can trust our family completely, J.T. You are a member of that family, you know. And a member of our clan. They would never betray you." Planting her hands on her hips, Elena glared at her brother. "Besides, Kate and Ed are very fond of Joanna. She has stayed with them several times when she's gone to the reservation to work on her sketches and paintings."

"Calm down, little sister, I didn't mean to rile you. I'm sure your cousins—our cousins—are fine, trustworthy people," J.T. said. "It's just that the fewer people who know exactly where Joanna and I are, the better."

"Kate and Ed raise sheep, but Ed works at the NFPI sawmill," Elena said. "Their house is pretty isolated, but neighbors will see you and Joanna as you travel the road to Kate's house, so Kate has asked her brother, Joseph, to speak to these neighbors, most of them friends and family, and caution them to tell no one of your presence on the reservation."

"I appreciate all you've done to help us." Joanna hugged Elena. "Maybe the FBI will capture Lenny Plott soon and this nightmare will be over for all of us."

"J.T. will keep you safe." Elena glanced at her brother and smiled. "And he will have Ed nearby, as well as Joseph, who is very handy with a gun. And we both know that Joseph would do anything for you, Jo."

"Speaking of Joseph reminds me that I promised to do a sketch of him as well as one of the children next time I came to visit," Joanna said.

"Who's this Joseph?" J.T. frowned.

"Joseph is Kate's younger brother." Elena ran her fingers through her long dark hair, pulling the flyaway strands off her face. "He's been sweet on Joanna since the first time they met."

"Elena!" Joanna's green eyes widened. Her cheeks flushed.

"Joseph is our cousin," Elena told J.T. "His mother and our mother were sisters, so that makes Joseph the great-grandson of Benjamin Greymountain, too."

"Is that right?" J.T. deliberately avoided eye contact with Joanna, knowing exactly what his sister was trying to do. She wanted to elicit his jealousy over another man's interest in Joanna. And not just any man, but another direct descendant of Annabelle Beaumont's one true love.

"Well, why don't you two finalize your plans for the trip." Elena grabbed Alex's arm. "I'll get one of the guest bedrooms ready for you for tonight, Jo." She pulled Alex toward the door, halting just before walking out into the hall. "Let me know if you want my help packing. I can run over to your house with you and J.T. before supper."

When Elena and Alex had left, Joanna turned to J.T. "I'm sorry about that. Elena wasn't very subtle, was she?"

"Subtlety isn't one of Elena's strong points." J.T. rubbed his chin. "Have you ever dated my cousin Joseph?"

"Have I ever...?" Joanna smiled, bit down on her bottom lip and then covered her mouth, trying to suppress her laughter.

"Why do you find the question so amusing? All I asked was whether or not you'd ever dated Benjamin Greymountain's other great-grandson."

"Yes, Joseph and I have *dated* a few times," Joanna said. "I've dated several men since I moved to New Mexico. Cliff Lansdell for one, and Joseph for another. I like Joseph a lot, I just don't like him in *that* way."

"He's a full-blooded Navajo just like Benjamin Greymountain," J.T. said. "If you've been looking for a lover like the one your great-grandmother had, what was wrong with Joseph? Is he ugly or stupid or a jerk or—"

Joanna kissed J.T. on the mouth very quickly, then tilted her head just a fraction and looked directly at him. "Joseph Ornelas is a handsome, intelligent, sweet man and I think of him as a friend, but there is no magic between us. Not the way there is between..." Joanna shut her eyes, escaping the hard look on J.T.'s face.

J.T. pulled her into his arms. "Not the way there is between you and me." His kiss proclaimed his barely contained jealousy as well as his need to brand her as his own.

Joanna gave herself over to his possession, accepting his momentary domination, realizing that he had no idea how revealing his actions were. Did she dare hope that at the very core of his protective, possessive desire, the seeds of love had taken root?

JOANNA FLUNG BACK the covers and jumped out of bed. There was no use trying to sleep; she had tried for over two hours. Sleep wouldn't come. She couldn't stop thinking, couldn't stop worrying, couldn't stop wishing tonight was last night, when she had become J. T. Blackwood's woman in every sense of the word.

Not bothering to turn on a lamp or put on her robe, Joanna walked across the room and slumped down in the chair beside the windows. Tucking her bare feet up under her, she sighed, leaned back and stretched.

If only there was a switch inside her brain that could be flipped on and off; she'd flip it off right this minute and put an end to her thoughts. Her mind kept running the gamut from the night Lenny Plott had raped her to today when she and J.T. had made love in Annabelle and Benjamin's special place. She had struggled diligently to put the past behind her, to come to terms with the brutal violation that had forever changed her life. But with Lenny Plott free and bent on revenge, she couldn't help reliving that horrible night when she had come home to her apartment after working late at the museum.

Don't think about it! Don't remember! It happened nearly five years ago. Put it in the past where it belongs. Don't allow Lenny Plott's threats to force you to relive what he did to you. That's what he wants—for you to recall the terror and the pain and the humiliation. He wants you to think about how it could happen again.

But it wouldn't happen again. She wouldn't let it happen again! And J.T. would never allow anyone to hurt her. He'd made her a solemn promise to protect her. She had to trust him, had to believe in him and his ability to keep her safe.

J.T. J.T. J.T. She had put her life in his hands. She had given him her heart. And yet she could not bring herself to trust him fully, completely, to have faith in their future together, when he had made no lasting commitment to her.

Would hiding away on the Navajo reservation keep her hidden from Lenny Plott, or would he find her regardless of where J.T. took her? And what would happen if Plott came after her, if he confronted J.T.? J.T. might have to kill him.

Joanna shuddered. Pulling her knees up against her, she wrapped her arms around her legs. Unless the FBI apprehended Lenny Plott before he found her, a showdown between J.T. and him was inevitable. On some purely primitive level, she gloried in the fact that her mate was a brave warrior who would defend her to the death. And yet there was a part of her that personally wanted to rip out Lenny Plott's heart and feed it to the buzzards.

How did such creatures as Leonard Plott III come into being? What malevolent twist of fate turned a man into an inhuman monster capable of physically, sexually and emotionally brutalizing woman after woman and deriving immense pleasure from subjugating them to his cruelties?

Joanna's stomach churned. Bitterness coated her tongue. Her body quivered. Tears gathered in her eyes.

The door to the guest bedroom slowly opened. Joanna snapped her head around, staring at the silhouette in the doorway. Biting down on her bottom lip, she tried not to cry aloud.

Moonlight filtered through the sheer curtains, spreading a soft, muted glow over the room. J.T. glanced at the bed, saw that it was empty, and visually searched the room.

"Jo?" he whispered, then saw her huddled in the chair by the windows.

Swallowing her tears, she tried to answer him, but couldn't. He closed the door behind him, walked over to the chair and knelt beside her.

"What's wrong, honey?"

Cupping her chin in his hand, he lifted her face. She pulled away from him. Her long, fiery hair covered her features when she lowered her head. Slipping his hands under her neck, he swept up her hair, then let it fall through his fingers and down onto her shoulders.

"I couldn't sleep, either," he said. "I kept thinking about how much I wanted to be with you. Wanted to hold you in my arms."

Placing his arms around her stiff body, he pulled her toward him. "Talk to me, Jo. Let me help you. You don't have to be alone, unless you want to be. Just tell me, do you want me to stay or go?"

Joanna grabbed J.T., clinging to him fiercely. Wrapping herself around him, she allowed him to slide his big body into the chair as he lifted her onto his lap. She gasped for air, then laid her head on his shoulder and wept.

"Stay...please...stay." She cried softly, quietly, but with heartbreaking force.

J.T. stroked her back, kissed the side of her face and whispered comforting words, telling her it was all right to cry, to be angry, to be afraid.

Holding her, he encouraged her to vent her feelings, and when she was spent and lay exhausted in his arms, he lifted her and carried her to bed. He laid her in the middle of the huge oak bed, then sat down beside her, pulling her upward to rest again in his arms.

"Would it help to talk to me, to tell me about it?" he asked.

"I thought I'd put it behind me," she said, cuddling against him. "I had to tell the police, the rape counselor, the district attorney, my own therapist and...worst of all, I had to sit there in a courtroom with Lenny Plott watching me and tell the jury what he'd done to me."

"You were very brave," J.T. told her. "It took more courage than most people have."

"I wanted him dead!" Joanna clung to J.T., pressing against him, seeking and finding comfort.

J.T. couldn't hold her close enough. He wanted to weld her to him, to encompass her completely and make her a part of him. "Plott deserves to die."

"I testified against him for the same reasons Melody and Claire and Libby did. We wanted him punished and we wanted to make sure he could never hurt another woman. And now Melody is dead and Claire is missing."

"It isn't fair," J.T. said. "Sometimes there's just no rhyme or reason to life."

"The FBI have to find him and stop him before he... before he—"

J.T. placed his finger over her lips. "Hush, honey. Don't think about it. It isn't going to happen. They'll find Plott." J.T. slid his finger over her chin and down her neck.

"But if they don't—"

"Then I'll take care of Plott."

"I don't want you to have to kill him." Joanna jerked away from J.T. and sat up ramrod straight in the bed. Closing her eyes, she hugged herself, gripping her elbows in the palms of her hands. "If anyone should kill him, I should. But I'm not sure I could...that I'd have the guts to."

"The night he attacked you, would you have killed him, if you could have?"

"Yes. Yes. A thousand times, yes." Joanna covered her face with her hands.

J.T. touched her trembling back. Wiping the tears from her eyes, she turned around and looked at him.

"While he was beating me...touching me...I kept thinking that if only I had a gun...or if only I was strong enough to take his knife away from him. Yes, I would have killed him."

J.T. rubbed her back, but didn't try to pull her into his arms again. He waited, unsure what to say or do to comfort her. Tonight she had reverted to the past, to the most horrible night of her life, and only by allowing her to tell him about Plott's vicious attack, could J.T. truly help her. But, God in heaven, he wasn't sure he was strong enough to hear the details without completely losing control. Already, there was a part of him that wanted nothing more than to hunt Plott down and take him apart, piece by piece.

"I tried to fight him, you know," Joanna said. "He liked that, my fighting him. He beat me. God, how he beat me." She swallowed the tears, pushing back the emotions threatening to overcome her. "The first blow was to my stomach. I'd never been hit before. Not ever. It took me by surprise. And it hurt. Oh, how it hurt."

J.T. wanted to take her in his arms and beg her not to tell him anymore. He had read a copy of the police report, and that had been more than enough reality for him.

"And when I doubled over, he shoved me down on the floor and kicked me." With each word she spoke, her voice became calmer, her face more somber, her eyes glazed with an unemotional stare. "I fought him even harder when he tried to rip off my clothes. That's when he hit me in the face, over and over again. I—I think I passed out. All I remember is his tearing my clothes and pawing me. Squeezing. Biting. Hurting me." Joanna clutched her throat. "And cutting me."

J.T. clenched his teeth. The roar of his own pain rumbled inside him—an agonized, wounded bellow forced into silence.

"And when he...when he... I wanted to die. In that one moment, I prayed to God to let me die." Joanna clutched the bedcovers, wadding them up in her fists. "But when he crawled off me, I prayed to God to let me live, to let me live long enough to kill him!"

She had to stop talking! J.T. told himself. He couldn't bear to hear another word. But, dear God, if just listening to her tell about what Plott had done to her hurt J.T. more than anything ever had, how must Joanna feel? What indescribable suffering she must have endured, and must still, at this very moment, be enduring!

Slowly, cautiously and with the utmost gentleness, J.T. eased his arms around Joanna. A loose, tentative hold. One from which she could readily escape. He kissed the side of her face over and over again, soft, delicate touches along her forehead, down her cheek and to her jaw. "Will you let me hold you?" he asked, strengthening his precarious clasp about her waist. "Will you let me lie here in this bed and hold you in my arms all night? I want to show you that you can trust me. That you're safe with me. That I'll never let anyone hurt you ever again."

Joanna gave herself over to J.T.'s kindness, knowing in her heart that he meant every word he'd said. He could give her his comfort and his promise of protection. He could guard her against the threat of Plott's murderous scheme. He could hold her in his arms and make her feel cherished and desired. But he could not give her his love, when he had none to give. She could be J. T. Blackwood's woman on a temporary basis in the same way Annabelle had been Benjamin Greymountain's woman. And Joanna knew that she, as her ancestress had done, would go to her grave, still in love with a man who could never be truly hers.

CHAPTER TWELVE

J.T. HAD RETURNED to the Navajo reservation only three times since old John Thomas had taken him away when he was five. Once when his mother was dying. Then for her funeral. And a final trip to get Elena. Now, after all these years, here he was, back on the land where he'd been born, back among his mother's people. Elena's suggestion to bring Joanna here for safekeeping had made perfect sense to J.T., but he'd known that his sister's plan included more than keeping her best friend safe. Elena was hoping a stay on the reservation would open his mind and his heart to a part of his heritage he had been taught to shun.

Following Joanna's instructions, J.T. drove along the endless stretch of road leading to Kate and Ed Whitehorn's place. Finally he saw their mobile home, the metal gleaming brightly in the hot morning sun. He pulled the Jeep up in front of the corrals where Ed kept his sheep and cattle when they weren't grazing. A small dark-eyed boy sat on the fence, cradling a baby lamb in his arms. Jumping down, he ran toward the Jeep, calling out a greeting to Joanna.

"That's Eddie, Kate and Ed's oldest child," Joanna said. "He helps Ed with the sheep and cattle."

"He seems awfully young for that kind of responsibility." J.T. opened the door, rounded the hood and assisted Joanna out of the Jeep.

Little Eddie ran up to Joanna, skidding to a halt before

running right into her. "Mama said you were coming back for a visit, and you and Elena's brother will be staying at Aunt Mary's house." Eddie stared up at J.T., his dark eyes sparkling with interest. "Are you my cousin? Mama says you are, that you're of our clan. If you're Elena's brother, why haven't I ever seen you before?"

Eddie wore faded jeans and a white cotton T-shirt. A strip of light-colored cloth wrapped around his forehead kept his chin-length black hair off his full face. When J.T. looked at the boy, he saw himself as a child and couldn't help wondering what his own fate would have been, had his grandfather not taken him away from the reservation. Would he have helped tend the small herds of sheep and cattle that had to be moved often from pasture to pasture because of the sparse vegetation on this land? Would he have attended a contract school the way Elena had, where he could have learned to read and write in *Saad?* His mother's language. A language he had forgotten, except for a few words and phrases. Except for something he said to Joanna every time they made love.

"Yes, Eddie, this man is your cousin." Smiling at Eddie, Joanna stroked the lamb he held in his arms, then glared at J.T. "The reason you've never met him before is because he lives far away in Atlanta, Georgia, and is here in New Mexico only for a visit."

The front door of the mobile home swung open and a plump young woman carrying a toddler on her hip stepped out onto the lattice-trimmed porch. A little girl with huge brown eyes clung to her mother's leg.

"Joanna!" Kate Whitehorn called out as she walked down the front steps. "And J.T." She stared at her cousin, her smile fading from brightness to softness, a look of curiosity in her eyes. "I'm sure you do not remember me.

We met very briefly at Aunt Mary's funeral. I was just a girl then."

J.T. held out his hand to Kate, noticing the strong family resemblance between her and Elena. The two could be sisters. "I appreciate everything you've done to help us. Elena said she explained the situation to you and your husband."

"Yes. Ed is at work, but you will meet him during your stay here." Kate shook hands with J.T., then rearranged the child on her hip and petted the top of her little girl's head. "You've met Eddie. He's our oldest. And this young lady hanging on to me is Summer. She's very shy and quiet, much like her father. And this—" Kate hugged her youngest to her side "—is Joey."

J.T. could not resist touching the plump bronze cherub in his cousin's arms. He cupped the child's face between his thumb and forefinger. A thicket of black hair covered Joey's round little head and his big dark eyes sparkled as he looked up at J.T. and laughed.

J.T. had never had a family—not until he had brought Elena to the ranch. But in many ways, he and Elena still were not truly family, and he knew the strain between them was his fault. He had been raised a loner, taught to neither need nor expect anything from anyone, to be totally self-sufficient. Needing others was a sign of weakness.

But as he grew older, J.T. realized that keeping others at a distance doomed a man to loneliness. As Elena was family, so were these people. This woman and her children were his cousins, from his mother's clan, people who had offered a sanctuary to Joanna and him.

"You will come inside and have lunch with us?" Kate asked.

"Thank you," J.T. said. "But I'd like to go on over to my

mother's house and get settled in. Is there a corral there where we can put our horses?" He nodded at the horse trailer hitched to the Jeep.

Kate shook her head. "No, I'm sorry, there isn't. But we have a small corral. We once had several horses, but now only one. You are welcome to keep your animals there. Eddie can show you."

"Thanks." J.T. glanced at Eddie, who grinned from ear to ear. "Oh, yeah, I was expecting someone from the tribal police to meet us here. Has anyone stopped by?"

"Yes, Joseph is here. He came early to visit with the children and me," Kate said. "That's his truck." She pointed to the dusty red pickup beside the house.

J.T. looked at the truck, noticing the feathers attached to the rearview mirror, and remembered Elena telling him something about feathers being attached to Navajo vehicles to ward off evil spirits. Undoubtedly this Navajo policeman still practiced old customs. "You said his name is Joseph?"

"Yes, my brother, Joseph. Didn't Joanna and Elena tell you that he is a tribal policeman? He is off duty right now. When he discovered Joanna was in trouble, he asked to help, to be your police contact here on the reservation."

"Joseph Ornelas?" J.T. asked. "No one told me anything about him being a tribal policeman."

"Did I hear someone mention my name?"

Joanna turned at the sound of the man's voice. J.T. watched her smile at Joseph Ornelas as he walked out on the porch. Slipping off a huge white apron, Joseph draped it over the porch railing and took several giant steps toward Joanna. He grasped her by the shoulders.

"It is good to see you again, Joanna." Joseph slid his hands down her arms and took her hands into his. "It's good that you've come to us. We'll do all that we can to keep you safe."

Clearing his throat, J.T. stepped forward and placed his hand on Joanna's shoulder. He glared at Joseph Ornelas, a tribal policeman, his relative, a Navajo and the great-grandson of Benjamin Greymountain. His cousin was several inches shorter than him, but the man's big, muscular body compensated for his lack of height.

The two men looked at each other, then J.T. glanced down at Joseph's and Joanna's clasped hands, and at that exact moment Joseph stared up at J.T.'s hand resting possessively on Joanna's shoulder. Joanna pulled her hand from Joseph's and laid her open palm over J.T.'s hand resting on her shoulder.

Joseph looked directly into Joanna's eyes, nodded his head and smiled. "You must stay for lunch. We've prepared a delicious mutton stew. Come. Stay."

"It's up to J.T.," Joanna said. "But I'd love to stay."

Joseph held out his hand to J.T. "Enjoy a meal with your cousins and give us the opportunity to become better acquainted."

J.T. shook hands with Joseph, and both men were careful not to exert too much strength, keeping the exchange nonthreatening. "Kate—" J.T. glanced at her "—mentioned that she and I had met at my mother's funeral. Were you there, too?"

"Yes," Joseph said. "I was only a teenager, just a few years older than Elena. I was attending the Navajo Community College in Tsaile when Aunt Mary died, but I came home for her funeral."

"I'm sorry I don't remember either of you." J.T. removed his Stetson, ran his fingers through his thick hair and replaced his hat. "I don't remember much of anything about that day." *Except how out of place I felt. I was an outsider.* Mary Greymountain Neboyia had been his mother, and yet she had been as much of a stranger to him as he had been to her. Until Elena had told him the truth, J.T. had thought his mother had willingly given him to old John Thomas. That was one of the many lies his grandfather had told him. But even now, the bitter little boy who had hated both his Navajo mother and his white grandfather lived in J.T.'s heart. Knowing the truth and accepting it on an emotional level were two entirely different things.

"Let the women go inside and I will help you with your horses," Joseph said. "Then we'll eat and talk before you take Joanna to Aunt Mary's house."

J.T. squeezed Joanna's shoulder. "All right?" he asked her.

She nodded, stepped away from J.T. and followed Kate up to the porch.

"Joanna?" Joseph called out to her.

"Yes?"

"While you're visiting here, I promise that I will make time to pose for you, but it will have to be on my next off day."

Joanna swallowed, forced a smile and refused to look at J.T. "Wonderful."

"I will take you out to Painted Canyon," Joseph said. "The scenery there is beautiful and would make a good background for the picture."

"Anywhere Joanna goes, I go," J.T. said.

"Of course, I understand." Joseph placed his big, broad hand on J.T.'s shoulder. "You are Joanna's bodyguard and must be with her at all times."

"Come on, let's set the table for our meal." Kate hurried Joanna into the trailer.

Putting Joey in his high chair, Kate picked up Summer, handed her a pot and spoon and set her down in the middle of the kitchen floor.

"You are J. T. Blackwood's woman, yes?" Kate asked.

Staring wide-eyed at her friend, Joanna gasped. "What?"

"I saw it and so did Joseph, that you are J. T. Blackwood's woman. My brother is deliberately trying to make our cousin jealous because he is not pleased that you chose J.T. over him."

"Kate, I'm very fond of Joseph—"

"But you love J.T., yes?"

"I'll talk to Joseph."

"And say what?" Kate asked. "That your heart belongs to another? That somehow, against your will, even against your better judgment, you have fallen in love with a man made of stone?"

"You've been talking to Elena," Joanna said.

"She has told me what a hard man her brother is, how unhappy he is, but that now you have come into his life, she has hope."

"Sometimes I wonder if there is any hope for J.T.," Joanna admitted. "He's never faced the truth about who he is, never come to terms with his feelings for his mother or his grandfather."

"Perhaps there is no love or forgiveness in him." Kate opened an upper cupboard door and removed a stack of soup bowls. "Although I hope my brother marries a Navajo girl, I would not have been terribly disappointed to have you for a sister-in-law. Joseph is a good man. He will make a good, loving husband and father. Can you say the same for J. T. Blackwood?"

"I don't know. But it doesn't matter." Joanna took the bowls from Kate and set them around on the table. "I can't change the fact that I love him."

"WE CAN WASH up out here." Joseph led J.T. from the corral to an outside faucet beside the house, unbuttoned his shirt, turned on the water and threw several handfuls into his sweaty face. Rivulets of water ran down his leather-brown throat and hard, muscular chest.

J.T. watched while this man—his cousin, another great-grandson of Benjamin Greymountain—cleaned himself. All elements of a civilized man seemed to vanish. J.T. followed suit, tossing his Stetson on a nearby rusty barrel and thrusting his hands beneath the running water. He wet his head and face, lifting the sweaty black patch that covered his blind eye.

"Elena told us that you lost the vision in that eye by taking a bullet meant for another," Joseph said. "You're a brave man."

"I was just doing my job." J.T. unbuttoned his own shirt, allowing the water to cool his heated skin. "Being a policeman, I'm sure you understand."

"You're very good at guarding people, in risking your own life to save others. You would die to protect Joanna, wouldn't you?"

"Yeah, I would, but that doesn't surprise you, does it? I get the idea you'd be willing to do the same thing."

"Our Joanna is a very special woman." Joseph wiped his wet face with his shirttail.

"*Our* Joanna?"

Joseph grinned. "We, Elena's family here on the reservation, have adopted Joanna. She has a love for this land and for our people that endears her to us."

"She told me that you two have gone out together." J.T. lifted his face to the sun, soaking in the drying warmth. "And she said there wasn't anything serious between you."

"Her choice, not mine." Bending over, Joseph shut off the water faucet, then rose and faced J.T. "Is there something serious between the two of you? Have you made a commitment to her? Is that what you are trying to tell me?"

J.T. stared at the other man who would have gladly become Joanna's lover. If all she had wanted in a fantasy lover was a Navajo, why had she rejected Joseph Ornelas? He was young, handsome and intelligent, and seemed to be a good man.

"I don't think my relationship with Joanna is any of your business." J.T. turned his back on Joseph, walked away and finished buttoning his shirt.

Following him, Joseph laid his hand on J.T.'s shoulder. "Wait."

J.T. halted, but did not turn around.

Joseph removed his hand from J.T.'s shoulder. "Since Joanna has no father or brother to question your intentions, then perhaps I do have a right." When J.T. made no reply, Joseph grunted. "Joanna deserves marriage and children and a man who is unafraid to love. Can you give her what she wants and needs?"

Every muscle in J.T.'s body tensed. "Joanna is my woman. That's all you need to know…cousin." J.T. walked across the yard, onto the porch and into the mobile home, not once looking back at Joseph.

JOANNA KNEW SOMETHING had happened between J.T. and Joseph, despite Joseph's efforts at pleasant conversation during lunch. J.T. had been silent and withdrawn, speaking only when spoken to, his replies always the one-syllable variety. And he hadn't said a word to her on the ride from Kate and Ed Whitehorn's place to Mary's old house. Joanna hadn't even tried to talk to him, uncertain and a little wary of what he might say if she prompted him to speak.

He parked the Jeep at the back of the small, frame house. Peeling paint clung to the wooden surface. Several floorboards on the south side of the back porch had rotted. Joanna knew that this house had stood here, unoccupied since Mary's death, because Elena could not bear to part with her mother's home.

J.T. got out, but made no attempt to assist Joanna. Ignoring him, she walked around to the back of the Jeep. When she opened the lift gate, J.T. grabbed her hand.

"Leave the luggage. I'll get it later." He slipped the house key out of his jeans, then pulled Joanna away from the Jeep, almost dragging her as he headed toward the house.

She balked, digging her heels into the ground. "What's going on with you? What's wrong?"

"Not a damned thing you can't fix, honey." He growled the words in a deep, dark whisper.

She glared at him, wondering just who this man was and if inside him still existed any small part of the J. T. Blackwood she loved. "I don't understand what this is all about, but—"

He jerked her into his arms, staring at her with such intensity that she sucked in her breath. With their gazes still locked, he lifted her up in his arms and carried her onto the small wooden stoop, unlocked the door and kicked it open. Despite having been recently cleaned, the house reeked with the mustiness of disuse and abandonment. The living room windows had no curtains, allowing the afternoon sunlight to flood the small area.

With the front door wide-open and the whole room bathed in golden sunshine, J.T. lowered Joanna to her feet. Slowly. Allowing her to feel every inch of his big, hard body. She had never seen him this way—on the verge of passionate rage.

"J.T.?"

"Shh. Don't talk. I need you, Jo. I need you now." He covered her mouth with his, taking her with ravenous hunger, consuming her with his desire.

She trembled, unable to control her body's compliance, realizing that there would be no gentleness in his love-making, no consideration for her. And yet she did not fear his possession, understanding, as if by instinct, that this time she must be the one to do the giving. Whatever was wrong with J.T., she and she alone could ease his suffering and make everything right for him.

In his haste to uncover her body, he popped two buttons from her blouse as he ripped it open. Burying his face against her lace-covered breasts, he undid her bra and pulled it and her blouse down her arms.

While he unsnapped and unzipped her jeans, she worked feverishly to do the same to his. Suddenly taking fire, her passion and need kindled by his, Joanna wanted nothing more than to be J.T.'s woman, to give him pleasure, to take him into her body and become one with him.

The minute he jerked her jeans and panties off, he drew her up against him and leaned back into the wall, bracing his body. Her breasts crushed into his hard chest. She cried out. Her nipples hardened into tight, throbbing points.

He cupped her buttocks, kneading her firm flesh, pressing her intimately, upward and against his arousal. She placed her arms around his neck. He kissed her, thrusting his tongue into the sweet warmth of her mouth.

"I love you, J.T." She lifted her lips from his and whispered against his throat. "Only you. Always you."

Freeing his sex from his briefs, he lifted Joanna, positioning her legs around his hips, and drove into her with jackhammer force. Clinging to his shoulders, she cried out with the sheer pleasure of their joining, feeling as she had never felt before in her life. This was part of heaven and part of hell. Pleasure and agony combined. Bliss and torment. The promise of fulfillment grew stronger and stronger, increasing the savage ache at the very center of her being. Holding her hips in his hands, J.T. shoved her back and forth, taking her…taking her…taking her! And all the while she gave to him—all that was hers to give.

Passion to equal his raged inside her, threatening to consume her with its overwhelming power. She was a woman in all her glory. Ecstasy was hers to give or deny.

The desire within J.T. overflowed, spilling into her, drowning him in the hottest, wildest, most complete fulfillment he had ever known. His release washed over her, bathing her in its fiery flood, igniting spasms of pleasure inside her so intense, she thought she would die from the sheer joy of them.

Completely spent, sweat dripping from their bodies, J.T. and Joanna clung to each other, their lips seeking and finding one final sweet contact as the last ripples echoed through their bodies.

Lowering her to her feet, J.T. held her in his arms, caressing her naked back. "I'm sorry if—"

She kissed him quickly, passionately, silencing him, then drew away from him and smiled. "Did I give you what you needed?"

"You know you did, you little she-cat." He rubbed his cheek against hers. "You don't hate me, do you, honey, for taking you like that? I couldn't bear it if—"

"How could I hate you for needing me so desperately? Don't you think I figured out what this was all about?"

"Just what do you think this—" he rubbed himself against her "—was all about?"

"It was all about staking a claim," Joanna said. "I assume you let Joseph know that I was your private property—"

"Now, honey, don't go putting words in my mouth."

"As I was saying, you let Joseph know that I was your private property, but once that was done, you needed to make sure I knew just which man I belonged to."

"You make me sound like some jealous, outraged, rutting animal."

She cupped his cheek, caressing him with the tips of her fingers. "No, my love, you're just a man who doesn't want to share his woman."

Grabbing her by the shoulders, J.T. surveyed her from head to toe, taking in every delicious feminine inch of her lovely face and beautiful naked body. "Why me and not him? He's Benjamin Greymountain's great-grandson, too. And he's the kind of man who could offer you everything you want. Marriage. Kids. 'Forever after.' The whole works."

"Maybe a part of me wishes it could have been Joseph," she said, her voice a hushed whisper.

J.T.'s big fingers bit into her soft, womanly flesh. "Why not him? Tell me. Make me understand."

"How can I make you understand when I'm not sure I do? All I know is that Joseph doesn't make me feel the way you do. When he kissed me, it was nice, but that's all."

"He kissed you?" J.T. growled the question.

"From that first day, when I saw you astride Washington, I felt alive in a way I couldn't explain, not even to myself." She ran her hand down his neck and shoulder, gripping his tense, muscular arm. "And I heard the drums. The drums Annabelle heard when she was with Benjamin."

J.T. stared at her with disbelief in his eyes. "You didn't hear these drums when you were with Joseph?"

"No. Never." Breath-robbing love filled her heart as she looked at J.T., at that strong, manly face, and saw pure, undisguised satisfaction. "Don't you know that I tremble when you look at me? That I shatter into a million pieces every time you touch me? And when you make love to me, I die from the pure pleasure of having you inside me?"

"Honey, you shouldn't say things like that to a man. Just look what you've done to me."

She glanced down and saw that he was once again hard with desire. "How do I make you feel, J.T.?" She slid her hand down his chest, over his stomach and then circled his arousal.

He sucked in a deep breath. "You make me feel like a twenty-year-old." He covered her hand with his, tutoring her in the precise moves his body craved. Within minutes, he stilled her caressing strokes. "Too much, honey. I can't bear any more. Let's go find a bed before I take you standing up again."

He slammed the door shut, locked it, and lifted Joanna in his arms. Carrying her through the first door to the left, he found himself standing in a small, dark room. An old iron bed waited for them, the covers turned down. A fresh bouquet of wildflowers in a glazed pottery vase sat atop the chest of drawers.

J.T. laid Joanna down on the bed, divested himself of his clothes and gazed down at her. "Every time I look at you, I tremble inside from wanting you so much." He lowered himself to the bed, straddling her body, aligning himself to perfectly fit her. When his hardness touched her softness, she cried out. "And when we touch, I shatter into a million pieces." He spread her legs and entered her slowly, taking her with her full cooperation. "And when I'm inside you, making love to you—" he plunged in and then withdrew, only to delve deeper and harder "—I die from the pleasure of it."

Their second joining did not possess the raging hunger of the first, but the joy was even deeper and the aftereffects longer lasting.

J.T. STOOD JUST outside his mother's house gazing into the distance at the ragged, monolith-type stone formations reaching upward into the crisp, blue, morning sky. His mother had been raised in a fairly traditional Navajo family, or so Elena had told him. Her love affair with the son of a white rancher had been heartbreaking for her parents.

He had no real memories of his grandparents, could not put faces to the names Elena had given him. He thought he remembered a voice singing to him when he was a small child. Elena said it must have been their grandmother; she had often sung to her.

Glancing back at the house, he wondered if Joanna had awakened yet or if, naked, warm, and with his scent still clinging to her skin, she lay sleeping peacefully. He had never lived with a woman; had never wanted that close a relationship. He kept his affairs brief and uncommitted. But Joanna was different. And she made him different. Gut-wrenching jealousy was something new to him. He hated that anyone had so much power over him, but he could not deny the fact that the mere thought of another man touching Joanna sent him into a rage.

Maybe the coffee he'd put on was ready. He sure could use a shot of caffeine. Rubbing his hand over his face, he decided he should shower and shave after he'd downed the first cup of coffee. The small two-bedroom house had one tiny bathroom, with a shower stall and no bathtub. He didn't mind the idea of sharing a shower with Joanna. He could go back inside, kiss her awake, make love to her again and carry her to the bathroom.

Just thinking about her aroused him. Hell, he was

thirty-seven. He shouldn't be walking around in a state of partial arousal most of the time because of one sweet little redhead.

J.T. breathed deeply, taking fresh morning air into his lungs. Reaching upward, he stretched the muscles in his long arms, in his broad back and lean waist. The mud-roofed stone hogan about fifty yards from the house caught his attention. Elena had told him that their mother had been born in that hogan, which now, like her house, was unoccupied. Close by the hogan stood the remains of a ramada. Had his mother, like her mother before her, sat inside that brush arbor, shielded from the sun, weaving intricately designed rugs?

A cloud of dust a good half mile up the road alerted J.T. that a vehicle was approaching. Although he was reasonably sure their early-morning visitor had to be a family member, his gut instincts warned him not to take anything for granted. He unlocked the Jeep, lifted his rifle out of the back and turned to await their guest.

Joanna opened the front door and stepped outside. "J.T.?"

Snapping his head around, J.T. took in the sight of Joanna standing there wearing nothing but his unbuttoned shirt. "Go back inside, honey. And put on some clothes."

"Is something wrong?"

"Probably not, but you don't want to welcome our first guest that way, do you?"

Nodding agreement, she went back inside. J.T. watched and waited while the cloud of dust grew larger and thinner. Suddenly he recognized Joseph Ornelas's truck. Hell and damnation, what did that man want?

Joseph pulled his truck to a stop behind J.T.'s Jeep. Smiling, he got out and walked toward J.T., calling out the typical Navajo greeting.

"Yá' át' ééh," Joseph said.

"You're out and about mighty early." J.T. glared at his handsome, younger cousin.

"I have some news—official news—for Joanna." Joseph glanced at the house. "Is she still asleep?"

"What sort of official news? Something about Plott?"

"In a way." Joseph looked up when he saw the front door open. "Ah, there you are, *nizhóni*. I have good news for you."

When J.T. saw Joanna, he sucked in his breath. His cousin had been right to call her beautiful. She'd brushed her hair back into a hastily tied ponytail. Tendrils of red hair curled around her makeup-free face. Her billowing striped caftan hid the luscious curves of her body, the body J.T. now knew so well.

J.T. clamped his hand down on Joseph's shoulder, leaned toward him and whispered, "Any news for Joanna, good or bad, goes through me first. Remember that. You have my cellular phone number. From now on, use it."

"What sort of good news?" Joanna rushed out to meet Joseph, stopping abruptly when she saw the look in J.T.'s glittering eye.

Stepping out of J.T.'s grasp, Joseph glanced back and forth from his bare-chested cousin to Joanna. "Claire Andrews has been found. Alive."

"Oh, thank God." Without thinking, Joanna threw her arms around Joseph and hugged him.

Returning her hug, Joseph looked over her shoulder at J.T., who glared back at him. Joanna withdrew from Joseph, grabbed J.T.'s hand and smiled at him. Reaching out, he tenderly wiped the happy tears from her cheeks.

"Come inside and tell us everything," Joanna said. "Have coffee with us."

Joseph hesitated until J.T. said, "Join us for breakfast, cousin."

Joseph followed them into his aunt Mary's house, through the living room and into the small, neat kitchen.

"How did Claire escape from Lenny Plott?" Joanna asked as she set out earthenware mugs for the three of them.

"Plott never had her," Joseph said.

"What?" Joanna and J.T. said in unison.

"Seems she panicked and ran away without telling her boyfriend or anyone else. When she'd had a chance to calm down and think clearly, she realized what her parents, her boyfriend and everyone would think. She called her mother to let her know she's all right. Her mother told the FBI that Claire is in California, but she doesn't want anyone to know exactly where."

"But Lenny Plott will find her. She needs protection. Doesn't she realize that?" Joanna lifted the coffeepot and poured the hot black liquid into their mugs.

"If Plott can find her, the FBI can find her." J.T. ran the back of his hand across Joanna's cheek.

"Let's just hope that the FBI finds her first." Closing her eyes, Joanna pressed the side of her face against J.T.'s caressing hand.

He knew what she was thinking and wished he could erase the fear from her heart. But all he could do was guard her and wait. Wait for the FBI to apprehend Plott or for Plott to make a move on Joanna. Perhaps it would be easier on Joanna if the FBI found Plott and returned him to prison, but on a very primitive level, J.T. longed for a confrontation with the monster who had brutalized her.

CHAPTER THIRTEEN

J.T. CAME UP behind Joanna, slipped his arms around her and drew her up against his chest. *"Ayoigo shil hózhó."*

Leaning backward, she tilted her head. He nuzzled her neck, then kissed her on the jaw. "What did you just say to me?" she whispered.

"I thought Eddie was giving us both *Saad* lessons. Haven't you been paying attention in class? I just told you that I'm happy." J.T. gazed down at the sleeping child resting in the baby bed. Joey Whitehorn's fat little thumb lay in the corner of his open mouth. A pang of something unfamiliar hit J.T. square in the stomach. He had never thought much about having children of his own, hadn't really wanted any. But recently, since getting to know Kate and Ed's children and seeing the way Joanna acted around them, J.T. had begun to think about a family of his own. What sort of father would he be? He'd had no example set for him, hadn't known his real father and despised the kind of parental figure his grandfather had been.

"While Eddie has been giving you daily *Saad* lessons, I've been painting, or had you forgotten?"

"How could I forget, when I'm the guy who's posing for the damned thing?"

Taking his hand, Joanna led him quietly from the room, closing the door only halfway behind them. Once in the living room, she slipped her arm around his waist.

"Joseph offered to pose for me," she said. "If you don't want to continue as my model, I can ask him."

"Forget it, honey." J.T. jerked her around and into his arms, smothering her face and neck with quick, warm kisses. "I'm going to be the only naked Navajo brave you ever paint."

"You're painting J.T. without his clothes on?" Eddie Whitehorn stood in the kitchen doorway, his wide-eyed sister at his side.

Little Eddie had been appalled when he'd learned J.T. couldn't speak *Saad* and had made a point of coming by every day for the past four days to give him a lesson. When Joanna had volunteered for them to spend the day at the Whitehorns' taking care of all three children so Ed and Kate could spend their Saturday alone in Gallup, J.T. had opposed the idea. When he had reminded her of exactly why they were hiding away on the reservation, she pointed out that it was highly unlikely that Lenny Plott could discover their whereabouts, at least not this soon. So, J.T. had reluctantly agreed to help babysit. After all, he had thought, how much trouble could three little kids be?

J.T. groaned. "I thought you two were outside playing."

"We were, but Summer got thirsty and I had to bring her in for a glass of water." Eddie led Summer into the living room, then stopped and stared up at J.T. "If Joanna gets to see you without your clothes on, do you get to see her without hers on?"

Joanna covered her mouth, smothering a laugh behind her hand. J.T. cleared his throat. He didn't know anything about kids, had never been around any until he brought Joanna to the reservation a few days ago. How was he supposed to reply to Eddie's question? He had no idea how to handle this situation.

"I'm an artist," Joanna said. "You already know that, don't you, Eddie?"

The child nodded his head. "So?"

"Well, I went to school, to a college in Virginia, and took classes in art. Sometimes all the art students drew pictures of models who didn't have on any clothes. That's the way we learned how to draw the human body."

"Yeah?" Eddie twisted his mouth into a frown, scratched his head and blew out a huffing breath. "If I go to the Navajo Community College in Tsaile and take art classes, will I get to see people naked?"

Smiling, J.T. looked at Joanna as if to say, "You started this, honey. Finish it."

The sound of Joey whimpering saved Joanna from thinking of an appropriate reply. "I'll go get him," she told J.T.

"I'm hungry," Summer whined. "When are we gonna eat supper?"

"Go get Joey," J.T. said. "I'll handle this."

"Could we have some ice cream?" Eddie asked. "Mama's got some in the freezer."

"Fruit," Joanna called out from the hallway. "One apple each, but no ice cream until after supper."

"Ah," both children groaned in unison.

After Joanna changed Joey's diaper, she brought him into the living room, sat down in the rocker near the window and began singing to him. His little eyelids fluttered, but every time he heard his older siblings' voices, his eyes opened wide and he tried to sit up.

Coming out of the kitchen, J.T. tossed Eddie and Summer an apple apiece, then motioned for them to follow him out onto the porch. When J.T. sat down on the steps, Summer crawled up in his lap and Eddie sat down beside him.

"Tell us a story, J.T.," Summer said, looking up at him with big brown eyes he found impossible to resist.

"I'm afraid I don't know any stories," J.T admitted. "What about you, Eddie, do you know a story you could tell Summer and me?"

"What do you mean you don't know any stories?" Eddie asked. "Surely you know about *Asdzá Na'adleehe* and her two sons?"

"Who was this *Asdzá*—?"

"Changing Woman, the mother-creator of our people. J.T. you don't know anything, do you? You can't speak our language and you never heard of Changing Woman."

"Why don't you tell me about her?"

Eddie eagerly recited the myth of Changing Woman, her husband, the sun, and their offspring—the story his parents had taught him since early childhood. J.T. listened with great interest, realizing that he truly wanted to know more about the Navajo legends. The truth of the matter was, deny it all he wanted, he *was* half Navajo; a part of his mother and a part of these people.

Hours later, after the sun had set and the two younger Whitehorn children were asleep, Eddie and J.T. checked on the animals before Eddie went to bed. Then, alone in the living room, J.T. and Joanna slumped down on the sofa and stared at each other.

"I don't remember the last time I've been this tired," J.T. said. "Kids can wear you out, can't they?"

"They certainly can," Joanna agreed. "I suppose that's why it's a good idea to have them while you're still young."

"I feel as if I've been playing twenty questions all day. They want the answers to everything immediately. How on earth do Kate and Ed cope?"

"I suppose they do what all parents have done since the

beginning of time," Joanna said. "They do the best they can and pray their best is good enough."

Kicking off her shoes, Joanna scooted to one end of the sofa, lifted her feet and put them in J.T.'s lap. He massaged her insteps. She sighed.

"I want children of my own someday," she said.

"Do you?" He caressed her ankles.

"Uh-huh. Have you ever thought about it? About having children?"

"I'd probably make a lousy father."

"Why do you say—" The ringing telephone interrupted Joanna midsentence. Gasping, she shuddered.

"It's okay, honey. It's just my phone." He lifted her feet so he could stand, then rested them back down on the sofa.

He picked up his cellular phone from where he'd laid it on the knickknack shelf filled with Kate's pottery collection. "Blackwood. Yeah. When did it happen? Is she all right? What about Plott?"

Joanna jumped up from the sofa and rushed over to J.T. Tugging on his arm, she mouthed the words, "Who is it?"

"Hold on a minute," he told the person at the other end of the line. "It's Dane Carmichael," he said to Joanna.

J.T. slid his arm around her waist, drawing her to his side as he finished his brief conversation. He punched the off button on his phone and laid it down on the shelf, then kissed Joanna on the forehead.

"What's wrong?" she asked.

"Plott found Libby Felton."

Joanna gasped. "No. Please, J.T., what happened? Did he—"

"She's all right, just badly shaken. Libby's husband and an FBI agent were both shot, but they saved Libby from Plott."

"Is Libby's husband dead? And the FBI agent?"

"No. They're both in the hospital. Libby's husband is in stable condition and the agent is in critical condition, but he's expected to live."

"When—when did all this happen?" Joanna asked.

"Before daybreak this morning."

"Plott escaped, didn't he?"

"Yeah, honey, he did."

"He won't go back to Texas after Libby anytime soon after what happened," Joanna said. "And it'll take him a while to find out where Claire is, so that means…that means he'll come to New Mexico. He'll go to the ranch."

"Only a handful of people know where we are and none of them are about to tell Plott."

"He'll find out. Somehow, he'll figure out a way to find out where I am and when he does, he'll come after me."

J.T. grabbed her by the shoulders. "Dane is calling in more agents. The FBI will be in full force in Trinidad. No way will Plott get past them."

"I hope you're right. Dear God, I hope you're right."

J.T. hoped so, too, but any doubts he had, he intended to keep to himself. While reassuring Joanna and keeping things as normal as possible for her, he planned to prepare himself for the worst.

LENNY PLOTT SEEMED to have vanished from the face of the earth since attempting to kidnap Libby. No one had any idea where he was or what he was plotting, but Joanna knew it was only a matter of time before he resurfaced.

Minutes had turned into hours and hours into days as Joanna and J.T. fell into a flexible routine. They went horseback riding every day, exploring the land nearby and becoming acquainted with the neighbors, all members of

Mary's Bitter Water clan. And every day, Eddie gave J.T.
a *Saad* lesson.

Joanna's portrait of J.T. had begun taking shape, but
she had refused to let him look at it. She had no idea how
he would react when he saw the way she had depicted
him. All primitive naked male, as rugged and wild as the
landscape surrounding him.

And they made love. In the mornings when they first
awoke. In the middle of the day when they couldn't go
another minute without touching each other. And at night
after Joanna covered J.T.'s portrait and the ghosts of their
great-grandparents hovered in the darkness.

Each night Joanna read to J.T. from Annabelle Beaumont's diary, and the more they shared their ancestors'
love story, the more they became a part of Annabelle and
Benjamin's doomed affair.

Tonight they sat on the threadbare sofa, as they did
every night, Joanna nestled between J.T.'s legs, while she
read to him. He wore nothing except his jeans, and she
her striped caftan. The side of his face rested against hers,
and from time to time, he kissed her temple.

> *"Benjamin's son is ill—not seriously, thank the
> dear Lord—but being a good father, he has trav-
> eled to his mother-in-law's home to visit the
> child. I find it strange that these people have
> such a matriarchal society, where although
> children are said to be born for their father's
> clan, they are born in their mother's clan. And
> in a case like Benjamin's, when a man loses his
> wife, he must give his child over to be raised by
> his mother-in-law.*
>
> *"I have not seen Benjamin in four days and
> I am dying from the agony of being apart from*

him. How will I be able to endure living when the time comes for us to part forever? He has become as essential to me as the air I breathe. Had I known the extent of anguish true love could bring, I would have done all in my power to have escaped its cruel clutches. No. No, I lie. Knowing all I know now—the pain as well as the ecstasy—I would change nothing. To have lived and died and never to have known this pure joy would have been a tragedy indeed.

"He has promised, if his son's health has improved, that we will meet tomorrow in our special place. I have a gift for him—a book of my favorite poems by Christina Rossetti. And I plan to ask him to allow me to cut a lock of his long black hair. I will braid it with a lock of mine and give it to him as a keepsake. Something to remember me by when I am gone."

Joanna's shoulders quivered. J.T. reached around her, closed Annabelle's diary and lifted it out of her hands.

He couldn't bear to see her cry and yet her tender, romantic heart was part of what made her so special. He would change nothing about her. She was as close to perfect as he would ever want a woman to be.

He laid the diary on the end table and turned off the table lamp, leaving only the dim light from their bedroom casting a shadowy glow into the living room. Cradling her in his arms, he hugged her fiercely and kissed her neck.

"Why do you do this to yourself, honey? You've already read that diary from beginning to end more than once. I don't see why you want to read aloud from it every night."

Resting her head against his chest, she closed her eyes

and sighed. "If I didn't read it to you, you'd never read all of it, and I want you to know Benjamin and Annabelle's story. I want you to feel about them the way I do."

"Honey, I've already admitted that I was wrong about them." J.T. lifted her clasped hands to his lips. "What happened to them was tragic, but nothing we say or do can change the past. Annabelle and Benjamin are dead and buried, and their great love with them."

How could she ever make J.T. understand the way she felt and what she believed? Yes, Annabelle and Benjamin were dead, but not their love. Didn't he realize that love never dies, especially the kind of love their great-grandparents had shared? Annabelle's and Benjamin's spirits were together, forever; their love was still alive. It was a part of J.T. A part of Joanna. And a part of what they felt for each other.

In her heart of hearts, Joanna believed that Annabelle had sent her to New Mexico, that her great-grandmother had opened her heart to the hope and dream of love at a time when she had thought there was nothing left worth living for. She had been destined to meet J.T., to love him and to heal his troubled soul. He belonged here in New Mexico, where both his mother's people and his father's had fought and died to claim this land. His birthright was here, and if he could ever embrace his mixed heritage, he could find peace in his soul. He could be both Navajo and Scotsman, both cowboy and Indian. Why couldn't he accept the fact that he did not have to choose, that indeed he couldn't choose between the two? He was a unique man, and she loved him as she would never love another. He was, as Benjamin had been to Annabelle, the other half of her.

"I wish we could go back to their special place," Joanna

said. "Tonight…right this minute…and share the magic of what we feel with them."

"We don't need to go to Annabelle and Benjamin's special place," J.T. told her. "And just as their magic existed only between the two of them, ours exists only between the two of us. It can't be shared."

"It's going to end for us, just as it ended for them." Joanna pulled out of J.T.'s arms and jumped up from the sofa.

"Jo? Honey?" He reached for her, but she moved too quickly for him to grab her arm. He stood and watched her. She ran to the door, unlocked it and grasped the knob.

"When this is over and Lenny Plott is either dead or behind bars, you'll go back to Atlanta, back to your job and your life there. And I'll stay here in New Mexico, except when you come home to visit Elena. Then I'll have to go away because—" she swallowed the tears trapped in her throat "—it will be unbearable for me."

She flung open the door and ran outside into the cool, starry night. A full moon spread a soft creamy blush across the land. J.T. raced after Joanna, calling her name as she fled from him. Following her, he cursed himself for hurting her this way. He understood only too well the desperation she felt, knowing that what they shared couldn't last forever. She was right. It had to end. She wanted eternity, a love that lived beyond death, and all he could give her was the moment—because that's all he believed in.

"Jo, stop running," he called after her. "Please, honey. You're going to hurt yourself."

But she kept running until he chased her down and pulled her into his arms. She struggled to free herself, but he tumbled her onto the ground and pinned her arms over her head as he straddled her.

"I can't stand to see you hurting this way." He tried

to kiss her, but she turned her face away. "Accept what there is between us. It's real. It's magical. It's passionate. Maybe it isn't what you want, but it's all I can give you."

Turning to face him, she stared up at him, the moonlight illuminating her features in gold-tinted shadows. "You could give me everything I want and need if you'd only let yourself," she said. "But you're afraid. So afraid to let yourself love me the way you really want to."

He pressed his arousal against her feminine mound. "Why can't this be enough for you? It's never been like this with anyone else. Never been this good…this right."

"Oh, J.T., I love you. I love you so." She arched her body up and into his.

He groaned, then took her mouth with savage hunger. Squirming beneath him, she thrust her tongue into his mouth, engaging it in a duel with his. Releasing his hold on her wrists, he caught the caftan zipper between his thumb and forefinger and whipped the garment apart. Shoving the caftan off her shoulders and down her arms, J.T. lifted her, removed the caftan and laid her naked body down on the flowing robe's silky softness.

She touched his chest with one hand and lifted the other to his head, threading her fingers through his hair. Rising up just enough to grab hold of his zipper, he opened his jeans, jerked them down his legs and kicked them into the dirt.

"This is the magic, Jo." He lifted her hips and plunged into her. "This is the ecstasy. It might not last forever, but it's more than some people ever know."

"Yes. Yes." This was the ecstasy, but what J.T. could not admit to himself was that the love they shared was what made it magical for them.

He rolled over, placing his body against the hard, dusty earth as he lifted her into the dominant position. They mated, there on the ground, beneath the stars; primitive man and woman, joined in nature's most basic, instinctive ritual. Each of them giving and taking in equal measure, sharing the earth-shattering pleasure when their climaxes claimed them.

Leaving their clothes lying on the ground, J.T. lifted Joanna in his arms and carried her back to the house and to the bed they shared in his mother's house. Neither of them said a word as he cradled her in his arms. They lay together in silence, listening to each other's heartbeats until they fell asleep.

Hours later, J.T woke, eased her from his arms and slipped out of bed. Quietly striding into the living room, he stood in the darkness for several minutes, then turned on a table lamp and walked over to the easel Joanna had placed in the corner. He lifted the cover slowly. Groaning, he closed his eyes, but he could not erase the portrait from his mind. In that one brief glance, he had seen himself as Joanna saw him, and if he had ever doubted that she loved him, he no longer did.

Opening his eyes, he stared at the beautiful, noble man Joanna had painted. Straight blue-black hair hanging to his shoulders. Glistening bronze skin stretched over taut, well-developed muscles. An ageless man. A man of yesterday and today and tomorrow. A perfect man, seen through the eyes of love.

He did not deserve Joanna's love. He was unworthy of such pure sweet devotion. How was it possible that she loved him so deeply and completely and saw in him the man he longed to be? Did he have the courage to accept what she was offering, and the strength to become the man she wanted and needed?

He knew that if he didn't find that strength and that courage, he would doom them to a fate as tragic as the one that had befallen their great-grandparents.

CHAPTER FOURTEEN

RITA GONZALES GRUMBLED to herself when she heard the door chimes. "No company. We are not at home. Go away."

Leaning the mop against the kitchen counter, she wiped her pudgy, damp hands on her apron and waddled into the hallway. The chimes rang again.

"Who would be bothering people so early in the morning?" She peered through the peephole in the solid wooden door. A tall, dark-haired man with a thick mustache stood on the front porch. She didn't recognize the man, but then she didn't know all of Elena and Alex's friends and business acquaintances. Rita unlocked and opened the door enough to take a better look at the stranger.

When he saw Rita, he smiled and nodded. She liked his smile, and although she was unaccustomed to seeing men in suits and ties, she liked his neat appearance.

"Morning, ma'am. Sorry to bother you so early, but I'm here on official business. I'd like to see Mr. and Mrs. Gregory." He reached inside his coat pocket and pulled out his identification to show Rita. "I'm Eugene Willis, one of the FBI agents working with Dane Carmichael in Trinidad."

"Agent Carmichael has been here on the ranch several times," Rita said, then shook her head. "I'm sorry but Elena and Alex are not here. They went to Santa Fe on business yesterday."

"Oh, that's too bad. I have some news for them and needed their help in contacting Joanna Beaumont."

"Your Mr. Carmichael knows how to reach Joanna and J.T." Rita eyed the man suspiciously.

"Yes, we've been trying to call them, but can't get through. We thought perhaps the Gregorys would have another number where they could be reached."

"Something must be wrong with J.T.'s little phone—"

"His cellular phone? Yes, that's what we think."

"If Mr. Carmichael can't reach J.T., why hasn't he called the tribal police? Since J.T.'s cousin, Joseph Ornelas, is a policeman, he would gladly take the message to them himself."

"I'm sure Dane will have thought of calling the tribal police by the time I check in with him," Eugene said. "It's just that we're all so pleased about the good news we have for Ms. Beaumont that we wanted to reach her as quickly as possible."

"What good news?" Rita opened the door fully and stepped out onto the front porch.

"We've apprehended Lenny Plott. Caught him in Trinidad before daylight this morning."

"Oh, my, this is good news." Rita stuck her fat finger in Eugene's face. "You make sure that man is put back in a thick cell with many locks so he can never escape again."

Eugene grinned. "Yes, ma'am, that's just what we intend to do."

"You tell Mr. Carmichael to keep trying to call J.T. on his little telephone and if there is no answer, call the tribal police and ask for Joseph Ornelas." Rita snapped her fingers. "Perhaps Elena's cousin, Kate Whitehorn, would know how to contact J.T. and Joanna. Joanna has visited the Whitehorns many times when she goes to the reservation to paint."

"Kate Whitehorn. Yes, ma'am. Thank you. And please, give Mr. and Mrs. Gregory the good news when they return from Santa Fe."

"Yes, I'll do that." Rita stood on the porch and watched Eugene Willis get in his gray sedan and drive away.

Moments later, Cliff Lansdell drove in from the opposite direction, slowed his four-wheel drive in front of the ranch house and stopped.

"Who was that, Rita?" he asked, watching the car drive away.

"An FBI agent named Willis," Rita said. "He came here to talk to Elena and Alex. They've caught that man, that Lenny Plott, who wanted to kill Joanna. But they can't get J.T. to answer his little telephone to give them the good news. I told him I didn't understand why they didn't just call the tribal police."

Cliff flung open the door, jumped out and ran up onto the porch. "Rita, did you see that man's identification?"

"What?"

"Did he show you proof that he was an FBI agent?"

"Do you think I'm a stupid old woman?"

"No, I do not think you're old or stupid."

"He showed me his badge, showed me his picture. It was him. Big black mustache and all. And his name was Willis. Eugene Willis."

Cliff let out a deep breath. "Good. Good."

"I wouldn't talk to nobody who wasn't the police." Rita placed her hands on her wide hips. "Anyway, I didn't tell him anything he didn't already know. The FBI knows that Joanna is on the Navajo reservation."

"But no one off the reservation, except Elena and Alex, knows exactly where J.T. took Joanna," Cliff said. "Not even the FBI."

"I'm glad this whole thing is over and that awful man will be put back in prison," Rita said. "Now, Joanna can come home and not have to be afraid anymore."

JOANNA SLIPPED HER sketch pad and pens into the saddle-bag and closed it. "I'm glad it isn't hot today. Maybe we can stay out longer than we did yesterday and I can fin-ish these sketches."

"Too bad you need sunlight to sketch," J.T. said. "If you could learn to draw in the dark, we could go out at night when it's cool."

"Ha, ha. Very funny." Joanna adjusted her hat, tight-ening the drawstring under her chin.

J.T. dropped his Glock into his saddlebag, then slid his Remington into its sheath attached to his saddle. Patting his shirt pocket, he double-checked to make sure he had his cellular phone, then he mounted Washington.

"Kate's planning that get-together this weekend," Joanna said. "We really need to give her an answer today. It's important to her that we be there. She wants you to meet other members of your mother's family."

."I've met more relatives than I can count already." J.T. motioned Washington into a slow trot. "Half the Bitter Water clan seem to live in this area and I think we count relatives down to tenth cousins."

Joanna laughed. "Hey, we Southerners do the same thing." She wondered if J.T. realized that he had said "we" when he had spoken of the Navajo. Probably not. But Joanna had noticed that he was beginning to relate to his mother's people and seemed to enjoy not only the *Saad* lessons Eddie gave him, but the history lessons, too.

She urged Playtime into a trot alongside Washington. "We need to let Kate know something by tonight."

"Hey, we didn't come to the reservation so I could socialize with my relatives," J.T. said. "I brought you here to keep you out of harm's way until the FBI catch up with Plott."

"There's no reason that while we're here we can't socialize. No one is going to talk to a stranger and give away our hiding place. Joseph told you that he's spoken to everyone in this area, cautioning them to contact him if anyone they don't know comes around asking questions."

"You're as determined as Elena that I accept my Navajo heritage, aren't you?"

"I want you to be happy, and I don't think you can be until you resolve all the hang-ups you have about being part Native American and part Scotch-Irish."

"You're beginning to sound like a psychiatrist."

"I suppose it comes from having gone through months of therapy after the rape," Joanna said. "I'm not sure how long it would have taken me to break away from Mother's domination if I hadn't reached a point in my therapy where I admitted that she had always run my life, that I had never made one decision on my own."

The afternoon sun warmed them as they traveled several miles from Mary's house. The land was dotted with yuccas, creosote bushes and mesquite. And the colors were sharp and pure; the earth itself was alive with vibrant hues.

When they reached Painted Canyon, J.T. searched for the spot Joanna had chosen several days ago when they'd first ridden out this way. He saw the huge rock where she liked to sit and look down over the plateau. He recognized the area because a scattering of cottonwood trees grew nearby.

He helped her dismount and retrieve her supplies, then

spread a blanket down for her to sit on. "I'm going to walk around awhile. I won't go far and I'll keep you in sight every minute."

"I know this must be boring for you," she said.

Leaning over, he took her face in his hands, drew her to him and kissed her soundly. "I'm never bored when I'm with you. But if I stay too close, I might distract you."

Smiling, she rubbed his nose with hers. "You just might." He released her. "Go on off and explore."

J.T. climbed higher up the canyon, feeling as if when he reached the summit, he'd be able to touch the sky. He glanced down at Joanna, who was busy sketching.

"Help! Somebody, please help us!"

J.T. heard the loud cry. His heart raced. He recognized that voice. Eddie. Eddie Whitehorn.

"Eddie?"

"Help! Help!"

"Where are you, Eddie?"

"Down here!"

"Where?"

"J.T., is that you?"

"Yes, Eddie, just keep talking and I'll find you."

Within minutes, J.T. had located his young cousin. The boy sat at the bottom of a ravine, wedged between two steep sandstone formations. Eddie held a lamb in his arms.

"Good God, boy, how did you get down there?" J.T. guessed the boy was a good eighteen to twenty feet down.

"I came looking for a couple of the little lambs that got lost yesterday," Eddie said. "Don't tell Mama I got in trouble. She told me I couldn't come out here by myself looking for them."

"How'd you get down there?" J.T. asked.

"I climbed down here when I saw the lamb, but now, I

can't climb back up and carry the lamb with me. And… and I think…well, I hurt my leg. I think I sort of sprained it."

"Stay put," J.T. said. "I've got to go tell Joanna. She can call your mother. I'm sure Kate is worried sick about you."

"No, J.T., don't tell Mama."

J.T. called out to Joanna, who turned sharply and stared up at him. He waved at her, motioning for her to come to him. She laid down her sketch pad and pen, then stood and climbed up the hill.

"Is something wrong?" she asked.

"Eddie's down in that ravine over there," J.T. told her. "He came out looking for a couple of lost lambs and found one, but he's hurt his leg and can't climb back up."

"Oh, my goodness. Kate will be terribly worried."

"Here." J.T. pulled his cellular phone from his pocket and handed it to Joanna. "Give Kate a call and let her know Eddie's all right and we'll bring him home in a little while." J.T. grasped Joanna's wrist. "I've got to climb down the ravine and get him and the lamb. After you call Kate, go get my rifle and keep it with you until I come back up."

"Go get your… Surely you don't think anything could happen to me in the few minutes it'll take you to rescue Eddie." Joanna caressed his cheek. "We're out in the middle of nowhere, and Lenny Plott has no idea we're on the Navajo reservation."

"I don't believe in taking chances. Get the rifle. Pacify me, honey."

"Okay. I'll call Kate and then I'll get your rifle."

DANE CARMICHAEL FINISHED off the last bite of his ham-and-cheese sandwich, then washed it down with the strong coffee they served at the Trinidad Café. He wished to hell they could wrap up this case. He hadn't had a decent night's sleep in over a week. Sooner or later Lenny Plott was going to come back to Trinidad, and Dane's guess was it would be very soon. Since his attempt to kidnap Libby Felton had failed, and it would take him time to track down Claire Andrews again, his next likely target was Joanna Beaumont.

Between his agents and the local and state authorities, they pretty much had Trinidad sealed off. He doubted a fly could sneak by without being caught in their trap.

Just as Dane reached for his bill, one of his agents, Jim Travis, slipped into the booth across from him. "I need to talk to you, and I'd like what I tell you to be off the record, at least temporarily."

"What's wrong?" Dane asked.

"It's about Eugene Willis."

"Yeah, what about Willis?"

"He met a girl the first day we got in town and he's been messing around with her. You know Willis. He's a ladies' man. He can't leave 'em alone and they can't leave him alone."

"The damned fool!" Dane wadded his bill in his fist. "Look, I don't know why Willis hasn't been dismissed before now, but if he messes up while under my command, he won't get a second chance."

"Yeah, well, I tried to tell him that you weren't anybody to mess around with, but... Hell, the guy went out to get us some breakfast this morning and he hasn't come back. I figure he's off somewhere with that girl, since he had—"

"What time this morning?"

"Around six-thirty."

Dane glanced at his wristwatch. "It's twelve-thirty."

"Yeah, I've been trying to track him down, hoping I could find him before—"

"I don't want any explanations. You're off this case, and so is Willis. As a matter of fact, both of you are history in the agency as far as I'm concerned."

JOANNA CLOSED J.T.'s cellular phone and slipped it into her shirt pocket, then walked over and removed J.T.'s Remington from its scabbard on Washington's saddle. Although she was a fairly good shot with a handgun, she wasn't accustomed to the feel of a rifle.

She climbed back up the side of the canyon, looked down into the ravine and saw J.T. slowly, cautiously making his way toward Eddie.

"I called Kate. She was half out of her mind with worry," Joanna told J.T. "She'd already called several family members to have them search for Eddie."

"Did you get my rifle?" J.T. asked.

She held up the Remington so he could see it. "I told Kate we'd bring Eddie right home."

J.T. chose his steps carefully, knowing how dangerous these steep ravines could be. Eddie was damned lucky that he hadn't slipped and injured himself badly. A sprained ankle would mend soon enough.

J.T. heard a distinct rattling. His heartbeat accelerated. Without moving or saying a word, he visually searched all around him, looking for the poisonous snake whose bite could prove deadly. And then he saw the rattler slithering across the tip of Eddie's boot. The boy saw the snake, too; his face paled.

"J.T.?"

"Hush," he warned. "Don't talk. Don't move." J.T. slid his hand into his pocket, feeling around for his knife. Slipping the knife out of his pocket, he continued watching the snake as it curled around Eddie's leg.

Eddie swallowed. "J.T.!"

"Shh." He opened the knife.

The lamb in Eddie's arms nuzzled his nose against the boy's side. Overhead an eagle soared. The snake crawled up Eddie's leg and onto his arm.

"What's wrong?" Joanna called out as she hovered near the edge of the steep embankment. "What's taking so long?"

Tears welled up in Eddie's brown eyes. J.T. gauged the distance. He was an expert shot, but his skills with a knife were rusty. If he missed, he could wind up stabbing Eddie.

The rattler coiled to strike. Eddie cried out. J.T. hurled the knife through the air. The blade sliced through the snake. Eddie dropped the lamb and clutched his arm. J.T. ran over, lifted the snake by the knife handle and flung its limp body against the canyon wall.

"Did it bite you?" J.T. jerked Eddie's hand away from his arm. "Damn!"

"Am I going to die?" Eddie's bottom lip quivered. Tears trickled down his dusty cheeks.

"No, you aren't going to die," J.T. said. "But we'll have to move fast and get you a shot to counteract the snake's venom. We'll have to leave the lamb down here, but I'll get someone to come back and get him."

"You promise."

J.T. nodded. "Come on, Eddie—" J.T. squatted "—crawl on my back."

Eddie obeyed J.T.'s command.

"Joanna!" J.T. called out to her.

"What's wrong?"

"A rattlesnake bit Eddie. Get on the phone and call

Kate, tell her to contact the clinic and have them send out some antivenom for a rattlesnake bite, then go get our horses ready!"

Joanna stuck the rifle under her arm, the barrel pointed to the ground. She pulled the cellular phone from her pocket. Her hands trembled so badly when she tried to dial the phone that she dropped it on the ground. When she bent over to pick it up, she heard the sound of an approaching vehicle. Standing, she gazed off into the distance and saw a cloud of red dust rising in the air, then clearing as a gray sedan came to a screeching halt a few yards away from where they'd tethered the horses. Playtime whinnied. When a tall dark-haired man in a suit got out of the car, Washington rose on his hind legs, then lowered his front hooves and pawed the ground.

"J.T.!" Joanna cried. "Somebody's here. A man with a black mustache, driving a gray car."

"Keep the rifle on him until I get up there," J.T. told her.

The man waved at Joanna. She slipped the phone back in her pocket and pointed the rifle at him.

"Don't shoot, ma'am, I'm an FBI agent. My name's Eugene Willis." He kept walking toward Joanna. "If you'll let me, I can show you my identification."

"Who sent you?" Joanna asked.

"Dane Carmichael. You are Joanna Beaumont, aren't you?"

"I might be."

"Well, if you are, I've got some good news for you."

"Don't come any closer. Just get out your ID, and do it very slowly."

"Yes, ma'am." Willis very cautiously pulled out his ID and held it up for Joanna to see, then took several more steps in her direction.

The sun glinted off the agent's ID. Joanna blinked. "What sort of news do you have?"

"We've apprehended Lenny Plott. He was taken into custody earlier today and Carmichael sent me out here personally to tell you."

Joanna let out a deep breath. "Thank God. Look Mr.—"

"Willis, ma'am. Eugene Willis."

"Mr. Willis, we have a young boy down in a ravine over there. He's been bitten by a rattlesnake."

"I'll do what I can to help. We can use my car."

"Thank you." She turned sideways and called out to J.T. "The FBI have captured Lenny Plott. This man's an agent named Eugene Willis. He can drive us back to Kate's." Joanna lowered the rifle, resting it against her hip, as she pulled the phone out of her shirt pocket and began dialing Kate's number with her thumb.

Willis jerked the rifle away from Joanna, whirled her around and slid the barrel under her neck as he dragged her back up against his chest.

"Drop the phone," he told her, "or I'll break your neck."

DANE CARMICHAEL STORMED into the Trinidad police station. "What's so damned urgent it couldn't wait?"

"A city worker found a body in one of the Dumpster trash containers about an hour ago," Police Chief McMillian said.

"Don't keep me in suspense," Dane said. "I take it the identity of this body will have some significance to me."

"Yeah, if he's who we think he is. He didn't have any type of identification on him. His wallet was missing. But we did find a motel key."

"A motel key?"

"Yeah. And since Trinidad only has two motels, it wasn't hard to trace the key. Seems the key is from the

Tumbleweed and the room was registered to one of your agents."

"Let me guess. Eugene Willis?"

"Yep."

"You need me to identify the body?" Dane asked.

"Yep."

CHAPTER FIFTEEN

"TELL BLACKWOOD THAT you're all right." The man pressed the rifle harder against her throat. "If you don't, I'll shoot him and the boy the minute they're in sight."

He brought the rifle outward, a half inch from her neck. Joanna gasped for air. Her throat ached. She licked her lips. Dammit! How could she have been so stupid?

"Joanna!" J.T. bellowed from below. "What the hell's going on?"

"Don't do anything you'll regret," her captor warned. "I really don't want to hurt any innocent people. I came for you, not your protector or that child."

"Nothing's wrong." Joanna's voice quivered. "I'm just overcome with...with the news about Plott."

"Good girl," the man whispered in her ear. "Now, you and I are going to leave and take a ride. If we hurry, we won't have to involve Blackwood and the little boy."

Joanna nodded agreement, not resisting, not putting up a fight of any kind. When J.T. surfaced with Eddie, he would be unarmed. He and Eddie would be sitting ducks.

Lenny Plott, disguised as an FBI agent! And she hadn't recognized him. Not with black hair, a thick mustache and sunglasses shading his eyes. Not when she hadn't been expecting him. She'd thought she was safe, hidden away on the reservation. How how Plott found them? Who had given away their location?

The cellular phone Joanna clutched in her hand rang.

Plott braced the rifle under his arm, grabbed the phone away from her, then clasped her wrist, jerking her up against him. The two of them stared at the ringing telephone.

Plott flipped open the telephone. "Yeah?" He placed it to Joanna's ear.

"J.T.?" Joseph Ornelas said. "Listen, Plott killed an FBI agent and assumed his identity. Eugene Willis. Plott's wearing a black wig and mustache and he knows Joanna is on the reservation. Don't let her out of your sight. Dane Carmichael is taking a helicopter from Trinidad, and I'm on my way."

Lenny jerked the phone away from Joanna's ear, punched the off button and then the power button. "We'd better get going."

He dragged her to the car, opened the door and shoved her inside. "Stay put if you want to live just a little longer, and if you don't want anyone else to get hurt."

She heard J.T. frantically calling her name. He knew something wasn't right. By the time he brought Eddie up out of the ravine, J.T. would be half out of his mind with worry. And when he discovered that she and the "FBI agent" were gone, he would know what had happened.

Plott unlocked the trunk, tossed J.T.'s rifle and phone inside and then removed Eugene Willis's 9-mm from the shoulder holster. Opening the driver's-side door, Plott got in the car and started the engine.

"I didn't think it would be this easy." He backed the car up, turned and headed away from Painted Canyon. "I figured I'd have to kill Blackwood to get to you or maybe kill you both from a distance. But that wouldn't have been any fun for us, would it, baby doll?"

The sound of the endearment on his lips chilled her. The night Plott had raped her, he'd called her "baby doll" over and over again. Her stomach churned. Salty bile rose in her throat. Holding her hands in her lap, she knotted them into tight fists. She had to go with him. She had to protect J.T. and Eddie. But no matter where he took her or what he tried to do to her, she was not going to let him win. Even if he killed her, she was going to put up the fight of her life.

And all the while Plott drove her farther and farther away from Painted Canyon, she kept praying that J.T. would save Eddie and then come after her—and find her before it was too late.

As J.T. BROUGHT Eddie up from the ravine, fear ate away at his gut. Joanna wasn't answering him, and he'd heard a car engine roar to life. Cautiously, J.T. peered upward, scanning the area before showing himself. In the distance a cloud of thick dust swirled in the air. He swallowed hard. Whoever had approached Joanna, wasn't an FBI agent.

"Where's Joanna?" Eddie asked. "Did she call my mama?"

"No, Eddie, I don't think she got a chance to call Kate."

"Where'd she go?"

"She went with the…the FBI agent."

What the hell was he going to do? He had a dying child in his arms. If Eddie didn't get an antivenom injection soon, he wouldn't make it. But if J.T. allowed Plott much of a head start, he knew he might not get to Joanna in time to save her.

J.T. carried Eddie to the horses, mounted Washington, and pulled his young cousin around to sit in front of him. When J.T. motioned the big Appaloosa into a full gallop, Playtime followed. The sun burned hot and bright in the western sky. Dust swirled about the horses' legs.

He could not—would not—let himself think about what

was happening to Joanna or how she must be feeling. If he thought about it, he'd go crazy. He knew what he had to do—what Joanna would expect him to do.

While riding as if the demons of hell were on his heels, J.T. bargained with the Almighty. *Keep her safe until I can find her, and I'll do everything I can to be the man she wants and needs. Don't let anything happen to her. Please. I haven't even told her that I love her.*

HE WAS LOST! Dammit to hell, this godforsaken country had tricked him. Everything looked the same. Every damn little dirt road. Every mesa. Every canyon. Every stupid shrub and bush.

Wide-open space. Never-ending sky. And a car with less than a quarter of a tank of gas. He had to take Joanna somewhere undercover and finish her off before finding his way out of this Indian hellhole. If he wasted too much more time trying to find the road he'd come in on, he'd run out of gas and Blackwood would have gathered his forces and come after him.

Lenny took the road to the left, slowing the car as he turned. Joanna grabbed the door handle and swung open the door. He reached for her, but she jumped out just as he clutched a handful of her shirt. The soft cotton material ripped right off her back.

Joanna fell onto the ground, knocking off her hat and momentarily stunning her as she rolled over and over. Breathless, she rose to her knees.

Plott slammed on the brakes. "Son of a bitch," he muttered. He flung open the car door and stomped around the hood. He lifted the black wig off his head and hurled it to the ground, revealing the thin, matted strands of his silver-blond hair.

Joanna lifted herself up from her knees and ran.

"Where the hell do you think you're going, baby doll? You can't get away from me. If you keep running, I'm just going to have to hurt you when I catch you." Plott scratched his head.

Joanna kept running and Plott chased her. Sweat seeped through his shirt—Eugene Willis's shirt. Plott cursed under his breath. When he caught her, he'd make her sorry she'd ever run from him.

She didn't look back. Not once. She stumbled, but didn't fall. Plott ran faster. When he got closer, he reached out for her, calling her name. His hand just missed grasping her long red hair.

Panting, sweat drenching her body, loose tendrils of hair plastered to her face, Joanna ran and ran. Lenny Plott reached out again. This time he caught a handful of her hair. She screamed. He jerked her backward. She whirled around, prepared to fight. He yanked on her hair, pulling her forward. Ramming into her with the full force of his body, he knocked her to the ground and trapped her beneath him.

"You women are so stupid." Lenny smiled at her. "When will you ever learn?"

LESS THAN TWO miles from Painted Canyon, J.T. saw dust clouds in the distance and heard the rumble of vehicles. Within minutes, a truck, a Bronco and a patrol car surrounded him. Joseph Ornelas jumped out of the patrol car and ran toward J.T. Several men climbed down off the truck bed and stood watching. Kate Whitehorn flung open the door of her neighbor Peter Yazzi's Bronco and followed Joseph.

"Plott's taken Joanna," J.T. said. "He's got a head start. We're going to have to track them." J.T. slid off Washington and lifted Eddie down into his arms. "Eddie's been bitten by a rattler. He needs to be taken to the clinic as fast as possible."

Opening her arms, Kate ran to J.T., who handed over her son. Peter Yazzi walked up behind Kate. "We will take care of Eddie. You go and save your woman."

"Peter," Joseph called out to the older man. "I'll radio ahead to the clinic and have them meet you with the antivenom serum." He turned to J.T. "Get in the patrol car. I'll send Agent Carmichael word on our general location." Joseph turned to one of the men near the truck. "Donnie, take care of these horses for us. The rest of you can follow, but you're to stay behind us and don't make a move without my orders. Understand?"

J.T. removed his 9-mm Glock and holster from his saddlebag, strapped the gun on and walked toward the patrol car.

The youth named Donnie ran over, mounted Washington and trotted off, Playtime following. J.T. jerked open the passenger door of the patrol car and slid onto the seat. Joseph got in, started the engine and turned to J.T.

"Painted Canyon," J.T. said. "He was heading west."

LENNY PRESSED HIS body onto Joanna's. She tried to wriggle, but the harder she tried to move, the harder he pressed. She struggled to slip one of her arms free.

Plott grabbed her face in both hands and squeezed, squishing her cheeks inward, compressing her lips into a fish mouth. Lifting her head, he held it for a second, then slammed it down against the ground. Joanna gasped. He repeated the head-slamming three times. She cried out, the pain momentarily blinding her.

Releasing her face, he loosened his tie, unknotted it and slipped it off his neck. Joanna slid her arm, freeing half of it, but her hand remained trapped under Plott's chest.

The minute Joanna slid one arm completely free, Lenny shoved himself up, straddled her hips and grabbed her wrists. She tried to lift her knee. He sat down on her, knocking the breath out of her.

He bound her hands together with Eugene Willis's silk tie, stood and yanked her to her feet. "Come on, baby doll, it's too hot out here and not nearly private enough for what I have in mind."

Joanna kicked Plott. He slapped her across the face. "You stupid girl. The more you fight, the more I'm going to hurt you." Leering at her, he grabbed both of her breasts. She kicked him again and again. He tightened his hold on her breasts, squeezing until she screamed. Then he kicked her in the stomach with his knee. Doubling over, she fell to the ground. Plott grabbed the ends of the silk tie, jerked her onto her belly and dragged her for several yards. Stopping abruptly, he pulled her to her feet, lifted her and slung her over his shoulder.

He slammed her up against the side of the car, ripped her ragged shirt off her and tore it into a long strip. Giving her a hard shove, he pushed her into the car, leaned down and grabbed her feet. He bound her feet with the tattered material of her shirt, then locked and closed the door.

When he got inside the car he sat there for several minutes, staring at her. She was scared to death. He could see the fear in her eyes. Green eyes. Hot green eyes. He could smell her fear, too, and the smell was delicious. No matter how brave they tried to act, sooner or later, they all succumbed to their fears. The ones who had testified against him and sent him to prison knew what it meant to fear him. Joanna Beaumont knew. He had given her the sweetest kind of pain, the kind she'd never be able to forget. And he would give it to her again before he killed her.

But he had to find a hiding place before Blackwood found them. Surely there was a safe place somewhere out here in this damned desert.

"WE'LL FIND THEM," Joseph said. "It's obvious Plott doesn't have any idea where he's going."

"Yeah, well, I'm not sure that's a comforting thought." J.T. wanted to rent the air with his fury, yell at the top of his lungs from the highest peak on the reservation. He wanted to lash out and smash something—anything. If he had to contain his anger and fear much longer, he'd lose his mind. "If Plott's lost, then he's probably upset and taking his frustration out on Joanna."

"Stop thinking about it, okay?" Joseph gripped the steering wheel with white-knuckled ferocity.

"How the hell do I stop thinking about it? I promised to protect her. Vowed to her that I'd never let Plott get anywhere near her, and look what I let happen."

"You didn't let this happen. Quit beating yourself up. What were you supposed to do? Leave Eddie down in that ravine, or let him die from the snakebite once you brought him up? Besides, how do you think you'd have caught up with them on horseback?"

J.T. hadn't cried since he was five years old—not since he'd been ripped from his mother's arms. A real man didn't cry, didn't show emotion. Hell, old John Thomas had taught him that a real man didn't even feel any emotion.

The tears lodged in J.T.'s throat. *Dear God, please. Please.*

"Look, over there," Joseph said. "Thank God, the fool

isn't trying to cover his tracks. See, it looks as if he's turned off on the trail leading up to the old mine."

Joseph stopped the car, got out and walked around, taking note of the tire tracks. J.T. got out when the truck filled with half-a-dozen relatives and neighbors pulled up behind the patrol car.

"There's been a car turn here recently," Joseph said. "If Plott took this road, then we've got him trapped. There's only one way out and that's the way he came in."

J.T. looked around, wondering how long ago Plott and Joanna had come this way. Long enough for him to have hurt her? Long enough for him to have raped her? Killed her?

J.T. spotted a wad of black fur lying on the ground. He walked over, picked it up and examined it. "Damn! Look at this. It's a black wig."

"Plott's wig." Joseph lifted the hairpiece from J.T.'s hand, then waved to the men in the truck. "He's gone toward the old uranium mine. Stay behind us and don't take any action on your own."

"Once he's figured out he can't get out of this alive, he'll kill Joanna." J.T. followed Joseph back to the patrol car and got inside. "We shouldn't go storming in there."

"Man, start thinking with your brain instead of your heart." Joseph tossed the wig into the backseat, then slid under the wheel. "He's planning on killing her, regardless. If he knows we have him trapped, he might be willing to bargain for his life."

J.T. didn't want to admit that he wasn't thinking straight, that at this moment he was far more lover than protector. Gritting his teeth, he shook his head. "How far is this mine?"

"Not far. About two miles up into those hills." Joseph turned on the ignition and shifted gears. "The place was abandoned years ago. Radioactive contamination to the workers caused a lot of our people to die from cancer."

"He'll take her inside the mine," J.T. said, but he wasn't actually talking to Joseph, just thinking aloud. Before he could close out the thoughts, he pictured Joanna's face, her terrified green eyes, and a surge of sour bile rose from his stomach to his throat.

He was going to rip Plott apart, piece by piece. And if Plott had harmed Joanna, he was going to take his sweet time killing the man.

When they reached the old mine, they saw a parked car with both front doors standing wide open. The late-afternoon sunshine glinted off the windshield of Eugene Willis's dust-coated gray sedan. Joseph slammed on the brakes of his patrol car, flung open the door and jumped out. J.T. swallowed the bitter juice coating his mouth and got out on the passenger side, then looked up toward the old, abandoned mine.

"Is there another way out of there?" J.T. asked.

"Yeah, around on the back side."

"Then it's possible Plott could try to escape that way."

"He won't know about the back entrance, and it could take him hours, maybe days to find it," Joseph said. "Besides, where's he going to go? I told you, there's only one way out of this canyon, unless the guy can climb better than a mountain goat."

"We'll need some sort of light." J.T. checked his gun.

Joseph stared at his cousin. "I've got a couple of flashlights and I'm sure they—" he nodded toward the men getting out of the truck "—will have one or two if we need them."

"I want you to show me the way into the back of the mine. I'm going in alone. Understand?" J.T. waited for a reply, but Joseph only nodded agreement. "If you can keep him distracted from this side, I should have a good chance of sneaking up on him."

J.T. knew that this could be their only hope of getting Joanna away from Plott—alive!

CHAPTER SIXTEEN

JOANNA'S EYES HAD become accustomed to the partial darkness and the eerie silence inside the old mine. Thankfully, Plott hadn't taken them very far inside. She could still see glimmers of sunlight toward the entrance. She lay quietly on the ground where Plott had tossed her, humming softly to herself.

If she thought she had a chance of escaping, she would try to crawl. But she'd never make it past Plott to get to the entrance, and if she tried to go in the opposite direction, she would be lost in total darkness.

Plott gazed around, turning his head from side to side. "Isn't this an appropriate place to die? Almost like being in a grave already, isn't it?"

Joanna shuddered at the thought. Was she really going to die like this? Wasn't there anything she could do to save herself?

Plott shone Eugene Willis's flashlight up, down and around, then dropped to his knees beside Joanna. She didn't move a muscle, didn't even breathe for several seconds. He laid the flashlight on the ground, within arm's reach.

"I'm going to untie you, baby doll, so we can have a little fun before I decide exactly how I'm going to kill you."

When he reached for her, Joanna scooted away from him. He threw back his head and laughed, then grabbed

her by the feet and hauled her up and under him, straddling her hips.

"I want you to be free to fight me the way you tried to
do the last time we played. Remember?" Lifting himself
off her, he pivoted around until he faced her feet. "I'll
never forget how much fun I had that night at your apartment. I bet you won't ever forget, either. Not as long as
you live." Reaching down, he began untying her ankles.

His diabolical laughter echoed off the rock walls.
Joanna raised her arms, aimed her bound hands and
pounded Plott on his head and back. Twisting his body
around enough to knock her hands away from him, he
leaned backward and slapped her across the face. Then,
after kicking the loosened strands of her ripped blouse
away from her feet, he rubbed his hands up and down her
legs.

Joanna shuddered. She couldn't bear for him to touch
her intimately that way. She would much rather he beat
her. The physical abuse didn't hurt her nearly as much as
his sexual caresses. But his caresses weren't truly sexual.
She understood that, now better than ever before. Plott's
every touch, whether he was beating her or caressing her,
was a form of brutalizing manipulation. To him it was all
a matter of power.

Plott stood, removed Eugene Willis's suit coat and
tossed it on the ground. Joanna glared up at him, seeing
only his dark, shadowy outline as he loosened the shoulder holster, took it off and laid it down beside the flashlight. Joanna's eyes focused on the gun. She swallowed.
If there was some way she could get hold of that gun...

Unbuckling his belt, Plott lowered himself back down,
straddling Joanna's hips again. When he touched her
cheek, she spat on him. He laughed, and the sound made
her want to scream.

"So much to do," he said, "and so little time to truly enjoy ourselves."

He unbuttoned her jeans. She bucked upward, trying to throw him off, then lifted her arms and brought them down against his chest. Grabbing her wrists, he flung her arms over her head and spread himself out on top of her. He insinuated one hand between their bodies and slid it between her thighs.

"Just think, baby doll, your last moments are going to be spent with me on top of you. My face is the last one you'll see. What I've done to you will be the last thing you remember."

"No!" she screamed. Her adamant denial echoed in the empty caverns of the abandoned mine.

J.T. HEARD HER scream at the same moment he saw the beam of light. A flashlight lying on the ground! All he wanted to do was go flying toward the sound of her terrified voice, but he stopped dead still and listened to his gut instincts and to his years of professional training. He checked his gun.

He had to take Plott unaware. It was the only way. Suddenly J.T. heard the rumble of men's voices. What the hell? Then he realized the sound wasn't people talking, but a distinct, synchronized chanting in a language with which he had recently become reacquainted. Why were they chanting? What purpose did it serve other than to alert Plott to their presence?

The rhythmic thumping of what sounded like a drum blended with the voices. A picture of men painted and ready for battle sprang into his mind.

Realization dawned on J.T. Damn, but Joseph Ornelas was a wily fox. The chanting and drumming would not only draw Plott's attention, they just might spook him. This was J.T.'s chance to strike. He had to act quickly and silently.

LISTENING, LENNY PLOTT lifted his head, turned left, right and left again. "Do you hear that?"

Joanna heard the chanting and the drumbeat. "They've found us. J.T. isn't alone. You'll never get away, now."

"Shut up! I need to think."

"Do you have any idea what they're going to do to you if you kill me?" Joanna wanted to cry out, to tell J.T. to come for her now, that she couldn't bear being trapped like this another minute. But she would not allow herself to panic.

"I said shut up!" Lenny grabbed her by the wrist, jumped to his feet and jerked her up beside him. "We'll go deeper into the mine. If they try to come after us, I'll be able to kill a few of them before they get me."

He bent over, clutched the 9-mm in one hand and picked up the flashlight with the other. Joanna jumped on top of his back, the sudden impact knocking him flat on his face. Even with her wrists bound, she tried to grab the gun out of his hand. Before she could reach it, Lenny threw her off him and moved a couple of feet away from her.

"You just don't know when to quit, do you, baby doll?" Standing, he aimed the gun at her and grinned. "Maybe I'll use all my bullets on you before those savages come in here and rip me apart. I can make your dying a slow, painful ordeal."

Joanna simultaneously heard the feral growl and saw the huge shadowy form of a man behind Lenny Plott. She sucked in her breath. J.T.! She bit down on her bottom lip to keep from crying out to him.

With the 9-mm in his hand, Plott spun around and faced J.T. The two men stared at each other for a split second in the semidarkness.

J.T. glanced down quickly at Joanna lying at Plott's

side, directly below his hand that held the semiautomatic. Could he shoot Plott and put him out of commission before Plott could shoot Joanna?

Plott spread out his leg until his calf touched Joanna's shoulder. "Shooting me won't save her life." He pointed the gun squarely at Joanna's head, then smiled at J.T.

The moment Plott directed his attention on J.T., Joanna scooted slowly backward, inching her hips across the smooth rock surface. Plott glanced in her direction, then jerked around toward her. J.T. flung himself at Plott, knocking him over. The two rolled around on the ground, both men holding on to their weapons. Joanna scrambled to her feet and backed up out of the way. Lifting her bound wrists to her mouth, she bit into the silk material and began pulling on the tight knot.

She glanced up from her task and saw two forms rise to their feet. She heard fists striking flesh, grunts, groans and curses, then the rattle of metal hitting the rock wall, then another loud clank as something hit the ground. An earsplitting gunshot echoed in the darkness.

Neither man slumped to the ground. She had no way of knowing whether one of them had been hit or whose gun had been fired.

She watched the two figures continuing their struggle, moving farther and farther back inside the tunnel and away from her. Giving a final tug on the silk knot, she managed to loosen the binding completely, and slipped her hands free.

Bending over, she picked up the flashlight Plott had brought into the mine with them. She pointed the beam inside the mine, but J.T. and Plott were almost out of sight. She shone the light all around over the ground, looking for one of the guns. When the light reflected off the barrel of J.T.'s 9-mm Glock, she ran over and picked it up, gripping it firmly in her hand.

Using the dim glow from the flashlight to guide her, Joanna headed back inside the mine. She saw J.T. throw Plott against a wooden support beam. If only she were closer, she could shoot.

A rumble drifted from inside the mine, then a loud crash. Joanna pointed the flashlight in the direction of the noise and saw Plott lift his fist, then suddenly stop and stare up above his head.

She shone the light toward the ceiling and screamed when she saw the heavy, rotted beams cracking. Huge, loose chunks of old timber fell, knocking both Lenny Plott and J.T. to the ground. Joanna ran toward J.T. He didn't move.

Dear God, please, don't let him die!

When she neared, she heard J.T. groan. She glanced over at Plott, who seemed to be unconscious. Kneeling over J.T., she wedged the flashlight between her breasts, sticking the handle inside her bra. Holding the gun, she laid her hand flat over it as she placed it on the ground.

"J.T.?" She turned him over on his side and saw several small rivulets of blood streaking his face.

He groaned. She wiped his sweaty, blood-smeared face with her palm and called his name again. His eyelids fluttered.

Pain shot up from her hand to her arm. She looked down at the big foot crushing her hand that held the Glock, then she glanced up at Lenny Plott who stood towering over her. She tried to hold on to the gun, but knew she had lost it the minute Plott bent over and lifted her hand. He picked up the gun. Joanna's heart beat frantically. J.T. moaned, then opened his eyes. Plott jerked Joanna up and shoved her in front of him. She clutched the flashlight that she'd stuck between her breasts.

What was Plott going to do? Would he shoot her and then J.T.? Was there any way she could stop him? What if she hit him in the head with the flashlight? She might not be able to strike, but even if she did, the blow probably wouldn't stun him.

"Let her go, Plott." J.T. struggled to lift his head.

"You're in no position to bargain," Lenny said.

A rifle shot hit the wall behind Plott's head, sending shattered pieces of rock crashing down onto the ground. "But I am." Joseph Ornelas's deep voice echoed in the stillness of the dark mine.

"I'll kill her!" Plott yelled. "Whoever the hell you are, stay back or I'll put a bullet in her head right this minute."

"Do what he says," J.T. shouted.

"Yeah, you'd better listen to your friend."

Using Joanna as a shield, Plott backed farther into the mine. Taking her one free hand, Joanna reached inside her bra, pulled out the flashlight and tossed it toward J.T. Plott cursed her, but didn't stop moving, backing farther and farther into the darkness.

J.T. rose to his knees, grabbed the flashlight and stumbled to his feet. He pointed the beam toward the mine entrance where Joseph Ornelas stood waiting. He motioned the other man to come on inside, then turned and followed Plott deeper into the mine.

Joanna knew she wasn't going to die without putting up a fight. Turning on her assailant in the darkness, she jerked out of his grasp and pelted him with her fists. He reached for her, but she escaped his grasp. He grabbed her arm. She cried out as his fingers bruised her flesh.

He jerked her toward him. She shoved against his chest, pushing him with every ounce of her strength, but he held on to her arm as he staggered backward. He screamed when the ground disappeared beneath his feet and continued screaming as he dropped straight down into an open shaft, dragging Joanna with him, but unable to keep his hold on her wrist.

When she realized what was happening, Joanna reached out, praying for something—anything—to grab on to to stop her deadly fall. She clutched a jutting piece of timber sticking out from the rock wall.

Plott's scream ended when his body hit the bottom of the deep shaft.

With her feet dangling over the precipice, Joanna struggled to hold on to the edge of the wooden beam with both hands. J.T. thrust the flashlight into Joseph's hand, fell to his knees and called out to Joanna.

Joseph flashed the light over the edge of the shaft. Joanna gazed up at J.T., her eyes wide, her mouth trembling. The tight emotion-formed knots in J.T.'s stomach constricted painfully. One wrong move on his part and Joanna would fall to her death.

"Hang on, honey. I'm going to pull you up."

Lying flat on his stomach, J.T. leaned over the shaft and stretched out one hand. Instantly he realized he couldn't reach her.

"You're going to have to give me your hand," he told her. "Just reach up to me with one hand."

"No! I can't! If—if I let go, I'll fall." Sweat dampened her palms. The wooden beam felt moist. What if her hands slipped off? What if she couldn't continue holding on?

"You won't fall, honey. I'm right here. See how close I am—" He wiggled the fingers of his right hand. "See how easy it'll be to just reach out to me."

What if she let go and lifted her hand to him and he still couldn't reach her? What if he caught her hand and couldn't hold on to her? "I can't, J.T. I can't. Please, think of something else. I just can't let go."

"She's scared," Joseph said. "She's not thinking straight."

"Joanna, hold on. I'll find a way to get you." J.T. looked up at Joseph. "I'm going to have to lean over farther to reach her. I need the light to see her, but I also need you to anchor me to keep me from falling into the shaft."

"No, J.T., don't risk your life," Joanna yelled. "Can't you go get a rope or—" The beam she clutched with all her might groaned, loosening just a fraction from the rock wall and sending a shower of granular sediment cascading down over her. "J.T.!"

"Give me your hand, Jo. Now!" He leaned into the shaft, stretching out his hand as far as he could. "Trust me. Believe that I can save you."

"I want to trust you, to believe."

"Lift your right hand and give it to me."

Joanna looked at his hand and saw Benjamin Greymountain's silver-and-turquoise ring on his finger. J.T. noticed the way she stared at the ring. "This was meant to be a wedding band," he told her. "Just like the one you're wearing. A symbol of a love to last a lifetime and beyond." He slammed the palm of his hand against the rock wall of the shaft. "You can't hang on much longer. If your hands slip, you're going to fall. Do you understand what I'm saying to you?"

"I know! I know!" Joanna panted, taking in short, choppy breaths. "Don't let me fall, don't let me die."

"Either give me your trust and lift your hand up to me, or I'm going to risk coming over the edge far enough to grab you."

"No! Don't! You could fall."

"Yeah, I know." He leaned over just a fraction farther.

"Don't do it," she pleaded.

"Honey, haven't you figured it out? If you don't come out of this alive, there's no reason for me to live. Either we both get out of this damned mine together or we die down there together. It's your choice."

J.T. held his breath. Joanna closed her eyes. She couldn't let J.T. risk his life any more than he already had. Her only chance to save him and maybe save herself, too, was to put her complete trust in him, to truly believe that he could save her.

She eased her right hand to the edge of the wooden beam, released it and shot her arm straight up. J.T. clasped her wrist, tugging her upward.

"That's it, honey."

Letting go of the beam completely, she gave herself over to J.T.'s strength as he lifted her up and out of the shaft. With both of them on their knees, J.T. hauled her up against him, hugging her fiercely. Weeping, she clung to him. Tears stung his eyes.

He lifted her to her feet, then swept her up into his arms. "It's over," he said. "And you're safe. Safe in my arms forever."

She laid her head on his shoulder and closed her eyes. "He's dead, isn't he? Really dead?"

"Yeah, he's about as dead as a man can get." Joseph shone the flashlight down into the shaft where Lenny Plott had fallen. "If you want to be sure, take a look," he said. "But I warn you, it's not a pretty sight."

"You don't have to look at him if you'd rather not," J.T. told her.

"I want to see," she said. "I need to see him dead."

Held securely in J.T.'s strong arms, she peered over the edge of the shaft. The flashlight illuminated just a fraction of the deep shaft, but enough for Joanna to see the lower half of Lenny Plott's lifeless body impaled on a sharp, jagged rock formation. She shuddered.

"My God!" Joanna gasped.

"Yeah." Joseph nodded. "I'd say the Great Spirit had a hand in Plott's demise."

"I'm getting you out of here," J.T. said. "The sooner we put all of this behind us, the better."

Joanna clung to J.T., rejoicing in their being alive, as he carried her out of the mine and into the light. Squinting against the glare of the late-afternoon sun, she stared at the Navajo men waiting in a straight line just outside the mine entrance.

J.T. carried her to the patrol car, opened the back door and slid inside, holding her in his arms. "After we get you thoroughly checked over at the clinic, we'll stay tonight on the reservation at my mother's house," J.T. said. "I'm sure the FBI will want to question all of us. But tomorrow, I'm going to take you home, back to my ranch. And as soon as you and Elena can do whatever you women do to plan a wedding, we're getting married."

"What?" Joanna gazed at him in disbelief.

He looked at her dirty, tear-streaked face and knew that no power on earth or in heaven would keep them apart. If Benjamin Greymountain had loved Annabelle as much as J.T. loved Joanna, the man would have found a way to keep her. Maybe their ancestors hadn't been able to fulfill the promise of their love, but J.T. intended to make sure he and Joanna reaped all the benefits from this once-in-a-lifetime love they shared.

"We're getting married as soon as possible," he said.

"Is that what you call a proposal?"

"It's all you'll get from me." With a shaky hand, he reached out and touched her beautiful face. "I'm not much of a romantic, honey, but you already know that. And I won't be much of a bargain as a husband, but I have a feeling you'll whip me into shape without too much trouble. Heck, by the time we have kids, I'll probably be downright domesticated."

"J. T. Blackwood, you are without a doubt the most irritating, infuriating—"

"Should I take that to mean you'll marry me?"

Joseph pecked on the window. J.T. motioned him away. Joseph opened the car door, stuck his head in, propped his booted foot inside and held up his cellular phone.

"I just talked to my sister, and I thought you'd like to know that Eddie's going to be fine. Or at least he will be until Kate takes a switch to his skinny little legs."

"I doubt she'll have the heart to whip him," Joanna said. "I know that if he were mine, I wouldn't."

"Maybe this has taught him not to go off alone again." J.T. motioned with the side of his head, indicating for Joseph to get lost. Removing his foot, Joseph stepped back and closed the door. Smiling, he turned around to wait for the helicopter carrying Dane Carmichael to land.

"I can think of only one thing I'd rather have from you than a marriage proposal." Joanna kissed J.T.'s lips softly, her breath mingling with his.

"Name it and it's yours."

"Don't agree too hastily," she told him. "This might be something you can't give me."

"You'll never know until you ask."

"All right." She lifted her head from his shoulder and looked directly at him. "More than anything, I'd like to have a declaration of love from you."

"A what?"

"A declaration of—"

"Yeah, I heard you." Shaking his head, he grunted. "During the past few hours I've said it over and over again. 'I love Joanna. I love her more than anything on earth. I love her so much it hurts. I never thought it possible to love anyone the way I love her. If she dies, I don't want to live.' I've said it to myself so many times, I guess I just forgot that I hadn't told you."

"I think you just did."

He lifted her right hand in his, interlocking their fingers. They both glanced down at their matching rings.

"Yeah, I guess I did." J.T. looked at her with longing. "*Ayói óosh'ni*, Joanna." And this time he knew exactly what the words meant. *I love you*.

Cupping the back of her head in his hand, he covered her mouth with his, claiming her, possessing her, telling her more eloquently than words ever could what was in his heart.

Joanna thought she heard the sound of drums, way off in the distance. Just a faint echo, as if the sound had traveled a span of decades to reach this moment in time.

EPILOGUE

Richmond, Virginia
June 1965

> *I shall soon join my beloved Benjamin. The*
> *years that have separated us will vanish. Not*
> *one day has passed that I have not thought of*
> *him, yearned for him, loved him beyond all*
> *reasoning. Although our time together was so*
> *brief, I would not give up one precious, stolen*
> *moment for a lifetime with any other man. I*
> *have lived my life in the only way I knew how.*
> *Benjamin understood that I could not desert*
> *my sons. And once the boys were grown, Ben-*
> *jamin was gone. If I have but one regret, it is*
> *that Benjamin and I did not have a child. A*
> *child would have made our love immortal.*

JOANNA WIPED THE tears from her eyes. Glancing down at
the last entry in Annabelle Beaumont's diary, she traced
her great-grandmother's handwriting with the tips of her
fingers. There, beneath the final entry, Annabelle had
neatly penned a stanza from her favorite Christina Rossetti poem.

> *Yet come to me in dreams, that I may live*
> *My very life again though cold in death:*

Come back to me in dreams that I may give
Pulse for pulse, breath for breath:
Speak low, lean low,
As long ago, my love, how long ago?

Joanna closed the diary and placed it inside her desk, then, one by one, she turned out the lights in the living room of the new house she and J.T. had built shortly after their wedding seven years ago. Hesitating briefly in front of the fireplace, she looked up over the mantel at her most recently completed portrait—an oil painting of her three children, which she had hung between her prized portraits of her great-grandmother and J.T.'s great-grandfather.

These three strong, healthy offspring of hers and J.T.'s were the true legacy of love, one they knew in their hearts they shared with their ancestors.

Six-year-old John Thomas, with his black hair, green eyes and tall, sturdy body already taking on the long, lean proportions of his father's, was their firstborn. The twins, Annabelle and Benjamin, had just turned three last week, and still possessed chubby toddler forms. A riot of red curls circled their little brown faces, which possessed their father's strong Navajo features.

Joanna flipped off the last lamp, walked down the hallway and stopped by John Thomas's bedroom, peeping in on him. Her heart always caught in her throat whenever she looked at him. He was so beautiful, so absolutely perfect. She went on to the next door, stopped and walked into her twins' bedroom. In a few more years, they'd want separate rooms, but for now they were happy being together twenty-four hours a day.

Her precious little Annabelle and Benjamin. Born of a love that would live forever. She pulled up the blanket Annabelle had kicked to the foot of her bed. She'd been a restless sleeper since infancy. Occasionally, Joanna would find her completely turned around in her bed, with her feet resting on the headboard.

Joanna tiptoed out of the twins' room and down the hallway. Opening the door to the master suite, she deliberately ignored J.T., who lay stretched out naked in the middle of the bed. She slipped off her silk robe, letting it puddle around her feet, then reached out and picked up J.T.'s tan Stetson from the dresser where he'd placed it. She set it on her head, turned around and put her hands on her hips.

J.T. sat up in bed, bracing his back against the headboard and crossing his arms behind his head.

"Howdy, partner." Joanna swung her naked hips provocatively as she walked to the foot of the huge four-poster bed. "Want to play cowgirl and Indian?"

J.T. grinned. "I might, if I like the rules of the game."

"The rules are very simple," Joanna said, taking off the Stetson and holding it in her hand. "The first part of the game is ringtoss. If I can circle the object of my choice with this cowboy hat, I win a free ride."

"And if you lose?"

"Then you get to tie me to a stake and set me on fire."

J.T. blew out a deep breath, lifted his hips up off the bed and laughed. "What the hell are you waiting for, woman? Toss that hat!"

Joanna sized him up, taking note of every inch of his masculine beauty laid out before her in naked splendor. She swung the Stetson around and around on her finger, lifted it and whirled it through the air. It landed right on target, sitting up straight over his arousal.

"Looks like you win, honey." He held open his arms. "Come get your free ride."

Joanna crawled onto the bed, lifted the Stetson, tossed

it to the floor and circled J.T. with her hand. He groaned deep in his throat.

"You'd think after seven years of riding, I'd have you broken in by now." She licked him intimately.

J.T. grabbed her by the shoulders and lifted her on top of him. Joanna giggled, then sighed when he placed her over his erection and eased himself into her body.

"Ride 'em, cowgirl," he said.

And she did.

* * * * *

ROARKE'S WIFE

CHAPTER ONE

"SHE'S OUTSIDE." Dane Carmichael stood in the doorway of Simon Roarke's office. "The lady brought her aunt with her."

Roarke nodded to his boss, who had recently taken over the reins as head of Dundee Private Security. Raking his fingers through his thick, brown hair, Roarke shoved back his chair and stood. "I'll be damned if I don't feel like some Thoroughbred stallion about to be paraded around and sized up to see if I'd make a good studhorse."

Dane chuckled. "I think the lady's pretty much made up her mind that you're the man she wants for the job. This little inspection is probably just a formality."

"I haven't accepted her proposition. I'm not sure that I can. She's asking an awful lot for her million dollars."

"I wouldn't do it." Dane clamped his big hand down on Roarke's shoulder. "But then, we're very different men, with totally different agendas. I'm not eager to retire from this business, and I'm not paying the bills for an ex-wife's medical treatment."

Roarke tensed at the mention of his former wife. Dane was one of the few people he'd ever told about Hope. He had always felt that his relationship with his ex-wife was nobody's business.

"I might as well get this over with." He took a deep breath and tried to grin at Dane. Was he a fool even to consider hiring himself out as a husband to a woman he'd never met?

"I'll tell the two Miss McNamaras to come in."

"Hey," Roarke called out.

Hesitating at the closed door, Dane glanced back at Roarke. "Yes?"

"What does she look like?"

"Does it really matter?" Dane asked.

"Yeah, it really matters. Good Lord, man, if I take her up on her offer, I'm going to be having sex with her for the next few months."

Dane cleared his throat in an obvious effort not to laugh. "She's okay, I suppose, if you like the type."

"And just what type would that be?"

"A petite redhead in a business suit, with an attitude so frosty that I could have chipped icicles off my fingers after our handshake."

"Damn," Roarke groaned. It might have made things a little easier if she was a luscious blond bombshell, the kind who could raise a man's temperature just by walking into the room.

"What did you expect—a hot-blooded temptress?" Dane asked. "Don't forget that she'd rather pay a man to marry her than seduce one with her charms."

"This particular woman is paying for more than just a husband," Roarke reminded him. "Ms. McNamara expects her money to buy her a husband, a bodyguard and a sperm donor."

CLEO MCNAMARA SHIFTED uncomfortably in the straight-backed chair. She couldn't remember a time in her life when she'd been so nervous. But then, a lot was riding on her interview with Simon Roarke. If he accepted her offer, she could save McNamara Industries and the jobs of several hundred employees. If he refused…? No, she wouldn't allow herself to think in negative terms. Cleo, more than most women, knew the power of money. After all, she had been born with the proverbial silver spoon in her mouth. Few men could turn down a million dollars for less than a year's service.

"Cleo, dear, will you sit still?" Beatrice McNamara patted her niece's quivering hand. "You'll make yourself sick if you don't calm down."

"I cannot believe I'm actually doing this," Cleo said. "I'm about to hire myself a husband. If the matter wasn't so dead serious, it would be hilarious. I'm sure Daphne will laugh herself silly if she ever finds out."

"Let Daphne laugh," Beatrice said. "Let the whole family laugh. It doesn't matter. The only important thing is that by fulfilling the stipulations in Daddy's will, you'll be able to retain control of McNamara Industries. Besides, there's no reason for anyone to know this marriage isn't a love match."

"If Uncle George hadn't been such an old-fashioned male chauvinist, he wouldn't have put me in this situation."

"Now, dear, give credit where credit is due." Beatrice straightened the soft neck bow on her silk blouse, her tiny fingers touching the material with delicate finesse. "Daddy might have been a bit old-fashioned, but if he'd been a true male chauvinist, he never would have allowed you to become CEO of McNamara Industries in the first place."

"I know, Aunt Beatrice, but—"

"He simply didn't want to see you wind up an old maid like me." Beatrice sighed dramatically. "Besides, when he made out his will, I'm sure he thought you'd marry Hugh."

Cleo supposed it was reasonable for Uncle George to have thought she would marry Hugh Winfield in order to fulfill the stipulations of the will. But she had dated the man only to please Uncle George, who'd been determined—for years—to see her marry. She'd known Hugh most of her life and had always liked him, but she certainly wasn't in love with him. In all honesty, if he had dumped her—a week before Uncle George's death—for anyone other than her cousin Daphne, she would have been relieved.

Beatrice fidgeted with the braid trim on her lavender jacket. "I'm most eager to see what Mr. Roarke looks like, aren't you? His credentials are quite impressive, but one can't really judge a man until one meets him face-to-face."

"I don't see that Mr. Roarke's physical appearance matters much one way or the other," Cleo said, lying to herself as well as to her aunt. "He meets all the qualifications I need in a temporary mate. He's intelligent and healthy. And he's a seasoned bodyguard."

"Well, say what you like, but I know that if I were planning on having—" Beatrice lowered her voice to a whisper "—sex...with a man, I'd want him to be at least passably good-looking."

Before Cleo could think of a reply, the inner office door opened and Dane Carmichael invited them into Mr. Roarke's office.

Standing, Cleo stiffened her spine, and when Aunt Beatrice grabbed her hand, she squeezed tightly, trying to reassure them both. She stepped back, allowing her aunt to enter first, then followed her into the plainly decorated, modern office.

The man stood with his back to them. A very large, wide back. He wore a long-sleeved blue shirt, the sleeves rolled up to the elbows, exposing dark, hairy forearms.

He was a big man, broad and thickly muscled beneath his clothes. He turned slowly. His blue eyes captured Cleo in their mesmerizing glare. The bottom dropped out of her stomach. She swallowed hard.

Beatrice McNamara gasped, then said ever so softly, "Oh, my, my."

My, my, indeed, Cleo thought. Simon Roarke was, without a doubt, the most masculine man she had ever encountered. He stood six-three, a good foot taller than she. With his top shirt buttons open, his thick, dark chest hair was partially exposed. Despite telling herself not to stare, Cleo could not stop herself from inspecting the man.

There was a rugged, almost fierce beauty in his appearance. His face was not a pretty one by anyone's standards, but a strikingly handsome, extremely manly one. A five o'clock shadow darkened his jawline.

"Roarke, this is Ms. Cleo McNamara," Dane said. "And her aunt, Miss Beatrice McNamara."

Gathering up her courage, Cleo stepped forward. She tilted her chin defiantly, daring anyone to think that she wasn't strong, capable and fearless.

"Mr. Roarke." She offered him her hand.

Simon glanced down at her small hand, tiny almost and quite delicate. Pale. Creamy. Soft. Unadorned. Well manicured, the nails painted with clear polish.

He accepted her greeting, his own big hand swallowing her small one when he grasped it. He felt a barely discernible tremor when their palms touched, but it was so slight he thought he might have imagined it. He realized he wanted this woman, who was trying so valiantly to appear tough, to show him some sign of weakness. But his gut instincts told him that Cleopatra McNamara seldom allowed anyone to see her vulnerable.

"Ms. McNamara. Won't you sit down?" He found himself strangely reluctant to release her hand, so he guided her to the chair and assisted her in sitting.

Dane had been right about her. Cleo was a frosty little redhead in a neatly tailored black business suit. But where Dane had failed to notice Ms. McNamara's nicely rounded behind and the high thrust of a pair of not-too-inadequate breasts, Roarke *did* notice. Maybe if a man knew he was destined to bed a woman, he paid closer attention to her physical attributes.

Cleo was no ravishing beauty—that was true. But good Lord, there definitely was something about her that stirred Roarke's baser instincts. Maybe it was because she was so small, so thin, that he could easily break her in half with his bare hands. Or maybe it was the fact that she was trying so damn hard to show him how strong and tough she was. A lot of women in her situation would have used the "I'm so helpless and need a big strong man like you" approach. Whatever the cause, Roarke found himself interested in and oddly attracted to this woman who could soon be his for the taking.

Cleo stared up at him with fearless, moss-green eyes, her expression questioning him, his honesty, his sincerity. And for the briefest instant he felt as if she were warning him not to hurt her.

"We haven't any time to waste," Beatrice said in her authoritarian, schoolteacher voice. "It's taken us nearly three weeks to find you, Mr. Roarke, and Cleo *must* be married within thirty-one days of Daddy's death." Beatrice stood behind her niece's chair, her fingertips biting into the leather surface.

Roarke glanced at Beatrice McNamara, a softer, older version of her niece. He knew she was sixty-three, but would have guessed her a good ten years younger. Although her auburn hair was streaked with gray, she kept it cut stylishly short, and her petite body was still youth-fully slender.

"I understand the urgency." Roarke spoke directly to Beatrice, then turned his attention to Cleo. "You must be desperate to retain control of your uncle's little fertilizer plant if you're willing to marry a man you don't know and have him father your child."

What sort of woman must she be, Roarke wondered, to pay such a high price for the stewardship of a small chemical plant in a one-horse Alabama town? If she didn't marry within a month of her uncle's death and become pregnant within a year, she wouldn't lose her inheritance, just control of the company. In fact, by selling the busi-ness, as the other family members wanted to do, she'd be a far richer woman than if she kept the company and lived off the quarterly dividends.

"If I don't fulfill the stipulations of Uncle George's will by marrying and getting pregnant, then McNamara In-dustries will be sold. And the company that wants to buy it plans to downsize drastically. That will mean hundreds of River Bend residents will lose their jobs. Our 'little' fertilizer plant is the major employer in the county, Mr. Roarke."

"I see." Roarke scanned Cleo's face for any sign of de-ception and found none. So Cleo McNamara was a do-gooder. A wealthy businesswoman who actually gave a damn about her employees.

Beatrice cleared her throat. "You understand that your background in the Green Berets and here at the Dundee agency is what tipped the scales in your favor as our choice for a husband. Cleo needs a full-time bodyguard."

"I'm well aware of Ms. McNamara's reasons for select-ing me over the other candidates." Roarke glared at Dane

Carmichael, who stood by the wall, his arms crossed over his chest and a smirky grin on his face.

"We're quite certain that someone in the family is trying to kill Cleo," Beatrice explained. "Two days after Daddy's funeral, someone tried to shoot her. And with one of Daddy's rifles, too! The sheriff checked every weapon in Daddy's collection immediately after the shooting and discovered one of the rifles had been fired recently. The bullet they found in the wall behind where Cleo had been standing was a match."

"But according to the report you sent me, there were no fingerprints, other than your father's, found on the rifle."

"That's right." Beatrice nodded.

"And the authorities don't have a clue as to who fired that shot?" Roarke posed his question to Cleo.

"Not a clue," she said. "But it had to have been either a family member or someone they'd hired. Only Aunt Beatrice and I want to keep McNamara Industries a family-run business. The rest of the family want to sell it."

"Is saving your uncle's company worth risking your life?" Roarke fervently wished he didn't find Ms. McNamara to be so damned noble. There was certainly something irresistibly appealing about a strong, intelligent, noble woman.

He realized that he'd never met anyone quite like her, and it was at that very moment he decided to take Cleo McNamara up on her offer of marriage. Even though he'd be doing it for the money, perhaps by making it possible for her to fulfill the stipulations of her uncle's will, he, too, would be doing something just a little noble.

"Yes. Saving McNamara Industries is worth any price I have to pay." Balling her hands into tight little fists in her lap, she stared up at Roarke. "Do we have a deal? As Aunt Beatrice pointed out, I don't have any time to waste."

"Has your lawyer drawn up all the documents?"

"Yes. I have them with me. In my briefcase."

"Then leave them and I'll read over them tonight. Come back tomorrow morning and, if you haven't changed your mind, we'll sign the papers."

"I won't change my mind," Cleo assured him. "Once we've finalized our deal, I'll want you to return to Alabama with me and we'll be married immediately."

Cleo stood and offered her hand to Roarke. Reluctantly, he accepted, once again holding on to her longer than necessary.

"I want one thing understood up front," Roarke told her, his thumb caressing her knuckles. "I'll marry you, father your child and protect you while we try to discover who wants to kill you. But I won't be around once the child is born. That's the only way I'll agree to this deal."

Cleo couldn't understand how a man could father a child and then desert it, never wanting anything to do with it. But for her sake and the child's, she was glad Simon Roarke wasn't the sentimental type. She had wondered how she'd handle the situation if he asked for visitation rights. Obviously, that wouldn't be a problem.

"You never want to see the child?" she asked. "Never want to be a part of his or her life?"

"That's right." Roarke clenched his jaw; the pulse in his neck bulged and throbbed. "The child will not be mine. It will be yours—completely yours."

"Very well. We have a deal." She pulled her hand free, squared her shoulders and turned away from him.

Roarke watched while Dane escorted the McNamara ladies out of the office. The moment the door closed behind them, he turned toward the window, took a deep breath and thought, *Good Lord, am I making the biggest mistake of my life?*

For a good thirty minutes, he stood looking out the window. His thoughts raced backward in time. To another marriage. To a twenty-one-year-old soldier madly in love with the prettiest girl in the world.

The pain rose inside him, a deep, twisting knot of agony that started in his belly and spread through him like an insidious poison. With unsteady hands, Roarke removed his wallet from his pocket and slipped out a frayed photograph. Blue eyes identical to his own stared back at him from the face of a golden-haired angel. His little Laurie. The picture had been taken only a few weeks after her third birthday. Her last birthday. Roarke had been halfway around the world in an insect-infested jungle when his daughter had died. If his military career hadn't been more important to him than his child, Laurie would still be alive. And Hope might not be vegetating in a mental hospital.

CLEO LAY IN the double bed in Atlanta's Doubletree Hotel, listening to Aunt Beatrice's wispy breathing as she slept peacefully. Cleo could not imagine life without her aunt, who actually was her father's first cousin. Beatrice, whom she'd referred to as *aunt* all her life, had been the nearest thing to a mother Cleo had ever known. When she was three, her father had been killed in Vietnam and her mother, young, beautiful and a bit wild, had deserted Cleo.

She had grown up on the McNamara estate in River Bend, a sleepy little Alabama town in northwest Alabama, near the Tennessee River. Aunt Beatrice had adored her and taken over her upbringing. And because she not only looked like the McNamaras but Uncle George believed she had the McNamara brains and grit, she soon became his favorite. "You're your father's daughter," he'd told her often. Uncle George had thought the world of young Jimmy McNamara Jr., his only brother's son.

Cleo couldn't ever remember wanting for anything money could buy. If she wanted it, needed it or asked for it, it was hers. But she would never forget the nights she had prayed her mother would return for her and love her the way mothers should love their daughters. But the beautiful, wild Arabelle had never returned. And when Cleo was nineteen, they received word that her mother had died accidentally of an overdose of drugs and alcohol.

She supposed one of the reasons she'd fallen in love with Paine Emerson and had agreed to marry him at twenty was that she'd longed for the kind of family life she'd been denied. She'd seen herself as a happy homemaker and the mother of half a dozen little Emersons. She'd been such a young fool. More in love with love than with Paine. And totally infatuated with the dream of being the kind of mother she'd never had.

She had thrown herself into their relationship with total abandon, giving Paine her virginity as well as her heart. She didn't know which she regretted losing the most. But in the long run, it didn't matter. She had retrieved her broken heart and mended it quite well. And her lost virginity was of little importance, since, for all intents and purposes, she was still what some would call a semivirgin, a woman with very little sexual experience.

She had hated Daphne for quite some time after her cousin had seduced Paine into eloping. But when Paine had left Daphne for another woman only four years into their turbulent marriage, Cleo had actually felt sorry for her cousin. She had welcomed Daphne home, if not with open arms, at least with civility.

She couldn't remember a time in her life when Daphne

hadn't wanted what she had. If Cleo got a pony, Daphne wanted a horse. If Cleo got a new dress, Daphne had to have two new dresses. When Cleo became engaged to Paine Emerson, Daphne promptly seduced him into eloping with her. So why had Cleo been surprised that, less than six months after she started dating Hugh Winfield, she found him in bed with Daphne?

Cleo supposed Uncle George had known that the only reason she dated Hugh was to please him. He'd made it perfectly clear how much he wanted to see her married. One of his greatest regrets had been that his only child, Beatrice, had remained single and childless. Understanding his reasoning and his assumption that she'd marry Hugh, Cleo could almost forgive her great-uncle for placing her in such an awkward predicament.

Tomorrow she and Simon Roarke would sign the documents that sealed their fate and doomed them both to a temporary marriage. She had weighed the pros and cons of this situation again and again. She didn't want to get married. And she certainly didn't want to bring a baby into this world with only one parent. Her actions would be unfair to her child. But she and Aunt Beatrice would surround the child with love, and she was wealthy enough to afford to raise a child alone. When she had considered taking Aunt Beatrice's advice to hire a husband who could father her baby, she'd thought the man would want to be a part of the child's life after the divorce.

What sort of person could walk away from his own flesh and blood? *A person like Arabelle McNamara,* she told herself. Was Simon Roarke as callous and unfeeling as her own mother had been?

Cleo wasn't sure what she had been expecting when she'd met Mr. Roarke. She knew a great deal about him, but only superficial information. His age, birthday, weight, height, schooling, occupational background, financial situation, medical history. But she knew absolutely nothing about the man himself. About Simon. She supposed, considering their marriage was a business arrangement and would be of short duration, that she really didn't need to know the things a woman usually wanted to know about her husband.

But their child was bound to ask about him someday. What would she tell her son or daughter? *The only reason I had you was so that I could save McNamara Industries. Your father and I were strangers who married each other for strictly business reasons, and he wanted no part in your life.*

Dear God in heaven, am I making a terrible mistake? Should I sell the company? That would make the rest of the family happy and no doubt end the threats on my life. Then there would be no need to marry a man I don't even know and conceive a child who would be born out of necessity and not out of love.

Reaching to the foot of the bed, Cleo grabbed her yellow cotton robe and slipped into it. She got up and walked quietly across the room, hoping not to disturb her aunt. Opening the drapes enough to allow the moonlight to filter through the sheer curtains beneath, Cleo then pulled a chair over to the window and sat down, placing her feet on the bottom cushion as she hugged her knees to her chest.

No, she hadn't known what to expect when she'd met Mr. Roarke today, but she certainly hadn't anticipated her reaction to him. She had long since passed the age of being a silly romantic and she'd never considered herself a very sexual creature. So why had every feminine instinct within her come to full alert the moment he'd touched her? Falling for the man she married wasn't part of her plan.

But how on earth could any woman be immune to a man like Simon Roarke?

"I don't know," she answered herself aloud, her voice a whisper. "But, Cleo, my girl, if you want to come out of this marriage with your heart intact, you'd better find a way."

"Do you, Simon Alloway Roarke, take this woman to be your lawfully wedded wife?"

Simon listened to the Alabama judge's words, reciting the marriage vows and making the appropriate responses when called upon to speak. Not long after he'd taken Cleo McNamara's hand in his, a soothing numbness had claimed him. Thankfully the event, being a civil ceremony, wouldn't last very long. He didn't think he could have endured anything elaborate. Lucky for him, Cleo was a sensible woman, not one for turning their wedding into a major production.

Of course, once they arrived at her home, they would have to begin acting the parts of madly-in-love newlyweds.

"My family may suspect the truth—that I bought and paid for you," Cleo said. "But I will not give them the satisfaction of knowing for sure. Whenever we're around others, I expect you to pretend to be in love with me. Aunt Beatrice has told the family that you used to date a college friend of mine, that you and I were acquainted years ago. And when we met again, by chance, while Aunt Beatrice and I were on our Atlanta shopping trip, you and I found ourselves attracted to each other. You simply swept me off my feet in a whirlwind courtship."

Roarke wasn't too sure how sharp his acting skills were, but he'd give it his best shot. After all, Cleo was paying him for his services, and it wouldn't exactly be a hardship to fake affection for a woman as appealing as Cleo.

"And do you, Cleopatra Arabelle McNamara, take this man to be your lawfully wedded husband?" the judge asked.

"I do," she said clearly in her deep, raspy voice that Roarke thought was very sexy.

Cleo and Roarke exchanged the simple gold bands she had purchased at the local jewelry store in River Bend earlier that day. He made sure he didn't hold her hand longer than was necessary.

Remembering a first wedding on the day of a second wedding might be only natural, but Roarke refused to allow himself to remember anything about his first wedding. It would be unfair to Cleo to compare her with Hope. And it would be unfair to him to have to recall the circumstances that had led to the demise of his former marriage.

Simon didn't look at his new bride. He hadn't made eye contact with her at all. What was the point? They both knew why they were there and what they had to do. This was a business arrangement, one that would benefit them both.

All the legal documents had been signed beforehand. The equivalent of one year's salary plus a nice bonus had been deposited in a bank account in Simon's name and Cleo had agreed to a million-dollar divorce settlement once he had successfully fulfilled his part of their bargain.

And that was the reason he was going through with this farce—for the money. If he was ever going to free himself from a life of danger and violence and still continue to meet his obligations to Hope, he needed money. A lot of money.

Cleo McNamara had offered him a small fortune to marry her—and to keep her safe. In the weeks, possibly months, ahead he would be not only her husband, but her bodyguard. Being her bodyguard, no matter how difficult, would be the easy part. Being her husband would be a complicated situation. But he could handle it. He could handle just about anything if it meant making sure Hope would be taken care of for the rest of her life. The most difficult part of the bargain would be dealing with Cleo's pregnancy. No matter how painful it would be for him, he could force himself to father Cleo's child—as long as he never saw the child, never became a part of its life, never allowed himself to love it.

He and Cleo were virtual strangers, having met only three days ago. But now they were man and wife. Legally bound in an unholy alliance. He had married her for money. She had married him for control of her family's business. No matter what the mitigating circumstances, no matter who else would benefit from their marriage, they had gone into this most sacred union without an ounce of love or commitment between them.

He kept reminding himself that Cleo wasn't his type, but he couldn't deny that she was attractive. Slender. Elegant. Cool. Controlled. Bossy and independent. It hadn't taken him long to size her up and decide that he liked her. But there wasn't much chance of her stealing his heart. Hell, he wasn't sure he even had a heart anymore.

His lips twitched slightly, but he didn't smile. He was no longer very susceptible to women in general. Once, he had preferred his women soft, warm, sweet and needy. Hope had been like that. But he had learned his lesson—learned it the hard way. Now he steered clear of emotional entanglements.

He didn't love anyone, and he never would love anyone. Not ever again.

But he had to admit that a part of him was intrigued by the challenge of melting the ice princess, of finding out if there was any fire inside Cleo.

"You may kiss your bride," the judge said.

Roarke looked at Cleo then, and for just a split second her expression was soft, almost tender. He noticed a damp glaze covering her moss-green eyes. Tears? Surely this steel magnolia wasn't crying.

"Well, Boss Lady, do you want a kiss?" Roarke asked, looking down, staring directly at her and determined to start this marriage off on the right foot. He reminded himself that this was strictly a business arrangement and she was his employer.

Cleo's expression hardened instantly. Taking a deep breath, she closed her eyes, then opened them to face him with a chilly glare.

"That won't be necessary." She pulled her hand out of his loose hold. "There are only three things this job requires of you, Roarke, and kissing me isn't a mandatory part of any of them."

"Well, I can see where marrying you and protecting you don't necessarily require kissing, but I'm afraid playing the part of your lovesick husband *will* require a few kisses. And getting you pregnant is definitely going to require more than a handshake."

The judge coughed several times and then cleared his throat. Cleo glared at Roarke. He met her glare head-on, neither flinching nor smiling.

Roarke had to continue thinking of getting her pregnant as just part of his job. He would never allow himself to think of the child as his. The baby would be Cleo's— Cleo's alone—from the moment of conception. Things had to be that way. Otherwise, he'd never be able to go through with their deal.

He took a good, hard look at the woman he had just married. Even on her wedding day, she wore a simple navy blue suit with a cream silk blouse. No frills. Not even a bouquet or corsage. She had dressed as if this were a business merger, not a wedding.

The fact that she had taken no pains to make herself feminine and alluring, hadn't bothered with flowers, music or even a little dab of perfume, made Roarke want all the more for her to act like a woman, a bride—his bride. Dammit, how could any female not wear something lace or satin on her wedding day? How could she not at least pin a rose on her lapel? And why the hell wouldn't she want to be kissed?

Maybe she did, he thought. Maybe she was just too proud to ask.

Before Cleo had a chance to object, Roarke slid his arm around her tiny waist and drew her up against him. Gasping, she gazed up at him, her cheeks coloring slightly.

"What—" She started to question his actions.

Quickly lifting her off her feet, he leaned over to meet her open mouth, capturing it in a kiss that left her breathless and shocked. When she jerked her head back, trying to end the kiss, Roarke deepened his attack, thrusting his tongue inside. She struggled momentarily, then melted into him, her lips softening, her moist warmth accepting him.

When he felt himself growing hard, Roarke slowed his pace. Tracing her lips with the tip of his tongue, he looked into her eyes and saw desire. And something more.

Good Lord, what had he done? The last thing he wanted was for this woman to care about him, and he figured that Cleo was the kind of woman who'd tie lust and love together in one neat little package.

"Why did you do that, after I'd expressly told you it wasn't necessary?" she demanded.

Roarke set her on her feet, then clutched her chin, tilting it upward so that she was looking directly at him.

"Every bride should be kissed on her wedding day, Mrs. Roarke, and every groom should have the pleasure."

"Oh" was all she said before pulling away from him.

Dammit all, he had desperately wanted to kiss her. He'd warned himself not to give in to the temptation, to his need to discover just how deep Cleo's frigid, controlled exterior went.

Well, he had just found out. His wife's icy facade was only skin-deep. Buried just below the surface was a volcano of passion waiting to explode. And heaven help him, he was glad that he was the man who was going to set off that explosion.

CHAPTER TWO

THE IRON GATES swung open, admitting Cleo's sleek, green Jaguar. Roarke could barely see the Steadman-McNamara house from the road. Cleo had told him that Jefferson Steadman, Aunt Beatrice's maternal grandfather, had built the country manor house around the turn of the century.

"How many acres have y'all got here?" Roarke asked, taking note of the vast, well-manicured green lawn, the huge, old trees that lined the driveway and the wooded areas in the distance.

"Three hundred and fifty acres," Cleo replied. "At one time this place was a working farm. We still have the fruit orchards, and Pearl cans and freezes a great deal of the harvest each year."

Three hundred and fifty acres. Not enormous, but large in comparison with the sixty-acre farm he'd grown up on in Tennessee. He had hated the way his overbearing, religiously fanatical aunt and uncle had treated him—like an indentured servant. But he had loved the land, the animals, the clean air and sunshine. That's what he missed, what he wanted again someday. Just a small place where he could raise a crop or two and keep a few chickens and horses and some cattle. He might even buy himself a dog. When he was a kid, he'd wanted a dog.

"Brace yourself," Cleo said. "We're almost there."

A two-story portico added a certain grandeur to the facade of the old manor house. Glistening white in the afternoon sunshine, the home boasted three stories, neat black shutters and four brick chimneys.

Roarke let out a long, low whistle. "This is mighty fancy digs for an old country boy like me."

Glancing at the man sitting beside her, Cleo noted the way he rested in the leather seat. His big, long body lounged in a half sitting, half lying position.

A quivering sensation hit Cleo's stomach. She quickly returned her attention to the driveway ahead of her. Just because Simon Roarke was devastatingly masculine didn't mean she had to overreact to the mere sight of him. If she allowed her hormones to dictate her actions every time she was around him, she'd be a nervous wreck by the end of the week.

"Do you really still consider yourself a country boy?" Cleo asked, remembering that Roarke's personal history stated that he'd been born in Chattanooga, but had grown up on a farm outside Lawrenceburg, Tennessee. "After a career in the Special Forces and having lived in Atlanta for several years, I don't see how you can think of yourself as a country boy."

"You know the old saying." Roarke scooted his massive frame up in the seat and spread one long arm out above Cleo's shoulders.

When she widened her eyes in a quizzical expression, he grinned. "'You can take the boy out of the country,'" he said.

"'But you can't take the country out of the boy.'" Smiling, she completed the sentence for him.

Cleo had a nice smile, Roarke realized. Warm, genuine and sort of sexy. Her wide mouth parted at a slightly crooked angle, curving the left side up more than the right. Her full, pink lips were moist and very inviting. Roarke's body tightened. Groaning silently, he warned himself to concentrate on something other than Cleo's luscious mouth.

"One of the reasons I took this job as your hired husband is so I can buy myself a little farm somewhere and retire."

"Thirty-nine is a bit young to retire, isn't it?" Cleo asked.

"Not from my line of business," he told her.

"Yes, I suppose you're right. I can't begin to imagine the things you've seen, what all you must have endured, the types of people you've met."

Yeah, he'd probably seen just about everything, experienced nightmares other people never even knew about. He wondered what Cleo would think if he told her that neither the horrors of being a professional soldier nor the dangers he faced in the private security business could compare with the never-ending hell a man lived in when he felt responsible for the death of his only child.

"Let's just say my life has been nothing like yours, Boss Lady."

"I wish you'd stop calling me that!"

"I'll be careful not to use the term around your family." He gave her shoulder a reassuring squeeze.

Suddenly realizing this homecoming was going to be a worse fiasco than she'd thought, Cleo groaned as they drove up to the house. The whole clan waited on the veranda, like a group of overeager fans prepared to pounce on their favorite rock star.

Smiling warmly and waving enthusiastically, Aunt Beatrice stood at the top of the steps. Several feet behind Beatrice, Oralie and Perry waited in front of the double doors. As always, Aunt Oralie, in her flowing silk dress and her thirty-inch pearls, looked the part of an aging Southern belle. She gazed at the approaching couple with cool, calculating hazel eyes, but put on a proper smile of welcome. Uncle Perry possessed a good poker player's face. One never quite knew what was going on behind his faded brown eyes.

Cleo pulled her Jaguar to a slow, smooth halt. Aunt Beatrice rushed down the front steps. Laughing giddily, she clapped her hands. "Congratulations, children, and welcome home."

Gripping the steering wheel, Cleo took a deep breath and willed herself to stay calm. If she was going to make this charade work, she could not allow anyone to suspect that she wasn't a deliriously happy bride.

"I thought you said you told your family that you didn't want any fuss made." Roarke surveyed the group of people hovering about on the porch.

The older couple had to be Oralie and Perry Sutton. Roarke thought that the woman's smile was too strained to be genuine, and he wondered what secrets lay hidden behind Sutton's unemotional demeanor.

The couple half-hidden behind one of the white columns were probably Trey Sutton and his wife, Marla. Young Sutton resembled his father a great deal, but he was a good three inches shorter. His wife looked very young and perhaps a bit too wholesome for this group of wealthy snobs.

"Knowing Aunt Beatrice the way I do, I imagine she's planned some sort of celebration." Releasing her tenacious hold on the steering wheel, Cleo turned to her husband of less than an hour. "I'll forewarn you. They're going to be suspicious and will probably ask far too many personal questions. My cousin Daphne will, no doubt, flirt outrageously with you today. And sooner or later, she'll invite you into her bed."

"I assume you would prefer that I didn't accept her invitation."

Cleo glared at Roarke, her dark green eyes glowing hotly. "You assume correctly. That is one advantage of your being my *hired* husband. You're my employee, and if you want to get paid, you follow my orders."

"I take it that your cousin Daphne isn't one of your favorite people," Roarke said. "Does that mean we should put her at the top of our list of suspects?"

"Other than Aunt Beatrice, all my relatives should be on our suspect list." Cleo opened the car door and stepped out, then plastered on a phony smile and turned to face her family.

Aunt Beatrice met Roarke the moment he emerged from the Jaguar. She slipped her arm round his waist and gave him an affectionate hug. "So wonderful to see you again, Simon, my dear boy."

Roarke's gaze swept the veranda and stopped on the tall, bosomy brunette who had slunk out from behind a white column. She had to be Daphne. Exotic. Sultry. Seductive. He'd known women like her before. And they were all pure poison.

Daphne's mouth curved into a mocking smile when her gaze met Roarke's. She licked her red lips. Roarke grinned.

When Cleo rounded the Jaguar's hood, Beatrice reached out, motioning her niece toward her. "Come, Cleo, everyone's waiting. They're all simply astonished by your whirlwind romance and marriage." Slipping her other arm around Cleo's waist, Beatrice whispered, "Oralie and Daphne have asked me a million questions, and Trey is fit to be tied. You're going to have to put on a good show to convince this—" Beatrice nodded toward the veranda "—skeptical audience."

Bending to reach Beatrice's cheek, Roarke kissed his bride's aunt, who blushed and giggled. "You leave everything to me," he told her.

Without warning, Roarke swept his wife up in his arms. Gasping, Cleo flung her arm around his neck and glared into his smiling face.

"What are you doing?" she murmured.

He nuzzled her neck. Cleo squirmed. His nose glided underneath her hair and circled her ear. Cleo swallowed hard.

"I'm convincing your family that you and I are madly-in-love newlyweds," he said.

"Don't you think we could find a less dramatic way of doing that?"

"Don't frown, Boss Lady. All those people waiting on the veranda are going to wonder why you look unhappy on your wedding day."

"Oh, all right. Proceed." She forced her phony smile back in place as Roarke turned around and walked toward the house. Aunt Beatrice, all smiles and fluttering hands, followed the couple.

When he put his foot on the first step, Roarke whispered to Cleo, "I'm warning you so that you'll be prepared. I'm going to move my hand down from your waist to your hip, then I'm going to caress you. And when we get to the top of these steps, I'm going to kiss you."

"Roarke, I—" The moment she felt his big hand gripping her hip, Cleo stiffened.

Her whole body tingled from his caressing touch. Relaxing, she gave herself over to these moments of sweet pretending. Almost unaware of her actions, she turned just enough to press her left breast against Roarke's hard chest and glided her fingers up his neck and into his thick, dark hair.

If only this were real, she thought. If only we were in love and wildly happy and unable to keep our hands off each other. If only this marriage *were* real and not a farce.

True to his word, the moment he reached the top of the stairs, Roarke took Cleo's mouth in a tongue-thrusting kiss that left her flushed, breathless and trembling.

For a split second, Roarke felt stunned himself and not quite in control. He had expected Cleo's acquiescence, but not her wholehearted cooperation. She had returned his kiss eagerly, her mouth opening in a warm, moist invitation, her tongue mating savagely with his.

He looked directly into her eyes—compelling green cat eyes—and saw a reflection of his own desire.

"You two might want to save that for later," a soft, saccharine, feminine voice said. "Right now, we have a little party waiting inside for the bride and groom."

Still slightly disoriented and sexually aroused, Cleo stared at her cousin. She focused on Daphne's moist, red lips, which were curved into a mocking smile. Daphne glared at Cleo, then turned to Roarke, and her expression changed. She sent him an invitation with her notorious come-hither look.

Cleo stiffened in Roarke's arms. She tightened her hold around his neck and glanced at her husband, who was surveying Daphne from head to toe. When he grinned at Daphne, Cleo wanted to scratch his eyes out. Dammit, wasn't there a man on earth immune to her sultry cousin?

Threading his big fingers through Cleo's short hair, Roarke pulled her face toward his. She quivered when his mouth touched her ear.

"If you laugh and then look longingly into my eyes, she'll wonder if I told you something about her," Roarke said.

As though on cue, Cleo smiled, then laughed and gazed

at Roarke as if he were the only man in the world. In her peripheral vision, Cleo noticed the smile on Daphne's face vanish, quickly replaced by a sullen frown.

Still carrying Cleo, Roarke headed straight for the double entrance doors. A tall, skinny, gray-haired man, wearing faded, patched work clothes, hurried ahead of them and opened the leaded-glass doors, then stood back and nodded a greeting.

"Oh, hello, Ezra," Cleo said. "Ezra, this is my husband, Simon Roarke. And this—" she smiled warmly at the old man "—is Ezra Clooney. He's worked here on the estate since before I was born."

"Nice to meet you, Mr. Roarke," Ezra said. "We're sure glad to see Miss Cleo got herself a husband."

"I'm glad that I'm the man she chose for a husband." Roarke carried his bride over the threshold and into the enormous foyer, where a sparkling crystal chandelier lit a hallway decorated with Persian rugs and antique furniture.

Once inside, he put Cleo on her feet, but kept his arm around her waist, securing her to his side. Beatrice McNamara scurried into the house behind them, followed by the other family members.

"Come on into the dining room," Beatrice said. "I have a little surprise for y'all."

"Heaven help us," Cleo moaned.

"Let's go see what Aunt Beatrice has done for us, darling." Following Beatrice's lead, Roarke led Cleo down the hallway and into the dining room.

A string quartet, set up in a corner in front of the Hepplewhite breakfront, played a Tchaikovsky composition. A classically romantic piece of angelic sweetness.

Cleo closed her eyes and said a silent prayer for the strength to see her through this ordeal. Wasn't it bad enough that she'd had little choice but to marry a stranger? Did she have to go through the motions of celebrating a marriage that was destined to end in divorce?

An enormous wedding cake awaited them in the center of the Sheraton dining table that was obviously large enough to accommodate a good two dozen persons or more. The four-foot cake was traditional in style, with a bride and groom perched on the top layer. Several bottles of champagne were waiting to be opened and a small feast had been placed on the sideboard. A variety of floral arrangements filled the room with a sweet, springtime aroma.

"This is lovely, Aunt Beatrice. Thank you," Cleo said, all the while wishing she and Roarke could escape upstairs to her suite and not have to endure this phony celebration. But it was her own fault, really, for letting her pride get in the way. Maybe she shouldn't have insisted on playing out this little drama with Roarke as her devoted lover.

Roarke glanced around at the assembled guests and discovered one person whose identity he couldn't discern. A blond man with a thin mustache. Somewhere in his mid-thirties. A three-piece-suit type. A slick, cultured pretty boy.

"Perry, you must do the honors as man of the house, now that Uncle George is no longer with us." Oralie Sutton slipped her arm through her husband's.

Perry Sutton opened the first bottle of champagne and filled flutes for everyone, then lifted his glass for a toast.

"To Cleo and her husband," Perry said. "We wish them every happiness."

There were several murmurs of "To Cleo" from among the small crowd.

Aunt Beatrice practically shouted, "Happiness to Cleo and Simon."

One by one, Cleo's family gathered around the table, waiting for the bride and groom to cut their wedding cake.

Slipping his arms around Cleo, Roarke placed the silver knife in her hands, then covered her hands with his, and together, they sliced the first piece of cake.

"You must feed it to each other." Beatrice's eyes glistened with unshed tears. "And I'll freeze the top layer for y'all to share on your first anniversary."

Of all the silly things for her aunt to have said, Cleo thought, when Beatrice knew good and well that there was no chance she and Roarke would celebrate their first anniversary. As soon as the identity of the would-be killer was discovered and Cleo was pregnant, Roarke's job would be completed.

Continuing their charade of being happy newlyweds, Cleo put a piece of cake up to Roarke's mouth and he bit into the delectable concoction. Without thinking, she lifted her hand to the side of his mouth and wiped away a smudge of frosting. Realizing what she'd done, Cleo stared into Roarke's sky-blue eyes—eyes that were smiling at her. He grasped her hand, brought it to his mouth and slid her finger between his lips, licking off the frosting. Cleo shivered. Her mouth gaped. She sucked in a deep breath.

For the next hour and a half, Roarke and Cleo gave award-winning performances. All the while Cleo prayed for deliverance, Roarke observed the group of suspects. And that's how he thought of Cleo's family. As suspects. After all, one of them had already tried to kill her.

He wasn't sure what lay at the root of Cleo and Daphne's problem, but even to an untrained eye, the animosity Daphne felt for her cousin was obvious. Roarke's gut instincts told him that a man was involved somehow. He couldn't help wondering if that man wasn't the pretty boy, whom he'd found out was a lawyer named Hugh Winfield, the son of the head of the law firm that handled all of the McNamaras' personal and business concerns.

Daphne had kept herself draped around Winfield like a vine around a trellis. But the odd thing was that Cleo seemed totally unconcerned. Maybe Winfield wasn't the man.

Cleo leaned over and whispered to Roarke. "I can't take much more of this. My feet are hurting. I've got a killer headache, and if I have to keep smiling this way much longer, my face is going to crack."

"Would you like for me to swoop you up in my arms and carry you upstairs?"

"No! I think we've put on enough of a show for one day," Cleo said. "Why don't you see how many more of Trey's and Aunt Oralie's questions you can answer, while I run out to the kitchen and ask Pearl to bring our supper upstairs to my suite? I think everyone will understand that we want to be alone on our wedding night."

"Do you suppose Pearl could round up some beer for me? I'm not much of a wine drinker."

"If necessary, I'll have her send Ezra into town to buy some. Any particular brand?"

"Anything domestic will do." Roarke grinned.

When Cleo started to walk away, he grabbed her wrist and pulled her up against his chest, then kissed her. "Don't be long, darling," he said loud enough for everyone to hear.

The moment Cleo exited the room, Trey Sutton, dragging his thin, blond wife with him, approached Roarke on one side, while Oralie Sutton closed in on him from the opposite side. Across the room, Daphne ran the tips of her long, red nails up and down Hugh Winfield's chest while she stared provocatively at Roarke.

"So, you knew Cleo when she was in college?" Trey asked. "Surely you weren't a student, too."

"No, I wasn't a student," Roarke replied.

"How did the two of you meet?" Oralie smiled ever so sweetly as she played with her cultured pearls.

"Mr. Roarke was dating a friend of Cleo's, Mother," Trey said derisively, his hazel-brown eyes twinkling with humor. "Don't you remember Aunt Beatrice telling us the whole story? Cleo and Mr. Roarke were attracted to each other years ago, but didn't pursue a relationship because he was dating a friend of hers."

"Oh, yes, of course." Oralie patted her son's arm affectionately. "But then, Beatrice is such a romantic little creature and prone to…well, shall we say…fantasies."

Oralie's mocking chuckle got on Roarke's nerves far more than Trey's unmannerly inspection. What the hell was the guy doing—measuring him for a suit or a coffin? From the short time he'd been around Cleo's family, Roarke already knew one thing. He didn't like any of them. With the exception of Beatrice.

"I'd love to hear your version of this wild, whirlwind courtship." Daphne sauntered across the room, her long, curly black hair swaying with each movement of her broad shoulders. "I've never thought of Cleo as the type who could inspire such hot passion in a man. Especially a man like you."

Oralie's cheeks flushed. She cleared her throat. "Daphne! What a vulgar thing to say."

"Was I being vulgar, Mr. Roarke?" Daphne brushed by Marla Sutton, who clung to her husband's arm, her eyes wide with wonder and her mouth slightly parted.

Slipping her arm through Roarke's, Daphne manacled his wrist. She scratched his skin just above his wristwatch.

He grasped her hand, holding it tightly, then tilted his head downward enough so that he could whisper in her ear.

"I find everything about you vulgar, Ms. Sutton." He spoke so low only Daphne could hear him. "Especially the way you're coming on to me." He jerked her hand away from his wrist and smiled when he saw the look of disbelief on her face.

Roarke stepped back, away from the smothering bodies and the prying eyes. He saw Aunt Beatrice looking forlornly at him from across the room where she stood beside Perry Sutton. With her eyes, she pleaded with him to continue the charade, to consider Cleo's pride before speaking.

"I think we should get a few things straight. Up front," Roarke said.

Aunt Beatrice's mouth opened on a silent gasp. Her green eyes widened in fear. She took several hesitant steps in Roarke's direction.

"I'm a private man and I don't think the details of my relationship with Cleo are any of your business. But since y'all are her *family*—" he practically snarled the word "—and know all about Uncle George's will, then I should tell you that Cleo and I rushed into this marriage so that she could fulfill the stipulations of that will."

Beatrice gasped. Tears glazed her eyes. Oralie nodded, a self-satisfied smile on her face. Trey laughed aloud.

"I knew it!" Daphne stared at Roarke.

"Oh, you misunderstand, Cousin Daphne," Roarke said. "If it hadn't been for Uncle George's will, Cleo and I would have had a chance for a longer courtship, but the end results would have been the same."

"What do you mean?" Trey asked.

"Cleo and I would have married. We just wouldn't have been in such a hurry. You see, I've been waiting all my life for a woman like Cleo." Roarke glanced at Daphne. "I'm damn lucky she agreed to marry me."

Silence hung heavily in the room, like a rain-filled cloud on the verge of explosion. Roarke scanned the room, quickly taking note of each person. Seeing Beatrice's bosom heave with a sigh of relief. Catching the little secret glance between Trey and Daphne. Observing the tightening of Hugh Winfield's soft jaw. Noting Marla's nervousness. Detecting Oralie's vaguely disguised anger. And recognizing Perry's unemotional demeanor for what it was—a habitual mask he used to hide behind.

"While I have y'all's undivided attention, I might as well go ahead and make something else perfectly clear," Roarke said.

A communal hush filled the air, as if everyone had taken a deep breath and were waiting for his revelation before exhaling.

"I know that someone in this family took a shot at Cleo right after her uncle's funeral. Let me warn you. If you're smart, you won't ever try to harm my wife again. Because if you do, when I catch you—and I will catch you—you're mine."

"How dare you accuse one of us of wanting to harm Cleo!" Oralie said.

"Just who do you think you are, coming in here, making threats like that?" Trey lifted his chin defiantly, but made no move to shorten the distance between himself and Roarke.

"I'm Cleo's husband." He crossed his arms over his broad chest, stretching the material of his dark blue suit taut over his wide shoulders. "And in case anyone doubts that I'm capable of backing up my promise of retaliation, I think you should know that I spent over a dozen years in the Special Forces. I know a hundred and one different ways to kill a person."

Oralie and Beatrice gasped in unison. Marla cried out. Trey, his face ashen, instinctively stepped backward. Daphne licked her lips. Perry remained silent.

"Now, if y'all will excuse me, I'll go out in the kitchen and find Cleo. We would appreciate not being disturbed tonight."

When Roarke exited the room, he paused briefly in the hallway, trying to discern where the kitchen might be. Hugh Winfield's voice rang out loud and clear.

"I'll speak to Father about what can be done legally to rectify the situation. Surely once I tell him about this man he'll be more forthcoming with information about Cleo's personal legal matters. And I'll run a check on Simon Roarke immediately."

Roarke grinned. *Yeah, you do that. Unless you've got some powerful friends, you'll never get any information on me. My army files won't be available, and Dane Carmichael will make sure you learn only what I want you to know.*

He heard Aunt Beatrice making angry, mother-hen sounds about respecting Cleo's marriage, but he didn't hang around to listen to anything else.

The kitchen had to be on the first floor somewhere. It was just a matter of opening a few doors. Suddenly, he wanted to whisk Cleo away from all the madness downstairs, away from her suspicious, uncaring family. Part of his job as Cleo's hired husband was to act as her bodyguard, to protect her from harm. And he intended to do just that. But after meeting her relatives, Roarke wanted to do more than simply protect her physically. He wanted to protect her emotionally. His gut instincts warned him that Cleo's kindred felt very little love for her.

If Roarke had his way, that bunch of vultures would never get their claws into Cleo again. They would never rip her apart and leave her bleeding. In the weeks to come, he would do everything in his power to take care of Cleo and keep her safe.

But what he intended to do right now was find his wife, take her upstairs and enjoy his wedding night.

CHAPTER THREE

"WHY DIDN'T YOU come out and meet my husband?" Cleo watched Pearl while the housekeeper hand-washed the pots and pans she had used in preparing the upcoming evening meal.

Other than Aunt Beatrice, Cleo supposed she loved Pearl better than anyone else in the world. Pearl had been Cleo's true friend for as long as she could remember.

"I don't approve of this hasty marriage of yours." Pearl kept her back to Cleo. "No matter what you or anyone else tries to tell me, I know why you married that man."

So, that was how it was, Cleo thought. Pearl had never been one to mince words, to keep her true feelings to herself. Uncle George had relished his and Pearl's heated disagreements over everything from politics to religion. Pearl came from a long line of Southern Baptist conservatives and would fight to the death for her convictions.

Taking one tentative step at a time, Cleo made her way across the polished wooden floor, past the tile-topped center island and toward the row of daffodil-yellow cabinets.

"And just why do you think I married Roarke?" Cleo halted a couple of feet behind Pearl.

"You married him because of your uncle George's will." Pearl placed the last pan in the drain board, wiped off her age-spotted hands on the large, white apron and turned to face Cleo. "You went and bought yourself a husband. That's what you did. You paid for a man to get you pregnant. And as soon as he does, you'll get yourself one of them quickie divorces."

"Is that what Aunt Beatrice told you?"

"Your aunt Bea said this Mr. Roarke swept you off your feet and the two of you were madly in love." Pearl frowned, turning the corners of her wide, thin lips downward and creating a row of wrinkles across her brow. Looking directly at Cleo, her sharp gray eyes narrowing, she shook her head and grunted. "Yep, that's what she told the rest of 'em, too, and they didn't believe her any more than I did."

"Don't you think I'm special enough that some man would fall madly in love with me and sweep me off my feet in a whirlwind romance?"

"Child, I doubt that the man's been born who's good enough for you." Swallowing her sentimental emotions, Pearl tilted her silvery white head to one side and surveyed Cleo from head to toe. "You deserve better than a bought husband. You deserve a man who'll worship the ground you walk on."

"Oh, Pearl!"

When Cleo threw her arms around the old woman's thick waist, Pearl wrapped Cleo in her embrace, stroking Cleo's hair as if she were a child.

"Your uncle George was a stubborn old fool to have written such nonsense in his will." Pearl wrapped her arm around Cleo's waist and led her over to the pine drop-leaf table. "He thought sure you'd marry Hugh Winfield. Had that boy all picked out for you, he did. I tried to tell him that old Hubert's son wasn't man enough for my Cleo Belle. I told him, one morning when he was sitting at this very table…I said to him, a Thoroughbred filly like our Cleo needs her a rogue stallion, not some 'lead him around by the nose' gelding."

Pearl's comment made Cleo smile, not just because she had fairly accurately described Hugh Winfield and Simon Roarke, but because her comparing people to animals reminded Cleo of the game she and Pearl had been playing since she was a small child.

"I'm sure if Uncle George hadn't taken ill suddenly and been in the hospital when I found Hugh in Daphne's bed, he would have reconsidered the stipulations in his will." Cleo pulled out one of the maple splat-back chairs for Pearl, and after the housekeeper sat, Cleo pulled out another chair and joined her.

"Now, there's a pair for you." Pearl's round, fat face crinkled with tiny lines when she smiled. "Daphne and Hugh. I'd say those two deserve each other. A black widow spider and a cockroach."

Cleo burst into laughter, the action releasing all the bottled-up tension inside her. "And Trey is a weasel and poor little Marla is a timid mouse and—"

"Your aunt Oralie's been a snake all her life, and all the years they've been married, Perry Sutton's been a whipped dog. And dear Beatrice has always been a little lamb. Even now, and her sixty-three years old." Pearl reached across the table and took Cleo's hands in hers. "Mr. George was so afraid you'd end up an old maid like Bea. It near broke his heart that she never married and had children."

"Aunt Beatrice has no idea you told me about what happened all those years ago." Cleo squeezed Pearl's hands, then released them and took a deep breath.

"She was brokenhearted when she lost her man." Pearl shook her head sadly. "And the way it happened. Poor little lamb ain't never gotten over it. But thank the good Lord, you're made of tougher stuff. When that Emerson fellow up and eloped with Daphne, you didn't roll over and play dead for the next thirty years like Bea did."

Cleo needed Pearl's support as much as she needed her aunt Beatrice's. She realized she should have talked things over with Pearl before getting married, made the old woman understand the necessity of her drastic actions. But when Aunt Beatrice had suggested the idea of hiring a bodyguard who could also double as husband and potential father, Cleo hadn't been one hundred percent certain she would be able to go through with the plan. Only after a weeklong search and nearly two weeks of screening half a dozen contenders did Cleo decide she'd found the perfect man. Simon Alloway Roarke.

"Pearl?"

"What is it, Cleo Belle?"

"You can help make things a lot easier for me if you can accept my marriage to Roarke."

"What sort of man can this Roarke of yours be if he's willing to be bought and paid for? That's what I want to know."

"I'm sure he has his reasons for accepting my offer," Cleo said. "Can't you see that he's essential to me right now? You don't want McNamara Industries to be sold and half the employees to lose their jobs, do you?"

"No, of course I don't."

"And you want me to be protected against the person who tried to shoot me, don't you?"

"I suppose this Roarke fellow is a bodyguard as well as a hired husband."

"That's exactly what he is, Pearl. He's a former Green Beret and has worked for the past several years as a top agent for Dundee Private Security."

"You must be paying the man a small fortune for all his expertise." Pearl slapped her meaty hand down on the table. "I don't approve of divorce. You know that. But… well…all things considered, I'm willing to hold off making a final judgment until after I get to know this Simon Roarke of yours."

Cleo let out a sigh of relief. "You'll go along with our little charade, then? You'll accept Roarke as my husband and cooperate with us?"

"I won't let on like I know a thing," Pearl agreed. "But you've got to know that the whole bunch suspects something's fishy about your marriage to a man none of them ever heard of before yesterday."

"It doesn't matter what they suspect, as long as they don't know for sure."

"You'd have been better off to have told them the truth—what you did and why. And that if they didn't like it, that was just too bad. Wasn't no need for you to go letting your pride get in the way of the truth." Pearl reached out and tenderly caressed Cleo's cheek. "It's Miss Daphne you don't want knowing that you had to hire yourself a husband, ain't it?"

"I could lie and say that I don't care what Daphne thinks, but—"

"But you're human and you do care."

Smiling sadly at Pearl, Cleo shoved back her chair and stood. "The agency Roarke works for not only provides security, in my case a highly trained bodyguard, but it also does investigative work. While my new husband is protecting me, he's also going to work on discovering the identity of the person who tried to kill me."

"I know there's little real love lost between that bunch of vipers and you, but it's hard for me to believe that one of them is capable of murder," Pearl said.

The kitchen door swung open. Cleo and Pearl turned abruptly to see who might have overheard their conversation. Pearl's eyes narrowed to a squint as she observed their intruder.

Smiling warmly, Cleo crossed the kitchen. She rushed over to her husband and took his arm. "Come meet Pearl. She's been running this house since before I was born."

Roarke allowed Cleo to lead him over to where the plump, elderly woman was rising out of her chair.

"Pearl, this is Simon Roarke. My husband." Cleo waited for the housekeeper to say something, but when Pearl kept staring at Roarke, obviously evaluating every inch of him, Cleo cleared her throat. "Roarke, this is my dearest and oldest friend, Pearl Clooney, Ezra's wife and our house-keeper for the past forty years."

"Nice to meet you, Mrs. Clooney." Roarke held out his hand in greeting.

She tilted her head, then grunted and smacked her lips. "Call me 'Pearl.'" She didn't accept his outstretched hand.

"Yes, ma'am."

"You're going to take good care of my Cleo Belle?" Pearl's words were part statement and part question.

Realizing the old woman wasn't going to shake his hand, Roarke withdrew it, then slipped his arm around his wife's waist and drew her up against him. "Yes, ma'am, I plan to take good care of Cleo."

Letting her gaze travel from Roarke's intense blue eyes to the tips of his size-twelve shoes, Pearl pursed her lips and then grunted again. "Yep, I do believe you just might be man enough, all right."

Shaking her head, Cleo rolled her eyes heavenward. Roarke grinned.

"You two escaped your own wedding reception, huh?" Pearl asked. "Can't say I blame you. A little of that bunch goes a long way."

"We're planning to go upstairs and stay there," Cleo

said. "Do you suppose you can serve our dinner in my room?"

"Getting an early start on your wedding night?" Pearl looked directly at Roarke.

"Yes, ma'am. You understand how it is with newly-weds," he said.

"I'll bring supper up around six," Pearl said. "That should give you time to unpack. Ezra done took your bags upstairs."

"Roarke likes beer," Cleo said. "Do we have any?"

"Ezra's got some." The corners of Pearl's mouth lifted in an almost smile. "You let me know what else your man likes to eat and drink, and I'll be sure to pick it up at the grocery store."

Cleo pulled away from Roarke, gave Pearl a big, loving hug, then turned back to her husband. Arm in arm, they walked across the room and opened the door.

Pearl called out to them, "A wife should use her husband's Christian name. If she doesn't, people wonder why." With that said, the housekeeper turned her back to them and busied herself by checking the apple pie in the oven.

Neither Cleo nor Roarke replied. They looked at each other and smiled.

"She's right," Cleo said. "I've got to stop calling you 'Roarke.' It's just that somehow I don't think of you as Simon."

It had been a long time since anyone had called him "Simon." He preferred to be called "Roarke," even by the women he dated. Using his last name was more impersonal. And that's the way he liked his relationships. Impersonal.

Roarke led her out into the narrow hallway between the kitchen and the sunroom. "Maybe it would be easier for you to call me 'honey' or 'darling' or something like that instead of forcing yourself to call me 'Simon.'"

"No, I'll call you 'Simon.' I suppose this is just the first in a long line of concessions I'll have to make while we're married."

"We're both going to have to make some concessions for the duration of our marriage," Roarke said. "After I unpack and we settle in upstairs, I think it would be a good idea for us to discuss setting up some ground rules. Each of us needs to know exactly where we stand, so that we can present a united front to your family and to your employees."

Roarke followed Cleo up the back staircase. "Pretending to be happily married isn't going to be easy, is it? Maybe Pearl was right. Maybe I should have been totally up front with everyone. Just told them that I hired you."

"I overheard you admitting to Pearl that it matters to you what your cousin Daphne thinks," he said. "And I have a hunch that it matters to you what your employees think. You'd prefer for people to speculate about our marriage than to pity you for having no choice but to buy yourself a man."

Directly in front of the door leading to her suite, Cleo whirled around to face Roarke. "I did not have to buy myself a husband. I know at least half a dozen men who would have jumped at the chance to marry me. I chose to hire you because none of the men I know had your particular skills. I need someone who can protect me and unearth my would-be killer."

"I didn't mean to imply that you couldn't attract a man, my dear Ms....pardon me...my dear Mrs. Roarke."

"No matter whom I married, it would have been a business arrangement."

"Even if you'd married Hugh Winfield?"

"How do you know about Hugh?"

"I guessed right, then, didn't I?" Roarke's broad chest rumbled with laughter. "You and Daphne both wanted Fancy Pants Winfield, and your cousin won the prize."

"Hugh Winfield is no prize." Cleo opened the door to her suite. "Please come in and make yourself at home. We'll share these rooms for however long our marriage lasts."

She took a step forward, only to be swept up in Roarke's arms once again. When she glared at him, he only smiled.

"It's customary for the groom to carry the bride over the threshold."

"You did that downstairs," she reminded him.

"That was for your family's benefit," he said.

"Oh? And for whose benefit is this little show, Mr. Roarke?"

"It's for your benefit, Boss Lady. I thought it might help you get in the right mood for our wedding night."

Feeling the heat rise in her face, Cleo looked away from Roarke as he carried her through the open door. She should have said something to him earlier about not wanting to rush into having sex. Obviously, he intended to take that part of their marriage seriously. Of course she realized that she'd have to have sex with him sometime if she wanted to get pregnant. She'd considered asking him to go through an artificial insemination process, but had changed her mind. Everything about her marriage to this man was a charade and as impersonal as a relationship could be. She didn't want the process of creating a child to be a clinical, impersonal act. She wasn't quite sure why it mattered so much; it just did.

Roarke carried her across the room and deposited her in the middle of a mahogany spindle bed. Placing his knees on the quilt coverlet, he braced himself with both hands spread out beside her hips. Leaning forward, he kissed her. She pulled back and sucked in a deep breath.

As she scooted toward the headboard, he followed her, trapping her against the ornately carved wooden surface. "It's been a while since you've done this, hasn't it?" he asked.

"What?" Her eyes widened, the dark irises glistening like polished jade.

"Sex," he said, resting his body beside hers, his head against the headboard. "You haven't had sex in a long time. You're too skittish for an experienced woman. You act as if you're afraid of me." Laying his head on her shoulder, he cocked it to one side and looked up at her.

Every muscle in her body tensed at his accusation. Every nerve rioted, sending shock waves of embarrassment through her entire system. "Just because I'm not quite prepared to—to—"

"Jump my bones." Roarke chose the words for her.

"Okay. Just because I'm not quite prepared to jump your bones right this minute does not mean that it's been years since I've been intimate with a man. It simply means that I can't rush into having sex with a man who's a stranger to me."

Lifting his head off her shoulder, he shrugged. "You don't have to know a person to have sex with him. Believe me, you can have great sex with a perfect stranger."

"I'm sure you would know. But unlike you and, from what I understand, most men, sex for me isn't just some bodily function, it's—"

"A deep and profound emotional experience?"

"I do not appreciate your making fun of me. And I don't appreciate your implying that I'm practically a virgin!"

Uh-oh, Roarke thought. He certainly had pushed all her buttons, hadn't he? He had hoped that Cleo McNamara wouldn't turn out to be the type of woman who couldn't separate her physical needs from her emotional needs. But just as he had suspected, she was a romantic under that icy exterior.

He had no intention of becoming emotionally involved with this woman. He hadn't allowed himself to care about anyone, really care, since Laurie died. Loving others meant pain and suffering when you lost them. His divorce from Hope had made him cynical. His daughter's death had made him emotionally barren.

He didn't want Cleo to care about him, didn't want her confusing good sex with love. It would make things easier for him if she'd had a legion of lovers, men who had meant nothing to her. But no, just his luck, she had admitted to being inexperienced. Just how inexperienced was she? *Practically a virgin?* What did that mean?

His stomach did an evil flip-flop. Practically a virgin usually meant only one former lover. Winfield? No, Roarke thought. Not Winfield. Someone else. Someone a long time ago. Someone she had loved.

Roarke scooted to the edge of the bed and stood. "I'm sorry if I sounded like I was making fun of you. I wasn't. Not at all. I just thought that since I'm going to be your lover, it would be better for both of us if I knew it had been a while since you'd been with someone."

"All right. Yes, it has been a while…years," she admitted reluctantly, her gaze fixed on the carved back of the needlepoint-upholstered French chair that sat behind her desk at the foot of the bed. "Ten years. He was my fiancé." She swallowed, bit down on her bottom lip and crossed her arms, hugging herself about the waist. "A few weeks before we were to be married, he eloped with Daphne."

That would explain, in large part, the animosity between Cleo and Daphne. And it explained Cleo's cool, controlled attitude. Apparently, Daphne was no longer married to this man, whoever he was. What Roarke wondered was whether Cleo still loved him. Surely not. Not after ten years. But the hurt would still exist. And the awful humiliation.

He, perhaps better than anyone, knew that sometimes old wounds never healed. Not completely.

Roarke walked over to the French doors that led out to a balcony overlooking the backyard. Lined drapes in an expensive floral fabric hung on each side of the doors. He glanced down at the brick patio and the small flower garden. Off in the distance, he saw the orchard Cleo had told him about earlier in the day.

"Any man who'd dump you for Daphne is a fool." Roarke's voice was deep, calm and totally void of emotion. "You're better off without him."

"Yes, I know." She got out of bed, removed her navy heels and slipped into a pair of green satin house shoes.

When Roarke opened the French doors and stepped out onto the balcony, she followed him. "You've been with a lot of women, haven't you?" she asked.

He grasped the white wooden banister that circled the balcony and leaned over, looking straight down at the screened back porch. "Several."

"How many are several?" She stood directly behind him, a couple of feet away.

"I don't know. Half a dozen before I got married, then more after my divorce. Not very many in the past five or six years. If you're worried, don't be. I always practiced safe sex."

"Did you ever love anyone other than your wife?"

"Not really. A couple of heavy involvements before I got married. Kid stuff, really. Hormones, mostly." He couldn't remember the last time he'd spoken so openly, so honestly with anyone, least of all a woman. But Cleo had been honest with him, had shared probably the most painful and humiliating experience of her life. He owed her the truth. He'd answer her questions. As long as she didn't start probing into his marriage, asking about things he couldn't bear to remember.

"Simon?"

A sudden hot, searing pain hit him square in the gut. It was as if she had branded his name into his flesh. The women he'd known in the past fifteen years had called him "Roarke" or "honey" or "lover," if they'd called him anything at all.

Hope had called him "Simon." She still did, on the rare occasions that she recognized him when he visited her at the sanitarium.

"Yeah?" He'd have to get used to Cleo calling him "Simon." It was all part of the act. This was just a job, he reminded himself. When it was over, he would walk away and forget he'd ever known Cleo McNamara. Forget that he'd left her with his child growing inside her body.

"I can help you unpack, if you'd like," she said. "I'll empty a couple of drawers in the chest for you. And I have an enormous walk-in closet with plenty of room for your clothes."

"I travel pretty light." He turned slowly and faced her, thinking how very pretty his new wife looked in the fading early-evening sunlight. Her red hair shone like bronze silk. He had the sudden urge to reach out and pull her into his arms. "I've got two suits. The blue one I'm wearing and a black one. Some dress pants, a sport coat, a couple pair of jeans and a few shirts. Other than socks and underwear, that's about it."

"We'll have to get some new suits made for you," she

said. "Uncle George has a tailor in town that all the men in the family use."

"Tailor-made suits?" Roarke widened his eyes in mock surprise, lifting his dark, thick eyebrows in the process. "You really want me to look the part of your husband, huh?"

"Let's just call any new clothes you acquire during our marriage a bonus," Cleo said. "Besides, we'll have to find something for you to do at McNamara Industries to explain why you're going in to work with me every day and nosing around at the plant. You'll need to look like a successful businessman."

"I'll certainly live up to the image of a kept man, won't I? We're living in your family's mansion. You're buying me new clothes and giving me a job. What else? Are you giving me a car, too?"

"Would you prefer using my Jaguar or my Mercedes?" she asked. "I prefer the Jag, but if you'd rather drive the Mercedes, then I have no objections."

"We'll use the Jag," he said. "Since I doubt I'll be going anywhere without you, we'll just use your favorite vehicle."

"Maybe everyone will think we're so in love that we can't bear to be apart, not even for a few minutes."

Moving closer, he clutched her shoulders in his big hands. "Look, Cleo, I know this situation isn't easy for you. And I know you have the noblest of reasons for choosing this course of action. I intend to do whatever I can to make things as easy for you as possible, and if that means convincing the whole world that we're madly in love, so be it."

She laid her hands on his chest, intending to push him away. But once she touched him, she felt the warmth of his body, the steady beat of his heart. "Thank you…Simon."

"We need to discuss each member of your family." He released her shoulders, then grasped her hands, which lay on his chest. "The more information you can give me, the better. I'll have to find out everything about your aunt and uncle and cousins, including Trey's wife."

"Surely Marla isn't a suspect. She's harmless. She doesn't make a move without Trey's approval."

"Then she'd do whatever he asked her to do, even try to kill you."

"Everyone is a suspect?"

"Everyone, including Hugh Winfield." He clasped her hands tighter, pressing them against his chest.

"Hugh?" Cleo gazed directly into Roarke's eyes, and for one brief moment longed to stand on tiptoe and find his mouth with her lips.

"He's involved with Daphne, and if he marries her, her inheritance will be his, too."

Cleo was looking at him as if she wanted to be kissed. But he wouldn't kiss her. He was beginning to know this woman—his wife. Her eyes might be begging for him, but she would deny their hunger if he attempted to give her what she wanted.

"Aunt Beatrice is above suspicion, and Pearl and Ezra, too, I hope."

"Probably. I don't think Beatrice would have suggested bringing in a bodyguard who could fulfill the stipulations in her father's will if she wanted you dead. And I don't see that either Pearl or her husband has a motive."

Cleo had to get away from Roarke—Simon—before she embarrassed herself. She couldn't figure out what was wrong with her, why she was acting like some female animal in heat. Maybe their discussion of their respective sex lives had triggered the rush of hormones that had her practically climbing the wall. This would never do! How was she going to convince her husband that she wanted to wait a couple of weeks before consummating their marriage if she went up in flames every time he touched her?

"I think I'll shower and change clothes before Pearl brings up dinner." Cleo shoved on Roarke's chest, and for a couple of seconds she thought he wasn't going to release her.

He dropped his hands to his sides and waited for her to remove her hands from his chest. "Sounds like a good idea. As soon as you finish up, I'll take a shower."

Lift your hands, she told herself. Lift your hands, turn around and walk away.

He kept looking at her, his gaze moving over her face, then down to her chest. He was staring at her breasts, at the pebble-hard nipples pressing against her sheer bra and silk blouse. A gripping sensation throbbed intimately within Cleo, sending tingling desire radiating from her feminine core to her taut breasts and then throughout her body. Balling her hands into fists, she shoved against his chest. He stepped backward, putting a few inches between their bodies.

Without saying a word, she turned and ran into her bedroom, leaving Roarke alone on the balcony. The moment she slammed shut the bathroom door, he let out a long sigh, then cursed under his breath. He was aroused to the point of pain. Somehow he had to make it through dinner and a discussion of the suspects. How many hours would that take? How long would it be before they went to bed? He could wait a little longer, if he had to. A few hours. Waiting would make the loving all the sweeter. For both of them.

CHAPTER FOUR

ROARKE FINISHED OFF his second beer, placed the bottle on the table and leaned back in the French bergère chair. Crossing his arms over his chest, he looked at Cleo, who sat in a matching chair across the round Sheraton table in her sitting room. She played with a piece of Pearl's delicious apple pie, destroying the flaky crust with the tip of her fork. She had picked at her entire meal, leaving most of it on her plate. Roarke wondered if she always ate so light or if she was nervous tonight.

His cast-iron stomach was all right; he never had a problem eating. As a matter of fact, all Roarke's appetites were in top form, and there was one particular appetite that he was more than ready to appease.

Cleo hadn't said much to him after they'd showered and changed clothes. Unfortunately, they'd showered separately. In the future, he'd have to rectify that situation. Before he'd had a chance to unpack, Ezra had delivered their dinner on an enormous silver tray, and Cleo had busied herself arranging the meal on the table in her sitting room.

Cleo's suite consisted of three rooms: a large, luxurious bath; a huge bedroom decorated with antiques; and a small sitting room, with a table and two chairs, a fat, overstuffed love seat and a Queen Anne wingback in the corner. All three rooms had been done in pale, delicate shades of green, peach and cream. Although there wasn't any lace or bows or satin or frilly touches in the suite, the rooms were decidedly feminine. The orderly neatness, the expensive decor, the cool, fragile colors corresponded with similar traits in Cleo herself. She was cool, neat, fragile and rich.

She gazed nervously at him, and Roarke instinctively knew that while they'd shared supper, she'd been thinking about tonight. About their first night together. Once or twice, he had noticed her glancing into the bedroom, at her bed. The bed she would share with him during their marriage.

"If you're finished, I'll ring for Pearl to clear away these things."

"I'm through. Pearl's a fabulous cook." Roarke laid his linen napkin on the table. "You didn't eat much. Weren't you hungry?"

"Not really. Nerves, I guess," Cleo admitted. "It's not every day that I get married."

"Or every night that you share your bed with a husband."

"Yes, I'm afraid I'm not accustomed to having someone share my suite, and certainly not my bed." She stood abruptly. Her napkin fell from her lap and landed at her feet on the soft, thick carpet. She crossed the room hurriedly, pulled open a drawer in the mahogany inlaid-and-banded chest, then turned to him. "I'll rearrange a few things so that you can have this drawer. And there's plenty of room in the closet—" she nodded toward the door that led to the room-size walk-in closet "—for you to hang your clothes."

"Thanks." Roarke couldn't help but notice how different Cleo looked after she'd changed out of her navy blue suit and into a pair of jeans and oversize top. Young. Fresh. Innocent. She'd washed away any residue of makeup, leav-

ing her face scrubbed clean. And she had removed her
gold jewelry, the earrings, watch and bracelet—everything except the wide gold wedding band.

He looked down at his left hand, at the band circling his
third finger. Eighteen years ago, Hope had slipped a similar ring on his finger and he had promised to love her forever. He'd been so sure their love would last a lifetime—it
hadn't survived the first year. Now he was married again,
but not for love. This time he knew in advance that this
marriage was headed straight for the divorce courts.

Cleo notified Pearl that they had finished dinner, then
she emptied the second drawer in the chest for Roarke.
She opened the closet door and, after flipping on the light
switch, walked inside and pushed some of her suits down
the rack on the left. Although she watched Roarke while
he unpacked his suitcase, she pretended to be otherwise
occupied.

Roarke was even more masculine, more devastatingly
male in a pair of tight, faded jeans and an Atlanta Braves
T-shirt than he'd been in his suit. His shoulders were massive, his arms bulging with muscles, his stomach flat and
his butt tight. She didn't believe she'd ever spent as much
time assessing a man's body as she had the past hour inspecting her husband.

After his shower, he hadn't bothered putting on any
shoes. When he'd commented on how soft the carpet was,
Cleo had stared down at his big feet. Even his feet looked
masculine. Large. Wide. His toes sprinkled with brown
hair.

After he'd emptied his underwear and a pair of blue-
and-white-striped pajama bottoms from a duffel bag and
placed them in the chest, he pulled out a shaving kit.

"Would you mind putting this in the bathroom for me?"
he asked.

"Of course." When she walked out of the closet, he tossed the kit to her.

Entering the bathroom, she paused to look at her very private domain, one that would be private no longer. For the next few months, she would have to share her living quarters with Roarke. Even her bathroom was no longer sacrosanct. She placed his shaving kit on the vanity, alongside her cosmetic basket. Her hand trembled. Marrying a stranger to fulfill the stipulations in her uncle's will had seemed the only solution to her problems, and she'd been certain she would be able to adjust to sharing her suite with a man. But she wasn't as sure now. Now that Simon Roarke's underwear was in her English mahogany chest. Now that his razor and toothbrush and aftershave rested on her vanity. Now that she had to face a night alone with him in her bed, lying beside her, his big body only inches away. What would happen if they accidentally brushed against each other during the night?

Stop worrying, she told herself. You're the boss. He's the employee. Once you explain that you want to wait a couple of weeks and become better acquainted before you have sex, then he'll have no choice but to comply with your wishes.

Exiting the bathroom, she halted in the doorway when she saw Roarke remove a gun and trim leather holster from his suitcase. She sucked in her breath. A gun! Of course he'd have a gun. He was a professional bodyguard.

With the holster in his hand, he looked across the room at Cleo. "Under normal circumstances, I would have worn this today, but... I'd like to put it in the nightstand, on my side of the bed. And I'll need to start wearing it whenever we're out of these rooms."

"Do you really think that's necessary?" If others saw

his pistol, what would they think? How would they ever explain why her husband was carrying a gun?

"Yes, Boss Lady. It's a necessary part of my protecting you." He pulled the gun from the holster and lifted it up so she could get a better look at it. "Do you know anything about guns?"

"Not a great deal," she said. "Uncle George had a small collection of rifles that he kept in a gun cabinet in his study downstairs."

"Come here." He motioned for her to come to him.

She complied with his request, crossed the room and stopped at his side. He grabbed her hand and laid the gun in her palm. She quivered.

"A gun is no better or worse than the person who uses it," he told her. "This gun will be used only for your protection. It's not your enemy."

She handed the gun back to him. "I'm not afraid of guns, Roarke. It's just that I'm not used to living with someone who carries one."

Roarke returned his Beretta to the holster, then gave it back to Cleo. "Put this in the nightstand, will you? I don't know which side of the bed you want me to sleep on."

Holding the gun cautiously, Cleo carried it to the nightstand on the left side of the bed, opened the drawer and carefully placed the holster on top of several paperback books.

"How will you explain wearing a gun if someone in the family or at the office notices?" Closing the drawer, she glanced across to where Roarke stood in the closet, hanging his clothes beside hers.

"I brought along that model of Beretta, a Cougar 800, because it's compact and easy to conceal, but uses a high-powered 9 mm clip. No one should notice it, but if someone does, I'll just say I'm wearing it to protect my wife."

She nodded agreement. What sort of man was he, this husband of hers? A former Green Beret. A private security agent. A professional bodyguard. He had nothing in common with the men of her acquaintance. Ordinary men, who lived ordinary lives. No danger. No violence. No weapons.

"You know a lot about guns, don't you?" she asked.

"In my line of business, it pays to know a lot about guns."

A loud, distinct knock at the bedroom door ended their discussion. Before Cleo could reply, the door opened and Pearl sauntered in, a large, empty basket in her hand. She looked Cleo up and down, then gave Roarke the same visual treatment.

"Your aunt Oralie was complaining that y'all didn't join the family for dinner," Pearl said. "Bea told her that she suspected you two wouldn't be joining the family for meals for several days."

When Pearl turned her gaze on Roarke, her eyes narrowing as she inspected him, he grinned at her and winked. Grunting, she spread her lips in a closed-mouth smile.

"Y'all's ears ought to be burning." Pearl chuckled quietly. "They've been discussing the two of you. Taking y'all apart, piece by piece. They're trying to figure out whether this marriage is for real or not."

"And what have they decided?" Roarke asked.

"Well, before y'all showed up this afternoon, they were one hundred percent sure that Cleo had hired herself a husband. But now they're not so sure. Not after the way they said you two were carrying on downstairs at the reception."

"We were not carrying on," Cleo said.

"From what they were saying, I'm sorry I missed seeing Mr. Roarke carry you up onto the veranda. That must have been some sight."

"What can I say, Pearl? How could a man keep from being romantic with his new bride?" Roarke grabbed Cleo around the waist and drew her to his side. "Especially when his bride is as lovely as our Cleo Belle?"

Cleo gasped at his use of Pearl's pet name for her. She had wanted and asked for Pearl's understanding and support, but, dammit, it wasn't necessary for Pearl to actually like Roarke.

"What I really hate that I missed was hearing you warn off that bunch of vultures," Pearl told Roarke. "I'd have given just about anything to see their faces when you told them that nobody had better try to hurt Cleo again, and that you knew a hundred different ways to kill a person."

Gasping loudly, Cleo clutched Roarke's arm. "Oh, my God, you didn't say that to my family, did you?"

"I said it and I meant it," Roarke admitted. "I thought that a little warning up front was in order. If we're lucky, just knowing that you have a protective husband watching out for you might give our potential murderer second thoughts."

"Couldn't you have discussed this with me before you went and shot your mouth off?" Cleo's short, neat nails bit into his forearm.

"I'll just go get those dishes cleaned up." Pearl nodded toward the sitting room. "Cleo, why don't you come help me, if you can tear yourself away from your handsome husband for a few minutes?"

Cleo knew Pearl wanted something other than her assistance in clearing away the remains of her and Roarke's meal. More than likely the housekeeper was going to preach her another sermon on marriage, something along the lines of a wife being subservient to her husband. Cleo laughed silently. As if Pearl Clooney had ever been sub-servient to Ezra one day in her life!

Once they entered the sitting room, Pearl and Cleo cleared away the table, placing the china, silver, crystal and linens in the large wicker basket. Cleo set the basket on the floor.

Pearl pulled a soft rag from her apron and ran it across the inlaid tabletop. Cocking her head so she could look at Cleo, she continued wiping the table. "By the looks of him, I'd say you got yourself some man there, Cleo Belle."

"Do you think so, Pearl?" So, that's what this was all about, Cleo thought. Pearl was on the verge of giving Roarke her seal of approval.

"A smart girl like you should be able to figure out a way to keep that man." Pearl swiped her rag across the wooden trim along the backs of the bergère chairs. "When you get pregnant with his baby, he's bound to want to stick around."

Cleo glanced into the bedroom. The look Roarke gave her chilled her to the bone. His blue eyes darkened to a deep indigo when he glared at her, reminding her that he had said he wanted nothing to do with any child she con-ceived. Roarke stomped across the floor and disappeared into the closet.

Lifting the basket off the floor, Cleo walked Pearl to the door, then opened the door and handed the housekeeper the wicker basket.

Pearl leaned close to Cleo's ear and whispered, "I be-lieve Simon Roarke just might be that rogue stallion I told your uncle George you needed."

For several minutes after Pearl disappeared down the hallway, Cleo stood in the open doorway. Earthy, erotic images danced wildly in her mind. A stallion and a mare.

Lightning illuminating a dark sky. She and Roarke, standing in the rain, naked, their bodies straining to touch.

She had to stop thinking like this, stop wondering what it would be like when she and Roarke made love. No, it wouldn't be making love. It would be sex. They would be lovers, but only in the most basic, animalistic sense.

"Would you care for a brandy?" she called out to him as she closed the door.

He walked out of the closet and stood on the other side of the room. "Sure, if you're having one."

"In the sitting room," she told him. "Why don't we go sit down, have our drinks and discuss the details of how we plan to handle our situation?"

Roarke nodded agreement, but waited several minutes before joining her in the sitting room. He needed a little more time to erase Pearl's words from his mind: *When you get pregnant with his baby, he's bound to want to stick around.*

He could never allow himself to think of the child Cleo would conceive as his baby. Getting her pregnant was just a part of his assignment, a part of the package deal that meant lifetime security for him and for Hope. He would never see Cleo's child, never be a part of his or her life. It had to be that way. He'd been a father once, and he'd done a lousy job of it. He had failed his little girl and his failure had cost Laurie her life.

A man could die a hundred ways and a thousand times, but Roarke doubted that any agony could equal the pain a man felt when he lost a child and knew he could have prevented the tragedy.

Roarke joined Cleo in her sitting room. She sat curled up, in her sock feet, on the fat, pale green love seat, a brandy snifter in her small hand. Her leather loafers lay half-hidden beneath the sofa's fringed edge. His brandy waited for him on the table. He lifted his glass, saluted her with it and slumped down into the corner wingback. He placed his feet on the needlepoint footstool and took a sip of the brandy, savoring the smooth taste of the aged liquor.

"Good stuff," he said, and took another sip.

"Uncle George's private stock. He bought only the best."

"Did he think he'd bought Hugh Winfield for you?" Roarke asked. "Is that why he put those ridiculous stipulations in his will?"

Cleo supposed she should feel insulted, but she didn't. How could she? In a way, what Roarke had suggested was true. "I was dating Hugh when Uncle George made out his new will, and yes, I'm sure he thought that I'd marry Hugh and that Hugh would jump at the chance to marry an heiress."

"What went wrong?"

"You already know the answer to that question."

"Daphne?"

"When Uncle George was in the hospital, dying, I discovered Hugh in Daphne's bed. She had seduced him and set things up so that I'd find them together." Lifting the snifter to her lips, Cleo slowly downed the remainder of her brandy. "Hugh was embarrassed, but not all that remorseful. He even accused me of being to blame."

"How the hell could he blame you?"

"He said that he would never have turned to Daphne if I hadn't refused to have sex with him."

"Aaa…hhh. A reasonable excuse for a man caught with his pants down," Roarke said.

Cleo laughed, despite the vividness of the humiliating memory of that night less than a month ago. "I think at the time Hugh believed one potential heiress was as good as another, so why shouldn't he choose the one willing to sleep with him? Of course, he had no way of knowing that Uncle George would make me his major beneficiary and leave me complete control of McNamara Industries."

"Did Hugh change his tune once your uncle's will was read?"

"He tried once, but I didn't give him a chance," Cleo said. "I would have given up McNamara Industries before I would have married that…that…that weasel!"

"So, Hugh stands to profit only if he marries Daphne and the family can force you to sell McNamara Industries?" Roarke finished off his brandy and set the snifter on the small cloth-draped, glass-topped table beside his chair.

"Hugh's not a bad man." Cleo smiled when she noticed Roarke's widened eyes and raised brows. "He's a weak man. Nothing like his father. Hubert Winfield was Uncle George's attorney for years and he trusted him implicitly. Hugh is a junior partner in his father's firm, but he's not the brilliant lawyer Hubert is. Hugh works exclusively with McNamara Industries. That's about all he can handle, and his father keeps pretty good tabs on him to make sure he doesn't screw up. And Hugh is not privy to any of my personal legal affairs."

"And this is the man your uncle chose for you?"

"Uncle George knew Hugh's bloodlines. Our families have been associated for several generations," Cleo explained. "Besides, I *was* dating Hugh. Uncle George wanted me to find a man, and Hugh was…well, he was there."

Roarke stretched his arms, threaded his fingers together and placed his entwined hands behind his head. "What do you suppose Uncle George would think of me as your husband?"

"I shudder to think. More likely than not, his first re-action would have been the same as Pearl's, but then, just as Pearl has done, once he had a chance to size you up, he'd advise me to hang on to such a prime specimen."

Roarke laughed, the sound a mixture of embarrass-ment and amusement. Relaxing, he burrowed into the big, comfortable chair and took a long, hard look at Cleo. He liked what he saw. Liked it far too much. Instead of sit-ting there discussing potential suspects, he'd much rather carry his wife to bed, undress her slowly and make love to her all night long.

Later, he told himself. Be patient. First things first. Business before pleasure.

Idiot, he reprimanded himself. Pleasuring Cleo would be business. Part of his job was to impregnate her.

He had to get his mind off making love to Cleo. "Does your cousin Daphne hate you enough to kill you?" he asked, determined to get back to the business at hand—gaining more personal information about the suspects.

"I honestly don't know." Cleo shifted uncomfortably, then bent one knee, lifting it high enough to drape her folded hands around it. "Daphne and I have had a love-hate relationship all our lives. Since we were children, whatever I had, Daphne wanted. For years, I couldn't un-derstand why she was jealous of me.

"I envied her so much. She had two loving parents. A mother who doted on her. A brother who adored her. And she's always been beautiful and the center of attention."

"So why do you think she's so jealous of you?" Roarke asked.

"Because of Aunt Oralie's insecurities. My father was Uncle George's favorite and Aunt Oralie resented that. Then when I came to live with Uncle George and Aunt Beatrice, I became Uncle George's favorite."

"Would you say that Oralie Sutton hates you?"

"No, of course she doesn't. I'm her brother's only child. In her own way, she loves me. It's just that…well, she's an unhappy woman, very fragile and high-strung. Uncle Perry is so protective of her, and he resents me a great deal. I'd say if anyone in this family truly hates me, it's Uncle Perry. He hates me because my existence has caused so much pain for Aunt Oralie and kept his children from being the only McNamara heirs."

"Do you think Perry Sutton tried to shoot you?"

"I don't know," Cleo said. "But I think it's possible."

"Why not Trey? Or even Marla?"

Shaking her head, Cleo giggled. Her short, cinnamon hair gleamed with healthy vibrance in the soft glow of the lamplight. "Marla wouldn't hurt a fly. She's too sweet and timid. And I doubt that Trey knows one end of a rifle from the other."

"Whoever tried to shoot you might have been hired by one of your relatives," Roarke told her. "Of course, since the shooter missed his target, I'd say he wasn't a trained professional. But Trey or Perry or even Daphne could have hired some local hoodlum who wasn't a very good shot."

Crossing her arms over her chest, Cleo rubbed up and down her arms. "I hate to think that one of my relatives is willing to kill me in order to sell the company. Can you imagine how that makes me feel? Knowing that someone I've lived with most of my life, someone I've loved and trusted, wants to see me dead."

"I won't kid you, Cleo. These next few months aren't going to be an easy time for you. But I promise that I'll do everything in my power to keep you safe."

"Roarke, I…"

"What?"

"Thank you for agreeing to this arrangement." She slid

to the edge of the sofa and stood. "I know that acting as my bodyguard is what you're trained to do, but the other... the personal terms of our business deal... Well, I'm grateful that, for whatever reasons, you decided to take me up on my offer, you were willing to marry me and...and—"

"I did it for the money," Roarke said unemotionally. "I'm nearly forty. I've got my share of battle scars, some obtained when I was in the Special Forces and some since I've been with Dundee. I'm tired. I want to retire. Invested wisely, the million you're paying me should take care of me for the rest of my life."

"Yes. I understand." She walked past him, pausing briefly before exiting the sitting room. "There's more brandy in the cabinet—" she pointed to the chinoiserie cabinet beneath the window "—if you'd like more. And there's a television in the armoire in my...our bedroom, and a fairly good selection of books on the bottom shelves. Please, make yourself as comfortable as possible."

"In other words, make myself at home, huh?"

"Yes, certainly." She glanced at him briefly and wished she hadn't. The way he looked at her made her feel all fluttery inside, as if a dozen tiny butterflies had been set free in her stomach. "I'm tired. I think I'll turn in."

Before she had taken three steps out of the sitting room, Roarke called out to her, "It's been a long day for both of us. I might as well call it a night, too."

Tell him, dammit, Cleo! Tell him that you are not going to have sex with him tonight.

Maybe he doesn't expect to have sex with you. Since you're his employer, maybe he plans to wait for your explicit orders.

"Roarke?"

"You take the bathroom first." He raked his hand over his jaw. "I need to shave before I go to bed."

Nodding agreement, she hurried to retrieve her gown and robe from the closet, then rushed into the bathroom, closing the door quietly behind her.

While preparing for bed, she thought about the fact that this was her wedding night. She almost cried. No, she told herself, don't give in to self-pity. Things could be a lot worse. What if Hugh Winfield was the bridegroom who would join her in her bed tonight? Heaven forbid!

At least with Roarke, she would be the one in charge. There were certain advantages to buying yourself a temporary husband.

The moment she walked out of the bathroom, Roarke, who sat on the edge of the bed, stood and smiled at her. He looked her over from head to toe and almost laughed aloud. She certainly hadn't dressed like a bride on her wedding night. No sheer, see-through nightie. No lace teddy. Nothing the least bit sexy or provocative. But dammit all, if there wasn't something appealing about little Miss Cleo Belle in her unadorned, pale lavender cotton gown and matching robe that skimmed the floor as she moved toward him.

"The bathroom's all yours," she said, then glanced away shyly.

He liked that about her. That hint of timidness. He'd already figured out that some of what people considered coolness in Cleo was actually shyness.

"I usually sleep in the raw," he told her, and couldn't repress a muted chuckle when he saw her mouth gape in a silent gasp. "But until you get used to me, I'll make a concession and sleep in these." He held up a pair of blue-and-white-striped pajama bottoms.

"Thank you for your consideration," she said.

She waited until he disappeared into the bathroom before she removed her robe, draped it over the desk chair at the foot of her bed and turned down the covers.

Roarke usually slept naked. She tried valiantly not to think about how he would look—tall, muscular and completely unclothed. Perspiration broke out on her upper lip. Moisture coated her palms. Her nipples puckered painfully. And her femininity tightened and released, then tightened again.

She crawled into bed, turned off the lamp on her nightstand and pulled the covers up to her neck. She lay there quietly, trying not to move. She should have told him that they were not going to have sex tonight. She should have told him!

Less than ten minutes later, Roarke emerged from the bathroom, clean-shaven and whistling some unfamiliar tune. Cleo tensed. Suddenly, she felt very hot.

She hazarded a glance in his direction. Dear Lord, he was magnificent. Dark brown hair curled over his chest, narrowed down to a V across his flat belly and disappeared beneath his low-slung pajama bottoms. His massive shoulders looked six feet wide and his big, muscular arms bulged with power.

Two ugly, semicircular scars, located below his right pectoral muscles, marred the absolute perfection of his chest. How had he gotten those scars? she wondered. In the army? Or on an assignment for the Dundee agency?

"Do you prefer the light on or off?" He sat down on the left side of the bed.

"Off, please," she said.

He turned off the lamp, then slipped under the covers and slid across the bed. Cleo lay there beside him as rigid as a corpse. Good God, what was wrong with her? Roarke wondered. Was she afraid? If she'd had only one other lover, she might be feeling more than a little uncertain about their making love.

"It's all right, honey." He reached out and ran his fingertips softly over her cheek.

She sucked in her breath and held it. He raised his head and leaned over her. She gazed up at him, able to see the outline of his face in the faint moonlight coming through the French doors. What would she do if he kissed her? she wondered. *Oh, please, don't let him kiss me.*

Roarke ran his fingers down the side of her neck, slowly caressing her soft skin as he lowered his hand over her shoulder. "Relax. We'll take things easy. I'm not going to do anything you don't want me to do."

Releasing her breath, she turned and buried her face against his shoulder. He lifted her body just enough to take her in his arms and hold her close. She trembled. He soothed her with long, sensitive strokes across her back.

"What's the matter, Cleo? You're trembling."

"I—I—" Tell him, you ninny! Tell him!

He felt the wild beat of her heart, the quivering of her fragile body, the tightening of her nipples as they pressed into his chest. He could not resist the urge to kiss her, but realizing how nervous she was, he tempered his passion with tenderness and took her mouth gently. She responded instantly, her lips softening and opening. He could tell that she wanted him.

Go slow, he told himself. Take it easy. She's not an experienced woman who takes lovemaking lightly. He continued the kiss, deepening it by degrees, gauging her reaction moment to moment. When she made no protest as the level of his passion increased, he cupped her breast in his hand, squeezing it tenderly.

Cleo broke the kiss and cried out. Shoving against his chest, she struggled to free herself from his embrace. He allowed her to withdraw from him. When she sat straight up, he took a deep breath and sat up beside her.

"What is it? What did I do wrong?" he asked.

Bowing her head, she stared down at her clasped hands resting in her lap. "I'm sorry. This was my fault. You didn't do anything wrong. I should have told you before we came to bed, but I thought that…maybe…you wouldn't… I mean, since I hired you to be my husband, to take your orders from me—"

Roarke grabbed her shoulders and shook her just enough to get her attention. "Stop babbling, Cleo, and just say whatever it is you're trying to say."

"I want us to wait to have sex." She looked directly at him. "I should have said something before we came to bed. I thought a great deal about the situation and decided that, since we're practically strangers, it would be easier for me to have sex with you after I got to know you a little better. I think we should wait a couple of weeks."

Dammit to hell! Why hadn't she told him sooner? Before he'd worked himself up into a sexual frenzy. He was hard and throbbing. She hadn't protested when he'd taken her in his arms and kissed her. She had responded eagerly. She wanted him! Dammit, he knew she wanted him.

Releasing her instantly, Roarke shot out of bed and stomped across the floor. He opened the French doors and went outside. He gripped the banister with white-knuckled anger. Frustration rioted inside his body.

Suddenly and without warning, he felt Cleo's hand on his shoulder. The rush of adrenaline roaring in his ears had blocked out every other sound, including her footsteps on the balcony. He tensed at her gentle touch.

"You're angry with me, aren't you?" she asked.

"No, Boss Lady, I'm not angry with you." He kept his back to her and measured each word he spoke very carefully. "You call the shots in this relationship. If you say no sex for two weeks, then we wait two weeks."

"Please understand why I need some time. My body may want you, but—" She hadn't meant to say that, to be so candid. What would he think of her? Did he already consider her a tease?

She did want him! He knew she did! He turned slowly, anger and frustration still riding him hard. The moment he looked into her tear-glazed green eyes, the anger vanished, but the frustration deepened. She was incredibly lovely standing there in the moonlight, her ivory skin gold kissed, her auburn hair shimmering like mahogany silk and her eyes darkened to a deep, dark jade.

"Go on back to bed, Cleo," he told her. "I'm fine. We'll wait until you tell me that you're ready for us to have sex."

"I want you to sleep with me," she said.

"What?"

"I want us to sleep in the same bed for the next two weeks, even though we won't be—"

"Yeah, sure. It wouldn't do if Pearl realized I was sleeping on the chaise longue or on a pallet on the floor. Or if a member of the family caught us sleeping separately."

"Yes, that's one of the reasons I think we should sleep together."

"One of the reasons? What other reason could there be?"

When she looked down, averting her gaze from his face, Roarke grabbed her chin, lifting it, forcing her to look at him.

"If we sleep together every night, we'll get used to each other." She tried to look away from him, but he held her chin tightly. When she could find no other way to escape his visual assessment, she closed her eyes. "I'll become accustomed to your body lying next to me."

Did she have any idea what kind of effect she was having on him? Did she know how badly he was hurting? It had been a long time since he'd wanted a woman the way he wanted her. And it was his own damn fault for assuming he would have sex with his wife on their wedding night.

"I understand," he said, and he did. But understanding her reasons didn't lessen his desire to take her—here, now, where she stood.

"Come back to bed," she said. "Please."

"Yeah, sure. In a little while." He released her chin. "You go on. I need some more fresh air."

"All right." She left him alone on the balcony.

He had meant to stay only a few more minutes, but by the time he had his body under control and his mind calmed, over an hour had passed. When he crawled into bed beside Cleo, he thought she was asleep, but within a few minutes, he realized she was still awake. He had a feeling neither one of them would get much sleep that night.

CHAPTER FIVE

ONE WEEK DOWN and one week to go, Roarke thought. Dammit, he hadn't been this preoccupied with sex since he was a teenager. But he had never slept beside a desirable woman night after night and been *ordered* not to touch her. Well, actually, she hadn't ordered him not to touch her—he *had* touched her, and that was part of the problem. But she had made it perfectly clear that they were not going to have sex for the first two weeks of their marriage.

He'd never been a Don Juan with the ladies, but he certainly hadn't led a celibate life, either. He wasn't accustomed to having someone dictate the terms of his sex life. But then, his sexual partner had never also been his employer. This arrangement with Cleo was frustrating, to say the least, with the potential to become explosive.

For a week now, they had lain in bed together every night, kept apart by nothing except Cleo's edict and his own willpower. But every morning they awoke to find their bodies touching, often lying spoon-fashion, her back to his chest, his arms draped around her, or vice versa, with her breasts pressed against his back, her hand lying on his stomach. This morning when he awoke, her leg had been draped over his, her fingers twined in his chest hair and her head on his shoulder.

He had found it damn near impossible to let her slip away from him, but he'd had no choice. She always seemed slightly embarrassed to discover that her body had sought the warmth of his during the night.

They continued their charade of being a happily married couple, but Cleo had seen to it that they'd had their breakfasts and dinners alone in her suite. She used their newlywed state as an excuse for them not to share mealtimes with her family. But being alone so much only added to Roarke's frustration, and he suspected Cleo wasn't immune to the sexual tension pulsating between them.

Roarke sat on the leather sofa in Cleo's office, trying his damnedest to concentrate on the files she'd asked him to look over. Maybe, if he wasn't aware of what she looked like first thing in the morning, with her hair mussed and her slender body clad in nothing but a thin cotton gown, he could look at the prim-and-proper Ms. McNamara—correction, Mrs. Roarke—sitting behind her impressive desk and see nothing more than a neatly attired businesswoman. She certainly didn't dress provocatively. She had a dozen simple little suits that she wore with matching heels and handbags and accented with pearl, diamond and gold jewelry, all small and delicate, like the lady who wore it.

Every time he looked at her, he saw a desirable woman. A woman he had a legal right to claim. But not a moral right.

Trey Sutton stormed into Cleo's office, disregarding the dire warning from Cleo's secretary that Mrs. Roarke was not to be disturbed. Audrey Woodward raced in behind Trey, waving her arms and threatening to do him bodily harm.

Trey marched straight over to Cleo's desk, pounded his fist on the wooden surface and glared coldly at his cousin. "You had no right to invent a position here at McNamara Industries just so you could give your husband a job."

"I'm so sorry, Mrs. Roarke," Audrey said. "I tried to stop Mr. Sutton, but he wouldn't listen to me. Do you want me to call Charlie?"

Roarke tossed the file folder on the sofa, uncrossed his legs and watched his wife very closely.

Cleo calmly laid aside the computer printout she'd been reading and looked up at Audrey. "No, there's no need to call the guard. After all—" she glanced meaningfully at Roarke "—our new head of security is sitting right here in my office."

"Yes, of course. I'd forgotten."

Audrey smiled at Roarke, and he thought once again, as he had when they'd first been introduced, how very young and sweet she seemed.

"Head of security, my rear end." Trey turned his heated glare on Roarke. "McNamara's never needed more than a guard at the front gate and a night watchman. Why, suddenly, do we need a head of security? You can hardly call a guard and a night watchman a security force."

Cleo smiled faintly, not parting her lips, and Roarke knew she was preparing to strike. In the ten days he'd known his wife, he'd learned the meaning of her different smiles.

"Why do we *suddenly* need a head of security?" Cleo asked mockingly. "Because, *suddenly,* after Uncle George's death, someone took a shot at me. And I have been informed that in the past two weeks, we've *suddenly* had a rash of phone calls from regular customers concerning inaccurate billing. Someone has gone into the computer system and altered the accounts. And in a plant that has been accident-free for over three years, we've *suddenly* had two mysterious accidents since Uncle George's funeral. If I didn't know better, I'd say someone was suddenly trying to sabotage McNamara Industries—someone who would like to see me forced into selling the company."

"Why do you assume that someone is monkeying around with our computer system? More than likely an employee simply made a mistake in billing and is too frightened of losing his job to own up to it." Standing straight, his back ramrod stiff, Trey bent his neatly manicured fingers into his palms, stopping just short of making tight fists. "And accidents do happen, you know? An electrical hoist can short-circuit. Mechanical equipment can and does fail."

"I'm well aware that equipment can malfunction. But not without a reason. As well-maintained as our maintenance crew keeps this plant, two of our workers shouldn't be in the hospital right now, recuperating from 'accidents' that never should have happened."

"All right, even if someone deliberately screwed with the accounts and there's no logical explanations for those two accidents, that's no reason to put your husband in charge of the investigations. I'd like to know just what his qualifications for the job are." Trey's tanning-bed brown face flushed scarlet. He kept his gaze focused on Cleo, not once glancing in Roarke's direction.

"As CEO of McNamara Industries, I do not have to justify my actions to you, a senior vice president, but as my cousin and a stockholder, I'll tell you this—" Cleo pushed her swivel chair away from her desk and stood "—I am satisfied that Simon is qualified to head up security, and that's all that matters. As soon as possible, he will be hiring several new people to form a small security force. We've been behind times for years now. I'm simply bringing us up to date."

"Don't you think you're going overboard in forming a security force, in hiring new employees, when it's all we can do to afford the people already on the payroll?" Trey asked. "We should be downsizing, not hiring!"

"The decision has been made," Cleo said. "There's no point in discussing this further. Whoever is behind the accidents, the computer tampering and the attempt on my life is not going to succeed in forcing me to sell this company!"

Roarke rose from the sofa. Standing to his full six-feet-three-inch height, he towered over a much shorter Trey Sutton. "And you don't have to worry about Cleo's safety." Roarke's deep, commanding voice vibrated through the room. "The only way anyone is going to be able to get to her is over my dead body."

"Well, I...er...I'm relieved to know that as Cleo's husband, you're taking her safety so seriously." Trey cleared his throat. "But I still think Cleo is going too far in forming a security force."

Roarke placed his hand on Trey's back. The younger man tensed. Roarke patted his back. "Well, why don't you let Cleo worry about running this company? After all, her uncle did leave her in charge, didn't he?"

"Right." Nodding agreement, Trey took a step away from Roarke's big hand, then glanced at Cleo. "You'll keep me notified of any developments?"

"Of course," Cleo said.

The moment Trey left her office, Cleo sat down on her desk, letting her short legs dangle off the edge. "He's afraid of something, isn't he?"

Roarke walked directly in front of Cleo, leaned toward her and braced his hands on top of her desk. His arms straddled her hips. With his face only inches from hers, he said, "Do you think Trey is our man?"

For a split second Cleo couldn't breathe, couldn't think. Roarke was too close, his body almost touching hers, his breath mingling with hers, his lips a hairbreadth from hers.

Night after night they lay together—man and woman— and Cleo's body cried out for his, longing for his possession. But she had made such a big deal out of waiting two weeks, to become better acquainted before they consummated their marriage, that her pride wouldn't allow her to back down now. Besides, Roarke had not made the slightest effort to pressure her or seduce her. If he really wanted her, wouldn't he have tried to persuade her to give in?

"What—what did you say?" She looked up into his mesmerizing blue eyes and fervently wished she were alone with him in their bedroom.

"I asked if you thought Trey might be behind the problems here at McNamara Industries and if he could have been the person who tried to shoot you."

"Oh. I don't want to think Trey is capable of either, especially not of trying to kill me. But I suppose it's possible." Cleo found that she could not stop herself from leaning forward toward Roarke. "We used to be close, when we were younger. Trey even occasionally took my side against Daphne. But once I started moving up the corporate ladder here at McNamara's faster than he did, he began to resent me."

"When Sam Dundee hired Dane Carmichael to run the Dundee agency for him, Dane extended the agency's services to include private investigation as well as private security."

Roarke wanted to take Cleo right this minute. Right there on her big desk. He wanted to spread her legs, strip off her stockings and panties, grab her lush little behind and thrust into her welcoming warmth.

"Morgan Kane is one of our top investigators," Roarke said. "I want to bring him over from Atlanta to train your new security force and to give your guard and night watchman refresher courses."

"If you want to bring in someone from the Dundee agency, then bring him in." Cleo's feminine instincts told her to open her legs, to stretch out her arms, to enfold Simon Roarke, to take him into her body and accept all that he could give her. If only he would take her. Not even ask her permission. Just know that she wanted him and act on that knowledge. "I'll cooperate fully with you in whatever steps you think necessary."

"I want every employee to know that I'm heading up a security force to investigate McNamara's problems," he said. "It's possible that whoever is creating havoc here at the plant will think twice about doing anything else if he or she knows."

"Whatever you want," Cleo told him.

Roarke could feel her heat, could sense her desire. What the hell was she trying to do—drive him crazy? Or was she, in her own inexperienced way, trying to seduce him? Dammit, why didn't she just come right out and tell him that she'd changed her mind, that she wanted to have sex with him and she wanted it now?

Or was she trying to push him over the edge so that he'd make the first move? No way. He wasn't going to make it that easy for her. She was the one who had set up the ground rules for their marriage. She'd have to be the one to change them. No matter how much he wanted her— and he wanted her bad—he wasn't going to take her until she asked for it. Maybe not even until she begged for it.

Lifting his hands off the desk, Roarke stood and took a

step backward, stopping less than a foot away from Cleo. He didn't break eye contact as he distanced himself from her.

Come get me if you want me, honey. His hardened sex strained against his slacks. *You've got to know I want you. All you have to do is say the word and I'm yours.*

Cleo crossed her ankles. Her heels rested on the side of the desk. She had thought Roarke wanted to kiss her, but just as she was about to reach up and put her arms around his neck, he pulled back, moving away from her.

"I think tomorrow will be soon enough to bring in Mr. Kane and start hiring people for the security force," Cleo said. "This afternoon, I'd like to continue our tour of the plant. By the end of the week, I want you acquainted with all our employees and them with you."

"You really care about these people, don't you?" he asked.

"McNamara Industries wouldn't exist without our loyal, hardworking employees. Uncle George taught me how important it is to take care of this company, and that means taking care of the people who make it run."

"Come on, Boss Lady. Lead the way." Roarke willed his body under control.

When he took her arm and draped it through his, Cleo hesitated momentarily, allowing herself time to adjust to the feel of him, his warmth and strength. "We'll end our tour in shipping and receiving, at the loading platforms."

Roarke followed Cleo out of her office and into the elevator leading three stories down to the plant level. He watched her closely as she led him through the laboratory. She stopped to speak to every technician, introducing each by name just as she'd done in the plant yesterday. Running three shifts, seven days a week, McNamara Industries employed nearly three hundred people, and there wasn't a one Cleo didn't know.

McNamara's was a small chemical plant, as plants go, but it was the life's blood of River Bend. And those nearly three hundred employees and their families depended on this little family-owned business.

Cleo carried a heavy burden on her shoulders—the fate of hundreds of McNamara employees and their families as well as the responsibility of a group of ungrateful, manipulative, dependent relatives. Roarke decided his wife was one of the strongest, most in-control women he'd ever known. She was the total opposite of Hope, who had been weak and dangerously emotional. As long as he lived, he would never forgive himself for not realizing sooner how mentally unstable Hope had been.

But Cleo was as different from Hope as sunlight is from darkness. In one short week, Roarke had learned to admire Cleo greatly. His speculation about her nobility had been correct. She was a woman with a mission, and that mission was to save the livelihood of her treasured employees and keep McNamara's a family-owned-and-operated business.

"We have people working here now whose grandfathers once worked here for Uncle George and my grandfather, before World War II." Cleo led Roarke into the shipping and receiving department, where raw materials needed to produce McNamara fertilizer were brought in and the finished product sent out.

"Hey, Blake." Cleo waved at an attractive man with black curly hair. "Come meet my husband."

A tall, lanky man in his mid-thirties turned around and smiled. "Ms. McNa—I mean Mrs. Roarke."

Carrying a clipboard in his hand, he limped toward

them. That's when Roarke noticed the heavy brace on the man's leg.

Cleo and Blake exchanged a hearty handshake, then Cleo turned to Roarke. "Simon, this is Blake Saunders, our shipping and receiving foreman. He's the man who keeps everything moving in and out of McNamara Industries. Blake, this is my husband, Simon Roarke. Simon is going to head up a small security force here at the plant to investigate the accidents we've had and to look into some recent computer tampering."

"Rumors have been spreading like wildfire," Blake told them. "An accident-free plant with a top-notch maintenance crew doesn't suddenly start having accidents. At least not two in ten days."

"What are people saying?" Cleo asked.

"They're saying there's something fishy going on." Blake nodded toward the crew of workmen, each man busy at his job. "We know Mr. Sutton and his folks want you to sell McNamara's. And...well...some of us have been wondering just how far a person would go to try to persuade you to sell. Not saying anything against Mr. Sutton and certainly not accusing him of anything."

"It's all right, Blake. I understand. I have my own doubts. That's why Simon—Mr. Roarke—is going to begin an investigation and hire a small security force."

"May I tell the men?" Blake laughed self-consciously, then corrected himself. "I mean the crew. I keep forgetting that we've got Margie. She's so much like one of the boys, most of the time I forget she's female."

Roarke scanned the crew, trying to figure out which one was Margie. Then he saw her. Big, rawboned, with linebacker shoulders, Margie drove one of the forklift trucks that the crew used to stack the pallets of fertilizer sacks and to load those pallets onto trucks for shipping. When Margie lifted a stack of pallets and turned the forklift, Roarke noticed that she was young and not bad-looking. But there was a hardness in that face, a strength and determination that warned off intruders.

"I have an even better idea," Cleo said. "Why don't we let Roarke introduce himself to the crew and explain things."

Blake glanced at Roarke, the two men's gazes meeting squarely. In that one moment, Roarke sized up the other man and made an instant judgment call. Blake Saunders was an okay kind of guy.

"Listen up," Blake said loudly, getting the attention of several crewmen. Then slowly, one by one, the workers paused to listen.

"Why don't we go over to your desk so you can show me your new pictures of Michael," Cleo suggested. "I think Simon can handle this without any help from me."

"How'd you know I have new pictures of Michael on my desk?" Laughing, Blake followed Cleo across to the partition in the corner that created his work nook.

Cleo listened while Roarke introduced himself and explained about the problems McNamara Industries had been having and the steps he intended to take to investigate those problems and to prevent any future incidents.

Cleo lifted a gold-framed photo of an adorable one-year-old boy with his father's curly black hair. "How's Michael doing since the doctors put the tubes in his ears?"

"Great. We sure did appreciate those balloons you sent to the hospital, and the toys," Blake said.

Cleo and Blake chatted while Roarke spoke to the crew, then when Roarke finished speaking, he glanced around, looking for Cleo. When he saw her, he motioned to her. She nodded and smiled. Although the employees talked among themselves, they went back to work quickly.

"I forgot to congratulate you on your marriage, Mrs. Roarke," Blake said. "I hope you and Mr. Roarke will be as happy as Kristy and I are."

"Thank you." Cleo wished everyone would stop congratulating her on a marriage that was as phony as a three-dollar bill. She felt like a fraud. Dammit, she was a fraud. She'd been married over a week and still hadn't consummated her marriage. What difference did it really make how well acquainted she and Roarke were before they made love? The end result would be the same—divorce.

The telephone on Blake's desk rang. When he reached out to answer it, Cleo mouthed "Goodbye" and started walking toward Roarke, who had just stepped out onto one of the loading platforms.

Under different circumstances, she would be proud to be married to Simon Roarke. He'd certainly acquired the respect of all the McNamara employees. She'd seen it in their eyes when they'd met him, noted it on their faces when they listened to him speak. He was a commanding presence. Strong. Self-assured. Emitting an aura of power.

Roarke watched Cleo as she walked toward him. She took quick, short steps, her black heels tapping on the concrete floor. Behind Cleo, Margie turned the loaded forklift around and headed it in the direction of the loading platform on which Roarke stood. A truck waited at the end.

The forklift lurched forward. Margie yelled. Cleo swirled around just in time to see the forklift barreling down on her. Margie jumped out of the vehicle. Her robust body hit the hard concrete floor. She cried out in pain.

Cleo froze to the spot for one brief instant, then realized she was in danger. Before she could move, Roarke shoved her out of the forklift's path, pushing her so hard that they both toppled to the floor. As they hit the concrete, he lifted her so that his body took the brunt of the fall.

She clung to him, her heart in her throat. Gasping for air, she gazed into his eyes and saw genuine fear. He'd been afraid for her.

"I—I'm all right," she told him. "Are you hurt?"

He lifted her to her feet, steadying her with his strong arm around her waist. "I'm okay, but we're both probably bruised and we'll be awfully sore by morning."

The forklift rolled out onto the loading platform. Without a driver to guide its path, the vehicle veered to one side and dove headlong off the side of the platform, crashing onto the pavement below. Several pallets filled with sacks of fertilizer hit the concrete and broke apart.

"What happened?" Cleo caught a glimpse of the crew as several rushed toward her, while some hurried to help their injured coworker and others went to inspect the wrecked forklift. "Is Margie all right?"

"I'm not sure what happened," Roarke said. "Margie seemed to lose control of the forklift and you just happened to be right in the way."

"I didn't lose control," Margie said as Blake and another man helped her to her feet. "The damn brakes wouldn't work. I tried using the emergency brake, but I couldn't get it to work, either."

Jerking her head around, Cleo stared at Roarke. "Another unexplained accident?"

"Blake, have one of your men take Margie to the emergency room," Cleo ordered.

"I'll be okay," Margie said.

"Let's make sure of that," Cleo told her. "Regardless of what the E.R. doctor tells you, take tomorrow off."

"And Blake," Roarke called out to the foreman, "get

maintenance down here, pronto. I want that forklift gone over with a fine-tooth comb. I want a full report on my desk first thing in the morning."

Blake issued orders to a crewman to drive Margie to the hospital, then rushed over to his desk and called maintenance.

"The rest of you guys get back to work," Blake said once he'd hung up the phone. "Morton, get that mess cleaned up. Use another forklift and get any of the undamaged pallets loaded."

Leaning against Roarke, Cleo glanced down at his big hand lying across her waist. Blood pooled across his knuckles.

"You've hurt your hand." Turning in his arms, she lifted his hand and inspected it.

"It's nothing. I skinned it when we fell."

"We should go to first aid and let the nurse clean it," Cleo said, holding his hand tenderly.

"You can clean it for me when we get home." He jerked his hand away from her, placed it in the center of her back and nudged her forward. "We were planning on leaving straight from here, weren't we?"

"Yes, but—"

Blake walked up beside them. "Do you think the forklift was sabotaged?"

"I think it's likely," Roarke said.

"You believe someone intended for me to be run down?" Cleo asked.

"No." Roarke slipped his arm around her waist and pulled her up against him. "There's no way anyone would have known exactly when you'd be in shipping and receiving, and if this person tampered with the brakes, there would be no way of timing precisely how long it would take them to malfunction."

"So this was set up as another plant 'accident,'" Cleo said. "And another McNamara employee has been injured."

"Should I call the sheriff, Mr. Roarke?" Blake asked.

"Let's hold off on that until I see the maintenance foreman's report. If the brakes on the forklift were tampered with, then I'll notify the local authorities."

"Yes, sir." Blake looked at Cleo. "Are you sure you're all right? Is there anything I can do for you?"

Cleo held her trembling hands out in front of her. "Whew. I guess I'm still a little shaky, but I'll be fine. I need to get out of these dirty clothes—" she glanced down at her soiled linen suit, scuffed heels and shredded panty hose "—and maybe take a hot bath before my muscles start screaming."

"I'll handle things here," Blake said. "And, Mr. Roarke, I'll make sure that report is on your desk first thing in the morning."

"Fine." Roarke grasped Blake's hand and shook it firmly. Once Blake walked away, Roarke said in a low voice, for Cleo's ears only, "I'll have Kane fly in tomorrow, and we'll get an internal investigation under way as soon as possible."

Roarke didn't like the smell of this accident—it stank to high heaven. It made perfect sense to sabotage equipment in the plant and to create computer problems if all the assailant wanted was to pressure Cleo into selling McNamara Industries. But then if the person's motive was to kill Cleo, things didn't quite add up. The only incident that might have been an attempt on her life had been the rifle shots, which hadn't come close to hitting her. There was definitely more going on here than met the eye. He just hadn't quite figured out what. Not yet. But he would.

Then heaven help the person or persons causing trouble for Cleo.

"If you need another Dundee man, that's fine with me," Cleo said. "But with you already here, why do we really need someone else to investigate and to hire and train a security force?"

Roarke dropped his hand to her hip and squeezed gently. "Are you sore from the fall?" he asked.

"Not much. But I do feel a bit battered," she admitted. "I'm okay, Roarke. Now, answer my question."

"Because, Mrs. Roarke, I can't be in more than one place at a time."

"Meaning?"

"Meaning that I can't be with you twenty-four hours a day, protecting you, and handle all the details of a complete investigation, while hiring and training a security team."

"Oh. Yes, I suppose you're right."

With his hand on her back, Roarke guided her down the side steps, off the loading platform and into the private executive parking lot. When they reached her Jaguar, Cleo's steps faltered. Roarke steadied her instantly, one arm going around her waist as one hand clamped down on her shoulder.

"I thought you said you weren't injured." Roarke growled the words as he gazed down at the blood seeping through her scuffed jacket sleeve, staining the lavender linen.

The pavement beneath her feet swirled around and around. Moaning quietly, Cleo grabbed Roarke's arm and leaned against him. "I'm just a little dizzy."

Roarke swept her up in his arms, unlocked the Jag and deposited Cleo on the passenger side, then rounded the car and slid into the driver's seat.

"I'm taking you to the hospital!" He revved the motor, shifted into Reverse and zoomed the Jag backward, out of the parking place.

"No, please. I'm all right. Really. I'm not dizzy anymore. I think maybe it was just a tiny bout of delayed shock or something."

"If you don't want to go to the emergency room, then as soon as we get home, I'm going to check you over thoroughly myself. And if I think you need to see a doctor, you won't argue with me."

"Thanks." She reached over and clasped his forearm. "I agree to your terms."

Roarke shifted gears. Second. Third. Fourth. Fifth. He flew the Jag out of the parking lot and onto the highway.

"Roarke?"

"What, Boss Lady?" He hazarded a glance at her. Her face was too pale. Even if she wouldn't admit it to herself, Cleo was badly shaken.

"When we get home, if we run into Aunt Beatrice before we can clean up, would you please help me downplay the accident?"

"I'll do what I can to reassure her, but your aunt is no fool. She's bound to suspect the truth."

"Exactly what is the truth?" Releasing Roarke's arm, Cleo lay back in the seat and rested her head on the soft leather.

"The truth is that someone's damned and determined to get you to sell McNamara Industries," Roarke told her as he maneuvered her Jag along the highway, heading west toward home. "I think the shooting right after your uncle's funeral was only an attempt to frighten you, and I believe these problems at the plant are designed to wreak havoc and convince you that the safest course of action is to sell."

"I will not be intimidated into selling McNamara's!"

"Once this person realizes that the scare tactics aren't working, that's when your life will be in real danger."

He hated the very thought that someone might try to kill Cleo. Already, without meaning to, he'd become emotionally involved with his client. It was something he'd never done before. In the past he'd been too smart to let his personal feelings get in the way of performing his duty.

It wasn't as if he loved Cleo. But he did like her. And he respected and admired her. And he wanted her almost to the point of madness. Once he'd had her, everything would be all right. He could handle liking her, respecting her and admiring her and still do his job. But when it came to keeping her safe, he had to have his mind one hundred percent on protecting her. As long as he felt like a mongrel chasing a bitch in heat, he risked making a mistake. And one mistake on his part could cost Cleo her life.

She glanced at him. He saw her in his peripheral vision.

"I'm glad I married you," she said. "Having you at my side makes me stronger. I know I'm not alone. You'll help me save McNamara's."

"I'll do my best," Roarke said.

"Thank you...Simon."

Her use of his Christian name created a hard knot of apprehension in his belly. He preferred for her to call him "Roarke"—it kept their relationship on a business level—and despite their discussion about it on their wedding night, she usually used the less intimate name. But when she called him "Simon" in that sexy, raspy voice of hers, it made him want to hear her cry out his name in the throes of passion. Every time she called him "Simon," he knew it meant something to her—that she was beginning to care for him. And that could be dangerous. For both of them.

CHAPTER SIX

ROARKE OPENED THE bedroom door for the housekeeper and took the first-aid kit she handed him. "Thanks, Pearl."

She glanced down at Roarke's skinned and bloody knuckles, then peered across the room, where Cleo sat on the edge of the chaise longue. "Do you need any help?"

"No, thanks." Cleo removed her scuffed heels, then inspected her ripped panty hose, and realized that beneath the ruined nylon her left leg was badly scraped. "I'll make sure Simon's wounds are tended."

Pearl gave Cleo a once-over, pausing when their eyes met. "What about your wounds, Cleo Belle? You look pretty battered up to me."

"I'll take care of my wife," Roarke said. "She refused to go to the hospital, so she has no choice but to let me examine her and make sure she has no serious injuries."

"She's always been stubborn," Pearl told him. "Ever since she was no higher than my knee. Always wanted her own way. Knew what she wanted and figured out how to get it. I've discovered that the only way to handle her when she's being stubborn is with brute force." Pearl chuckled, apparently remembering times when, as a child, nothing short of physical restraint had saved Cleo from harm.

"I'll keep that in mind." Glancing at Cleo, Roarke grinned. "If you hear her hollering, you'll know I've had to resort to letting her know who's boss."

Cleo stuck out her tongue at him. His grin widened.

"Don't listen to Pearl," Cleo said. "I was an angelic child. I never gave anyone a moment's trouble."

"Well, now, Mr. Roarke, if you believe that one, I've got some swampland in Florida I'll sell you real cheap." Pearl laid her pudgy hand on Roarke's arm. "She's as stubborn as the day is long. She might well have the soul of an angel, but as a child she had a mean, stubborn streak. And though she's learned to control it some since she grew up, it still rears its ugly head from time to time. You just watch out for it."

"I'll do that," Roarke said.

When Pearl started to leave, Cleo called out to her. "Wait."

Stopping immediately, the housekeeper glanced over her shoulder at Cleo. "When Aunt Beatrice returns from the bridge party at Mrs. Madden's, tell her that I'll see her at breakfast. There's no point in worrying her about what happened at the plant. I'll tell her in the morning. That way she'll be able to get a good night's sleep tonight."

"What if, during dinner this evening, Trey mentions the accident at the plant?" Pearl asked.

"Trey had a trip planned to Huntsville this afternoon, so I doubt he'll learn about the accident before I tell him in the morning," Cleo said.

"I'll do my best to handle things below." Pearl looked directly at Roarke. "You handle *things* up here."

"I'll certainly try," Roarke said, then closed the door behind Pearl when she walked out into the hall.

With the first-aid supplies in his hands, Roarke turned around and watched while Cleo removed her ripped jacket and tossed it on the floor. He clenched his teeth when he saw the two large bruises on her left arm.

He had to find a way to keep Cleo safe from any more plant "accidents." Although this one hadn't been planned to injure her, it had. And whoever was creating havoc at McNamara Industries was probably either the same person who had taken a shot at Cleo or was a cohort.

"I'll have to throw this suit away. I'm afraid it's ruined." Gripping her elbow, she lifted her arm, turning it slightly to get a better look at the darkening bruises. "Oh, they look awful, don't they? Like someone hit me really hard a couple of times."

Slowly, silently, Roarke crossed the room, laid the first-aid supplies at the foot of the chaise longue and removed his sport coat. He tossed the coat onto a nearby chair and reached out for Cleo. Without making a comment or asking permission, he began unbuttoning her blouse. She stared down at his big fingers working the buttons loose. The side of his hand brushed against her breast. Her nipple beaded instantly. She sucked in her breath and looked up at him. Their gazes met and held.

"I—I can unbutton my own blouse," she told him. But by the time she spoke, he was already pushing her short-sleeved, purple silk blouse off her shoulders.

His big hands felt like fine sandpaper, the palms callused from the physical workouts that kept his body in fighting form. Lifting her arm in one hand, he ran his fingers gently over the bruising, then up to her shoulder and across to her neck.

Her aching body tingled with awareness. She hadn't allowed a man to touch her this intimately since Paine Emerson had seduced her. And not even the girlish love she'd felt for her former fiancé had induced such a strong, physical need.

"If we'd gotten an ice pack on this, it would have helped," he told her as he ran his hand over her right shoulder and down her arm, inspecting it for damage. "Is it already sore?"

"Yes," Cleo admitted. "To be honest, I'm sore all over."

And I'm aching inside, she thought. I can't bear for you to touch me like this, and yet I don't want you to stop.

"It might be even worse in the morning," he said.

She nodded in agreement, knowing that by morning not only would her body be sore, but after another night of lying next to Roarke, she would be aching with longing.

He undid the closure on her skirt, then eased down the zipper. "Lift your hips up just a little, so we can get your skirt off."

Her heartbeat roared in her ears as the deafening flood of blood raced through her body. Obeying his command without a word of protest, she lifted her hips. He slipped off her skirt, then pushed up her silk slip. When his fingers slid beneath the waistband of her panty hose, she gasped and looked up at him.

Staring directly into her eyes, he said, "We've got to take these panty hose off so I can take a good look at your leg."

He took his time removing the hose, all the while stroking her hips and legs with his fingers as he maneuvered the tattered material downward. She closed her eyes, savoring the sensation of his gentle touch, while at the same time she tried to control her body's reaction. But she could no more stop her breasts from tightening and throbbing and her femininity from moistening and clenching than she could stop the sun from rising in the morning.

Blood had dried and stuck to the nylon along her lower thigh and upper calf, so he took extra precaution, being as gentle as possible. She winced and opened her mouth on a silent cry when he loosened the soiled and shredded panty hose from her scraped flesh.

After throwing the ruined hose on top of her discarded

clothing, Roarke lifted her leg and examined the injury. Without any warning, he scooped her up in his arms, picked up the first-aid kit and headed toward the bathroom.

"What—" She grabbed him around the neck. "I can walk!"

The scent of sweat and dried blood clung to him. Breathing in those warrior odors, Cleo shivered and fought the urge to rest her head on his shoulder.

"Quicker this way," he said as he sat her down on the vanity stool in the bathroom. "Doesn't look like anything serious. I'll clean these scratches and scraps." He laid the kit on the vanity and popped open the lid. "Other than having some ugly bruises and being sore for a while, you should be fine."

"What about you?" Cleo asked, looking at the dried blood on his knuckles. "You must have done that when you rolled me over on top of you and your hands skidded along the concrete floor."

"I'll make a deal with you, Boss Lady. You be a good girl and let me tend to your wounds, and when I finish, you can tend to mine."

"You're used to getting your way, aren't you?"

"I'd say that was something we have in common."

Turning his back to her, he rummaged in the first-aid kit and removed a small bottle of peroxide. Glancing up at him, she immediately saw bloodstains on the back of his shirt. Stains that had darkened a large circle across his shoulder blade and dotted a trail of droplets down to his waist. Her gaze focused momentarily on the hip holster that housed his sleek, deadly Beretta.

"Roarke?"

He turned around, peroxide and cotton balls in his hands. "Yeah?"

"Your back has been bleeding."

"I figured it had." He poured the peroxide on her scraped leg. "You can take a look at it for me." Once the peroxide bubbled on her wounds, he blotted the residue off with the cotton swabs. "I don't think this needs to be covered, but I'll check it again in a few hours and see."

Suddenly she felt quite vulnerable sitting there in her slip, with Roarke hovering over her. He played the role of protective and caring husband to perfection, but Cleo's instincts told her that his attentive actions went far beyond mere acting.

"Thank you," she said.

"You're welcome. It was my pleasure, Boss Lady."

Cleo stood on weak, trembly legs, wanting nothing more than to fall into Roarke's strong arms. "Now it's my turn to play nursemaid and see to your injuries."

He unbuttoned his soiled shirt, revealing his broad, hairy chest. Cleo watched, tantalized, as he removed the shirt and tossed it on the floor. He turned his back to her and waited. She grimaced when she saw the raw, red scrape across his right shoulder blade.

"Well, what does it look like?" He glanced over his shoulder and grinned when he saw the dismay on her face. "That bad, huh?"

"Oh, no, not bad at all. Just bloody." Forcing herself to concentrate on the task at hand and not on Roarke's incredible physique, Cleo picked up the peroxide bottle and doused his wounds. The excess liquid ran down his back, dribbling onto his slacks. "Damn!" Grabbing several cotton balls, Cleo swabbed at the trickling peroxide dampening his waist.

"What were you trying to do—give me a bath in that stuff?" he asked jokingly, then turned around and held

up his scuffed knuckles. "Just dab these with a little peroxide."

He had to know how nervous she was, and had probably guessed the reason. She felt foolish overreacting to
a man's gentle touch and the sight of his partial nudity.
It wasn't as if this was the first time he'd touched her or
the first time she'd seen him without his shirt. He slept
in nothing but his pajama bottoms every night. But this
was the first time she had given herself over to the pure
sensual pleasure of sight and touch.

Cleo cleaned his knuckles quickly, then recapped the
peroxide bottle and closed the first-aid kit. "There. I think
we'll both live."

She whirled around, prepared to leave the bathroom
and escape Roarke's nearness. In her haste, she didn't notice that he had eased toward her, and when she turned,
she brushed against his bare chest. Throwing up her hands
in surprise, she froze to the spot. Roarke grasped her
hands and laid them on his chest.

She felt the steady beat of his heart. Her hands quivered. Her stomach fluttered. She swallowed hard.

His gaze traveled from her flushed face, down her
throat and over the rise of her breasts, which pressed up
above the lace on the bodice of her lavender slip.

"You're a lovely woman, Cleo Belle." He slipped his
hand behind her head and grasped her neck.

She stared at him, hypnotized by the look in his piercing blue eyes. Of their volition, her fingers threaded
through the thick, dark hair curling over the center of his
muscular chest. She opened her mouth to speak. To tell
him that he was a handsome man. That it was a pleasure
just to look at him. But before she could utter one word,
Roarke tightened his hold around the back of her neck,

pressed her face upward and swooped his head down, capturing her mouth in a hot, wet kiss.

She gave in to the slow, damp, heated desire spreading through her like sweet honey over warm bread. As he deepened the kiss, she responded wildly, gripping his shoulders and pressing her body intimately to his. His sex pulsed against her. Her femininity tightened and released, then tightened again in greater awareness and stronger need.

Just when she thought she couldn't bear another moment of this tortured arousal, Roarke clutched her buttocks in his big hands and lifted her up and into his hardness. She cried out from the sheer agonized pleasure, the sound muffled by his lips on hers, his mouth devouring hers.

On the precipice, ready to plunge headlong into mindless sensuality, Cleo mumbled a complaint when Roarke ended their kiss and released her. When she continued clinging to him, he stepped backward. Her fingertips grazed his chest, then she retreated, lowering her arms and gazing up at him questioningly.

"Six days isn't long," he said, his deep voice calm and controlled.

"Six days?" Her mind couldn't seem to focus, refusing to comprehend the meaning of his words.

"We were married eight days ago today. In six days we will be married two weeks."

"Oh." Realization dawned.

"Have you changed your mind about waiting the full two weeks?" he asked.

"I…I don't…"

"You're in charge of this marriage, Boss Lady. I follow your orders."

"Yes, I know. I'm just not sure if we should—"

"Think about it and let me know," he told her. "I'm

going to go change into a pair of jeans, then make a call to Morgan Kane at Dundee's."

"You're going to call Mr. Kane this evening?"

"Yes. After the incident today, I don't want to delay bringing him in. If I can get in touch with him now, he can be here by breakfast in the morning."

"I see. Well...yes, of course. By all means, go call Mr. Kane."

For some odd reason she felt as if Roarke had deliberately thrown a bucket of ice water on her. Was he toying with her? Tempting her?

Had he taken Pearl's suggestions to heart and used *brute force?* Had the kiss been intended to show her that he, and not she, was really the boss of their marriage? Damn the man! She'd show him who was boss. If he thought she couldn't last six more days without his lovemaking, then he was wrong. She'd lived through a week of sleeping beside him, longing for him to reach out and take her, dreaming of what it would be like to belong to him. She could wait another six days. But while they were waiting, she was going to make him suffer as much as she did.

WHILE MAKING ARRANGEMENTS with Kane to fly from Atlanta to River Bend on the first available flight, Roarke watched his wife. She entered the closet, leaving the door ajar just enough to allow him a glimpse. Not once did she glance his way or acknowledge that she knew he could see her. Slowly, provocatively, she pulled her slip up over her head and discarded it. For a couple of minutes Roarke couldn't think, couldn't remember what he was saying to Kane. Actually, for about half a second, he didn't even realize he was on the phone.

Wearing nothing but a pair of lavender silk panties and

matching bra, Cleo searched through her clothes. She removed an item off the rack, looked at it and replaced it; then she repeated the procedure several times. Roarke's sex, which he'd just gotten under control, grew hot and heavy again. What the hell was she doing? If he didn't know better, he'd swear she was putting on a show for his benefit. To drive him crazy!

Cleo's petite body was slender, but not lacking in all the right curves. Her hips flared nicely and her butt was full and tight. And her breasts—ah her breasts. High, round and firm. And larger than anyone would suspect hidden there beneath her simple little suits.

"Huh?" Roarke hadn't heard what Kane had said.

"I said I'll be on your doorstep at the crack of dawn," Morgan Kane told Roarke. "Hey, buddy, what's wrong with you? You seem distracted."

"Sorry, I let my mind wander." Yeah, his mind, his libido and his sanity had all wandered into dangerous territory. "I'll work with you, but I'm going to need you to take charge of the investigation. My main function is protecting Cleo." What was she doing now? he wondered. No, she isn't going to. She wouldn't. She would! His body tightened painfully. Cleo unhooked her bra, removed it slowly and tossed it on top of her slip. He was going to kill her! "Huh? I didn't get that?"

"Dammit, man, if I didn't know better, I'd swear you were right in the middle of having sex," Kane said. "Where's your mind?"

My mind is on my wife's bare breasts, Roarke thought. Hell, she had to know what she was doing. Didn't she? Maybe not. Maybe she didn't realize she'd left the door cracked enough to put her body on display.

"Look, I've got to run. I'll see you first thing in the

morning." Not certain whether Kane made any reply,
Roarke hung up the phone.

He crossed his arms over his chest and stared at Cleo's
breasts. All he had to do was close his eyes or just turn
away to end his torment. But he did neither. His gaze
caressed her. His thoughts tasted her pink nipples. Instantly, as if she knew what he was thinking, her nipples
puckered.

Holding his hands at his sides, he balled them into fists
and silently cursed his own male weakness. Why was he
punishing himself like this, visually devouring a woman
he couldn't bed for six more days? If things continued
this way, he'd be a raving lunatic by the end of the week.
If he wasn't married to Cleo, if he hadn't made a bargain
with her, he'd sure as hell go out and find himself a willing woman as soon as possible.

Cleo pulled a pair of soft, yellow cotton slacks off a
hanger. Her breasts swayed when she bent over to drag
the pants up her legs. Roarke closed his eyes then, as his
mind flooded with thoughts of those luscious breasts dangling over him, of his mouth reaching up to taste their
sweetness. When he opened his eyes a few minutes later,
she had slipped a baggy yellow T-shirt over her head.

Find something to do, he told himself. Get your mind
off having sex with Cleo. Looking around the room, he
noticed the bookcase. That's it. He'd read awhile.

Cleo walked out of the closet and over to Roarke, who
stood in front of the open bookcase. She placed her hand
on his shoulder. He tensed instantly.

"Looking for something in particular?" she asked.

"No. Just anything to pass the time until Ezra brings
up dinner." If she didn't remove her hand, he was going
to either slap it away or jerk her into his arms. He knew

she wasn't wearing a bra, and if he pulled her up against him, he'd be able to feel her nipples pressing into his chest.

"I've got Stephen King's latest, if you like horror, and a couple of other bestsellers. And several archaeology books, if you're interested." Cleo reached inside the bookcase and pulled out a leather-bound volume. "This book belonged to my grandfather. It's a history of River Bend from the early 1800s to the mid 1930s."

When she held the book out to him, he accepted it, their hands just barely touching. He looked into her eyes and knew she'd felt the jolt of awareness that passed between them just as surely as he had.

"Thanks." *Get the hell away from her, man, before you're the one doing the begging!*

"Sure."

Cleo crossed the room, lifted her briefcase off the desk at the foot of her bed and removed a file folder. She slumped onto the floral chaise longue, then brought her knees up to use as a prop for her folder. Once she had it open, she flipped through the contents, stopping at the section she needed to study. If McNamara Industries' orders were being deleted from the computer, the person responsible might have left some evidence of the tampering.

She glanced over at Roarke, who had sat down on the bed and braced his back against the headboard. Why didn't the man button his shirt? Was he deliberately tempting her by giving her a partial view of his magnificent chest? Marvelously muscled. Gloriously hairy. And brutally scarred. She had to ignore him, to pretend he didn't arouse her.

She smiled secretly, remembering the nerve it had taken for her to undress down to her panties in front of him. He had no way of being sure she'd done it on pur-

pose. She'd closed the closet door more than halfway. She
had never in her entire life set out to purposely arouse a
man. But she'd rather enjoyed putting on a striptease show
for her husband. By the time he'd hung up the phone and
she'd come out of the closet to find him by the bookcase,
he'd gained some control over his body. But his nostrils
had been flared, his sex semierect, and a fine sheen of
perspiration glistened over his upper lip.

She loved knowing that he was attracted to her, that
he wanted her as she wanted him. But just as she knew
how he felt, he knew the same about her. It was as if they
were in a game of wills, to see who would give in first—
before the appointed two weeks were up. In retrospect,
she realized she'd been foolish to make such a decree,
considering how sexually aware she'd been of him since
the moment they'd met. But in fairness to herself, her reasoning had been sensible. She'd wanted to give them both
time—admittedly, especially herself—to adjust to being
married, before they consummated their union. Although
her sexual experience was limited to a brief relationship
with Paine Emerson, she had dated over the years and
been attracted to several men. But never—ever—had she
felt anything to compare with the way she felt every time
she looked at Simon Roarke.

For the next few hours, they gave each other plenty of
space, keeping to themselves except when they shared
dinner in the sitting room. While eating, they limited
their conversation to business, discussing the forklift accident, the computer tampering and Morgan Kane's expected arrival the next day. Cleo spoke briefly to Blake
and relayed the messages to Roarke. Margie Evans had
been released from the emergency room with a sprained
wrist and minor bruising. And maintenance's initial find-

ing was that someone had definitely tampered with the brakes on the forklift.

Roarke remained in the sitting room while Cleo returned to the paperwork waiting on her desk. He opened the armoire that hid a thirty-five-inch television. Slumping onto the sofa, he clicked the remote to ESPN and lowered the sound to just barely audible.

Cleo studied the information on McNamara Industries' orders for the past month until her vision began blurring. Pinching the bridge of her nose, she braced her elbow on the desk and rested her head.

A piercing scream shook Cleo from her restful meditation. Then she heard a second scream, followed quickly by a third. My God, who was screaming? And why?

Cleo rose so quickly that she knocked her briefcase onto the floor. Roarke flew out of the sitting room, dashed over to the nightstand and removed his Beretta. He met Cleo at the bedroom door and pushed her behind him as he eased the door open.

"I'll go find out what happened," he told her. "You close this door and lock it. And don't open it to anyone you wouldn't trust with your life. Is that understood?"

She nodded her agreement. The moment Roarke stepped into the hallway, she closed and locked the door. Waiting impatiently, she paced the floor. She heard voices in the hallway, but couldn't distinguish the speakers.

Someone tapped softly on her door. Gasping, she jumped, then shivered. "Who is it?"

"It's me, dear, Aunt Beatrice."

Cleo unlocked the door. Hurrying inside, Beatrice threw her arms around her niece and held her close. Cleo returned her aunt's hug, then grasped Beatrice's hands. "What's going on? Who was doing all that screaming?"

"Oralie," Beatrice said. "She swears she saw a man peeping in the windows."

"Downstairs?"

"Yes, in the front-parlor windows. And the hysterical fool wouldn't stop screaming." Beatrice huffed disgustedly. "Perry and I didn't see a thing. Oralie was working on her needlepoint and Perry and I were listening to a Mozart concerto."

"Where's the rest of the family?"

"They're all downstairs," Beatrice said. "Or they were a few minutes ago. They followed Simon down the stairs. Daphne and Trey are trying to comfort their mother. I think Marla poured Oralie some sherry."

"Where's Roarke?"

"Simon went outside to check the grounds. He asked me to come up and explain to you what happened and stay with you until he returned." Beatrice walked over and closed the bedroom door, then locked it. "I told him that Oralie had a delicate disposition and was prone to hysteria. But he said he wasn't going to take any chances where your safety was concerned." Beatrice patted Cleo's arm. "My dear, you are most fortunate in your choice of a husband. Considering the unusual circumstances, he is the perfect man for you."

"Yes, I believe he is." Cleo walked into the sitting room and looked out the row of windows. She had planned to wait until morning to tell her aunt about McNamara Industries' problems, but since it was unlikely anyone would get a good night's sleep after Oralie's outburst, Cleo decided there was no point in delaying. "We're having trouble at the plant."

"What sort of trouble?" Beatrice joined her niece, draped her arm around her shoulders and pulled her away from the window. "Simon said not to show yourself in front of the windows. Your silhouette would make a perfect target."

"He thinks of everything, doesn't he?"

"He's been trained for it, you know." Beatrice led Cleo over to the sofa and they sat side by side. "What's going on at the plant?"

"Someone tampered with the computer and deleted several big orders. Those orders were never shipped."

"How long has this been going on?"

"Only since Uncle George died."

"I see." Beatrice sighed loudly. "Daddy had no idea what a hornet's nest his will would stir, did he? Since Trey is an executive with access to the computers, I assume he's the chief suspect."

"One of the suspects, anyway," Cleo said. "But it's possible that whoever's behind the problem is paying an employee to delete the orders."

"What about Hugh and Daphne? He's weak enough to be influenced by her greed."

"There's more going on than computer tampering."

Sitting very still, her sharp green eyes studying Cleo's face, Beatrice laid her hand over her niece's. "Something more dangerous?"

"There have been three accidents at the plant since Uncle George's funeral. One today." Cleo hesitated, not wanting to upset her aunt. But she knew she couldn't keep the truth from Beatrice. "We're fairly certain that someone tampered with the brakes on a forklift. Margie Evans was injured. A sprained wrist and some bruising. And... well, when the forklift went out of control, I was directly in its path."

Beatrice grasped Cleo's wrist and looked anxiously into her eyes. "You weren't hurt, were you?"

"Roarke shoved me out of the way. I got a few scrapes from the fall on the concrete floor, but that's all."

"What does Simon intend to do about these problems?"

"He called another Dundee Security employee tonight and the man will be here by morning," Cleo said. "Mr. Morgan Kane will train a small security force for McNamara's and, under Simon's supervision, he will head up an investigation into the computer tampering and the accidents."

"While Simon guards you."

"That's right." Cleo shivered. "I hate this being suspicious and afraid, this second-guessing everyone and everything."

Beatrice wrapped her arms around Cleo and drew her niece's head down into her lap. She stroked Cleo's shiny red hair, so like her own. "I have every confidence in your husband. He'll protect you."

Lying contentedly with her head in her aunt's lap, as she had done so often when she was a child, Cleo wished that she could spare Beatrice the truth. But they both had to face reality. And the sooner, the better. "What makes this whole thing so difficult is knowing that someone in the family has to be behind everything—the problems at the plant and the attempt on my life."

A loud knock on the bedroom door brought Cleo and Beatrice up off the sofa. Side by side, the two walked into the bedroom.

"Yes?" Cleo called out.

"It's me, Roarke."

Cleo rushed to open the door. The moment her husband appeared, she let out a sigh of relief. "Did you find anyone?"

"Not a soul," he said. "I don't think there was ever anyone peeping in the windows. Mrs. Sutton's imagination must have gotten the best of her."

"That's happened before," Beatrice said. "Besides, she's been a nervous wreck ever since Daddy died. She made a nasty scene at the reading of the will."

"Well, Mr. Sutton said he'd given his wife a sedative and put her to bed. And Trey sent Marla to their room. The rest of them are downstairs waiting for us. They're demanding a family meeting."

"They're what?" Beatrice screeched.

"For what reason?" Cleo asked.

"They want to hire a night watchman for the grounds," Roarke said. "Daphne told me that she's felt uneasy ever since someone took a shot at you, and now that her mother has seen someone lurking about outside, the sensible thing to do is hire protection for the family."

"They're trying to throw suspicion off themselves," Beatrice said. "I wouldn't put it past Daphne to be at the root of all our problems."

"I think we should meet with them," Roarke said. "Cleo, you tell them that you think hiring a night watchman for the grounds is an excellent idea and you'll see to it immediately. Then we'll have Kane put one of his security people on the job."

"Do you think that's necessary?" Beatrice asked.

"If they're bluffing, we'll call their bluff," Cleo said.

"And we'll be putting one of our own men in place and not someone they hire." Holding the door open, Roarke nodded. "Shall we join the family powwow?"

"By all means." Cleo marched into the hallway, her head held high.

AN HOUR LATER, Roarke and Cleo returned to her suite, the immediate family emergency settled, if not to everyone's satisfaction, at least to Roarke's. As long as Cleo continued allowing him the power to make all security decisions, he felt relatively certain that he could keep her safe. And her safety was his top priority.

Daphne and Trey had protested Roarke's hiring the night watchman for the grounds, telling him plainly that he was a newcomer to the McNamara-Sutton family and had no right to take charge. Cleo backed Roarke a hundred percent, and since she held the purse strings, the others begrudgingly acquiesced to her wishes.

Daphne had pursed her red lips in a little-girl pout and huffed loudly. Roarke suspected he was the first man she'd been unable to twist around her little finger, and so was frustrated at not being able to get her way and seduce him into her bed.

"It doesn't matter to me who hires this security person," Perry Sutton had told them. "Oralie insisted that I speak to y'all about hiring someone and I promised her that I would. She refused to take her sleeping pill until I agreed."

Roarke locked the bedroom door as he did every night. Cleo retrieved her gown and robe from the closet, then headed toward the bathroom.

"I'm tired. This has been a long, difficult day," she said. "I'm going to take my bath and go to bed."

"Go ahead," Roarke told her. "I think I'll watch a little TV. I'll keep it low so it won't disturb you."

She paused in the bathroom doorway. "Simon?"

"Yeah?" Dammit, he wished she wouldn't call him "Simon" when they were alone. But he could hardly demand that she call her "Roarke." What could he tell her? That her using his first name aroused him?

"Thank you for taking this job. For marrying me," Cleo said.

Before he could reply, she hurried into the bathroom and closed the door. Every time she said something sweet and sentimental like that, the hairs on the back of his neck stood up. A warning? He was beginning to worry that Cleo just might possess the power to get through his defenses and make him feel something more than sexual desire. He couldn't let that happen.

Roarke picked up the remote and stretched out on the love seat, hanging his feet over the edge. He found a special on A&E about World War II.

No matter how tired he was, he intended waiting until Cleo was sound asleep before he took his shower and joined her in bed. It was difficult enough lying there beside her when she was asleep, but he couldn't bear it when he knew she was awake and could possibly turn to him and ask him to make love to her.

While one part of his brain registered the events on the television special, another part went over the entire day's events. As the minutes ticked by, he wondered how long it would be before she emerged from the bathroom, fresh, clean and warm from her bath. She'd taken a dark green silk teddy and robe into the bathroom with her. Did she intend to sleep in nothing but a lace teddy?

"Roarke!" Cleo's overly calm voice called out from the bathroom.

He jumped to his feet. "Is something wrong?" He rushed into the bedroom, stopping outside the closed bathroom door.

"I—I can't get out of the bathtub. There are spiders crawling around on the floor. And—and I'm pretty sure that they're brown recluse spiders."

"Stay right where you are," he told her.

"Please, Simon. Help me!"

CHAPTER SEVEN

NOT EVEN AS a child had Cleo been the type of female who was afraid of insects. Much to Aunt Beatrice's dismay, as a preschooler Cleo had been fascinated by grasshoppers and ladybugs and had often handled them with great delight. But spiders were something else altogether. She'd been taught that black widows and brown recluses could be deadly. Pearl had told horror stories about how her own little brother had almost died from a severe reaction to a brown recluse bite.

Cleo stood in the middle of the huge whirlpool tub, her wet, naked body shivering, her nerves jangling. She hadn't noticed anything unusual when she'd entered the bathroom earlier. Nothing out of place.

How could half a dozen spiders have crawled into the bathroom? They couldn't have. One? Unlikely, but possible. Six? Out of the question. Someone had to have placed them inside the large, fluffy towels stacked on the white-wicker shelves at one end of the tub.

Cleo shuddered, remembering how she'd reached out and picked up one of those towels and seen a brown recluse clinging to the terry-cloth surface. The tiny, brown spider had wriggled its eight legs. Cleo had gasped and dropped the towel, but not before she'd noticed the dark, violin-shaped mark on its back near the head. Pearl had been the one who'd taught her how to instantly recognize the poisonous creature.

Within minutes she had noticed other identical spiders crawling over the stack of towels. That's when she had called for help.

Roarke opened the bathroom door, stepped inside and closed the door behind him. Cleo crossed her arms over her breasts, but felt rather silly thinking about modesty at a time like this.

"Be careful," she cautioned him. "They're crawling all over the floor. I've counted six of them."

His gaze traveled the length and breadth of the twelve-by-twelve-foot bathroom, noting the location of all six spiders. "Stay in the tub. I'll get you out."

He had thought of little else but Cleo's naked body lying beneath his. And her little striptease in the closet earlier had certainly added fuel to the fire. For half a second, he looked at her, absorbing the fine lines of her body, the delicate, slender beauty of her feminine curves.

His sex grew hard and heavy. Dammit, he couldn't help how his body reacted, could he? After all he was a man, and Cleo was a lovely, desirable woman.

He crossed the bathroom and stopped at the edge of the tub. Deciding to do the gentlemanly thing, Roarke reached toward the wicker shelves, intending to pull out a towel and wrap it around Cleo.

"Don't," she screamed. He glared at her, his expression questioning her sanity. "The spiders crawled out of the towels. There could be more inside them."

He nodded his understanding, then glanced down at where a spider inched close to his right foot. Without hesitation, he raised his foot and smashed the thing.

"Let me get you out of here, honey," he said. "Then I'll come back in here and take care of these little pests."

Roarke lifted her out of the water and into his arms, bringing her naked body up against his chest. In his walk to the door, he ground another spider beneath his feet. Cleo clung to him, shivering, as much from fear as from the chill. After closing the bathroom door behind them, Roarke dashed over to the bed and set Cleo on the edge, then lifted the quilt coverlet and draped it around her shoulders.

When she looked up at him with her big, trusting green eyes, he could not resist the urge to kiss her. He brushed his lips quickly across hers.

"Stay put. I'll be right back." He headed toward the bathroom.

"Please be careful." She clutched the quilt in both hands, savoring the warmth and protection it provided.

He rewarded her concerned plea with that self-confident little grin of his that she had grown accustomed to over the past week. Then he disappeared into the bathroom.

Fidgeting nervously as she sat on the edge of the bed, Cleo wondered if she shouldn't do something. Call the exterminator? Phone the police? Warn the rest of the family that their home had been invaded by poisonous spiders?

No, there wasn't any need to alarm the rest of the household when she felt certain the spider infestation was limited to her private bath. And if she called the police, what would she tell them? One of my relatives is trying to kill me and I think they planted half a dozen potentially deadly spiders in my bathroom? And she'd wait for Roarke's assessment of the situation before she made a call to the exterminator this late at night.

Maybe she should put on some clothes. The lace teddy and robe that she'd intended wearing to torment Roarke lay on the vanity stool in the bathroom. She had other teddies. She could slip into one of them. No, Roarke had said for her to stay put. When he emerged from his spider annihilation mission, she would be right here, waiting for him.

In retrospect, things didn't seem as scary as they had just a few minutes ago when she'd been totally naked and surrounded by a troop of three-eighths-of-an-inch assassins. Odd, she thought, how completely she'd come to count on Simon Roarke, how totally she trusted him to protect her.

Even though she'd been fortunate enough to have been nurtured, loved and adored by Aunt Beatrice and Pearl and trained for success by a loving uncle George, Cleo had always possessed an independent streak. A need to take care of herself. A determination to do things without assistance, and to do them her own way. And yet here she was, relying on someone else—a man who, although he was her husband, was practically a stranger. But he didn't seem like a stranger. After less than two weeks' acquaintance, she had no doubts that she could trust Roarke with her life. And not simply because he was her employee, but because he was the kind of man who instinctively took care of his own.

"Mission accomplished." Roarke emerged from the bathroom like a conquering hero, having vanquished the foe. "We'll get an exterminator in first thing tomorrow, strictly as a safety precaution. I'm certain there's not a spider left alive. And Pearl's going to have a job straightening up the mess I made in there."

Cleo found that she'd lost her voice when she tried to speak, to verbally respond to Roarke. He stood there, his hair slightly mussed and damp, and grinned at her. His shirt was partially unbuttoned, enough so she could see his moist, curling chest hair. And his sex bulged against his jeans.

She rose up off the bed, mesmerized by the power

radiating from Roarke and urged into action by her own feminine needs. With the quilt draped around her shoulders, she clutched the edges together across her chest. She stared at him, wanting to ask him to make love to her, but her voice was mute. Only her eyes spoke for her.

Roarke halted, stopped dead in his tracks by the look in Cleo's warm green eyes. Was he reading her right? Was she asking for what he thought she was? Or had he let his own desperate need for her influence his perception?

"Cleo?" *Tell me, dammit! Say the words, honey. I want to hear you ask.*

With her gaze fixed on Roarke, she took several tentative steps toward him. The sound of her rapidly pumping heart roared in her ears. She felt hot and moist, and ached unbearably. All she knew was that she wanted Roarke. No, she needed him. Now.

Boldly, she released her grip on the quilt and allowed it to drop from her shoulders and slide down her body, forming a cotton mound on the floor. She stood before him, naked, unashamed and painfully aroused. Being a wanton seductress was something new for her. But then, wanting a man the way she wanted Roarke was also a new experience.

"Ah, Cleo Belle." Roarke tensed, every muscle tightening, every nerve fully alert. His sex grew hard and heavy. "Come here." He didn't open his arms, he simply stood unmoving, waiting for her to obey his command.

They kept their eyes focused on each other, their gazes locked. Cleo walked toward him, slowly, surely. And all the while she wondered if her weak legs could make the short journey. When she reached him, she broke eye contact, lowering her head shyly, needing for Roarke to make the next move. She had come this far, done this much. Now it was time for him to take charge.

"Let me look at you," he said.

Cleo shivered. Her breasts ached, needing his touch to bring them relief.

His gaze traveled over her, from the cap of red silk covering her head to the triangle of red fluff at the apex between her thighs. Small and delicately made, her skin like porcelain, Cleo possessed a perfect, petite body.

His instincts told him that she'd never done anything like this before, never served herself up on a silver platter, her body an offering to a man's desire.

"You're lovely," he told her. "The loveliest thing I've ever seen."

Throbbing, tingling, aching sensations created turmoil inside her. She didn't know how much longer she could stand here without crumbling, without crying out, without begging him to end her agony.

"Undress me," he said, and lifted her hands to his chest.

With unsteady fingers she finished unbuttoning his shirt and spread it apart. Gasping, she shut her eyes. The sight of his hairy, muscled chest took her breath away. She ran her hand over his chest, loving the feel. Tangling her fingers in the thatch of hair, she pressed her cheek against his chest and breathed in the rich, earthy aroma of an aroused man. Her man. Her husband.

She traced the thick scar tissue on the right side of his chest with her fingertips. "How did you get these?"

"Bullets. It happened on an assignment last year. I almost died."

"Oh." Lowering her head, she kissed his scars.

Threading his fingers through her hair, he grasped her head. "Finish the job, honey." Roarke's voice was thick with desire. "Undress me."

Opening her eyes and lifting her head, Cleo stared up at him. He was so tall he towered over her. He released her hair. She slipped the shirt down his shoulders, over his arms and let it drop to the floor. She stared at his belt buckle. She could do this. She had to do this. Roarke wasn't going to help her. He intended to make her strip him.

Struggling several minutes with the buckle, she finally undid it. Then she unsnapped and unzipped his jeans. His sex bulged against the exposed V of his cotton underwear. She gripped his hips and tugged on his jeans, pulling them down. When they reached his ankles, the jeans hung on his feet. Kneeling before him, Cleo unlaced his athletic shoes. Roarke kicked them off one at a time, then held up his left foot. She removed his sock, then the other when he lifted his right foot.

She glanced up the long length of his legs. Powerful, hairy legs. When she swayed forward, resting her head against him, Roarke reached down and lifted her hands to the elastic waistband of his briefs. Staying on her knees, she tugged his underwear over his hips, over his straining sex and down his legs. Roarke stepped out of his briefs and stood there before her, totally naked, fully erect and powerfully male.

Placing his hands under her armpits, he lifted her until her mouth was almost touching him intimately. Her warm breath felt like flames against his engorged shaft. She placed her lips on him, the first kiss hesitant, the next and then the next more eager, as she kissed him from root to tip and back again.

When he could no longer bear her moist, hot caresses, he grasped her head in both hands and drew her sweet mouth away from him. Groaning, the sound a ravaged statement of need, he threaded his fingers through her hair. When she looked up at him, her face flushed, her eyes glazed with passion and her damp lips slightly parted, Roarke thought he would explode.

He lifted her to her feet, his breath ragged, his heart thundering like a wild, racing stallion. Pulling her up to him and off her feet, he pressed his sex against her belly, her breasts against his chest. Then he devoured her mouth in a kiss that robbed her of her breath and of what little sense she had left.

She flung her arms around him, taking his kisses and returning them full measure. Clutching her buttocks in his big hands, he crushed her mound against his sex. She cried out. He moaned.

"Tell me, Cleo. Tell me and I'll put us both out of our misery."

"I want you," she said breathlessly. "Make love to me. Please."

Gathering her up and into his arms, he carried her to the bed and laid her in the center, then came down on top of her. He was hard and heavy and big. So very big. He made her feel tiny and helpless against his strength.

He kissed her savagely, conquering her mouth with his thrusting tongue. Moving hastily on to new territory, he attacked her breasts with tender fierceness, squeezing them gently as he lifted them. He pinched one puckered point, then the other. She moaned and writhed beneath him. Lowering his mouth, he sucked greedily, moving from one begging nipple to the other.

While his mouth ravaged her breasts, he stroked her belly, then moved his hand downward, probing the notch of her legs. When he touched her intimately, her hips rose off the bed. He slipped his hand between her thighs, parting them, then inserted his fingers into the damp, hot tightness. She buckled, her body undulating, pleading for his possession.

"Now, Simon. Now!" She gripped his buttocks, forcing him closer.

"Yes, Cleo. Now." His tongue plunged into her mouth the exact moment he removed his hand and thrust into her waiting warmth with his hardness.

Her body sheathed his, surrounding him snugly within a hot, fluid grip. She was as ready for this mating as he. As mindless with passion. As desperate with need.

He knew he couldn't make it last, for either of them. They were both too hungry, too starved for satisfaction. He moved in and out, increasing the pace with each lunge.

She gasped loudly. Her swollen femininity clenched him tightly. And then she cried out her release. Furious. Overwhelming. Earth-shattering. The spasms shook her body.

Roarke moved faster, his thrusts harder and deeper. And while she still quivered with the aftershocks of her release, he spilled himself into her. He shuddered, then his body jerked several times as it emptied the last drops of completion. Groaning with satisfaction, he stared down at Cleo, and the sight of her lying beneath him, so blissfully fulfilled, stirred his body.

Damn, he barely had the energy to breathe. He sure as hell wasn't ready for another wild ride. Not this soon. But his body was telling him that it wanted more. *Hey, you horny bastard, don't you know how old we are?* he asked the part of his anatomy over which he had no control. *We're nearly forty. So act your age, will you?*

Sliding off Cleo and onto his side, he brought her into his embrace and placed soft kisses all over her face.

"You've just proven an old adage," Roarke said.

"What old adage is that?" Snuggling against him, she laid her hand over his belly and caressed the line of dark hair leading down to his manhood.

Easing his hand between her legs, he petted her intimately and savored her small, breathless gasp. "The old adage that dynamite comes in small packages," he told her. "You, my little darling, are pure dynamite."

"Oh, that old adage," she said, moving her hand slowly downward until she encountered his renewed arousal. "I don't disagree entirely, but—" circling him, she stroked him intimately and grinned when he drew in a sharp breath "—I happen to know, firsthand, that a certain type of dynamite comes in a big package."

The combination of her seductive words and her talented hand brought Roarke's manhood to full readiness. He delved his fingers into her, manipulating her feminine core. She moaned her pleasure.

"You know I want you again, don't you?" he asked.

"Yes, I know."

"And you want me, too."

"Yes," she said.

"You aren't too sore from the first time, are you?"

"No, Simon, I'm not too sore."

Without saying another word, he lifted her on top of him, placing her gently, allowing her to make the final plunge that would completely unite them. She straddled him as if he were that untamed stallion Pearl had compared him to. And the moment she brought him totally inside, he lifted his hips and hoisted himself to the hilt. With his hands guiding her and his lips feasting on her breasts, Roarke encouraged her wild ride. Her tempestuous release hurled him over the edge into savage fulfillment.

She fell on top of him, their bodies bonded with perspiration and satiation. He stroked her hair, her neck, her back and her buttocks. They fell asleep with his big, dark hand cupping her hip as his body cushioned hers.

ROARKE AWOKE SUDDENLY, his heart racing at breakneck speed. Damn, he'd been dreaming. Just dreaming. Cleo was all right. She lay snuggled against him, her head on his shoulder, her hand resting on his belly. He breathed a sigh of relief. She was safe. Thank God. Easing his arms around her gently, trying not to wake her, he pulled her into his embrace. Her naked body was warm and compliant, and the very feel of her skin against his aroused him. He longed to make love to her again. She had been as hot and wild as he'd hoped she would be, giving herself completely, holding nothing back. And she had tempted him beyond all reason to give equally to her. But both times, in the end, he had held back, afraid to allow himself the freedom to experience the emotions clamoring for release.

No matter how much he wanted Cleo and she him, their time together was limited. Theirs was not a love match, not a lifetime commitment. She might cling to him passionately, giving herself to him as he knew she'd never given herself to anyone else, but nothing could change the fact that he was her employee. She'd hired him for three reasons—to protect her, to keep McNamara Industries a family-run operation…and to impregnate her. Once he'd served his purpose, his job would end and they'd both go their separate ways.

Being Cleo's husband had certain benefits, the least of which was being her lover, and he might be tempted to hang around after the job ended, if the circumstances were different. But they weren't. Once she told him she was pregnant, he'd make plans to leave. Surely by that time they would have discovered who was trying to harm Cleo and sabotage McNamara's.

But what if he'd gotten her pregnant tonight? They had made passionate love twice. Pregnancy was a possibility.

Shimmery moonlight shone in through the French

doors and floor-to-ceiling windows, illuminating the room with a soft, pale light. He looked at the woman in his arms, the strands of her short hair shiny cinnamon threads against his hard, leather-brown shoulder.

If she was pregnant—this soon—he couldn't leave her and her baby unprotected. But that didn't mean he would have to stay. It wasn't as if he was indispensable. He could easily turn his bodyguard duties over to Morgan Kane, or keep Kane on the investigation and bring in Gabriel Hawk. But could he really leave Cleo's protection to another man, no matter how well-trained that man was? No, of course he couldn't. Not after tonight. Tonight Cleo had become his, in every sense of the word. He'd just have to hope that he hadn't impregnated her already. Hanging around to watch her grow bigger with his child every day hadn't been part of their bargain. He'd made it perfectly clear that this child would be hers and hers alone.

He'd already been given one chance at fatherhood and he'd screwed up royally. Cleo's child deserved better. And so did Cleo. She deserved a man capable of loving her and committing himself to her for the rest of their lives. He wasn't that man. He knew himself too well. Inside, where it really counted, he was a burned-out shell. The fire of guilt and remorse and self-hatred had gutted his soul years ago. That fire had begun the day he'd received the news that Laurie had died. It had blazed inside him at his little girl's funeral. And the day he'd said goodbye to Hope at the private mental hospital where she'd been committed, that internal fire had raged. Day by day, week by week, year by year, the inferno had slowly destroyed him, destroyed any ability he'd ever had to love.

Cleo roused, opening her eyes and looking up at Roarke with tenderness. She smiled.

"You're awake," she said. "Couldn't you sleep?"

"I slept like the dead for several hours after…" Pausing, he stroked her cheek. "I'm not going to let anything happen to you. Whoever is playing these deadly games is going to lose. I'll see to it."

Stretching far enough for her lips to reach his, she kissed him, then pulled away. "I know you will." Bracing her elbow on the bed, she supported the side of her face with her hand and gazed adoringly at Roarke. "We both know that someone deliberately planted those spiders in the bathroom."

"Yeah. And tomorrow I'll have to call the local authorities. We'll have to bring them in on this and on the problems at McNamara Industries." He liked the way she looked at him, her eyes filled with tenderness and just a hint of passion. He supposed a lot of women got mellow after sex, and some, like Cleo, would get sentimental. He usually didn't hang around long enough to find out. He hadn't slept the night through in a woman's bed in a long, long time.

"This is just the beginning, isn't it? If I continue refusing to sell McNamara's, my life will remain in danger and the problems at the plant will only escalate."

"If you're having second thoughts, Boss Lady, now's the time to say so."

"No second thoughts," she said. "No second thoughts about any of my decisions."

He understood her meaning. She was telling him that she wasn't sorry she'd hired him as her bodyguard and her husband. Right now, he was glad Cleo McNamara had walked into his office and made him a proposition he couldn't refuse. But he knew that in a few months, when this job ended and he left River Bend, he *would* have second thoughts. For the rest of his life, he would wonder if he'd done the right thing, fathering a child and then deserting it.

He had deserted a child once before, giving his military career greater precedence in his life than he'd given his daughter's welfare. But this time, he was thinking of the child first, knowing that the best thing he could do for Cleo's future baby was to get out of its life and stay out.

"What's wrong?" Cleo asked. "You seem to be a million miles away."

"Fifteen years in the past." He'd spoken before he'd thought, but covered his slip by saying, "I was just considering how much my life has changed over the years. I've gone from a gung ho young soldier to a middle-aged warhorse who wants to retire to a farm somewhere."

"And the money I'm paying you will buy you that farm."

"Yeah."

The sheet that had barely covered Cleo's breasts slipped downward. When she reached out to grab it, Roarke jerked her hand away. The sheet drifted slowly to her waist, leaving her breasts exposed to the cool air and Roarke's hot appraisal. Her nipples puckered. He ran the tip of his finger over one jutting point and then the other. Cleo held her breath as shivers of awareness rippled through her.

"I didn't know it would be this way," he admitted, lifting himself up and over her, bracing his body with his hands planted, palms down, on the bed.

"What way?" she asked, her breathing quickening, her body straining upward pleadingly.

"I didn't know that once we made love, we wouldn't be able to keep our hands off each other."

"It's crazy, isn't it?" Cleo placed her arms around his neck and brought his head downward, his lips closer to hers. "I didn't realize that I could ever feel like this. It's a raging hunger, isn't it?"

"Yeah, that's exactly what it is." He parted her thighs and slid between them. "And I want to feed that raging hunger again right now."

"So do I." Spreading her thighs, she opened herself up fully to his invasion. The moment he entered her, she lifted her hips and draped her legs around his waist.

Roarke took control of their mating until the final moments when Cleo's body dictated the rules of release for both of them. She moved against him, taking his thrusts and returning them, bringing them both closer and closer to completion. When she tightened around him and cried out in earth-shattering pleasure, his body took its cue from hers and spiraled out of control into a jetting explosion.

CHAPTER EIGHT

"WAKE UP, SLEEPYHEAD."

Cleo opened her eyes and stared up into Roarke's handsome face. Smiling, she stretched like a contented cat, then reached up and draped her arms around his neck, bringing his mouth down to hers for a morning kiss.

Roarke took charge of the kiss immediately, knowing how easily it could get out of control if he didn't end it quickly. He wasn't sure he liked the way Cleo could turn him inside out, the way she could make him want her so desperately. He wasn't used to a woman having that much power over him.

He removed her arms from around his neck and sat down on the edge of the bed. She snuggled against him.

"Good morning, Simon."

"Good morning, Cleo."

She eased away from him and sat up straight. Allowing the sheet to slide down to her waist, she stared at him and smiled. "You've already showered and dressed. How long have you been up?"

He tried not to look at her full, round breasts that beckoned to him, pleading for his touch. Damn, if she didn't cover herself, he'd be lost. And this morning wasn't the right time to fall back into bed and make love to Cleo. This morning was the time for business—serious business.

He shot up off the bed, crossed the room and went into

the closet. Emerging with a blue satin robe, he tossed it to her. "Put that on. You're far too tempting the way you are right now, Cleo Belle."

Lifting the robe from where it had fallen over her lap, Cleo grinned at her husband, then slowly slipped into the robe. "There, is that better?"

"Much." Roarke sat back down on the edge of the bed. "We have a lot to accomplish today. I've been up a couple of hours."

Scooting to the edge of the bed beside Roarke, she laid her hand on his arm. "What have you been doing during the two hours you've been up?"

"I made some phone calls—" he nodded toward the sitting room "—from in there. I didn't want to disturb you. You were sleeping so soundly."

"I was exhausted. Your wore me out," she said teasingly as she stroked the inside of his wrist with the tip of her index finger.

He grinned, but quickly forced his mouth into a sober line and grasped Cleo's shoulders. "There's nothing I'd like more than to make love to you again right now, honey. But we're expected downstairs for breakfast in about twenty minutes, so unless you want to greet your family looking the way you do right now—"

"Why are we having breakfast with my family this morning?"

"Because it's time."

Standing, Roarke dragged Cleo up and out of bed, then gave her a gentle shove toward the bathroom. When she halted, turned around and gave him a questioning stare, he shook his head.

"Hey, do you believe I'd send you in there if I thought there was any danger? I checked the bathroom out thoroughly before I took my shower." Gently clamping his hands down over her shoulders again, he guided her forward. "Just ignore the mess."

She hesitated at the closed door. "Why is it time for us to have breakfast downstairs? And who did you call this morning?"

"I called the police and spoke to a Sheriff Bacon. He was very accommodating. Seems he knew your uncle George and thought highly of him. He's going to check into a few things for me."

"I see." When he gave her another shove, she balked. "Who else did you call?"

"I phoned the exterminator who regularly services the house. Someone named Roy Bendall. He'll be out this morning."

"Neither phone call explains why we're eating breakfast with the family," Cleo said.

"I remembered something from when I read over the information about the members of your family that I asked you to compile for me."

"What did you remember?"

"That your uncle Perry is a retired college professor, whose background was in entomology. He'd know everything there is to know about the brown recluse, wouldn't he?"

"You're planning to tell my family what happened last night and then watch how they react, aren't you? You're going to cross-examine Uncle Perry and see if you can make him sweat."

"Something like that."

"Do you think Uncle Perry is behind the threats on my life and the problems at the plant?" Cleo asked.

"It's possible, isn't it? He and his entire family would benefit if you were out of the way."

"Yes, I suppose you're right. Uncle Perry and I have never been close. He's always seemed to resent me."

When Roarke gave her another nudge, she opened the bathroom door and disappeared inside, closing the door behind her. She stood perfectly still for several minutes as she surveyed the area, noting the total disarray. There didn't appear to be an inch of her private bath that Roarke hadn't examined. She shivered as she remembered that there wasn't an inch of her own body that Roarke hadn't examined. Shutting her eyes, she leaned her head back against the door and sighed deeply. The moment she thought about their passionate lovemaking, Cleo's body responded to the memory. Her nipples puckered; her femininity throbbed. How was it possible to want him again so soon?

Making her way carefully across the cluttered tile floor, Cleo watched for any movement, the slightest sign that even one spider might have escaped annihilation. With an unsteady hand, she reached down and picked up one of the scattered clean towels from the floor. Reaching inside the glass-enclosed shower, she turned on the brass faucets and started the water flow.

Taking one final look around the room, she stepped inside the shower enclosure. Filling the net body scrub with scented liquid soap, Cleo washed her arms and shoulders, then hesitated at her breasts. They were a little tender, her nipples sore from Roarke's diligent attention. As she rubbed the lather over her breasts, she sucked in her breath as a tingling sensation spiraled outward and downward, reaching her feminine core.

She had never known that making love could be so all-consuming, so totally, completely, earth-shattering. Paine Emerson had been her first and only lover, but he'd been a boy of twenty-two, and she now realized that he'd been an inexperienced, inept lover. If she hadn't been so infatuated, so youthfully, foolishly in love with him, her intimate moments with him would have been a great disappointment.

Having had Simon Roarke as a lover, Cleo now understood how sexual desire could dominate a person's life. And if that desire was combined with other equally strong emotions, the results could be explosive. And that's exactly what her feelings for Roarke were—explosive. With each passing day she grew to like and respect her husband more and more. He was, as Pearl had told her, a fine man.

Yes, that's exactly what Simon was. A fine man. A man she not only needed in her life, but very much wanted.

As rivulets of water cascaded over her, Cleo circled her belly with the nylon net scrub. Was she already pregnant? Had her husband given her a child during their hours of hot, passionate lovemaking?

The thought of being pregnant, of carrying Roarke's baby inside her, created a warm happiness deep in her heart. Someday she could tell their child what a good man his father had been, could honestly say that their union had meant more to her than a business deal. But how could she ever explain why Roarke wasn't a part of his life? Why the child's own father hadn't wanted anything to do with him?

Stilling the circling motion of her hand, Cleo clutched the net scrub, then tossed it onto the floor. While she rinsed the foam from her body, she tried to stop thinking about being pregnant, about the possibility that Roarke's son—or daughter—could have taken root in her womb.

The longer it took her to become pregnant, the longer Roarke would remain a part of her life. He couldn't leave her until he fulfilled all his obligations. As much as she longed to be pregnant, she hoped that she wasn't. Not yet.

Not until she found a way to persuade Roarke to stay with her during her pregnancy and afterward help her bring up their child.

"THEY'RE EATING OUT on the patio, by the pool," Pearl said. "I'll bring your plates out directly. We're having blueberry pancakes this morning. Coffee and juice are on the serving cart out there, Mr. Roarke."

"Has everyone come down?" Cleo asked.

"Everyone," Pearl said. "Y'all are the last ones, but folks understand your being late, since y'all are still honeymooners."

Cleo willed herself not to blush. Before this morning there had been no truth to the charade they'd been enacting as happy newlyweds. But after last night, she felt quite a bit like a deflowered virgin bride, and was afraid the aftereffects of sexual pleasure hung over her like a bright, shiny halo, proclaiming her wedded bliss to the whole world.

"Pearl, I'm expecting several visitors this morning," Roarke told the housekeeper. "I believe all three of them will arrive while Cleo and I are at breakfast. I want you to be sure to announce each gentleman and bring him directly out to the patio."

"Three visitors this morning?" Narrowing her gaze, Pearl stared quizzically at Roarke. "Just what's going on?"

"Cleo had some unexpected guests in her bathroom last night." Roarke took Cleo's hand in his. "Someone planted half a dozen brown recluse spiders in her bath towels."

"Oh, my dear Lord!" Reaching out, Pearl patted Cleo's cheek. "Them little creatures are dangerous. My baby brother nearly died from one of 'em's bite. Are you all right, Cleo Belle? Why didn't—"

"I'm fine. Roarke killed all of them," Cleo said.

"One of our visitors this morning will be the exterminator," Roarke said.

"Good. You called Roy Bendall. We don't want to come across one of them spiders that might have escaped." Pearl grabbed Roarke's arm. "If somebody planted the brown recluses in Cleo's bath towels, then my guess is one of your other visitors will be a lawman."

"Sheriff Bacon," Roarke said. "I understand he was on friendly terms with the late Mr. McNamara."

"Phil Bacon's daddy used to be sheriff before him," Pearl said. "The McNamaras have always taken a friendly interest in local politics, if you know what I mean."

"Pearl, you make it sound as if Uncle George had the local law in his hip pocket." Cleo shook her head. "And you know that isn't true. Phil Bacon is as honest as the day is long."

"I suppose he's as honest as a politician gets, and that's what a sheriff is. Part lawman and part politician," Pearl said.

"You've got an opinion on everything and everyone, haven't you, Pearl?" Roarke squeezed Cleo's hand, then lifted it to his lips.

Pleased with her husband's genuine affection, Cleo shivered inside and the tiny shivers radiated pleasure through her whole body.

Pearl fixed her gaze on Cleo's and Roarke's clasped hands. "You're right about that. I'm an opinionated old woman. And with every passing day, my opinion of you gets better and better." She stepped directly in front of Roarke and looked up at him. "Who's this third visitor we're expecting this morning?"

"Morgan Kane," Roarke said. "He flew into Huntsville from Atlanta and is driving here. He's a private security agent and an investigator."

"Looks like it's going to be a busy morning around here." Pearl planted her hands on her hips. "I'm sure going to be close by so I can see how the Suttons deal with all the excitement."

Hand in hand, Roarke and Cleo walked through the double French doors and outside onto the patio area, near the pool. The entire clan quieted instantly when he and Cleo approached. Only Aunt Beatrice seemed pleased to see them. Cleo leaned over and kissed her aunt on the cheek. Roarke seated her at the far end of the table, then poured two glasses of juice and placed them side by side. After filling two cups with hot coffee, he put one in front of Cleo and the other next to her, then seated himself beside his wife.

He had deliberately placed himself where he could watch the others. Even the cleverest person sometimes gave himself away with a word or a look, a reaction to something unexpected. Three unexpected visitors might trigger a suspicious response in one of the Suttons. But which one? Roarke wondered as he surveyed the length of the heavy glass-and-metal table and he paused briefly to study each person.

Even though he automatically excluded Beatrice McNamara from his list of suspects, he let his gaze linger on her. Looking at this woman gave him a preview of what Cleo would probably look like thirty years from now. There was a strong family resemblance. From their red hair and green eyes to their petite bodies and small, delicate bone structure. Cleo could have easily been the child Beatrice never had.

"We're simply delighted that y'all decided to finally join the family for a meal," Oralie said as she lifted the Haviland china cup to her lips.

"I can't say that I blame Cleo for wanting to keep her

new husband all to herself." Daphne licked a drop of syrup from the side of her mouth. "I know if I had a husband like Roarke, I'd keep him locked in my bedroom for a month."

"Daphne!" Oralie scolded. "I will not tolerate such disgraceful talk at my breakfast table."

"Don't upset yourself, Mother." Trey folded the newspaper behind which he'd been buried and laid it on the table between his plate and Marla's. "You know as well as I do that Daffie loves to shock you almost as much as she loves to needle Cleo."

"What a thing to say." Oralie smiled faintly. "You'll give Mr. Roarke the wrong impression of our family, dear."

"I imagine Mr. Roarke has already formed an opinion of us, and our pretending to be anything other than what we are won't fool him," Daphne told her mother, then stared directly at Roarke. "Aren't I right about that, Simon?" She spoke his name in a sultry drawl, turning the pronunciation of his name into an invitation. "You've got us all sized up, haven't you? I'll bet you've even narrowed down the suspects, eliminating Aunt Beatrice because she adores Cleo so, and Pearl and Ezra for the same reason. And of course, no one would suspect sweet, mousy little Marla."

"Daphne, you're a bitch!" Trey snarled.

Marla Sutton's pale cheeks flushed. Dropping her chin to her chest, she gazed down into her lap. Roarke tended to agree with Daphne's assessment. It would be difficult to picture the quiet, shy, sweet young woman in the role of a potential murderess. Even the woman's sedate, old-fashioned page-boy haircut and expensive but plain attire added to her overall Jane Eyre appearance.

But appearances could be deceiving. Roarke had seen too much evil and cruelty, often disguised as sweet in-

nocence, to disregard the possibility that behind Marla
Sutton's gentle facade a killer existed.

Pearl breezed outside, carrying two plates stacked high
with blueberry pancakes. Roarke marveled at how easily
the elderly, overweight housekeeper maneuvered. She set
one plate in front of Cleo, the other in front of Roarke.

"Roy Bendall is here," Pearl announced.

"Ask him to come on out," Roarke said. "I want to
speak to him, give him some specific instructions before
he begins."

"Roy Bendall?" Perry Sutton looked at Roarke for the
first time. The fork he held quivered in his unsteady hand.
"Why is the exterminator here? He's already been here
this month, hasn't he?"

Roarke thought that Perry must have once been a very
handsome man. Remnants of that youthful beauty still lin-
gered on his lined face, in his large, dark eyes and in the
sturdy build of his body. But something had beaten this
man, whipped him into a shadow of what he'd once been.
Roarke had seen men like that before. Men who had allowed the spark of life to die inside them. Men who had
given away their strength and dignity to some carnivo-
rous force whose hunger could never be appeased. He had
come close to becoming one of those men. If he'd stayed
married to Hope, it could have happened to him.

"I called Roy Bendall earlier," Roarke said. "I want
him to give Cleo's suite a going-over."

"Why would Cleo's rooms need inspecting?" Oralie
asked.

"Here he is." Pearl showed the auburn-haired, freckle-
faced Mr. Bendall out onto the patio.

"Believe me, I don't know how any spiders could have
gotten in Ms. McNamara's suite," Roy said. "I can promise
you that they didn't crawl into the house by themselves.

Just ask Pearl. I do good work. There's not so much as an ant in the kitchen."

"No one is blaming you, Roy," Cleo said.

The short, stocky Roy relaxed his tense stance. "Why anybody would want to harm Ms. McNamara, I don't know, but I'd stake my reputation on the fact that those brown recluses were deliberately brought into this house."

"Brown recluse spiders!" Aunt Beatrice gasped. "In the house? In your rooms?" She turned her concerned gaze on Cleo. "When? How?"

Cleo reached across the table and laid her hand reassuringly over Beatrice's. "Last night Roarke killed half a dozen spiders that someone had placed inside one of my bath towels."

"Who on earth would have done something so despicable?" Oralie rested her hand over her heart.

"I think Mr. Roarke is accusing one of us, Mother," Trey said. "Isn't that right? You believe that planting the spiders was another scare tactic to try to frighten Cleo into selling McNamara Industries."

"Mr. Bendall, I want every inch of Mrs. Roarke's suite inspected and then sprayed," Roarke said. "Pearl will clean up when you're finished and air out the rooms."

Before Pearl could escort Roy Bendall back inside the house, Ezra appeared in the doorway.

"The sheriff's here," Ezra told them. "Said he's here to see Cleo Belle…er…that is, he's here to see Mrs. Roarke."

"Please ask Phil to join us for breakfast," Cleo said.

"You've called in Phil Bacon?" Perry Sutton set his cup down on the saucer so hard that coffee splashed over the sides.

"Someone is trying to harm my wife," Roarke said. "When I spoke to Sheriff Bacon, he assured me that his department has been involved since the day someone took a shot at Cleo. He wants to get to the bottom of this and arrest the person responsible."

As Roy Bendall exited, Sheriff Phil Bacon entered. Pearl poured the tall, robust young man a cup of coffee and handed it to him. Accepting the coffee with a gracious nod, the sheriff sat down beside Cleo.

"'Morning, folks." Phil greeted the entire family with one of his wide, toothy grins, then focused his attention on Cleo. "Your husband tells me that there was an accident at the plant yesterday and you nearly got run over by a forklift. And this wasn't the first 'accident' McNamara Industries has had since your uncle died."

"This is simply awful." Beatrice halfway rose out of her seat. "Cleo could have been killed."

Cleo eased her aunt down, petting her as she did so. "I told you that I wasn't hurt. I'm fine. Just a few scratches and bruises."

"And I understand that last night, you had a scare when you found a bunch of spiders in your towel," Phil said.

"Where do you suppose someone could get hold of half a dozen brown recluse spiders?" Roarke asked.

"I don't have any idea," the sheriff said. "But I sure as hel—heck, intend to find out. Whoever's causing trouble for Ms. McNa—that is, Mrs. Roarke isn't going to get away with it. Not in my county. I'll have a couple of my deputies look into those plant accidents."

"Thank you, Phil," Cleo said. "We'd appreciate all the help you can give us. You know how many jobs depend on my keeping McNamara Industries a family-run business. If anything happens to me, Aunt Beatrice won't have enough voting power to block a sale."

"Believe me, I understand." Phil gave Trey Sutton a hard stare, then turned his displeased look on Daphne.

"As soon as you have something to report on those spiders, I expect to hear from you," Roarke said. "Knowing where they might have been acquired could give us a clue to the culprit's identity."

"Oh, my." Sighing loudly, Oralie rubbed the sides of her forehead, pressing her fingertips into the edges of her salt-and-pepper hair. "Pearl, would you please bring me my stomach medicine? All this talk about spiders and accidents at the plant and suspects and culprits has made me quite nauseated."

Pursing her lips in a pout, Pearl tapped her fingers on the serving cart and gave Oralie a disgusted glare. "You want the liquid stuff or the little tablets?"

"The tablets, please. And do hurry." Holding her hand out to Perry, she looked at him, her expression pleading. "You know what a weak disposition I have. My greatest regret is that I've always been rather delicate."

Perry patted his wife's hand as if it were some inanimate object, his touch gentle and yet emotionally detached. "Yes, my dear."

Roarke wondered how many times Perry Sutton had spoken those three words. Hundreds? Thousands? How many times during his two-year marriage to Hope had he said, "Yes, honey," trying to comfort and pacify a woman who could not be consoled?

Pearl took her time leaving, her slow departure proclaiming her opinion on the true state of Oralie's health.

"I'm sorry if our discussing this nasty mess in front of you has upset you, Miss Oralie," Sheriff Bacon said. "I sometimes forget that there are still ladies around with delicate sensibilities. My daddy would never have made such an error. Please accept my apologies."

"Certainly, Phillip." Oralie lifted a trembling hand, then let it fall helplessly to her side. "I quite understand that a man in your position is exposed to all sorts of people."

"Unfortunately, that's true," the sheriff said.

Opening the French doors, Pearl stepped outside, then cleared her throat. All eyes focused on the housekeeper's face, everyone noting her closed-mouth smile.

"Where is my medicine?" Oralie demanded.

"I'll get it in a minute," Pearl said. "Just thought Mr. Roarke would want to know that there's a Mr. Morgan Kane here to see him."

"Who?" Beatrice asked.

"What the hell is this—Grand Central Station?" Trey shoved back his chair and stood. "What's going on, Roarke? Have you called in the damn marines now?"

"Not the marines," Roarke said. "The navy. To be specific, a former SEAL." He motioned to Pearl. "Tell Kane to come on out and meet the family. After all, he'll be staying here at the house and working at the plant. So there's no time like the present to introduce him."

"I'm afraid that I, for one, don't understand what's going on." Perry Sutton stiffened his spine and sat straight up in the padded patio chair.

"I think it's perfectly clear." Trey gripped the back of his wife's chair, his fingers biting into the cushion with white-knuckled intensity. "Cleo's husband is bringing in a professional."

"A professional what?" Oralie asked naively.

"Yes, Roarke, do tell us exactly what Mr. Kane does for a living." Daphne glanced at the doorway, where Pearl stood, a large shadow looming behind her inside the house.

"Kane." Roarke's command thundered in the sudden eerie quiet.

Everyone looked toward the French doors. The moment

Morgan Kane appeared, Cleo's mouth fell open and Daphne gasped, then purred. Cleo thought that Morgan Kane was probably one of the most devastatingly handsome men she'd ever seen. Almost beautiful, in a totally masculine way. Younger than Roarke by a few years, perhaps somewhere around thirty-five, the tall, broad-shouldered blond filled out his Armani suit like an athletic cover model.

He strutted out onto the patio with a military-trained bearing, his body honed to perfection. He stopped at the far end of the table, directly behind Perry Sutton, removed his dark sunglasses and stared at Roarke with cold, intense gray eyes.

"Morgan Kane, meet my wife's family. Everyone seated at this table is a suspect, with the exception of Aunt Beatrice."

Beatrice smiled shyly and nodded. "Are you from the Dundee agency, Mr. Kane?"

"Yes, ma'am," Kane said, his voice a deep baritone, his accent decidedly Southern.

"Just what is the Dundee agency?" Daphne slid back her chair and stood, giving their visitor a full view of her long, bare legs and her large, braless breasts. Her orange terry-cloth short-shorts and matching halter top only enhanced her dark, exotic beauty.

"Private security and investigation, ma'am," Kane said.

"I'm Daphne Sutton." She rounded the table slowly, making her way toward Kane and giving him ample time to appreciate the view.

"I've hired Kane to find out who's behind the accidents at McNamara Industries and to prevent any future problems," Roarke informed them.

"I resent the way you've taken over," Trey said. "At the plant and now here at home. Just who the hell do you think you are, running roughshod over all of us?"

"I'm—" Roarke said.

"He is my husband," Cleo told them, her voice deadly calm. "He has every right to go to whatever lengths he feels necessary in order to protect me and to protect McNamara Industries."

"For God's sake, Cleo, if you'd just sell the damn plant, none of this would be necessary." Trey's hazel-brown eyes glittered with fury. A dark, angry flush colored his cheeks. "Your stubbornness is putting your life in danger and destroying this family."

Daphne sauntered close to Morgan Kane, inspecting him as if he were a prized piece of horseflesh. "I would just love for you to personally investigate me."

"I intend to *personally* investigate every member of your family," Kane said. "When I get through, I'll know who flosses his teeth and who doesn't."

"Cleo, I object to this man's presence here. It's bad enough that your husband is a trained killer. Now, with Mr. Kane's arrival, we'll have two in the house," Oralie said, then glared at Pearl. "For goodness' sake, will you please go get my medication!"

Pearl hesitated momentarily, then slowly walked into the house.

"I'm sorry if my husband's and Mr. Kane's backgrounds bother you, Aunt Oralie," Cleo said. "But Mr. Kane isn't leaving until he completes his assignment."

"You're determined to make this situation as difficult for everyone as possible, aren't you, Cleo?" Perry Sutton asked.

"I don't want to make anything difficult, Uncle Perry, but I'm not going to let y'all have your way. Not this time." Jumping to her feet, Cleo flung her napkin down on the table. "There's a lot more at stake here than my getting my way on this issue. There are hundreds of jobs on the line. Doesn't anyone else care about these people? Are all of you so selfish that you aren't capable of seeing past your own needs?"

"Daddy cared about his workers," Beatrice said. "And that's why he left you in control. Because he knew you'd take care of his company and all his employees."

"Uncle George was getting senile," Trey said.

"He was not!" Beatrice screamed.

"Cleo was always Uncle George's favorite," Daphne said. "Senile or not, he would have left her in control. I just think it's amusing that he made sure she found herself a husband before he turned over all the power to her."

"I'm afraid Cleo would never have married otherwise." Oralie sighed dramatically. "Most men abhor aggressive, domineering women." She cast her sorrowful gaze at her niece. "I tried to guide you the way I did Daphne, instilling in you both all the ladylike virtues, but I'm afraid I failed."

"You did the best you could, my dear." Perry patted Oralie's hand.

"Good God, Mother, I believe you're getting senile yourself." Trey balled his hands into fists and pressed them against the sides of his thighs. "Don't you realize what the issue is? Unless Cleo sells the damn company, we're going to lose millions and wind up stuck with an unprofitable business."

"That's it!" Cleo marched around the table, halting directly in front of Trey. "McNamara Industries is not an unprofitable business! And no one is going to lose millions. Not in the long run." Cleo whirled around and glared at Oralie. "And I never married before now because I chose not to." Turning slowly, she smiled at Daphne. "Mr. Kane is staying to do his job. And if you get in his way or try to interfere in what he has to do, I'll kick your butt out of this house. Do I make myself clear?"

"Jealous, Cousin? Are you staking a claim on Mr. Kane?" Daphne grinned. "Isn't your husband enough for you?"

Cleo closed her eyes and counted to ten. She would not allow Daphne or anyone else in this family to push her over the edge. Uncle George had kept an uneven peace for as long as she could remember, his powerful personality as strong a deterrent as the threat of cutting someone out of his will. Since his death, the family had begun falling apart. The bitterness, anger and hatred that had been simmering just below the surface had finally bubbled to the top and boiled over onto everyone's lives.

"Phil, I apologize for my family," Cleo said. "Please let me know when you have any information on those spiders." She looked directly at Trey. "Mr. Kane will be leaving here shortly to go to the plant. I want you to give him your full cooperation and assist him in any way you can. Do I make myself clear?"

"Perfectly clear." Scowling, Trey clenched his jaw tightly shut.

"You're enjoying finally getting to play Lady of the Manor, aren't you?" Daphne brushed by Cleo, deliberately shoving her.

Temporarily losing her balance, Cleo swayed dangerously close to the pool's edge. She fought the unnatural fear, reclaiming her senses at the last moment.

"Grab her, Perry," Beatrice cried out. "Don't let her fall into the water!"

Perry Sutton, who was the closest to Cleo, knocked over his chair as he stood and reached out for his niece. He grabbed her arm, pulling her toward him and steadying her.

Roarke flew across the patio and jerked Cleo into his arms. Her breath came in gasping swallows. She grasped the front of Roarke's shirt, then laid her head on his chest.

"What's wrong, honey?" Why had his wife gone suddenly white? Why had the prospect of Cleo falling into the pool struck fear in Beatrice's heart and frightened Cleo senseless?

"You must be careful, Cleo, dear," Oralie said. "It was unwise of you to stand so close to the edge of the pool. Anything could have happened."

Lifting her head from Roarke's chest, Cleo looked toward the French doors, where Daphne stood watching, a slightly wicked smile on her face.

"Nothing would have happened, except Cleo would have gotten wet and ruined her neat little blue suit," Daphne said. "Her husband would have saved her from drowning."

Cleo whispered to Roarke, "I'm going upstairs to change, and then I'm going to the plant."

Roarke followed Cleo as she walked across the patio, her leather heels clipping loudly on the stone surface. The moment they entered the house, Roarke grabbed her and whirled her around to face him.

"Want to tell me what that was all about?" he asked.

"It was about Daphne playing childish games," Cleo told him. "I embarrassed her in front of Phil Bacon and Mr. Kane, so she felt compelled to embarrass me in return."

"I understand that, but what I don't understand is your reaction to almost falling in the pool."

"I used to be terrified of falling into the pool." She lifted her chin defiantly, her gaze meeting his head-on. "A few months after I came here to live, when I was a very small child, I almost drowned in that pool."

"You were allowed to play in the pool all alone? No one was watching you?"

"I—I don't know. I have no memory of even getting into the pool. Pearl found me and saved my life. I'd still be scared of the water if Uncle George hadn't forced me to learn how to swim. But everyone in the family knows about what happened years ago and that occasionally, I'm still wary of the swimming pool."

"Is it possible that someone tried to kill you all those years ago?" Roarke hated to ask, but he couldn't shake the feeling that someone in this household had wanted to see Cleo dead long before George McNamara had left her in control of his fortune.

"No. No. I—I…" Cleo slumped against Roarke. He wrapped her safely in his arms and stroked her back lovingly. "If that's possible, then there's more to the threats on my life than someone wanting me to sell McNamara's. Someone hates me. Truly hates me."

CHAPTER NINE

CLEO RUBBED THE bridge of her nose, then ran her hand over her face and down her neck. Her back hurt, her shoulders ached and she felt the beginnings of a headache. Laying aside the file folder Roarke had given her less than fifteen minutes ago, she shoved back her chair and stood. Things were worse at McNamara Industries than she'd thought. The sabotage was more widespread, and the damage far more extensive. Someone had truly created havoc with the company's computer system. And it had all happened since Uncle George's death.

It had taken Morgan Kane less than forty-eight hours to discover the extent of the damage. He'd handed Roarke a complete report when he'd come in from the plant thirty minutes ago. And after reading the report immediately, Roarke had turned it over to Cleo and left her alone to absorb the information. He'd assured her that since Kane was now on the job and had already assembled a security force of two men and one woman, no one would have the opportunity to tamper with the computer system again. Right now, their main objective was to straighten out the present mess.

At moments like this, Cleo wished she could escape from her own life, from the burdens of being CEO of McNamara Industries, from the responsibility of caring for others. If she could escape to some deserted tropical island, she would want Roarke to go with her. They could frolic in the ocean, bask in the sunshine and make love under the stars. No past. No future. No worries. Just endless happiness.

But she couldn't escape, couldn't run away from the danger that threatened her and her company. She had little choice but to stay and face whatever lay ahead, to confront the person who wanted to destroy her life and ruin the family business. She had to fight and win this battle.

There was another battle she wanted to win. But in her heart, she feared it was a lost cause. She wanted to win Simon Roarke, and she was willing to fight whatever demons plagued him, whatever tormenting memories held him prisoner. He stayed at her side during the day, guarding her diligently, and at night he held her in his arms and made mad, passionate love to her. But there was a part of himself that he held back, a private, tortured part of his soul that he would not share. He protected her and possessed her with equal fervor, but where she was unable to control her emotional response to him, he never relinquished complete control. Only in the throes of passion did she possess him as surely as he possessed her. And those moments were fleeting—an ephemeral ecstasy soon ended.

Roarke knocked on the door, opened it and walked into the study. He saw her standing in front of the empty fireplace, her red hair glimmering in the honeyed glow of the pewter chandelier that hung from the vaulted ceiling. A spiral metal staircase led from the ground level up to a mezzanine library level lined with rows of bookshelves.

"Have you read Kane's report?" He closed the double pocket doors behind him.

"Yes, I've read it." Turning slowly, she picked up the file folder from the enormous Jacobean desk that dominated Uncle George's private study. "Where's Kane now?"

"He's in the kitchen. Pearl's serving him a late dinner."

"Pearl approves of Kane," Cleo said. "She constantly amazes me. At first she objected strenuously to our marriage, but you won her over quickly. Then I was certain she'd disapprove of Kane, and now here she is, clucking over him like a mother hen."

"He doesn't know how to handle her mothering." Roarke chuckled. "Kane's a cold, solitary son of a bitch. I've never known him to succumb to any type of emotion or let any woman get to him, whether she was trying to mother him or trying to seduce him."

"Have you known him long?"

"Long enough to know that I can trust him, and that he's one of the best at what he does." Roarke glanced at the manila folder Cleo held in her hand.

She lifted the files, shaking the folder. "Well, your Mr. Kane certainly pinpointed all of our computer problems."

"All the security codes are being changed and Kane is working with the computer expert he brought in. They're putting safeguards in place to make sure this doesn't happen again."

"We've already lost thousands of dollars, maybe tens of thousands, if I can't make things right with several of the companies who do business with us." Cleo dropped the file on the nineteenth-century silver tray that topped the coffee table. Sitting down on the tufted, oxblood leather sofa, she crossed her legs at the ankles, rested her head on the plush back and laid her hands in her lap.

Roarke watched her, noting the worry lines across her forehead and the slightly drooped corners of her mouth. She pinched the bridge of her nose, then spread her hand across her forehead and rubbed her temples with thumb and forefinger.

"Do you have a headache?" He crossed the room, stopping directly behind Cleo. Reaching down, he ran his fingers into her hair and massaged her head. She sighed. "You'll find a way to straighten things out. Just don't make yourself sick worrying," he said.

"I am on the verge of a bad headache, but you're helping prevent it. Thanks." She loved the feel of Roarke's strong yet gentle hands easing the tension from her head and neck. In a relatively short period of time, she had come to depend on him, to rely on his strength, his protection and his understanding. She could not allow this dependency on her husband to become a weakness. If she found that she couldn't live without him, she would be lost. Simon hadn't said or done anything to indicate that their relationship had become anything more than what it was meant to be—a business arrangement. But it had become more to Cleo—much more. If she wasn't very careful, she'd find herself in love with a man who didn't love her.

"At least Kane caught the payroll inaccuracies before this week's checks were printed," Roarke said. "That's one disaster you can avoid."

"I shudder to think what would have happened if he hadn't discovered the problem before checks went out."

Releasing Cleo's head, Roarke rounded the sofa and sat down beside her. "Luckily, all the lab data are on backup disks. Without those disks, months of research would have been lost."

"Who's doing this? Dammit, who?" Knotting her hands into tight fists, Cleo lifted them into the air. "The payroll messed up, lab files deleted and a rash of orders either erased or altered where the wrong amounts were sent out or were sent to the wrong companies or not delivered at all. Whoever is doing this doesn't care anything about the company, and is willing to do anything, cause any amount of chaos to force me to sell."

Taking her fists into his hands, he drew them to his lips and kissed her knuckles. "We'll find out who did this. Trey is the most obvious suspect. On the other hand, Hugh Winfield, who as a company lawyer has access to all the computer files, minored in computer science in college."

"Don't narrow it down to Hugh or Trey," Cleo said, pulling her hands out of Roarke's grasp. "Anyone could have hired someone within the company to sabotage the computer system."

"That's true, but—"

"Marla!"

"What?"

Cleo shifted her body around to face Roarke, bracing her back against the sofa arm. "Marla worked at McNamara Industries as a secretary. That's how she and Trey met. Marla is very knowledgeable about computers and she'd know our system inside out."

"I'll be sure Kane knows that. He's got the situation under control," Roarke assured Cleo, "and whoever was behind the problems won't be able to do any more damage. And if he...or she...is foolhardy enough to try anything again, they'll be caught in a trap, just like that." Roarke snapped his fingers.

"I almost wish whoever it is would try something." Cleo rested her head on Roarke's shoulder. "I want this person caught and stopped. I want this nightmare to end."

Roarke slipped his arm around her waist and lifted her onto his lap. Circling her neck with one arm, she laid her head back down on his shoulder.

"Cleo? Honey?"

"What?" She lifted her head and stared into his troubled blue eyes.

"There's a possibility that whoever's behind the problems at the plant isn't the same person who's threatening your life."

"You really believe there are two members of my family out to destroy McNamara Industries and me?"

"It's possible. And they could be working together or separately."

"So catching the saboteur at McNamara's won't necessarily end the danger to me, will it?"

"We'll have to wait and see." Roarke encompassed Cleo in his big arms, holding her possessively. "In the meantime, I'm going to do everything in my power to keep you safe. Just don't take any chances and don't trust anyone in your family, except—"

"Aunt Beatrice."

"Sooner or later, they're going to make another move. We have to be very careful because we don't know what form the next attack will take or when it will come."

A knock on the door thundered through the room. Cleo jumped. Roarke's body tensed. Cleo sucked in a deep breath.

"Oh, God, I'm jittery," she said.

"It's all right, honey. My nerves are pretty frayed, too."

The knock sounded again. Cleo looked at Roarke and smiled. He eased her off his lap and back onto the sofa.

"Yes?" Cleo said.

"Cleo, it's Uncle Perry. May I have a word with you?"

She exchanged a curious stare with Roarke and when her husband nodded affirmatively, she sighed.

"Yes, of course, Uncle Perry. Please come in."

As her uncle spread apart the double pocket doors, he hesitated momentarily when he saw Roarke. "I was hoping to speak to you in private."

Roarke rose from the sofa. "Whatever you have to say—"

"I think that can be arranged," Cleo said. "Simon, darling, I don't think Uncle Perry would be foolish enough to try to harm me with you just outside in the hall."

Roarke grumbled. He didn't trust Perry Sutton any more than he trusted the man's hotheaded son. But Cleo was right. The man was no fool.

"I'll be right outside." Roarke glared at Perry as he slowly exited the room. Pulling the doors together, he didn't quite close them completely.

Scanning the hallway, he found it empty. Trey and Marla had excused themselves and gone straight to their suite after dinner. Daphne was out on the town with Hugh. And the last he'd seen of them, Beatrice and Oralie were in the parlor together, Beatrice reading and Oralie doing some sort of needlework.

He couldn't put his finger on the problem, but his instincts warned him that something wasn't quite right, that trouble was brewing. He hated getting these gut feelings. Nine times out of ten, they were right on the money. He always seemed to have a sixth sense for danger.

When this assignment ended, he was going to quit this business and put the past behind him. He wasn't going to second-guess a person's every action, wasn't going to question everything other people said and did. He was going to buy the farm he'd always wanted and live a peaceful, solitary life. No danger. No suspicions. No constantly watching his back. He'd had enough—more than enough. And he wanted out.

But every day he spent with Cleo made him question his great plan for the future. The sooner he wound up this assignment and left River Bend, the better off he'd be. He'd already let Cleo get under his skin—something he should never have allowed to happen. Every time he took her in his arms, she melted against him. Every time he kissed her, she surrendered. And every time he made love to her, she gave him all she had to give. The problem was that she expected the same from him and knew he was holding back. And each time, it became a little more difficult not to give in completely, a little harder to regain absolute control.

No matter how much he wanted Cleo and enjoyed their physical relationship, he could not—would not—allow her complete power over him. And he would never allow himself to care for her, not in a way that would endanger his emotions. He could not survive loving another woman and child and losing them forever. And if there was one thing Simon Roarke was, it was a survivor.

"WHAT DID YOU want to talk to me about, Uncle Perry?" Cleo faced Trey and Daphne's father, a man she'd known all her life and yet really didn't know at all. In all the years that they'd lived under the same roof, Perry Sutton had never made any effort to be a real uncle to Cleo. Other than the times when he'd staunchly supported his wife and children whenever Uncle George had taken Cleo's part in any disagreement, Perry had pretty much ignored Cleo. Of course, he hadn't paid a great deal of attention to his own children, either. Before his retirement, he'd practically lived at the local college where he taught, and when he was at home, he'd spent most of his time in his greenhouse, tending to his precious flowers.

"I did not place those spiders in your bath towels," he said, a slight tremor in his deep voice.

"Has someone accused you, Uncle Perry?" Cleo asked. Eyeing him speculatively, she noted that sweat dotted his upper lip. He stuck his hands into his jacket pockets. Were his hands trembling? she wondered.

"Since Sheriff Bacon reported to your husband that he's convinced the brown recluses that were put in your bathroom came from an experiment in Covenant College's science lab, Mr. Roarke has all but accused me." Perry took a tentative step toward Cleo. "He's questioned me repeatedly. He says things like 'As a retired professor, you stop by the campus fairly often, don't you?' and 'No one would think anything about your visiting the science lab, would they?' He thinks I'm the one trying to harm you, doesn't he?"

"Uncle Perry, if you are innocent…if you have nothing to hide, then there's nothing for you to worry about."

"If I'm innocent?" His voice rose to a loud, vibrating pitch. "My God, Cleo, do you think I'd actually harm you?"

"I don't know," she said honestly. "Your entire family has a great deal to gain if I die."

"George McNamara is somewhere down in hell right this minute, laughing his head off." Perry removed his hands from his pockets and rubbed them together nervously. "He's enjoying seeing me suffer. He always did like to see me sweat. And I'm sweating now, Cleo. Does that give you pleasure, too?"

"No, Uncle Perry, seeing you sweat gives me no pleasure. And I'm sorry that your relationship with Uncle George was so detrimental to you. What I don't understand is that if you and Uncle George hated each other so much, why did you stay here? Why didn't you leave years ago?"

Removing his hands from his pockets, Perry wrung his hands repeatedly and paced the room. He stopped abruptly by the Palladian windows. "If I'd been more of a man, I would have left. I'd have taken my wife and children and gotten as far away from River Bend as I could have. If I had, maybe Trey and Daphne wouldn't be… Maybe Oralie and I…"

"Did you stay for the money?" Cleo asked. "Did you think Uncle George would disinherit Aunt Oralie and Trey and Daphne if y'all weren't living here in his home?"

"The money didn't have a damn thing to do with my staying." He glared at Cleo, his eyes overly bright, a fine mist of tears coating their dark surface. "I had…personal reasons for wanting to stay. And Oralie never would have left. You know how much her social position here in River Bend means to her. Being a McNamara is what her life is all about."

"Yes, I'm well aware of how much being a McNamara means to Aunt Oralie," Cleo said. "She wanted desperately to be Uncle George's favorite and resented him and Aunt Beatrice because they both adored my father so. But she thought she'd finally won Uncle George over when she saw how he loved her twins. Then when my father died and my mother deserted me and I came to River Bend to live permanently, Aunt Oralie resented my intrusion into her perfect little world."

"Oralie can't help being the way she is." Perry hung his head, sadness and defeat overcoming him.

"You've always resented me, too, haven't you, Uncle Perry? You dislike me a great deal. I've always felt it, but pretended otherwise. My existence has made life much more difficult for you, hasn't it?"

Lifting his head just a fraction, he moved his eyes upward and glared at Cleo over the rim of his glasses, which were perched on his nose. "Yes. Yes. Anything that creates a problem for Oralie makes my life more difficult." He tilted his chin up and stared directly at Cleo.

"But I haven't tried to harm you. You must believe me. Beatrice loves you so dearly. Despite everything, I would never... Please, Cleo, ask your husband to stop tormenting me. I am guilty of many things—foolishness, stupidity, cowardliness—but not of trying to kill you."

"I'll speak to Simon, but—"

Roarke opened the pocket doors. "Sorry to interrupt," he said.

Aunt Beatrice stood in front of Roarke, a small silver tray in her hands. "It's my fault, I'm afraid. I insisted on bringing you your evening tea, my dear."

"It's all right," Cleo said. "Come on in. Maybe you can persuade Uncle Perry that no one has accused him of trying to harm me."

Roarke looked over Beatrice's head, his stare questioning Cleo. Her return gaze reassured him that everything was under control. He stepped back into the hall, but left the double doors open.

"Why on earth would anyone accuse Perry, of all people?" Beatrice set the silver tray down on the Jacobean desk, lifted the small china teapot and poured the hot liquid into a matching Lenox cup. "Perry wouldn't hurt a fly."

Beatrice glanced at Perry and the warm smile disappeared suddenly. He gazed at her, the look melancholy and wistful. She returned his gaze with the same tender longing. Tears gathered in the corners of her sad, green eyes. Cleo felt like a voyeur witnessing this bittersweet moment between two people who had once been in love. She remembered the first time she'd noticed this type of heartbreaking exchange between them. She'd been thirteen and had asked Pearl what it meant. Now she often wished that Pearl had never told her about Aunt Beatrice and Uncle Perry's past relationship.

"Mr. Roarke has been harassing me ever since Sheriff Bacon reported to him about the brown recluses being taken from the science lab at Covenant College," Perry told Beatrice. "I've been pleading with Cleo for understanding. Bea, you know I'd never do anything to harm her. You know I wouldn't."

Beatrice set the teapot down and turned to her niece. "You must put a stop to this immediately!" Tilting her head, she looked out into the hallway, where Roarke stood guard, his back to them. Snapping her head around, she faced Cleo. "I can't believe you could possibly think that Perry is capable of attempted murder."

"Aunt Beatrice, no one has accused Uncle Perry of anything. Roarke has simply been asking him questions in an effort to get to the truth and find out who put those spiders in my bathroom."

"Well, Perry most certainly didn't do it!"

"Beatrice, don't upset yourself this way." Perry took a hesitant step toward her, then stopped abruptly. "There's no need for you to fight my battles with Cleo the way you always tried to do with your father."

"I—I simply can't bear to…" Beatrice breathed deeply. Tears trickled down her cheeks. "I can't bear to see you suffer."

Perry cleared his throat loudly. He blinked away the mist covering his eyes, nodded to Beatrice and hurried out of the room. Roarke stepped inside the study and closed the pocket doors.

"Aunt Beatrice, I know that you believe Uncle Perry is incapable of harming me, but—"

"There are no buts! He knows you're like my own child, that I love you more than my own life. He'd never… never…" Tears streamed down Beatrice's face. Her small, delicate hands trembled.

"Oh, please don't do this to yourself." Cleo rushed to her aunt's side, slipped her arm around her waist and led her to the wingback chair opposite the sofa. "Sit down."

Beatrice eased down into the huge chair. Cleo knelt in front of Beatrice and took her aunt's quivering hands into hers.

"I'm sorry, dear," Beatrice said, squeezing Cleo's hands. "I didn't mean to act so silly. It's just that I know the kind of person Perry really is and the thought of… No, no, you must never suspect Perry." Beatrice pulled her hands free and clasped Cleo's face. "Life has been so unkind to him, you know."

"Yes, I know." Cleo rose to her feet, glanced across at Roarke, who stood silently at the closed doors. She smiled sadly at him. He nodded.

She walked over, picked up the cup of tea her aunt had poured for her and brought it to Beatrice. "Here, drink this. Tea always soothes my nerves. That's why you fix it and bring it to me when I've had a difficult day."

Beatrice accepted the tea. The saucer shook in her unsteady hands. She lifted the cup to her lips and sipped.

"Better?" Cleo asked.

"Yes, dear." Beatrice continued sipping the tea.

Cleo sat down on the sofa. "Don't worry about Uncle Perry anymore. I promise Roarke won't harass him."

Cleo felt Roarke tense. She glanced up instantly and saw the disapproving look in his eyes. If only she could explain her promise to Aunt Beatrice. Take me on faith, she tried to convey to him. Believe that I know what I'm doing. As she stared at Roarke, she saw his big body gradually relax and she knew that on some level, she had reached him with her thoughts.

When Beatrice finished the tea, Cleo jumped up, took

the cup from her and placed it on the tray. "Everything's all right now. Right?"

"Yes—" Beatrice gasped for air. "Oh, dear. I'm afraid I—" Her face twitched. She laid her hand on her cheek. "My—my cheek is numb."

"What's wrong?" Cleo rushed to her aunt's side. "Roarke, come here—quickly! Something's wrong with Aunt Beatrice."

When he reached Beatrice, she was breathing erratically. Checking her pulse, he found it irregular. His mind sorted through his past experiences. Erratic breathing. Irregular pulse. Facial twitching and numbness.

Beatrice grabbed Cleo's hand. "I'm going to be sick." She tried to get out of the chair, but before she could rise to her feet, she swayed backward, then promptly threw up.

"Oh, my. My," Beatrice moaned.

"I'm calling 911." Cleo dashed toward the telephone on the Jacobean desk.

"No!" Roarke said.

Cleo stopped, her hand hovering over the telephone.

He'd seen this sort of thing before. Men. Women. Children. Animals. Poisoned. The symptoms varied, depending upon the type of poison used, but the results were usually the same. Death.

Roarke stripped off Beatrice's soiled blouse, then lifted her into his arms. "Get that afghan." He nodded at the cream knit shawl lying across the back of the leather sofa. "We don't have any time to waste. We've got to get her to the hospital immediately."

"Why?" Cleo jerked the afghan off the sofa and followed Roarke out of the study. "What do you think's wrong with her?"

Roarke carried Beatrice down the hallway and into the foyer. "Open the door and go get a car. Any car. Just hurry."

"What's wrong with her?" Cleo demanded.

"I'm pretty sure she's ingested some kind of fast-acting poison," Roarke said. "Every minute counts. Do you understand?"

Cleo flung open the door and ran outside. Trey's silver Mercedes was in the driveway. She opened the door and said a silent prayer of thanks that, as he often did, Trey had left the keys in the ignition.

Roarke laid Beatrice in the backseat. Cleo crawled in beside her, putting her aunt's head in her lap. Beatrice groaned, then gasped for air.

Roarke got in on the driver's side, reached inside his pocket and pulled out his cellular phone. He tossed it to Cleo.

"Call 911 and have them notify the hospital to expect us," Roarke said. "The hospital's on Madison Street, isn't it?"

"Yes, two blocks off Main," Cleo replied.

Roarke started the engine, shifted the gears into Drive and raced around the circular driveway and down the private road leading to the highway.

"After you contact 911, call the house and speak to Kane," Roarke told her. "Have him go into the study and get the cup Beatrice drank from, along with the teapot. Tell him to ask Pearl where the loose tea is kept. Then have him call Sheriff Bacon."

"The tea?" Cleo trembled as realization dawned.

"Yeah, honey. That'd be my guess."

The tea had been poisoned! The tea Aunt Beatrice had brought to her. The tea she'd given her aunt to drink. Cleo's private blend. No one else in the house drank that special blend. Of course! That had to be what had happened. Whoever doctored the tea hadn't meant to harm Aunt Beatrice. They'd meant to kill Cleo!

CHAPTER TEN

CLEO PACED BACK and forth in the emergency room waiting area, her soft leather sandals silent against the tiled floor. What were the doctors doing for Aunt Beatrice? Would they be able to save her life? Dear God, if she didn't find out something soon, she'd lose her mind!

How could this have happened? It wasn't fair. Aunt Beatrice had never done anything to harm another living soul. Why was she being punished this way?

Roarke draped his arm around Cleo's shoulder, bringing her frantic pacing to a halt. "Come on, honey. Let's sit down. You're not doing yourself or your aunt any good working yourself into a frenzy like this."

Turning into Roarke's embrace, she buried her face against his chest. He encompassed her in his arms. "Oh, Simon, why did I give her that damned cup of tea to drink? If only I'd gotten her a glass of water, instead."

Roarke cupped Cleo's chin in his hand and tilted her chin. She looked up at him. "This isn't your fault. You didn't poison the tea."

"You're sure, aren't you, that the tea was poisoned?"

"Yeah, I'm pretty sure. I've seen the symptoms before. My guess would be cyanide or something related to it. That's what I told Dr. Iverson." Roarke led Cleo over to a green vinyl sofa in a corner of the room, away from the other people waiting for emergency care. "Whatever was used had to be water soluble. My guess is a powder of some kind."

Resting her head against Roarke's shoulder, Cleo relaxed. Roarke took her hand in his. "Who were you talking to on your cellular phone when the nurses forced me to come back out here?" she asked.

"Kane."

Her whole body tensed. Cleo lifted her head and stared directly at Roarke. "What did he tell you?"

"He and Sheriff Bacon are waiting at McNamara Industries lab while Dave Hibbett runs some tests on the tea," Roarke said. "Bacon agreed with Kane that your lab and technicians could get results quickly, whereas waiting on the police lab could waste time that we simply don't have."

"Knowing what type of poison it was could save Aunt Beatrice's life, couldn't it?"

"Yeah, honey, it could."

Cleo relaxed against her husband again, and together they waited. Time stood still for Cleo. The minutes seemed like hours. Just as Dr. Iverson emerged from the cubicle where nurses and another doctor still worked with Beatrice, the emergency doors parted and the entire Sutton clan stormed in like a threatening tornado.

"Where's Beatrice?" Perry Sutton demanded. "That Kane fellow said y'all had rushed her to the hospital."

"What happened?" Oralie asked. "She was perfectly fine earlier this evening."

"Was it a heart attack?" Trey asked.

"A stroke?" Daphne slipped her arm around her mother's waist. "Is she still alive?"

Leaving Trey's side, Marla approached Cleo. "Is there anything we can do? The minute Mr. Kane told us that

Aunt Beatrice was ill and y'all were en route to the emergency room, we rushed here as quickly as we could."

"Thank you, Marla," Cleo said. "But there's nothing any of us can do, except wait and pray." Cleo stood, brushed past Marla and walked slowly over to Dr. Iverson.

Following Cleo, Roarke waited behind her, his hands on her shoulders when she faced the doctor. She trembled. He tightened his hold on her shoulders, giving them a reassuring squeeze.

"How is Aunt Beatrice?" Cleo asked, a slight tremor in her voice.

"We need to find out exactly what type of poison she ingested. I've begun some preliminary treatment, but—" Dr. Iverson hesitated briefly. "She's having great difficulty breathing, and I'm afraid she could go into respiratory failure at any time. Until we know what kind of poison she ingested, all we can do is treat the symptoms."

"We have Dr. Hibbett, from the company lab, running tests on the tea Aunt Beatrice drank shortly before she became ill," Cleo said.

"Sheriff Bacon is at the lab and he'll phone the hospital as soon as they have the results." Roarke watched Dr. Iverson, wondering if he had told them everything. But Roarke didn't have to be told that time was of the essence. Proper treatment could save Beatrice's life, but at this point, the doctor would be playing a guessing game.

"What are you talking about?" Oralie nudged Daphne in the ribs and loosened her daughter's hold about her waist. She pushed past Trey and Perry. "Are you saying that Beatrice drank some sort of poisoned tea?"

"Yes," Roarke said, without glancing at Oralie. "Beatrice drank the tea she'd prepared for Cleo."

"But no one ever drinks that stuff except Cleo." All eyes turned to Daphne when she spoke. Her cheeks colored slightly. "Well, it's no secret. Everyone knows that Pearl buys that special brand for Cleo."

Dr. Iverson reached out and took Cleo's hands. "We're moving Miss McNamara up to ICU, Cleo. I promise you that we'll do everything possible to save her."

"Dear God, you're saying that Beatrice could die." Perry's voice quivered. His eyes filled with tears.

Cleo glanced at her uncle and saw genuine fear and great sorrow on his lined face. Quickly she turned back to the doctor. "Thank you."

Dr. Iverson disappeared behind the private emergency room door. A nurse emerged and came directly toward the family.

"Mrs. Roarke?"

"Yes," Cleo replied.

"Y'all can go on upstairs to the ICU waiting room. We'll be transferring Miss McNamara immediately."

"May I see her?" Cleo asked.

"Not until we have her in ICU, and then only if... Well, we'll just have to wait and see."

Roarke draped his arm around Cleo's shoulder as she turned to face the Suttons. Surveying the group, he wondered which one of them had deliberately poisoned Cleo's tea.

Perry Sutton looked as if he might crumble at any moment. His tall, slender body suddenly seemed haggard and his handsome face appeared pale and gaunt. Apparently, he was genuinely distraught over Beatrice's condition, but his concern did not rule him out as a suspect.

Cleo had been the target, not Beatrice. Only a chance happening had prevented Cleo from drinking the tea.

"Why on earth would Aunt Beatrice drink your tea?" Daphne asked. "She has always preferred coffee, even in the evenings."

"She had brought the tea to me, as she often does when I'm working in the study," Cleo said. "But tonight, she was upset and I thought...I thought a sip or two of my tea might help calm her."

"You gave her the tea after I left?" Perry asked.

"What do you mean, after you left?" Oralie grabbed her husband's arm. Her neatly manicured nails bit into the sleeve of his jacket.

Roarke had never seen Oralie looking less than perfect. Her curly salt-and-pepper hair was cut stylishly short and fluffed into a soft halo around her square face. Diamonds, rubies and sapphires glistened on her fingers and two heavy gold bracelets jangled on her wrist.

Her hazel eyes glimmered as she glared at Perry, who tightened his jaw, grasped her hand and lifted it from his arm.

"I was speaking privately with Cleo when Beatrice came in with the tea," Perry said.

His explanation obviously satisfied Oralie, who turned her full attention on Daphne. "Where is Hugh? Did he come with you?"

"Hugh loaned me his car, but he simply couldn't leave the Andersons' dinner party," Daphne said. "I've promised to call him and let him know how Aunt Beatrice is doing."

Roarke glanced at Daphne. She still wore a silver satin tea-length dress. Amethyst teardrops dangled from her ears and a matching bracelet circled her wrist. She was a beautiful woman, but there was something cold and hard about her. He'd known her type. The kind who made a man pay with his life's blood for her favors. Like mother, like daughter? he wondered.

Cleo slipped her hand into Roarke's. When he looked at her, a tight knot of pain formed in his stomach. The very thought that it could have been Cleo on her way to ICU, that it could have been Cleo hovering between life and death right now, unnerved him far more than it should. As much as he liked and respected Cleo, the possibility of her dying shouldn't scare the hell out of him.

But she was his responsibility. His job was to protect her, to keep her from all harm. How could he have prevented the poisoning? Not even he would have suspected a cup of tea made by Aunt Beatrice's loving hand could prove deadly.

"Let's go upstairs," Cleo said. "I want to be there, just in case they'll let me in to see her."

"Come on."

Together they walked out of the emergency room and down the hallway to the elevators. The Suttons followed closely behind. Trey and Marla whispered to each other, while Daphne and Oralie openly discussed the possibility that Beatrice might be dying. Perry remained quiet. Roarke noticed that his eyes were filled with tears.

When the elevator doors opened, Roarke rushed Cleo inside and punched the close button quickly, shutting out the rest of the family. As the doors fastened, they heard Trey shouting at them.

"Thank you," Cleo gripped Roarke's hand. "I'd had about all I could take of them."

"They'll be right behind us," Roarke said. "I just gained us a few minutes of solitude. You'll have to face them all again once we get upstairs."

"One of them poisoned the tea. One of them is responsible for what happened to Aunt Beatrice."

"Yeah. At least one member of your family is capable of murder. But which one?"

"I wish it were anyone except a member of my own family, even Hugh," Cleo said.

The elevator stopped at the third floor. The doors opened automatically. Cleo closed her eyes, took a deep breath and said a quick, silent prayer for her aunt Beatrice.

A young blond nurse whose name tag read K. Mullins met them the moment they entered the ICU waiting room. "Are you Mrs. Roarke?"

"Yes." Cleo's heartbeat roared in her ears like a jet engine. "Has something happened to my aunt?"

"It's good news, Mrs. Roarke," the nurse said. "Dr. Iverson said to tell you and your husband—" she glanced up at Roarke and smiled "—that Sheriff Bacon called. The lab identified the poison."

"Oh, thank God." Cleo swayed unsteadily on her feet.

Roarke grabbed her, putting his arm around her waist and lifting her against him. "Did Dr. Iverson say what it was?"

"Yes. It was some sort of fluoroacetate. Dr. Iverson mentioned something about it being a rodenticide, I believe. But he said the stuff was banned years ago."

"What was banned?" Oralie asked, as she and her troupe descended upon the ICU waiting room. "Is there news about Beatrice?"

"Dr. Iverson will be out shortly," Ms. Mullins told Cleo, then excused herself and returned to the intensive care unit.

"What was that all about?" Trey asked.

"The lab identified the poison," Roarke said.

"So quickly?" Perry stood behind his wife and children, his shoulders slumped, his face moist with tears. "Does that mean they'll be able to save Beatrice?"

"It means that Dr. Iverson will be better able to administer whatever treatment is available for that type of poison, even though many poisons are similar." Roarke answered Perry's question, but his gaze never left Cleo. She was his main concern. Hell, she was his only concern.

He guided her farther into the waiting room, eased her down onto a brown vinyl cushion and then joined her on the row of backless seats attached to the wall.

Oralie and her brood chattered among themselves, occasionally throwing out a question or comment to Roarke or Cleo. Neither of them responded, and when Roarke finally gave them his killer stare, they stopped speaking to him altogether.

Perry Sutton stood by the windows facing the back parking lot. He didn't say a word and never once turned to reply to anything his wife or children said to him. Several times Roarke noticed the man's shoulders shaking.

Cleo held Roarke's hand, finding strength and comfort in his nearness. This man had been a part of her life for only a couple of weeks and yet she could not imagine turning to anyone else at a time like this. Simon Roarke was a solid, immovable rock. Powerful. Dependable. Trustworthy.

Over the next hour, Cleo watched the clock. Wondering. Waiting. Praying. She had ignored Aunt Oralie and her cousins entirely, tuning out their incessant jabber. But occasionally she glanced over at her uncle, who had sat down at the far end of the waiting room, physically separating himself from his family. He sat with his eyes closed, but Cleo suspected that he wasn't asleep.

"Mrs. Roarke?" Ms. Mullins appeared in the doorway.

Cleo jumped. "Yes?"

Roarke helped her to stand. "Easy, honey," he said.

"Dr. Iverson said that you may come in and see your aunt for a few minutes."

"Thank you." Cleo hugged Roarke, then pulled away from him and followed the nurse into the ICU.

"What's happened?" Perry opened his bloodshot eyes.

"They're letting Cleo go in to see Aunt Beatrice," Daphne told her father.

DR. IVERSON MET Cleo at the foot of Beatrice's bed. He patted Cleo on the back, a comforting, fatherly gesture.

"It was touch and go there for a while. She went into convulsions and I was afraid she'd slip into a coma, but since giving her an injection of calcium gluconate, the convulsions have stopped. It's possible that the symptoms will reappear later, but we'll treat them if and when that happens."

"Is she going to be all right?" Cleo glanced at her aunt. Beatrice looked so small and pale lying there, her petite body connected to an endless assortment of wires and tubes. Lifesaving devices. Dear Lord, please let them be just that.

"I can't guarantee her recovery," the doctor said. "But Beatrice is a fighter, and with God's help she should pull through."

Cleo eased around to the side of her aunt's bed. Hesitantly, she touched Beatrice's slender arm, then stroked her hand tenderly.

"I'm here, Aunt Beatrice. Right here at your side. You're going to be all right. Do you hear me? You're going to be just fine." Tears filled Cleo's eyes. When they spilled over onto her cheeks, she swatted at them with her fingertips.

Dr. Iverson laid his hand on Cleo's shoulder. "Stay only a few minutes, then when you go out one other family member may come in for a brief visit."

Nodding agreement, she slipped her hand beneath her aunt's and squeezed softly. She swallowed the sobs trapped in her throat. "I love you, Aunt Beatrice. You know that, don't you? You've been more of a mother to me than my own mother ever was. You hang in there, do you hear me? You fight hard to get better. I can't do without you."

Cleo knew she'd stayed longer than she should have when the nurse tapped her on the shoulder. She turned to face Ms. Mullins.

"I'm sorry, Mrs. Roarke, but if another family member wants to see Miss McNamara, you'll have to let him or her come in now," the nurse told her.

"Yes, of course. Thank you."

When Cleo exited the ICU, she found Roarke with a coffee cup in his hand, waiting just outside the door. He encircled her shoulders and pulled her against him.

"Dr. Iverson thinks she has a chance of surviving." Cleo's knees suddenly felt wobbly, her head light.

Tightening his hold on her, Roarke guided her to a seat, then knelt in front of her and handed her the cup of coffee. "Here. Cream. No sugar. Drink it, honey."

Clasping the foam cup in her hands, Cleo lifted it to her lips and took a sip of the warm, creamy liquid. After slowly downing half the cup, she looked across the room at her uncle, who sat on the edge of his seat, his head bowed. He held his hands between his legs in a prayerful gesture.

"Uncle Perry, you can go in and see Aunt Beatrice for a few minutes," Cleo said.

Perry shot to his feet, fatigue and anxiety falling miraculously from his shoulders. He ran across the room, totally oblivious to everyone and everything around him.

Before he reached the waiting room doorway, Oralie cried out, "Why is Perry being allowed to see Beatrice? Why not me?"

Perry walked out of the waiting room and straight into the ICU, as if Oralie had never spoken.

"It's all right, Mother. We'll all get a chance to see Aunt Beatrice." Daphne petted her mother's arm.

"No, I'm sorry," Cleo said. "No one else is going to see Aunt Beatrice tonight."

"On whose orders?" Trey asked.

"Dr. Iverson said only one visitor after me," Cleo told her cousin.

"Then why Perry?" Oralie asked sharply, bitterness in her voice.

"Because he truly cares about Aunt Beatrice, which is more than I can say for any of you." Cleo ignored Oralie's outraged gasp and Trey's angry curse.

Cleo calmly finished her coffee, then set the cup down on a side table to her right. She turned to Roarke. "If Uncle Perry is the one who poisoned the tea, he'll break under the strain of knowing he almost killed Aunt Beatrice."

"Exactly what is there between Perry and Beatrice? I've noticed some sort of invisible bond between them."

"That's a perfect way to describe it," Cleo said. "An invisible bond."

Oralie glared at Cleo. "What are you two talking about over there? I heard you mention Perry's name."

"Don't upset yourself, Mother," Daphne said.

"It's ridiculous for you to assume that my husband cares more about Beatrice than I do," Oralie said. "She's my own dear first cousin, isn't she? And she's only related to Perry by marriage."

Cleo looked directly at Oralie. "You know why I told Uncle Perry he could go in to see Aunt Beatrice."

"What does she mean by that remark, Mother?" Trey stirred from his seat beside Marla, who had fallen asleep and was awakened by her mother-in-law's outburst.

"I want you to march right in there and bring your father out!" Oralie said. "He has no business in there with Beatrice."

"What the hell's going on?" Trey looked quizzically from his mother to Cleo.

Before either could reply, Perry Sutton returned from the ICU, his face damp with tears. On some instinctive level, Cleo wanted to go to her uncle and put her arms around him. But she didn't.

"There you are," Oralie said. "I'm ready to leave, Perry. This has all been too much for me. I'm completely exhausted. You know what a nervous disposition I have."

Perry glanced at his wife, his face void of emotion. "Yes, my dear, I know."

"There's nothing we can do for Beatrice by staying," Oralie told him.

"You're quite right. There's nothing any of you can do for Beatrice by staying here." Perry looked at his son. "Trey, you and Marla take your mother home. Daphne, you go with them and see to your mother's comfort."

"Aren't you coming?" Daphne asked.

"You are not staying here!" Oralie rose to her feet. Glaring at her husband, she walked slowly toward him.

When Oralie stood directly in front of Perry, her cheeks bright with anger and her eyes wild with rage, he smiled. And that odd little smile on her uncle's face sent cold chills up Cleo's spine.

"Yes, my dear, I am staying." Perry's voice was deadly calm.

Oralie whirled around so quickly she almost lost her balance. Daphne grabbed her mother's arm. "Take me home immediately," she demanded. "I can't bear another minute of this."

Daphne guided Oralie out into the hallway. Trey and

Marla followed. Trey hesitated, then turned around and said, "Please call us if Aunt Beatrice's condition worsens."

"Yes, I'll call," Cleo said, and breathed a sigh of relief when her aunt and cousins boarded the nearby elevator.

Perry slumped into a chair by the door, crossed his arms over his chest and closed his eyes. Cleo watched him for several minutes, wondering if she should go over and talk to him, try to comfort him. She didn't.

"Do you want to tell me what that was all about?" Roarke asked.

"I asked Pearl a similar question when I was about thirteen," Cleo said.

"And what did Pearl tell you?"

"Years ago, when Aunt Beatrice and Uncle Perry were young, they fell in love and planned to marry."

"What happened?"

"Aunt Beatrice grew up in an age when nice girls didn't have sex before marriage, so she wanted to wait until after their wedding."

"And?"

"Aunt Oralie was jealous of Aunt Beatrice. She wanted Perry for herself and didn't have any qualms about seducing him in a weak moment." Cleo glanced across the room at Perry Sutton and her heart ached for him. "Aunt Beatrice would have forgiven him and married him anyway, except... Oralie was pregnant. With twins."

"Trey and Daphne."

"Of course Uncle Perry married Aunt Oralie and the rest, as they say, is history."

Roarke groaned. "God, what messes we make of our lives. We human beings find a way to screw up everything and destroy ourselves in the process."

Cleo touched Roarke's face, stroking his stubble-roughened cheek. "I'm glad that you're here with me. That I'm not having to go through this alone."

He took her in his arms. She went willingly. An overwhelming sense of belonging came over her. This felt so right. Being with Simon. Her husband.

ROARKE NUDGED CLEO. She purred in his arms like a sleepy kitten. He lifted her off his lap, where she'd slept most of the night, set her beside him on the vinyl sofa and shook her gently.

"Wake up, Cleo Belle. It's visiting hours. You can go in and see Aunt Beatrice in a few minutes."

Cleo opened her eyes slowly. The first thing she saw was Roarke's face. That wonderful, strong, handsome face. Smiling, she sat up straight and stretched.

"The last thing I remember is your lifting me into your lap and telling me to take a nap."

"That was around midnight last night," Roarke said. "It's nearly six o'clock."

"Did you get any rest?" Unable to resist touching him, she laid her hand on his chest. "You must have been uncomfortable with me lying on you all night."

"I got plenty of rest," he told her. "You're as light as a feather." He leaned down and whispered in her ear, "Besides, that's not the first time you've slept on top of me most of the night."

She made a funny little sound deep in her throat, a mixture of moan and laughter. "I probably look a fright." She stood, then reached down and picked up her shoulder bag. "I need to go to the bathroom." She glanced around the waiting area. "Where's Uncle Perry?"

"He's already gone in to see Beatrice."

"Oh. Okay. Could you rustle us up some coffee while I go freshen up?"

"I'll see what I can do."

Roarke walked down the hall to a small alcove where a row of vending machines stood. He removed a couple of dollars from his wallet and inserted one into the coffee machine, then punched a button. He repeated the process, then returned to the waiting room.

He set Cleo's coffee on the side table, then walked over to the windows and looked out at the parking lot. Lifting the cup to his lips, he sipped the hot, black brew.

Since Beatrice had lived through the night, her chances of recovery had improved. He was grateful that Cleo's aunt hadn't died. Cleo loved Beatrice deeply and was devoted to her. How different would his own life have been if his aunt Margaret had shown him the affection Cleo had received from Beatrice? His father's sister had been a cold, harsh woman who'd never once said a kind word to him. Not even when he'd first come to live with Margaret and Eddie Bullock, and had been a scared, lonely boy of nine whose father had just died and left him an orphan.

Roarke's life had been without love, without any human warmth and kindness, until he'd met Hope. She was beautiful, bright, bubbly, and he'd fallen for her so hard he hadn't had a chance of escaping. Hell, he hadn't wanted to escape. He'd thought she was everything he'd ever dreamed of, everything he'd ever wanted. He'd been wrong.

She'd wanted him to leave the army. He'd tried to explain what being a member of the Special Forces meant to him. She didn't understand. She didn't even try.

A year into their marriage, he'd known what a mistake he'd made. But Hope clung to him, begging him not to leave her, not to stop loving her. She was so needy, so desperately needy, and no matter how much he gave, it was never enough.

"Do I look better?" Cleo asked as she emerged from the bathroom. "I cleaned up a bit. Washed my face and combed my hair." She spied the coffee cup on the table. "Oh, good. Coffee."

"You look fine, honey. A little tired, maybe."

A tall, bony, middle-aged nurse appeared in the doorway. "Mrs. Roarke, your aunt is awake and asking for you and your husband."

"She's awake." Cleo laughed nervously. "Oh, she'll fuss at me for staying here all night." She smiled at the nurse. "Is my uncle still in with her?"

"Yes. He's waiting until y'all come in before leaving. I must say, your uncle is quite devoted to her, isn't he? Just watching the way he looks at her, you can see how much he loves her."

"Yes, I know exactly what you mean," Cleo said.

They followed the nurse into ICU. Perry sat beside Beatrice's bed, holding her hand. Beatrice glanced up and smiled when she saw Cleo.

"You gave us quite a scare last night." Cleo leaned over and hugged her aunt. Gazing into Beatrice's weak eyes, Cleo clenched her teeth to keep from crying.

Perry released Beatrice's hand, then bent over and kissed her forehead. "I'll be right outside."

"No, wait, Perry," Beatrice said. "I want all of you to go on home. I'm out of danger now, aren't I, Ms. Danton?" She glanced at the skinny nurse. "I'm going to be just fine."

"You've certainly come through the night with flying colors," Nurse Danton said. "We're hoping you'll be fully recovered and able to go home in a few days. If you continue to improve, Dr. Iverson will put you in a private room sometime late tomorrow."

"See," Beatrice told them. "Go home. Take baths. Eat

something. Tend to business. You can come back and see me this afternoon."

"I'll be back." Perry waved at Beatrice, then turned and left the ICU.

"I didn't want to say anything while Perry was here." Beatrice lifted her hand, reaching for Roarke. "Come here."

Roarke took her hand in his. "I'm right here, Aunt Beatrice."

Smiling, she sighed deeply. "I'm so glad that Cleo has you at her side. She's in real danger. If we had any doubts about how far this person will go, I think this incident should erase those doubts."

"Do you know what happened?" Cleo asked.

"I heard Rob Iverson and the nurses talking," Beatrice said. "Of course they didn't know I could hear them. I was poisoned, wasn't I? Or rather, the tea I prepared for Cleo had been poisoned."

"Yes, dear." Cleo stroked her aunt's forehead, brushing back a strand of silver-streaked red hair.

Beatrice clutched Roarke's hand. "You must find this person and stop him before he kills Cleo!"

"Don't upset yourself, Aunt Beatrice." Roarke turned her hand over and gave it several reassuring pats. "I'll take care of Cleo."

"Whoever did this must hate Cleo a great deal." Beatrice's eyes filled with tears. "Find the person who hates Cleo, before it's too late. It's not Perry, but it could easily be Oralie. Or Daphne. Or even Trey."

"I'm sorry," Nurse Danton said. "I'm afraid y'all are going to have to leave and let Miss McNamara get her rest. If you'd like to speak to Dr. Iverson, I'll have him call you at home, Mrs. Roarke, after he's seen your aunt later this morning."

"Yes, have him call her later," Beatrice said. "Now, Simon, take her home and see that she eats and gets some rest before you let her come back to this hospital."

Neither Simon nor Cleo said a word on the elevator ride down to the ground level of the hospital. When the doors opened, Cleo gasped. Sheriff Phil Bacon stood there, waiting for an elevator.

"I was on my way up to talk to y'all," he said.

"Why don't we go into the coffee bar over there." Roarke pointed to his left.

The three of them sat down at a small table in the corner. Cleo reached under the table and clutched Roarke's hand.

"Cleo, your private stock of tea was laced with a poisonous substance that your people at McNamara labs tell us was odorless and tasteless, and very deadly."

She gripped Roarke's hand even more tightly. "How would someone get such a poison?"

"Well, that type of poison, according to your Dr. Hibbett, used to be in rodenticides and stuff like that, but the government banned it years ago."

"Then how—" Cleo asked.

"There's still some of it around," Phil Bacon said.

"Do you have any idea where the amount put in Cleo's tea came from?" Roarke squeezed Cleo's hand.

"As a matter of fact, we do. And that's why I needed to talk to you."

"You found the source of the poison?" Cleo sucked in her breath. "So soon?"

"We did a search of your house and the grounds," the sheriff told her. "I've had my men out there all night."

"You found the poison at my house?"

"No, ma'am, we found it in your uncle's greenhouse."

"What?" Cleo bit down on her bottom lip.

"There was about a fourth of a bag of the stuff in the bottom of the trash. It was an old bag. Someone had wrapped it in a separate plastic bag and covered it with all sorts of debris."

"Uncle Perry's greenhouse." Cleo spoke slowly, trying to absorb the meaning of what she'd been told and praying, for Aunt Beatrice's sake, that the most likely suspect wouldn't turn out to be guilty.

CHAPTER ELEVEN

MAY HAD EXPLODED into fragrant bloom. Springtime flowers and shrubs littered the countryside. Nourished by several days of scattered thundershowers, the lawns were a vibrant green. Cleo hugged herself when she stepped out onto the screened back porch. "'God's in his heaven and all's right with the world,'" she quoted Browning. A shiver of apprehension quivered along her nerve endings. Despite the fact that Aunt Beatrice was home from the hospital and recuperating nicely, and despite the fact that for the past week absolutely nothing had gone wrong, either at home or at the plant, all was most definitely not right with the world.

Despite the appearance of normalcy, her life was anything but normal. My God, her family's company had been sabotaged, her aunt had nearly died from poisoning and she was paying her hired husband a million dollars to get her pregnant.

And they still didn't know who was trying to kill her!

Regardless of the peace and tranquillity at the house and the smoothly running operations at the plant, Cleo feared that this was all simply the calm before the storm. Even with Morgan Kane and his security force monitoring McNamara Industries seven days a week, twenty-four hours a day, Cleo kept waiting for another accident or another computer problem. It was like waiting for the other shoe to drop.

And Cleo couldn't remember a time when the Suttons

had been so eager to maintain family harmony. Trey had kept his temper under control and Daphne had refrained from her usual catty remarks. And even Aunt Oralie hadn't acted like a jealous harpy whenever Uncle Perry showed any kindness toward Aunt Beatrice. It seemed highly unnatural to Cleo, and she'd said so to Pearl, who had agreed with her wholeheartedly.

"There's something not right about all this sweetness and light coming from the likes of them," Pearl had said. "It's like a pit of vipers disguising themselves as a bunch of harmless grub worms."

Whether it was Aunt Beatrice's near death or the sheriff's questioning of Uncle Perry—which had fallen just short of his arresting him on suspicion of attempted murder—that caused the change in the Suttons, Cleo was uncertain. But one thing she knew for sure—it wouldn't last.

The Suttons were scared. The whole lot of them. And each for his or her own reason. Now that Hugh Winfield was at Daphne's side every moment he wasn't working, Cleo counted him as a Sutton, and equally suspect in the company sabotage and the failed attempts on her life. Six suspects. Three blood related, two relatives by marriage and another a family friend she'd known since childhood.

Coming up behind her, Roarke slipped his arms around his wife and drew her back up against his chest. Leaning into his body, she lapped her arms over his. He kissed the top of her head, then rested his chin in the softness of her hair.

"I'm ready for our ride," he said. "I haven't been on a horse in years. Not much opportunity in my line of business."

"You'll be just fine. Riding a horse is like riding a bicycle. Once you learn how, you never forget." Cleo breathed deeply, taking in the delicious aroma of the fresh early-morning air and the clean, manly scent of her husband.

"I still think there are better ways to spend a lazy Saturday morning than going horseback riding." He nuzzled the side of her face.

Giggling, Cleo squirmed out of his arms and turned to face him. Simon Roarke was the only man she'd ever known who could fill her stomach with fluttering butterflies just by looking at her. But then again, she'd never known a man like her husband. Standing here before her, the morning sunshine casting a golden glow on his thick, brown hair and richly tanned skin, Simon was a magnificent sight. His faded blue jeans hugged his lean hips and long legs. She shivered, remembering the feel of wrapping herself around his hips, the pleasure of having those long, hairy legs straddling her.

Lifting her chin, she looked up into his mischievous blue eyes. "I knew you'd wake up with lascivious thoughts on your mind this morning," she said. "That's why I got up and out of the bedroom before you awoke."

Roarke grasped her face, cradling her chin between his thumb and forefinger. "What's the matter, honey? Are you getting tired of me already?"

Knowing that he was joking, she tried to keep the smile on her face and think of some similarly jovial response. But her thoughts turned serious. Didn't he realize that she would never grow tired of him, of his passionate lovemaking, of the blissful moments she spent in his arms, possessing him and being possessed by him? Didn't he have any idea how much he'd come to mean to her, how much she wanted him to remain a part of her life, even after she was pregnant, even after she was no longer in danger?

"You're having to think that one over way too long, Cleo Belle. Does that mean—"

Standing on tiptoe, she flung her arms up and around his neck. "It means that I was trying to think of a response as equally silly and ridiculous." She rubbed against him like a sleek, sensuous cat. He cupped her buttocks and lifted her off her feet, pressing her into his arousal. "I might get tired of you, Mr. Roarke, in about a hundred years or so. But even then, I doubt it."

"So why didn't we spend the morning upstairs in our bed, making love?" He took her mouth in a hot, hungry kiss and acknowledged her fervent response by lifting her body up higher onto his and deepening the kiss, devouring her with his passion.

She draped her jean-covered legs around his hips, returning his passion in full measure. Her core throbbed against his pulsating sex. She knew, as he did, that only the barrier of their clothes kept them from mating there on the back porch, in broad daylight, where they could be interrupted at any moment.

Roarke reluctantly ended the kiss, realizing full well that this either had to stop or be taken to the limit. He brushed his lips over hers, then whispered against her mouth, "Either we go back upstairs and finish this…or we go riding."

"I want to do both," she said tauntingly.

When he began lowering her slowly, she loosened her legs from around his body and allowed him to set her on her feet. "You want to go back upstairs and then go riding later?"

"No, I want to go riding now and finish this out there—" she gazed toward the thickly wooded area to the east of the house "—in a very beautiful, secluded spot I know."

Roarke grinned. The bottom dropped out of Cleo's stomach.

"You, my darling wife, can be a very diabolical lady."

"If you say so. But I prefer to think of myself as inventive and adventurous. We haven't made love anywhere except upstairs in our suite. I thought a little variety was called for today. In celebration of a noneventful week."

"We've had variety," he told her, his lips twitching in an almost grin. "We've made love in the bed. You on top. Me on top. Side by side. From the edge of the bed. From the front. From the rear. We've made love in the shower, in the tub, on the love seat, in the chairs and even on the desk."

Cleo smiled broadly. Recalling each and every moment they'd shared, Cleo sighed. Her cheeks flushed a soft, delicate pink. "Yes, I know. But we've never made love outside. Hidden under the trees. With the smell of honeysuckle and wild roses all around us."

He grabbed her hand. "Come on, woman. What are we waiting for? Let's get down to the stables and saddle up old Paint."

Hand in hand, Cleo giggling quietly and Roarke grinning from ear to ear, they hurried off the porch, out of the backyard and down the unpaved lane leading to the stables.

"When I was a teenager, Uncle George kept over half a dozen horses stabled here," she said. "He loved to ride and he enjoyed having mounts for visitors. Of course, I've had my own horse since I was a child, just as Aunt Beatrice has. But now there's only Valentino and Sweet Justice."

"Let me guess. Valentino belongs to Beatrice and Sweet Justice is yours. Am I right?"

"Aunt Beatrice has had Valentino since he was two years old. He's fourteen now. You won't have any problem handling him. He's a gelding and has a sweet disposition."

"And Sweet Justice? Don't tell me he's a stallion."

"Sweet Justice is an Arabian filly. Uncle George gave her to me for my birthday last year. She's barely two years old. She replaced Candy Man, an Arabian I'd been riding most of my life."

The well-kept stables stood a half mile behind the main house. Willie Ross, whom Cleo had introduced to Roarke the first week of their marriage, met them just as they started to enter the enclosure. The sandy-haired man, with his wide, toothy smile, came out to meet them, walking with a slight limp. Cleo had told Roarke that as a child, Willie had been injured in an automobile accident that had left him physically and mentally impaired. But he was a gentle, loyal man, who had a knack for caring for horses as well as a deep love for animals in general. George McNamara had given him a job when he'd been a teenager and had kept him on at full salary even after he'd sold all but two of the horses. Cleo's uncle had remembered his stable hand in his will, requesting that Willie receive his wages as long as he lived.

"I was expectin' you down this morning, Cleo."

Willie spoke with a pronounced slur. When he said her name, it came out sounding like Clay-ee-o.

"Got Sweet Justice and old Valentino all saddled up and ready for you and Mr. Roarke."

"Thank you, Willie." Cleo patted the thin, frail man's arm. "Mr. Roarke and I plan to be out most of the morning. I'm going to show him some of my secret places."

"You going to take him over to the Great Mississippi?" Willie's laughter sounded like a grunting chuckle.

When Cleo smiled at him, the stable hand's face came alive with warmth and gentle affection.

"I'm going to show him the Great Mississippi and Sherwood Forest," Cleo said.

"He'll like 'em both." Willie looked up at Roarke. "I used to take care of Cleo, watch out for her when she was a little girl and played in Sherwood Forest and swam in the Great Mississippi."

"Sometimes Willie would play with me," Cleo said. "He'd be Little John and I'd be Robin Hood. And we used to sail a boat up the Great Mississippi."

"Sometimes I was Huck and Cleo was Tom, then next time she'd be Huck and I'd be Tom."

"Sounds like you two had quite a few adventures together," Roarke said.

"Yes, sir. That we did. Cleo's always been my friend."

Willie went inside and led Valentino out of his stall and into the stable yard. Roarke noticed a fine mist covering Cleo's eyes. He knew she ached inside with love for Willie and a deep sadness that a man of nearly fifty would forever have a little boy's mind.

The gray gelding Willie led had small, curved ears and large, expressive eyes. Roarke stroked the horse's long, arched neck as he accepted the reins. Valentino was a handsome fellow and obviously pampered. He nudged Roarke's hand.

"What do you want, buddy?" Roarke looked to Willie.

Willie pulled out a small apple from his baggy jacket pocket. "Old Val likes a treat. Whenever Miss Bea rides him, she always gives him an apple."

Roarke accepted the apple and offered it to Valentino, who took it greedily. Roarke laughed.

Willie rushed back into the stables, soon emerging with Cleo's mount. Sweet Justice was a magnificent specimen, a chestnut filly with a broad, muscular chest and deep girth. With her tail set high, she pranced toward Cleo.

"Here's my girl." Cleo hugged the beautiful Arabian. "Have you missed me, Sweetie?" The filly nuzzled Cleo's arm. "Yes, well, I've missed you, too."

Roarke waited for Cleo to mount, watching her graceful ascent. In the morning sunlight her hair shimmered a bright, rich auburn and Sweet Justice's shining coat was almost an exact match. Woman and horse seemed made for each other. Both were noble creatures. Proud, beautiful females. Aristocratic purebreds.

Roarke mounted Valentino and motioned the gelding to follow the filly's lead. Sweet Justice broke into a trot, taking free, straight strides.

"When I called Willie yesterday and told him to have the horses ready this morning, I asked him to give you Uncle George's saddle," Cleo said. "I thought it only fitting. Since you wouldn't be here in River Bend, wouldn't be married to me, except for Uncle George's will. In a way, as my husband, you're what Uncle George would have called the 'head of the household' now, and my 'lord and master.'"

Roarke laughed, trying to imagine anyone being lord and master of Cleopatra Arabelle McNamara Roarke. And the last job on earth he wanted was as head of a household that, until the past week's good behavior, thrived on jealousy, greed and hatred.

When Sweet Justice broke into a gallop, Valentino followed suit. The two Arabians struck a natural pace, floating across the ground with fast, free strides.

During the next hour, Cleo gave Roarke a grand tour of the estate then led him to what she and Willie had always referred to as the "Great Mississippi." In reality, the body of water was a large creek that bisected the McNamara property in half. But as a child, it had seemed vast, and had posed a challenge for her and Willie as they had ridden downstream in their old wooden canoe.

Roarke and Cleo slowed the horses. Cleo dismounted. "Well, what do you think?" she asked.

"This is the Great Mississippi?" he asked.

"To an eight-year-old it was," she told him. "And those woods over there—" she pointed behind them "—were Sherwood Forest."

"Why were you Robin Hood instead of Maid Marian?" Roarke dismounted.

"Because Robin Hood was the one in charge. He was the one who led the merry men. And as long as I can remember, I've always liked being the boss."

"Yeah, I can believe that. You're a real bossy butt, Cleo Belle. A lot of men wouldn't find that trait appealing."

She slowly unbuttoned her short-sleeved, turquoise-and-yellow-striped blouse. "But you do, don't you, Simon? You like the fact that I'm a take-charge kind of woman."

She removed her blouse and tossed it on the ground. Roarke didn't take his eyes off her, focusing for the moment on her yellow satin bra.

"Yeah, honey, I like it. As a matter of fact, your bossiness turns me on."

Her gaze focused on his broad, muscular chest. She sucked in a deep breath. "I brought you here so we could go skinny-dipping."

"Is that so?"

"I want you to take off all your clothes, and then I want you to undress me." She looked at him, unsmiling, a dead-serious gleam in her eyes. "Turnabout is fair play."

"Whatever you want, Boss Lady." He unbuttoned his blue cotton shirt and threw it on top of Cleo's blouse.

As he slowly took off his clothes, he watched her, and loved the reactions she couldn't hide. As soon as he stripped off his shirt, she clenched and unclenched her hands. He knew she wanted to touch him, to run her fingers over his chest.

He removed the leather hip holster and laid his Beretta on the ground. Cleo's gaze followed his every action.

He unbuckled his belt and unsnapped his jeans. Cleo swallowed hard. He lowered the zipper. Cleo's mouth opened to a soft oval. He sat down on the ground and removed his boots and socks, then rose to his feet. Cleo took a nervous step toward him. He dragged his jeans down his hips and over his long legs, then kicked them aside. Cleo sighed deeply. Turning around so that his back was to her, he bent over and eased off his briefs. Taking his time, he turned back around and faced her in all his gloriously naked splendor. Cleo licked her lips.

A fine film of moisture coated her upper lip and forehead. Roarke knew her perspiration had little to do with the warm sunshine and a great deal to do with sexual heat. Cleo's body was a low-burning fire, easily stoked to a full blaze by her desire for him.

He loved knowing how much she wanted him.

Roarke stood before her, unmoving, like some bronze statue, his body honed to perfection. He was tempting her, she realized, waiting for her to succumb, to give in to her own wanton longings. But this was her game, and they were damn well going to play by her rules.

If anyone begged for mercy, it was going to be Simon Alloway Roarke. She intended to make him as hot as she was. She wanted to see his big, hard body drenched with perspiration. And Cleo knew exactly what to do to make him sweat.

"Come here, Simon," she commanded, like a queen giving orders to a servant.

He strutted toward her, shoulders and back straight,

head held high, his long legs moving with the same muscular grace with which the Arabians trotted. Proud. Strong. Magnificent.

Control, Cleo cautioned herself. Control. She could so easily lose herself in Roarke's overwhelming masculinity. Everything female within her was drawn to that powerful male aura. When they were alone together, nothing existed except the two of them. No marriage of convenience. No plotting, conniving relatives. No family and business responsibilities. No regrets about the past. No plans for the future. Only the here and now. Only this wild, free passion that drove them to madness—and beyond.

When he was within a few inches of bringing their bodies close enough to touch, he stopped and looked down at her. "Is this where you want me?"

"Yes." She looked up at him. "Now, take off my clothes."

His gaze met hers. Radiant blue and warm amber-flecked green clashed in a battle of wills. They spoke without words, each understanding the other perfectly. Physically, he was much larger and a great deal stronger, but she possessed strengths that neither he nor any man possessed. She was woman. Keeper of men's souls. Guardian of untold treasures. Loving angel and vengeful she-devil. Earth mother and fiery temptress.

He clenched and unclenched his shaky hands, then reached out and loosened her leather belt. She shivered. He unsnapped and unzipped her jeans, then slipped his hands beneath the waistband, cupping the upper sides of her hips. He glanced up at her yellow bra. Her chest rose and fell with labored breaths. He eased her jeans downward, letting them ride low on her hips. Spreading his hands across her stomach, he rotated them in a caressing circle. When she sighed with pleasure, he knelt before her.

"You'd better brace yourself, Boss Lady." Lifting her hands, he placed them on his bare shoulders.

He picked up her right foot, tugged on her boot and jerked it and her sock off, and pulled her jean-clad leg free, then repeated the process with her other foot. Cleo gripped his shoulders, loving the hot, hard strength of his body.

Leaning low, he kissed first one and then her other knee. She swayed. He kissed a damp, moist trail up her right thigh, over her yellow satin bikini panties, across her naked belly and upward to the V of her bra. Reaching around her, he unhooked the scrap of yellow satin and slid the straps down her shoulders. Her high, firm breasts fell free, exposed to the sun's heat, the breeze's warm breath and Roarke's piercing stare. He threw the bra on the ground, then cupped her breasts.

Cleo's body tightened, then released. A purely feminine tingling radiated upward from her central core.

Using the pads of his thumbs, he played with her nipples until they peaked in hard, throbbing points and begged for his mouth. He answered their plea, tormenting one nipple with his tongue while his fingertips toyed with the other.

Cleo moaned, the painful pleasure was so intense. "Simon!"

Halting the sensual torture, he lifted his head and looked at her. "I'm sorry, Boss Lady. I got a little sidetracked by your beautiful breasts. Don't worry, I'm going to finish what I started." He slid his hands inside the back of her panties, kneading her buttocks.

He was killing her by slow degrees, but she knew, despite his iron-will performance, that he was getting closer and closer to losing control. He could not hide his aroused state. His manhood stood at attention, hard and pulsating, passionate moisture trickling from the tip.

He took his own sweet time removing her panties, his hands caressing their way downward, his fingertips giving off electrical energy that sent shock waves through her body.

When her panties fell down to her ankles, she kicked them aside and reached out for Roarke. When she touched him intimately, he growled like a beast in pain.

She smiled as she encompassed him, stroking him with her closed hand. He jerked. Running her thumb across the tip, she spread the juice around his shaft.

"Dammit, woman!" Roarke hauled her up against him, but when he tried to lift her, she pulled away, then quickly dropped to her knees. He gazed down at her, his vision slightly blurred from the raging desire boiling inside him. "Don't tease me, honey. Not about this."

And that was the last coherent thing Simon Roarke was able to say for quite some time. Cleo played with him, tormenting him with her tongue, promising but not fulfilling, until Roarke's big body trembled. He was a mighty oak ready to fall. All it would take was one tiny push. One sweet, sweet tiny little push.

He grabbed the back of her head, urging her to give what she had promised. Threading his fingers through her hair, he pressed her face toward his body.

She made love to him with her mouth, tenderly, thoroughly, learning from his grunts and sighs what he preferred and what he didn't want. She brought him to the very edge, then hesitated, her own body quivering with need. Then she pushed him over the edge, headlong into earth-shattering release.

When some measure of sanity returned to him, he lifted her off her feet and up into his arms. His mouth took hers in a frenzy, feeding off her passion. He tasted himself on her lips, on her tongue, and his body reawakened. How was it possible? he wondered. He was damn near forty years old. Maybe he should remind a certain part of his anatomy that men his age couldn't make such a quick recovery.

Roarke carried her to the edge of the creek and set her on the grassy bank, letting her feet and calves hang over into the water. He walked into the creek, then lifted her to straddle his hips and eased the two of them into the water. She cried out when he entered her, surprised that he was ready again so soon. He guided her movements, back and forth, splashing the water around them. With her legs wrapped around his hips and her arms draped loosely around his neck, Cleo allowed Roarke complete control. The sensations mounted inside her quickly. He plunged deeper and harder, pounding into her until she screamed her pleasure.

The aftershocks of her fulfillment pelted him. He drove into her repeatedly, with quick, hard lunges, then jetted his release into her receptive body.

They clung together, their bodies shaky, their breathing harsh. Roarke supported her weight with his strength, and she was glad because her bones had melted and offered no support.

Gradually their weakness diminished and Roarke carried her out of the creek and up onto the grass. The horses grazed contentedly nearby. Roarke looked around for a secluded spot and spied two weeping willows, their long, feathery branches overlapping where they touched the ground. He carried Cleo inside the verdant cocoon, placed her on the warm, soft grass and lay down beside her. She reached over and clasped his hand.

They lay there, side by side, for several minutes. Neither of them speaking. Each listening to the other one's breathing. They dozed off and slept until the sun was high in the sky.

Rousing from her nap, Cleo gently awakened Roarke. "Let's don't go back to the house," she said. "Let's stay out here all day. If anyone needs to find us, Willie knows where we are."

"I can't think of anything I'd rather do than lie here under this willow with you all day. Both of us naked." He stroked the underside of her wrist with his thumb. "But we can't hide out here forever. Sooner or later, we'll have to go back and face what's waiting for us."

"What's waiting for us is my family, who have suddenly started acting like a Stepford family. Like sweet, docile robots." Cleo shook her head. "And I dread the thought of Aunt Beatrice finding out that Uncle Perry is the sheriff's number-one suspect."

"She still loves him, doesn't she?" Roarke ran his fingers through his hair.

"Yes, I'm afraid she does."

"But you're not still in love with Paine Emerson and you were never in love with Hugh Winfield. Is that right?"

Cleo braced her elbow on the ground, placing her body in a half sitting, half lying position. She gazed directly into Roarke's questioning eyes. "That's right. Despite the strong family resemblance, I am not a carbon copy of my aunt Beatrice. I'm not the type to spend my whole life pining away for a man I could never have. Besides, I wouldn't have Paine Emerson now if he threw himself at my feet and begged me to forgive him."

Roarke positioned himself on one elbow and turned toward Cleo, his body mimicking the way hers rested on the bed of grass beneath them. "What about Hugh Winfield?"

"What about Hugh?"

"Any regrets where he's concerned?"

"Only that I ever dated him in the first place," she said. "We've been friends since we were kids, but I never seriously considered going out with him. Not until Uncle George suggested it."

"Uncle George wanted you to marry Hugh." Roarke broke off a blade of grass and put it in his mouth.

"Uncle George wanted to make sure I didn't make the same mistake his daughter made. He was damned and determined to see me married and a mother. He truly believed I'd never be happy otherwise."

"He must have hated Perry Sutton for hurting Beatrice the way he did. What I can't understand is why your uncle George allowed Oralie and her family to live with him." Roarke removed the blade of grass from his mouth and ran the tip up and down between Cleo's breasts.

Her nipples hardened instantly. "I'm sure Uncle George did hate Uncle Perry for years, but after time passed and he saw that Perry paid dearly for his mistake every day of his life, then Uncle George's attitude mellowed. He never forgave Uncle Perry, but I think, in the end, he pitied him.

"To understand the situation fully, you have to know that my father and Aunt Oralie had lived with Uncle George since their early teens, after their parents died. Uncle George was really a father to his brother's children as well as to his own daughter. Would you believe that at one time Aunt Beatrice and Aunt Oralie were like sisters? Uncle George allowed Oralie to continue living with him because Aunt Beatrice asked him not to kick her out. Uncle Perry had very little money at the time and Aunt Oralie has always had very expensive tastes."

"Beatrice is a remarkable woman," Roarke said. "Not many in her position would have been so generous."

"That's the kind of person she is. Loving and forgiving to a fault."

"Let's keep our suspicions and Sheriff Bacon's from Beatrice as long as we possibly can." Roarke ran the blade of grass across Cleo's tight nipples.

She gasped as the tingling sensation in her nipples raced downward. "I agree, but sooner or later, she's bound to find out. Especially if Uncle Perry really is guilty."

"You know, Cleo, despite all the circumstantial evidence against him, my gut instincts tell me that Perry Sutton didn't place those spiders in your towels and he didn't poison your tea." Roarke repeatedly raked the grass blade across Cleo's nipples.

She grabbed his hand. He looked at her and grinned, then pulled free and threw away the blade of grass.

"Why would an intelligent man, who is an entomology expert, with free access to the science lab where the spiders were kept, be foolish enough to take such a risk?" Roarke reached out and lifted an unruly strand of hair off Cleo's cheek. "And why on earth would a man use an outdated rodenticide, which he kept in his own greenhouse, to poison your tea?"

"It's almost as if someone were trying to set him up. But who? Why would Trey or Daphne set up their own father? And Lord knows, Aunt Oralie wouldn't. She couldn't survive without Uncle Perry's constant attention."

"If you're right, that leaves only Hugh Winfield. And he'd have nothing to gain unless he can persuade Daphne to marry him. Of course, I'm not as generous in my estimation of Daphne as you are. I believe she'd use anyone to get what she wanted. It's possible that she's capable of setting up her own father. Could be that she and Winfield are working together."

"Anything's possible, isn't it?" Cleo lay flat on her

back, looking up through a fluttering, feathery green curtain at the bright blue sky overhead. "We're really no closer to the truth than we were two weeks ago."

"Have I failed you, Cleo?" he asked. "Did you expect—"

She covered his lips with two fingers, silencing him. "McNamara Industries is secure and well policed by Mr. Kane and his security force. That was your doing." She traced the line of his jaw with her fingertip. "I'm alive and well and happier than I've ever been in my life. And that, too, is your doing."

"Ah, honey, you shouldn't say things like that to a naked man."

"Then you'd better put on your clothes," she told him.

"Later." He reached for her, grasping her by the shoulders and drawing her into his embrace. "I have something in mind that requires both of us to be naked."

"Oh, is that right?" She rubbed her breasts against his chest and smiled when he moaned. "Just what do you have in mind?"

"It involves a little payback for my loving wife," he said, slipping his hand between her legs.

"Payback? Tit for tat?"

He massaged the tiny kernel hidden in the apex between her thighs. Cleo lifted her hips up off the ground. "You've got the idea, honey," he said.

"You're going to give me what I gave you." Her body dampened against his fingers, surrounding them with moisture.

"Lick for lick." Roarke inserted his finger inside her welcoming warmth.

Cleo blew out a deep breath. "No one has ever…I mean… well, it'll be a new experience."

"What you did for me was a new experience, too, wasn't it?"

"Yes," she admitted.

"And afterward, we'll rest for a while, then later, I want us to go for a ride in your Sherwood Forest." Lowering his head, he kissed her belly. "And you're going to experience another first once we enter Sherwood."

"Another—" she gasped when he kissed her triangle of fiery curls. "Another first? When we ride into the woods?"

"When we ride into Sherwood Forest," he corrected her. "Today you're going to be Maid Marian."

"Oh, I am, am I?"

He spread her legs and lifted her hips. "Yes, my Cleo Belle, you are."

She swallowed hard. "I suppose that means you want to be Robin Hood."

"Yeah, I suppose so," he said.

He flicked her intimately with his tongue. She moaned, the sound reverberating in her throat.

"All right, just this once—" she gasped as his mouth moved over her "—I'll be Maid Marian and you'll be Robin Hood."

"Whatever you say, Boss Lady."

Roarke took her where she'd never been, into an erotic paradise of pleasure. His mouth worshipped her femininity, savoring the smell and taste of her body, reveling in the feel of her undulating against his tongue, loving the sound of her hot, ecstatic cries.

And when she fell apart, shattering into a million shards of pleasure, he lifted her on top of him and told her to ride him hard and fast, to pretend he was a wild stallion she had to tame.

And tame him she did.

CHAPTER TWELVE

ROARKE READ THE report Morgan Kane had given him, then glanced up over the edge of the manila folder, looking his fellow Dundee agent square in the eye.

"All this does is make me wonder if we're dealing with more than one person." Roarke flung the file on the desk. "And whether or not the attempts on Cleo's life and the problems at McNamara Industries have a common perpetrator or if we have two family members working independently of each other."

"My guess is that we're dealing with at least two individuals," Kane said. "And they have separate agendas. Whoever was behind the problems at the plant wanted to force Ms. McNa—that is, Mrs. Roarke..." Kane hesitated, but continued when Roarke smiled. "To sell her uncle's company. But I'd say the person threatening your wife wants to see her dead."

"Yeah, I'm afraid you're right." It had been a long time since an assignment had frustrated Roarke to such an extent. Hell, who was he kidding? Despite the failures and near failures he'd experienced, despite all the stress and frustration of his worst assignments, nothing compared with this one. But then, he'd never allowed himself to become so personally involved before.

It wasn't as if Cleo was nothing more than a client. Dammit, she was his wife, albeit only temporarily, but still she *was* his wife. She slept in his arms every night.

He worked at her side every day. And in stolen moments out of time, like yesterday's swim in the Great Mississippi, the hours spent shaded beneath the willow trees and an unforgettable trip into Sherwood Forest, he could almost convince himself that he and Cleo belonged together. But he knew better. He couldn't allow great sex with an incredible lady to cloud his vision of reality or give him any delusions that life actually offered people happily ever afters.

"Unfortunately all the evidence I've collected and the sheriff's department has collected is nothing more than circumstantial," Kane said. "The rifle that fired the shot that barely missed Mrs. Roarke belonged to her great-uncle and everyone in the house had access to the gun case. Since the person didn't hit the target, we don't know whether they were a poor shot or just didn't intend to kill in the first place."

Pushing the oversize leather swivel chair back away from the Jacobean desk in the study, Roarke motioned toward a chair across from him. "Sit down."

Kane slumped into the chair, his big, hard body filling it completely. "The brown recluse incident and the tea poisoning both point the finger at Perry Sutton, but there's nothing to link him to any of the problems at the plant. According to the guards and the secretaries at McNamara Industries, Mr. Sutton seldom even visits the place."

"My gut instincts tell me that Sutton isn't our man." Roarke tapped his index finger on the manila folder he'd tossed on top of the desk. "What I hate most about this situation is that there's not much we can do about unearthing this would-be killer until he or she strikes again. And I'll be honest with you, Kane. I hate like hell that Cleo is the only bait we can use to catch this person."

"I wouldn't want to be in your shoes." Leaning slightly

forward, Kane rested his arms on his thighs and allowed his hands to dangle between his legs. "Protecting a woman you're married to can't be easy. I mean, even if there's no love between y'all and the marriage is a business arrangement, the two of you having a relationship has to make it difficult for you to view things objectively."

Roarke wanted to vehemently deny Kane's observation, but there was no way he could. The man was right. "I'm trying to handle things, not to let what's between Cleo and me get in the way of my judgment or interfere with doing my best to keep her safe."

"Maybe we can't catch the person trying to kill Mrs. Roarke until another attempt is made on her life, but we can do something about catching whoever wreaked havoc at McNamara Industries."

Roarke glanced down at the folder. "Trey Sutton was a prime suspect, until I read your report. Now I have to place Hugh Winfield and perhaps Daphne Sutton at the top of my list."

"I know Ms. Sutton and Winfield are dating, but why suddenly, after her uncle's death, did she start stopping by the plant on the nights Winfield worked late, when she'd never done that before? Was she encouraging Winfield to tamper with McNamara's computer system? Were they planning the accidents that plagued the plant for weeks?"

"It's possible," Roarke admitted. "Very possible. But the fact that Marla Sutton started having lunch at the plant with her husband, in his office, a couple of times a week, is suspicious. According to Trey's secretary, his wife seldom if ever had lunch with him at the plant before George McNamara's death. And Trey wasn't known for eating in his office."

"That means that during her lunch visits, Marla Sutton could have been using her computer knowledge to do some major damage. Since she was once a secretary at McNamara's, she'd be familiar with their computer system."

"What do you suggest we do, short of eliminating all the security systems you've put into place, to catch our culprit?" Roarke asked.

"I suggest we set a trap for our big rat," Kane said.

"Using what as bait?" Leaning back in the enormous leather chair, Roarke narrowed his eyes and grinned. "Ellen Denby?"

"The fact that Ellen is a woman has worked to our advantage before when we've brought her in on a case. Men tend to make the mistake of believing that because she's an attractive female, she's not as smart or tough or capable as her fellow agents."

Laughing robustly, Roarke shook his head. "That's why you brought her in and pretended to hire her as part of McNamara's new security team. You wanted her in place, just in case we needed her."

"She can play the dumb blonde around Trey Sutton and Hugh Winfield. And when we think the time is right, we'll put her on night duty. Alone. She'll tell each one of our boys in advance."

"Hell, who knows, it just might work," Roarke said.

"It's worked before. Ellen can be mighty convincing when she wants to be."

"Yeah, but woe be it to any who gets fooled by her. Behind that pretty face and gorgeous figure, our little Ellen is a pit bull."

A knock at the closed door interrupted Roarke and Kane's private meeting. Both of them tensed instantly.

"Yes?" Roarke asked.

The pocket doors slid open. Daphne Sutton, dressed in a micromini, skintight, backless, red sundress, sauntered into the room. "I hate to disturb y'all, but Phil Bacon just called and said for Kane to call him right back. He's home from church, but he'll be leaving to go to his mother-in-law's for a late Sunday dinner in about thirty minutes."

"The sheriff wants to talk to Kane?" Roarke asked. "The phone in here didn't ring."

"I was walking by Kane's room and heard his phone ringing. Did you know you'd left your cellular phone lying on your bed?" Daphne asked. "The door was unlocked, so I went in and answered the phone for you."

"I'll go give Bacon a call," Kane said.

Daphne sashayed across the study, her slender hips shifting seductively. "When I asked Phil why he'd bother a body on a beautiful Sunday afternoon, he said he was just returning Kane's earlier telephone call. Something about his using the sheriff's department's firing range." Daphne sat down on the edge of the Jacobean desk and looked back and forth from Roarke to Kane.

"Yeah, I asked the sheriff if he'd set up a convenient schedule for me to get in a little practice." Kane rose from the chair, excused himself and exited the room, leaving the doors open behind him.

"I take it that our Mr. Kane is a crack shot and doesn't want his skills to get rusty while he's on an assignment." Daphne draped her body across the top of the desk, lifting herself in a semiupright position. "Are you a sharpshooter, too, Roarke?" She slithered across the desk until she reached him, then dangled her long, bare legs off the side.

"I'm not as good as Kane," Roarke said. "But I usually hit whatever I aim at."

"I can't picture a man like you married to my little cousin, Cleo." Daphne lifted one leg and stretched it out toward Roarke. The toe of her red sandal hit the edge of his chair. She tapped her foot repeatedly against the chair.

"What sort of man do you think I am? And why can't you picture me married to Cleo?"

"I'd say you're an adventurer, a man who's lived his life on the edge. And my bet is you like your sex hot and wild and as untamed as the life you've lived." Slipping her hips off the desk, Daphne grasped the side with her hands to balance her body, then slid her foot between Roarke's thighs, pressing him intimately when her foot hit its mark. "Cleo is a tame little tabby, who's never done anything exciting in her entire life. Business is the only thing that matters to her."

Roarke knocked Daphne's foot away so quickly that she almost lost her balance. While she struggled to climb back on top of the desk, he stood up and glared at her.

"That just goes to show how little you know your cousin," Roarke said. "My wife happens to be the most exciting woman I've ever known."

"Is she paying you to say things like that, too?" Daphne glowered at Roarke, her breathing harsh and her cheeks slightly flushed. "We all know that she went off to Atlanta on a shopping trip and bought herself a husband."

"Think what you want to," he told her. "The bottom line is that I'm Cleo's husband and I intend to take good care of her and protect her from any and all harm."

"Are you going to get her pregnant, too?" Daphne asked. "If she isn't pregnant within a year, she'll lose control of McNamara Industries, you know."

Roarke grinned. "Let's just say that we're doing everything we can at every available opportunity to make that happen."

Daphne's exotically beautiful face hardened. Her green

eyes sizzled with a barely contained anger. Slithering off the desk, she walked over to Roarke.

"Cleo must be paying you plenty to screw her." Daphne eased her arms around Roarke's neck and rubbed herself against him. "You must be getting pretty bored with all that cool, controlled sweetness."

Just as Roarke reached out to remove himself from Daphne's clutches, she pressed her lips against his and tried to force his lips apart with her tongue.

"Oh, excuse me," Cleo said as she walked into the room.

Roarke grabbed Daphne's arms and threw her away from him with such force that she almost fell. She caught the arm of the swivel chair and laughed, then turned around to face Cleo.

"We thought we were alone," Daphne said. "I'm afraid I don't know what to say. How to explain."

"Cleo, this wasn't what it looked like," Roarke told his wife.

"Oh, I think it was exactly what it looked like." Cleo walked across the study and rounded the desk. Opening a bottom side drawer, she withdrew a laptop computer. "I forgot and left this down here. I need to do a little work this evening." She took several steps toward the door.

"Cleo?" Roarke called out to her.

"Yes, dear?"

"Don't you want an explanation of what you saw?"

Hugging herself around the waist, Daphne nibbled on her bottom lip. "I'm really sorry, Cleo."

Cleo's loud laughter filled the room. She turned slowly and glared at her cousin. "Simon isn't Paine Emerson or Hugh Winfield. He's twice the man either of them ever was. And he's *my* man!"

"Well, your man is a wonderful kisser," Daphne said.

"How would you know?" Cleo smiled devilishly. "He didn't kiss you. You kissed him. Or you were trying to. And Simon was trying to push you away when you attacked him."

"You're deluding yourself if you think he didn't want me."

"No, Daffie, you're deluding yourself if you think he did."

Roarke stood there speechless as his wife turned around and walked out of the study. Daphne huffed loudly. Roarke chuckled. Well, he'd be damned. Cleo trusted him. She trusted him completely.

When he rushed past Daphne, she called out, "Where do you think you're going?"

"I'm going to find my wife so I can kiss her," he said.

He left Daphne in the study and raced up the stairs, catching up with Cleo in the upstairs hallway. Without saying a word, he scooped her up in his arms and carried her into their suite. He tossed her down on the bed, then came down on top of her, kissing her breathless.

They tore at each other's clothes, and when they had removed enough essential garments, Roarke took her hard and fast and wild. They reached their climaxes simultaneously, their bodies joined in ecstasy, their hearts beating in unison and their souls touching for one spellbinding moment.

They both treasured what they shared, but knew, despite the trust they had in each other, the magic couldn't last.

CLEO HAD DIFFICULTY concentrating. She couldn't seem to keep focused on the row of figures before her. Her mind kept wandering off in a decidedly different direction. The past weekend with Roarke had been so incredibly wonderful that she questioned if it had really happened. But it had. All she had needed to do to confirm the reality of their uncontrollable passion for each other was to glance across the room at Roarke. Every time he'd looked at her during the past few days, she'd seen the desire in his eyes and had known he wanted her. And just that one look had set her pulse to racing. Dear Lord, would it always be that way? Would she never get enough of loving and being loved by Simon Roarke?

With Roarke in the same room with her, she hadn't been able to think straight. She kept thinking about Saturday, when they'd gone riding and spent the day making love outside, in the creek, under the willows, in the woods. And Sunday, when she'd caught Daphne trying to seduce Roarke. How good it felt to know that she could trust her husband. After Roarke had carried her into their suite, they hadn't come out again until that morning, when they'd left for work.

Roarke had been such a distraction she'd finally asked him to leave, to send Kane or a member of his security force to guard her for a few hours. Roarke had put a man named Tom Brown outside her office, kissed her goodbye and told her he'd be back around noon with their lunch.

How could she be this deliriously happy when her life was in constant danger? Because she had fallen in love with her husband, that's how. She'd been attracted to him since the first moment she saw him in his Atlanta office, and with each passing day that attraction had grown. The more she got to know Simon Roarke, the better she liked him. He was everything a man should be. Intelligent. Strong. Courageous. Understanding. Loving. Gentle. And an incomparable lover. But her perfect husband had one slight flaw. He wasn't a man for long-term commitments. He hadn't signed on for the long haul.

She hadn't planned on falling in love with him. He'd been a means to an end. Their marriage a business arrangement. But somewhere between the judge pronouncing them man and wife and Roarke kissing her for the first time and this weekend, when their passion had known no bounds, she'd fallen head over heels in love with Simon.

How would she ever be able to let him go? Without him, her life would be meaningless. But when the time came she'd have no choice—if he chose to leave her. Maybe he was beginning to care for her. Maybe he wouldn't want to end their marriage. Whatever his reasons for stipulating that he wouldn't stick around to see her through the pregnancy might no longer be valid. Not if he loved her the way she loved him.

But Simon had never mentioned love, not even during their most intimate moments, when they were as close as two people could possibly be. She had no doubts that he would die for her, that he'd lay his life on the line to protect her, but what she didn't know was whether his actions would be prompted by duty or love.

Did she dare bring up the subject of their marriage? Question him about his true feelings? What if he didn't love her? What if he intended to follow through with the stipulations of their marriage contract and get a divorce?

A knock on the outer office door brought Cleo out of her thoughts. She glanced up just as Audrey opened the door.

"Mr. Winfield is here to see you, Mrs. Roarke."

Tom Brown stood in front of Hugh, obviously waiting for Cleo's answer before either stepping aside to allow Hugh entrance or escorting the man outside.

"Tell Hugh to come on in." Cleo checked her watch. Twelve-twenty. Roarke would return with their lunch shortly.

"Thanks for seeing me, Cleo." Hugh pranced into the office like some spirited young colt, blithely slamming the door in Tom Brown's scowling face. "We haven't had a chance for a private conversation since you married."

"Is that what this is—a private conversation?" Cleo asked. "I assumed you needed to speak to me about a business matter."

"I thought we were friends." He perched his skinny butt on the edge of her desk. "Can't friends have a private conversation?"

"Yes, of course." Cleo scooted her swivel chair up to her desk and looked at Hugh.

"We are still friends, aren't we?" he asked. "I mean you're not still upset about what happened between Daphne and me, are you?"

"No, Hugh, I'm not still upset. As a matter of fact, I was never that upset. I was disappointed more than anything else. Disappointed in your judgment. We've known each other since we were kids and I always thought you were a reasonably intelligent guy."

"You are still upset." He slid around the desk, grabbed her chair and turned her where she was directly facing him. "Cleo, sugar, Daphne is an exciting woman and very…well, shall we say, talented. But sleeping with her while I was dating you was a big mistake. And I'm sorry it happened."

"What's the purpose for rehashing old news? You've already apologized and begged my forgiveness." Cleo wondered just what Hugh wanted. He hadn't stopped by to renew their old friendship. He was after something else.

Leaning forward, Hugh reached out and grasped Cleo's chin in his hand. "It's not as if Daphne and I are in love or anything like that. I mean, if you'd accepted my offer when I found out you needed a husband, we could have worked something out. You didn't have to pay a stranger to marry you."

Cleo sucked in her cheeks, then relaxed them and ran her tongue over her teeth in an effort not to laugh in Hugh's face. The dirty dog. The scheming, lying cheat. He actually thought she would have preferred marrying him to marrying Simon Roarke. Obviously Hugh's ego was inflated. Didn't he know that he wasn't even close to being in Simon's league?

"What would you have done if I'd accepted your offer?" She tried desperately not to smile.

"Why, I'd have married you, of course. Obviously your uncle George wanted us to marry. What other reasons could he have had to put such ridiculous stipulations in his will?"

"But if I'd married you to fulfill the stipulations in the will, what would you have done about Daphne?"

"Well, I don't know. Daffie and I are pretty heavily involved sexually. But since my marriage to you wouldn't have been a love match—"

"Are you saying that you could have married me, gotten me pregnant to fulfill the stipulations of the will and continued your relationship with my cousin at the same time?"

"Well, when you put it that way, it does sound rather crude, doesn't it?"

"Hugh, let's cut to the chase. I'm not pining away for you. I never loved you. I never wanted to marry you. And the only reason I dated you was because it pleased Uncle George."

Her declaration wiped the smile off Hugh's face. "Well, I see. I see. But still, wouldn't it have been better to have married me than to have paid some stranger to marry you and get you pregnant? After all, what do you know about this Roarke character? Do you have any idea who his people are?"

Cleo grinned. Laughter bubbled up inside her. "For your information, Simon Roarke is the most wonderful man I've ever known and my marriage is a real one, despite what you and my dear family want to believe." Unable to contain it any longer, Cleo burst into laughter. "Why did you request this little private visit? What is it that you want, Hugh?"

"I certainly didn't request a visit so that you could laugh in my face."

"I'm sorry, it's just that you're so transparent." Cleo laid her hand on his shoulder. "You forget that I've known you a long time."

"Meaning?" Tilting his chin haughtily, he stuck his nose in the air and turned from her.

"You found Daphne irresistible, but you've finally figured out that she might have been using you to hurt me. After Uncle George died, you found out about his will, and hoped you could have me, my money and Daphne, too."

"How can you accuse me of being so mercenary?" He displayed a properly wounded expression.

"But recently, you've begun to wonder if maybe you made a mistake, that perhaps I'm going to win this battle and retain control of McNamara Industries." Cleo shot up out of her chair, placed her hands on her hips and looked Hugh square in the eye. "Is that why you've offered yourself to me again? Did you think I still wanted you?"

"You've made it perfectly clear that you don't want me, that you never did," Hugh said. "There's no need to rub it in."

She put her arm around Hugh's shoulder. "Thanks for the offer, old friend, but I already have exactly what I want. I'm married to Simon Roarke, and if I'm very lucky, I'll have his baby."

"God, Cleo, you're in love with him, aren't you?"

"What's wrong with that?" she asked coyly. "After all, he is my husband."

"Yeah, well, I hope he doesn't break your heart the way I thought I had." Hugh slipped his arm around her waist. "You know, you'd probably have been better off if you had married me. At least when our marriage broke up, neither one of us would have gotten hurt."

She knew that in his own misguided way Hugh might actually have meant what he said, and it was obvious that his statement had made perfect sense to him.

She kissed him on the cheek. "You can always marry Daphne. After all, she's a wealthy woman. Just not quite as wealthy as she would be if we had to sell McNamara Industries."

"You'd be better off if you did sell." He sighed, then hugged her to him. "But I know you won't ever do that willingly."

Just as Hugh kissed Cleo, a hasty, goodbye kiss, Roarke walked in. She glanced over Hugh's shoulder at her husband, who stood in the doorway glaring at her.

The sight of Cleo in Hugh Winfield's arms hit Roarke like a blow from a sledgehammer. He wanted to march across the office, rip Cleo from Winfield's arms and beat the hell out of the guy. How dared he touch Cleo! She belonged to him. She was his wife.

Some primeval instinct rose inside him, heating his jealousy to the boiling point. If Cleo knew what he was thinking, she'd skin him alive. He wanted to place a brand on her. One that read, Roarke's Wife.

Every muscle in his body tensed. He took several deep, calming breaths. Winfield was kissing Cleo, not the other way around. This was pretty much the same scene Cleo had walked in on in the study yesterday between Daphne and him.

Taking one more deep breath, Roarke lifted the two paper bags he held in his hands. "I brought lunch, honey. Are you finished with Hugh?"

Smiling at Roarke, Cleo stepped out of Hugh's embrace. "Yes, I'm finished with Hugh." Dismissing her former boyfriend without another word or glance, she motioned for her husband to come to her. "I'm starving. I hope you brought dessert, too."

"As a matter of fact—" Roarke ignored Hugh as he walked by him and over to Cleo and set both sacks on her desk "—I drove over to the River Bend Café."

"Lemon icebox pie?" She groaned. "Tell me you brought me a piece of lemon icebox pie, and I'll be yours forever."

"You're mine forever," Roarke said, then took Cleo in his arms and kissed her.

The kiss was long and wet and deep, and when he allowed Cleo to come up for air, Hugh Winfield was nowhere to be seen and the office door was closed.

Roarke removed the two lunch sacks, placing them in her empty chair, then lifted Cleo off her feet and set her down on the edge of her desk. Kissing her deeply, he pushed her skirt up her thighs until it bunched around her hips, then slid his hands inside her panty hose and bikini briefs and tugged them down and off.

"What do you think you're doing?" Her heartbeat drummed in her ears. Her body throbbed with anticipation.

"I want dessert, too," he told her as his lips moved down her neck and his hands unbuckled his belt and unzipped his slacks. "And I want mine before we eat our corned beef sandwiches."

"Am I your dessert, Mr. Roarke?" She draped her arms around his neck when he spread her legs apart and situated himself between them.

"Yes, Mrs. Roarke, you most definitely are." He cupped her hips and brought her forward, then thrust into her, bouncing her hips off the desk.

They made love with wild abandon, oblivious to the outside world. Later they ate their corned beef sandwiches, and when Cleo started to eat her pie, Roarke took it from her and fed it to her. In the middle of the sensual feeding, Cleo gasped.

"Oh, my God, Simon, we didn't lock the door. Anyone could have walked in on us."

"It wouldn't have happened," he said.

"Why wouldn't it have happened?"

"Because when I came in, I told Tom Brown that no one was to enter this office until I told him otherwise."

"You're a wicked, wicked man, Simon Roarke." Cleo smiled, then opened her mouth, asking for another bite.

"And you're glad that I am, aren't you, my Cleo Belle?" Roarke cut off a piece of the pie with the plastic fork and put it in Cleo's mouth.

THE FOLLOWING FRIDAY NIGHT, Hugh Winfield dined with the family. During after-dinner drinks in the front parlor, Oralie Sutton announced that Daphne and Hugh were engaged. Hugh made a big production of placing a rather large diamond on Daphne's finger. Cleo congratulated them and wished them well, and considered herself lucky not to have married Hugh.

While Oralie discussed plans for a huge engagement party at the country club, Daphne gloated, smiling cattily at Cleo. But when Roarke nuzzled Cleo's neck and she giggled, the glint of triumph died in Daphne's green eyes.

That night Roarke gave Kane orders to have Ellen Denby ready the following Monday night to spring the trap that would hopefully catch the McNamara Industries saboteur. The odds were even. Fifty-fifty. Especially now that Winfield had officially cast his lot with the Suttons.

Which would the trap ensnare? Roarke wondered. A hotheaded, angry young cousin or a money-hungry, disloyal old friend?

down until it lay over where his jeans were zipped.

Lord, please let me show him that I'm ready for an adventure of my own. Something with Simon. Something wild.

CHAPTER THIRTEEN

CLEO TOSSED BACK her head and laughed. Despite the overcast sky and the prediction of isolated showers, the day was perfect. Perfect because she was going to spend it with Simon, just the two of them alone together. Riding Sweet Justice and Valentino out to the Great Mississippi and into Sherwood Forest again this Saturday. Pearl had prepared them a picnic lunch that Cleo planned for them to spread out beneath the two willows. But what if it rains? she thought, then smiled secretly to herself. She'd never made love outside in the rain.

"What's that impish smile all about?" Roarke squeezed her hand as they walked down the path leading to the stables. "You worry me, woman, when you get that wicked look on your face."

"Wicked?" Pulling on his hand, she urged him to run with her. "Come on, and I'll show you wicked."

Releasing her hand, he grinned and checked his small backpack. "That's an invitation I can't refuse." Roarke raced with her, reaching the stables first. Not even winded from his run, he leaned against the fence and waited for her to catch up.

Breathing hard, but not out of breath, Cleo slowed her pace as she neared him. "No fair. Your legs are longer." She glanced at him, surveying him from the tip of his boots to his silver belt buckle, then moving her gaze down again to focus on where his jeans formed a triangle. "Much longer."

He grabbed her by the shoulders and pulled her up against him. "You are wicked, Cleo Belle. Wonderfully wicked."

Reaching up on tiptoe, she circled his neck with her arms and gave him a quick kiss. Thunder rumbled off in the distance. She tilted her head to listen. "It might rain."

"It might," he agreed.

"I've never made love outside in the rain," she said.

"You haven't?"

"If it turns out to be only a light summer shower, we could stay under the willows."

Lifting her off her feet, Roarke took her mouth hungrily. She clung to him, responding fervently.

Willie cleared his throat. "Excuse me, Cleo." He led Sweet Justice out of the stables. "Got Sweetie all saddled up and ready for you." He held out the reins to her.

Roarke set Cleo back on her feet. She eased out of his arms and took the reins from Willie. "Thank you." She smiled at Willie, who beamed with pleasure.

"I'll go get Valentino for you, Mr. Roarke."

Roarke threw up his hand in greeting. "Okay. Thanks."

When Willie returned to the stables, Cleo whirled around and faced Roarke. "How would you like to race over to the Great Mississippi? The winner gets to name his or her prize."

"I think this race just might be rigged," Roarke said. "Considering the fact that you'll be riding a young filly and I'll be riding a much older horse."

"What if I give you a head start?"

"How much of a head start?"

"Two minutes."

Willie led Valentino out of the stables. "Here he is, all ready for a good gallop this morning."

"Here are the rules," Roarke told her. "We mount at the same time, then you time yourself two minutes after I start off, and whoever gets to the Great Mississippi first gets to throw the other one in before he gets to name his prize."

Cleo clicked her tongue against the roof of her mouth, rolled her eyes heavenward, then pursed her lips. "Sounds fair enough, I suppose."

"Oh, yes," Roarke said. "There's just one more thing." He removed the backpack and held it out to her. "You have to carry our lunch with you."

Cleo groaned. "That won't be a disadvantage." She took the backpack and strapped it on, then lifted her foot into the stirrup and swung her leg over Sweet Justice's back.

Following Cleo's lead, Roarke mounted his horse. He glanced over at his wife, who smiled at him, then puckered her lips and blew him a kiss. He loved her smile—beautiful, joyous and genuine, like the woman herself.

Sunlight reflected off the decorative silver trim on Cleo's hand-tooled, leather saddle. The minute Cleo eased her bottom into the saddle, Sweet Justice whinnied loudly and reared her front legs into the air.

Roarke's heartbeat accelerated. What the hell had happened? Something had spooked Sweet Justice. But what? He hadn't heard or seen a thing. He sat in the saddle, watching helplessly while the skittish filly bucked Cleo off and onto the ground.

Dear God, it had all happened so quickly that Cleo must not have had a chance even to try to calm the panicked animal.

"Cleo!" Roarke heard the sound of his own voice as if coming from a great distance.

Willie rushed over to Cleo, who lay unmoving on her side. Roarke dismounted hurriedly.

"Don't touch her, Willie," he shouted. "Just get hold of Sweet Justice's reins and keep her away from Cleo." When the stable hand jerked around and looked at him with fear in his eyes, Roarke cursed under his breath. "I know you want to help her, but if she's injured, you would hurt her more if you try to move her."

Nodding his understanding, Willie grabbed the filly, who'd stopped prancing and casually kicked at the earth near Cleo's head. While Willie spoke softly to the horse, Roarke bent down and ran his hands over Cleo's prone body. She didn't move or speak.

He didn't think she'd broken any bones, but there was no way to be certain without X-rays. He stroked her cheek tenderly with the back of his hand.

"Cleo? Honey?" She didn't respond. "Cleo Belle, can you hear me?" She lay deadly still.

Roarke unzipped the backpack Cleo wore and removed his cellular phone. His hands trembled as he dialed 911. He told the operator what had happened. She warned him not to move Cleo and assured him that an ambulance was on its way.

"What—what can I do, Mr. Roarke?" Willie asked.

"Tie Sweet Justice to the fence over there," Roarke said. "Then go up to the house and tell Miss Beatrice what's happened. Tell her to call Sheriff Bacon. And Willie—" Roarke hesitated while his mind tried to absorb the implications "—don't let anyone get near Sweet Justice except the sheriff himself. Do you understand? Something caused Sweetie to throw Cleo off and I want the sheriff to examine the horse, her saddle and her food."

"I got all that." Willie kept nodding repeatedly. "I'll go tell Miss Bea to call the sheriff."

Roarke sat down on the ground beside Cleo, wanting more than anything to lift her into his arms and see her open her eyes and smile at him. God, please, don't let her be seriously injured. Maybe she'd just gotten the breath knocked out of her. No, if that was all it was, she'd be coming around by now and gasping for air.

He looked at her pale face, wishing that her long, dark auburn lashes would flutter. They didn't. Suddenly, he noticed fresh blood ooze out from underneath Cleo's head.

Closing his eyes against the sight, Roarke clenched his teeth and screamed silently. His hot anger raged, boiling inside him, threatening to explode. How could he have let this happen? Why hadn't he seen it coming? He should have done something to prevent this. Dammit, if anything happened to Cleo...

"Cleo Belle." He caressed her cheek, then checked the pulse beating in her neck. "You're going to be all right. The medics are on their way."

When Beatrice and Pearl reached the stables, Roarke sat beside Cleo, stroking her hand and speaking softly to her.

"God in heaven, she's not moving," Pearl said. "She's not—"

"Hush up, you silly goose," Beatrice scolded the other woman. "Of course she's not."

"I'll take care of Sweetie until the sheriff gets here." Willie untied the filly and led her toward the stables, stopping just before entering. "You'll take care of Cleo, won't you, Mr. Roarke? You're her husband and you love her."

Roarke swallowed hard, downing the pain and anger and regret. "Yeah, Willie. I'll take care of Cleo."

Beatrice rushed over to Cleo, Pearl on her heels. "Willie said Cleo fell off Sweetie. How could that have happened? She's a good horsewoman. She's been riding since she was a girl."

"Something frightened the filly," Roarke said. "Sweetie was fine until— Oh, God!"

"What is it?" Beatrice asked.

"Sit down here beside her." Roarke shot to his feet. "I don't want her to be alone. If she wakes, I want her to see a familiar face."

He helped Beatrice sit down, then called out to Willie. "Hold up there."

"Where are you going?" Beatrice asked.

"Sweet Justice was fine until Cleo sat in the saddle. The minute her back end pressed down, Sweetie reared up as if she'd been shocked." Roarke clamped his big hand down on Willie's shoulder. "Keep her still while I check out something."

"Yes, sir."

Beatrice and Pearl watched while Roarke ran his hand over every inch of the hand-finished, floral-leaf-patterned saddle. He tugged on the silver swell plates and did the same with the full cantle plates and the corner plates. He inspected the skirts, the stirrups, the fenders and the horn. Then he lifted the saddle and turned it upside down, running his hand over the leather belly.

His fingers encountered four small, circular objects about the size of quarters. He flung the saddle on the ground, kicked it and cursed loudly. "Dammit to hell!" He stomped the ground.

"What in heaven's name is wrong with you?" Pearl asked. "Must be something mighty bad for you to be cussing a blue streak."

"Did you find something on Cleo's saddle?" Beatrice looked up at him, her eyes misty with tears.

"Yeah, I found something, all right. Four small buzzers. The kind you can buy at any party store. A practical joker can put them in his palm and shock somebody when he shakes hands with them."

"Someone put them under Cleo's saddle deliberately," Pearl said. "Someone wanted Sweetie to buck Cleo off and kill her, yes?" The housekeeper's cheeks flared scarlet. Her wide, fleshy jaw clenched. "You've got to find out who's doing these things, Mr. Roarke, and put a stop to this person!"

"I've done a poor job so far." He blamed himself for this. Why hadn't he checked out Cleo's horse and saddle before she'd mounted? He should have realized that everyone in the family knew that he and Cleo were going riding this morning. Any one of them could have attached the buzzers. But he hadn't been thinking about the possibility that someone would tamper with the horses. All he'd been thinking about was spending the day making love to his wife.

He was too damn close, too personally involved, to do his job right. And if Cleo died—dammit, no! He wouldn't let himself think about losing her.

Roarke lifted Beatrice to her feet and resumed his place at Cleo's side. Beatrice and Pearl hovered over them, and Willie stood beside Sweet Justice, guarding Cleo's filly and her dust-covered saddle.

ROARKE PACED THE floor in the waiting room. No amount of reasoning from Beatrice or finger-shaking from Pearl stopped his relentless prowl. What the hell was taking those damn doctors so long? Didn't they have any idea what he was going through, not knowing if Cleo was alive or dead?

When the medics had moved her, Roarke saw blood on the hand-size rock that was three-fourths embedded in the ground. The side of Cleo's head had hit the rock when she'd fallen.

Please, God, don't let there be any internal bleeding. Don't! Don't! Don't! Roarke hadn't prayed in fifteen years. Not since the night he'd been notified that his ex-wife and daughter had been in a serious automobile accident. In those few moments between being given the information and being told that Laurie had died on impact, Roarke had prayed more fervently than he'd ever prayed in his life. He'd said one final prayer at his little girl's funeral, begging God to forgive him for not taking better care of the precious life that had been entrusted to him. After that Roarke had never prayed again. Not until tonight.

He'd never cared enough about anything to seek divine intervention again. His life hadn't been worth a prayer, and praying for Hope was useless. But Cleo was worth a thousand prayers, a thousand promises to God.

Tilting his head, Roarke lifted his eyes heavenward as he stood at the far end of the waiting room, his back to Beatrice and Pearl. *What do you want?* he prayed silently. *Whatever it is, I'll give it. Just let Cleo be all right.*

"Oh, Dr. Iverson," Beatrice cried out.

Roarke spun around just as Pearl and Beatrice rushed toward the doctor, who walked out of the E.R. examining room.

"How is Cleo?" Beatrice asked. "May we see her?"

"It's certainly taken you long enough," Pearl said. "We've been out here for hours."

"Mr. Roarke," Dr. Iverson said.

The sound of his blood rushing through his body momentarily deafened Roarke. His heartbeat accelerated. Sweat coated his palms. He moved forward, every step an effort.

"Cleo?" Roarke asked.

"Her vital signs are good," Dr. Iverson said. "We've done a series of tests and X-rays. There are no broken bones and no internal injuries, but…"

Roarke let out the breath he hadn't even realized he'd been holding. "But what?"

"She suffered a concussion and she's still unconscious. I think that's only temporary. I expect her to come around soon. She'll have a headache and probably be nauseated."

"What if she doesn't regain consciousness?" Beatrice asked.

Dr. Iverson patted Beatrice on the shoulder. "Now, Miss Bea, let's not borrow trouble." He looked at Roarke. "There's something else, though."

"What?" Roarke asked.

"Did you know that Cleo is pregnant?"

Roarke felt as if someone had punched him in the stomach. Shivers raced along his nerve endings. "Pregnant?"

"Oh, isn't this wonderful." Beatrice giggled. "A baby. My little Cleo is going to be a mother."

"Well, not for about eight more months," Dr. Iverson said. "I doubt Cleo realized she was pregnant."

"Did her fall jeopardize the pregnancy?" Cleo is pregnant, Roarke thought. Already.

"It doesn't seem to have caused any problems, but we'll keep her monitored," the doctor told Roarke. "You can go in and see her for just a few minutes before we transfer her upstairs to a room."

"Go on, dear," Beatrice said. "You're her husband. Pearl and I will wait here for you, and we can all go upstairs together."

Roarke followed Dr. Iverson into the E.R. cubicle where Cleo lay, her auburn hair gleaming red against the pristine whiteness of the sheet beneath her. She looked so small and helpless lying there with her eyes closed. Roarke neared the bedside, hesitating as he gazed down at her.

She was going to be all right. No internal injuries. Only a concussion.

He wanted to lift her into his arms and hold her. He wanted to kiss her awake and hear her sweet laughter. But he didn't even take her hand in his. He just stood there staring at her.

Did you know that Cleo is pregnant?

She was pregnant. Pregnant with his child. No! Not *his* child. *Her* child. Hers and hers alone.

"Talk to her," Dr. Iverson said. "It's possible that she'll be able to hear you. It might even help her come around sooner." The doctor put his hand on Roarke's back. "She should be all right. And there's no need to worry about the baby. Your son or daughter is safe."

No, my daughter isn't safe, Roarke wanted to shout. She's dead. She died fifteen years ago, and I wasn't even there to say goodbye.

Swallowing the emotions that threatened his sanity, Roarke took a deep breath. "Cleo. You're going to be just fine. You took a bad spill off Sweet Justice, but that hard little head of yours didn't get much more than a scratch."

A nurse and an attendant entered the cubicle. "We're all set to take Mrs. Roarke to the fourth floor. Her room's ready," the nurse said.

Roarke stepped back out of the way and waited until the attendant rolled Cleo out of the cubicle and toward the inside exit leading to the private elevators.

"Give them a few minutes to get her settled in," Dr. Iverson said, "then y'all can go on up."

Roarke heard Beatrice's voice before he entered the waiting area. "She's going to be just fine. But no thanks to one of you," Beatrice said sharply. "I wish I knew which one of you is trying to hurt Cleo. I'd—I'd—" She choked on her tears. "I'd strangle you with my bare hands."

"Yeah, and I'd help her," Pearl said.

When Roarke walked out into the waiting room, all eyes turned to him. Dammit, the whole Sutton clan had arrived, swooping down like a bunch of buzzards waiting for their next meal.

"What the hell's going on out here?" Taking each Sutton in turn, Roarke glared menacingly, giving each a deadly dose of his killer stare.

"How is Cleo?" Perry Sutton asked.

"Do you really care?" Roarke had just about had his fill of Cleo's bloodsucking relatives.

"How dare you question my husband's concern." Oralie puffed up like a bullfrog. She titled her head and lifted her nose with a regal air.

"Aunt Beatrice says that Cleo has a concussion," Daphne said. "Is she conscious?"

"Not yet," Roarke said. "But Dr. Iverson thinks she'll come out of this with nothing more than a bad headache."

"That's good to know," Marla said meekly.

"What happened to her?" Trey asked. "When we arrived home, Ezra said that Cleo had had a riding accident."

"Yeah, she did." Roarke paused, waiting to see if he could discern any type of suspicious reaction from Trey and the others. "I'll wait and let Sheriff Bacon fill you in on the specifics of what caused the accident, but I will tell you that something spooked Sweet Justice and she threw Cleo." Roarke looked meaningfully at Beatrice and then at Pearl, warning each silently not to reveal any specific information to the Suttons.

Oralie gasped and clutched her chest. "Oh, how dreadful. I've warned Cleo and Beatrice about riding those beasts. I despise the smelly creatures."

"There's no point in y'all being here," Roarke said. "I plan to stay with Cleo until she's released from the hospital. Aunt Beatrice, I know that you and Pearl want to see Cleo before you leave."

"We'd all like to see Cleo." Oralie strutted over and stood directly beside Beatrice, slipping her arm around her cousin's shoulder. "I, for one, will feel much better once I see for myself that she's all right."

Beatrice eased herself away from Oralie and glanced over at Perry, then lowered her head and looked down at the floor.

"Nobody's going to go in and see Cleo except Beatrice and Pearl. Then I'll send them home in a cab," Roarke told the Suttons. "The rest of you can leave now."

"We have every right to—" Trey said.

"If Mother wants to see Cleo—" Daphne spoke at the same time.

"Let me make this perfectly clear." Roarke's voice was deceptively calm and steady. A steaming volcano raged inside him, ready to erupt with the least provocation. "Someone has tried, unsuccessfully, four times to kill my wife. And each one of you is on my list of suspects. So there's no way in hell I'm going to allow any of you near Cleo until she's fully recovered. Do I make myself clear?" He spoke the last sentence slowly, enunciating each word.

"Well, I've never been so insulted in my life." Oralie huffed indignantly. "Take me home this instant, Perry. I will pray for Cleo's recovery and ask the Lord to remove Mr. Roarke from our lives. He's been nothing but a heartless bully since the day Cleo brought him home."

Confident that he'd made his point to the Suttons, Roarke dismissed them from his mind. He escorted Beatrice and Pearl out of the emergency room waiting area and into the hall. While they waited for an elevator, Pearl put her arms around Roarke and hugged him.

"I've been waiting a lifetime to hear somebody tell that bunch where they could get off." Pearl grinned from ear to ear. "Poor old Perry's too timid to control his own children, and Lord knows he's never been able to handle Oralie."

"Perry does the best he can," Beatrice said. "He's far

too gentle and easygoing for a woman as high-strung as Oralie."

"Yeah, you're right about that." Pearl glanced sadly at Beatrice. "What he always needed was a sweet, kind, loving woman like you."

The elevator doors opened and the three of them stepped inside. No one said a word during the ascent to the fourth floor.

CLEO CAME IN and out of consciousness several times during the afternoon. Once she called Roarke's name and smiled when he lifted her hand to his lips. He sat beside her bed waiting impatiently, his mind tormenting him with images of Cleo as her body gradually ripened with their child. As hard as he tried not to think of the child as his, he couldn't change the fact that he had ignited that tiny spark of life growing inside her.

Was the baby a girl? Would she have big blue eyes like Laurie's? Would she have the same loud, ear-splitting cry when she was a newborn and wanted attention?

Hell, what difference did it make if the baby *was* a girl? What difference did any of it make? He wouldn't be around to see her, to hold her, to rock and sing to her. He'd never see her smile or listen to her laugh or hear her call him "Daddy."

He had to destroy any paternal feelings that he had, and do it immediately. He could not allow himself to take any interest in Cleo's baby. They had made a bargain. And he intended to see that Cleo kept her word and set him free.

She awoke in the late afternoon, coming fully alert by degrees. Roarke held her hand and watched her. She smiled at him.

"Hi, there," he said. "How do you feel?"

"I've got a humdinger of a headache," she told him. "What happened to me?"

"Don't you remember?"

She thought for a minute. "We were going on a picnic, weren't we? We went to the stables and... Something scared Sweetie. She threw me! Roarke, what...who...? Did someone deliberately spook Sweetie?" She lifted her head, then groaned when intense pain exploded inside her brain.

"Don't get upset, Cleo. Lie back and rest." Taking her by the shoulders, he eased her down on the bed. "Dr. Iverson says you have a concussion, but no broken bones or internal injuries. You're going to be fine."

Reaching out, she sought his hand. He grasped her hand, squeezing reassuringly.

"I'll lie still and be good," she said. "If you'll tell me what really happened."

"All right. If you have to know right now, then I'll tell you." He sucked in a deep breath, held her hand tightly and looked directly at her. "Somebody stuck four whoopee buzzers under Sweet Justice's saddle, so that when you mounted her and put your weight on the saddle, the buzzers would give your filly a shock and make her go wild for a few minutes. Long enough, this person hoped, for Sweetie to throw you off. I'm sure the plan was for you to break your neck."

"When is it going to stop? When they've succeeded and I'm dead?" Jerking her hand out of his, she turned from him and buried her face in her pillow.

"I know I let you down." Getting up out of the chair, he stood beside her bed. "You could have been killed out there this morning. I had my mind on making love to you, instead of protecting you."

She turned around slowly, intensely aware of the pain

in her head, and looked at Roarke's haggard face, his bleary eyes and slumped shoulders. He was blaming himself for what had happened to her. She couldn't let him do that.

"Simon, this wasn't any more your fault than the spiders in my bath towels or the poison in the tea Aunt Beatrice drank. There was no way you could have predicted any of those things happening and no way you could have prevented them."

"You shouldn't be staying in that house. Hell, you shouldn't even be living in this town!"

"What are you talking about?" she asked.

"The danger is here, in River Bend. The Suttons are dangerous. One of them. Two of them. Or all of them. When you're released from the hospital, I'm taking you away from here until I can guarantee your safety."

"I can't leave River Bend. I can't go away at a time like this, when McNamara Industries is in trouble. People are counting on me. I can't let them down."

"Dammit, woman, don't you understand that I can't promise you that another one of these unpredictable accidents won't happen? The person behind these accidents is covering his tracks well. The police haven't turned up any real evidence against anyone other than your uncle Perry in the poisoning incident. And that evidence was circumstantial." Sitting down beside her, he leaned over and gently grasped her shoulders. "You've got to stop worrying about everyone else and start worrying about yourself."

"You sound as if you want to put me in some sort of glass bubble and not let me have any human contact."

"If I could do that, I would."

She reached up and stroked his face. He pulled away from her caressing hand. "I promise that I'll cooperate with you in every way possible," she said. "No more horseback riding. No more risks of any kind. But I can't leave River Bend. McNamara Industries can't do without me. Not right now."

"Damn McNamara Industries!"

"Roarke, how can you say such a thing when you know how much my company means to me?"

"If you can't leave your damn business behind in order to protect your life, then at least we can move out of the mansion and get you away from your 'loving' family."

"How will we ever catch the person or persons who are trying to kill me if I'm not available to them?" Cleo placed her hands over Roarke's where they gripped her shoulders. "Moving away isn't the answer. This isn't going to end until either they kill me or we catch them."

Releasing his hold on her shoulders, he lifted her hands in his and held them against his chest.

Hell, he knew she was right. But he didn't want to admit it. What if this unknown assassin tried again and succeeded? What if, despite his best efforts, he couldn't stop them?

"No more horseback riding," he told her. "At home, you'll eat and drink only what everyone else does. I'm going to do a thorough check of our suite every time we leave and return. At McNamara's, you'll run everything from your office and won't go out into the plant."

"I won't like it, but I'll do it," she said. "I don't want to be unreasonable about anything. It's just that I have obligations that I can't turn my back on, despite the risk I'm taking."

"Well, from now on you won't be just putting your life at risk." He released her hands.

She spread her palms out flat against his chest. His heart beat wildly. "What do you mean?"

"You're pregnant, Cleo," he said.

"I'm... Already?" Instinctively she laid her hand over her belly. "Oh, Simon. It's too soon. It shouldn't have happened. Not yet."

"I know. I was hoping our would-be killer would have tipped his hand by now. But whoever it is, is taking his own sweet time. He's not in any hurry because he knows he has a whole year."

Cleo realized that Roarke had misunderstood what she'd meant, although he was right about the fact that not only was she now in danger, but so was her unborn child. And whoever had attempted to kill her would want to see her child dead, too.

But Cleo had meant it was too soon to have to worry about Roarke leaving her. He'd made it clear that he wouldn't stay with her through the duration of her pregnancy. How soon would he leave and turn her case over to someone else? Surely he'd changed his mind. He wouldn't leave her now, not the way things were between them.

"Simon, you won't leave me, will you?"

"What?"

"Just because I'm pregnant, you won't leave me."

"No, Cleo, I won't leave you." Not now. Not yet. Not until I know that you and our...your child are out of danger.

She smiled contentedly. "I knew you'd change your mind. Everything is going to be all right for you and me and our baby. We're going to be so happy."

Now wasn't the time to tell her that nothing had changed. That as soon as she was safe and they had her would-be killer behind bars, he was going to leave. There could never be a happily ever after for Simon Roarke.

CHAPTER FOURTEEN

CLEO DUG HER bare toes into the soft love seat cushions and lifted her knees. Hugging the cream knit afghan to her, she draped her arms around her legs. Alone in the solitude of her sitting room. Ah, home sweet home. But since Uncle George's death this house hadn't seemed like home. Not even here in her own suite did she feel perfectly comfortable. Knowing that a member of her own family had tried to harm her—four times—created a morbid air of suspicion and hostility. She didn't want to believe that someone hated her enough to want her dead. But since Aunt Beatrice's close call with death after drinking the poisoned tea and her own riding accident yesterday morning, she could no longer delude herself. Someone wasn't just trying to scare her—someone was trying to kill her!

Simon had wanted her to stay another day in the hospital, but since Dr. Iverson had said she would be as well off at home, she'd insisted on leaving. Simon hadn't liked bringing her home, but he hadn't argued with her about it. In fact, since their heated disagreement about their leaving River Bend and his announcement that she was pregnant, her husband hadn't said much of anything. Every time she'd tried to talk to him about their marriage and their child, he had changed the subject.

Yesterday, she had chalked up his moodiness to his fear for her life and his ridiculous guilt over not foreseeing the accidents that had occurred. She'd tried to tell him that he was a bodyguard, not a mind reader.

Simon had stayed by her side at the hospital all night, sleeping in the chair beside her bed. Whatever she wanted, he was one step ahead of her, waiting on her hand and foot, with gentle patience. He had kissed her good-night and held her hand until she'd drifted off to sleep. And when she had awakened this morning, he'd been sitting there staring at her.

Cleo knew that something was wrong, something that had nothing to do with the threats on her life or with Mc-Namara Industries. Simon was worried. She hadn't known her husband long, but they had become so close, so intimately connected, that she could sense the change in his mood.

She wasn't sure what was wrong, but she suspected the worst. Her greatest fear was that he hadn't been completely honest with her when he'd told her that he wouldn't leave her. She had assumed that he was beginning to feel for her what she felt for him. Maybe he didn't love her—not yet. But she was certain that he cared deeply for her. Did he care enough to stay with her, to be a father to their child and a real husband to her for the rest of their lives?

When she'd tried to broach the subject this morning, he'd cut her off sharply, mumbled something about getting Kane to keep an eye on her while he went out for some fresh air. A couple of minutes later, Morgan Kane told her that he'd be right outside her door if she needed him.

Simon had been gone for hours. Something was definitely wrong. The massive oak grandfather clock in the hall struck twice. Cleo jumped. Her nerves were shot, and her husband's mysterious need to be alone had increased her anxiety.

She glanced at the lunch Pearl had brought up for her around noon. She'd taken a couple of sips of the iced tea, nibbled on the potatoes and taken a bite out of the yeast roll. The remainder of the meal lay untouched on the tray atop the round end table.

She glanced up when she heard the outer door open. Her heart skipped a beat when she saw Simon enter. Kicking the afghan off onto the floor, she stood up and walked to the open French doors that connected the sitting room to the bedroom.

"Simon?"

He looked at her, his face hard, his eyes cold. She shivered, apprehension spreading through her like wildfire.

"You shouldn't be up," he said. "Go back and sit down and rest."

"Where have you been? You've been gone for so long I'd begun to worry."

"I'm sorry, Cleo, if I worried you. That's the last thing I wanted." He moved across the room, taking slow, cautious steps, as if he had to be careful not to come too close. "I just needed time alone, to think things through."

"What things?" Her heart raced madly. She clutched the sides of her satin robe.

"You're recovering from a pretty bad fall, and you've just found out that you're pregnant. This can wait, Cleo."

"Wait until when?"

"Until you're better." He turned around, removed his jacket and tossed it on the bed.

She stood there in the doorway, looking at his broad back and his wide shoulders. He removed his hip holster and laid his Beretta on the nightstand by his side of the bed.

"I want to know now," she told him. "This mood you're in is all about my being pregnant, isn't it? About the bargain we made and the contract we signed when we got married."

"I said this can wait!"

When she gasped, he turned sharply and saw the stricken look on her face. Dammit, why was she pressing him so hard? Why couldn't she just leave it alone for now? He was going to have to tell her the truth; she was going to force the issue and make him hurt her. He hadn't planned for this—for her wanting them to stay married. In the beginning, he'd been sure she'd be able to handle ending their marriage without any messy emotional displays. Now he wasn't so sure.

"You're going to leave, aren't you?" She looked at him, all the pain and disappointment showing plainly in her misty green eyes.

"Eventually," he admitted. "But not yet. Not until I know you aren't in any danger. I'm going to stay as long as it takes for us to catch both our problem maker and our would-be killer."

"I see." She sighed deeply. "You still think they're two different people, don't you? Well, if that's the case, you might have to hang around longer than you'd intended. You wanted to be gone before my pregnancy became advanced, didn't you?"

"You knew from the beginning that this marriage was temporary," he said. "You hired me for specific reasons, and once I've done my job I'll move on. I have plans for my future that don't include a wife or a child."

Cleo could not control her tears. They gathered heavily in her eyes and spilled over, running down her face in torrents. "I—I don't mean anything to you, do I? What we've...these three weeks together, making love, sharing our days and nights, learning to truly like and trust each other. Has it all been a lie? Was being my passionate lover just a little something extra you threw in for no extra charge? Dammit, Simon, have you been pretending to care about me?"

Why was she doing this? Why couldn't she just accept things the way they were? Why did she have to analyze their relationship to death? Because despite her cool, levelheaded, businesswoman demeanor, Cleo was a loving, giving woman. A woman who felt things deeply. A woman who, when she gave herself fully and completely to a man, gave him her heart.

But he didn't want her heart. And he had no choice but to give it back to her, broken into pieces.

"I wasn't pretending," he said truthfully. "I do care about you, Cleo, just not the way you want me to care. And not enough to stay with you and be a father to your child."

She doubled over with the pain of understanding. She loved Simon Roarke. He did not love her. What could be more simple?

When he saw her double over, he rushed across the room and reached out for her. She jerked up and spread her hands in front of her, warning him off.

"Don't touch me." She spoke the words in a low, calm, chillingly frosty voice.

"I want you to understand." He dropped his outstretched hands to his sides. "I owe you that much."

"You don't owe me anything, except to finish your job." She turned around and went back into the sitting room.

Roarke followed her. "Don't walk away from me, Cleo. Even if you hate me right this minute, give me a chance to explain."

She sat down on the love seat and crossed her arms over her chest. "What's there to explain? I thought that there was something between us, something strong enough to build a real marriage on, but obviously I was mistaken. You want to finish this assignment and then you want out."

Roarke entered the sitting room. "Yeah, you're right. I want out. I don't want to be married. And I do not want to be a father."

"Fine. Good. We understand each other perfectly. Enough said." Cleo clenched her teeth, trying not to cry. A lump the size of Texas formed in her throat, threatening to cut off her breathing.

Roarke sat down in the wingback chair across from Cleo. "You know that I was married once, a long time ago." Why are you doing this? he asked himself. What good will it do to bare your soul to her? It won't change anything.

"Married and divorced," Cleo said. "Yes, I know. That information was in your files."

"What the files didn't tell you is why my marriage ended and why, sixteen years after my divorce, I'm still taking care of my ex-wife."

Cleo uncrossed her arms and sat up straight, staring inquisitively at Roarke. "What do you mean you take care of your ex-wife?"

Leaning forward, he rested his arms on his thighs and dropped his clasped hands between his legs. "My mother died when I was too young to remember her, and my father got killed in a tractor accident when I was nine. He'd been a good guy, treated me okay, but wasn't much on affection. His sister and her husband raised me. They treated me like a hired hand on their farm. I couldn't wait to get away, so I joined the army at eighteen and never looked back."

"What does your childhood history have to do with your ex-wife?"

"No one had ever loved me. Really loved me." He bowed his head, hesitant to make eye contact with Cleo. "I met her when I was on leave, on vacation, in Florida. She was blond and beautiful and she smothered me with love."

"Your ex-wife?"

"Hope. Hope Allister. We had a wild fling. I thought we were both in love. Before my leave ended, we got married. That's when things changed."

Part of Cleo wanted to know more, to know every detail of Simon's life, then maybe she could make some sense of what was happening to them. Another part of her wanted to tell him to stop talking, that she didn't want to know any more about Hope, the beautiful woman he'd once loved.

"How did things change?" Cleo asked.

"She wanted me to leave the army. She didn't want me going away on assignments. She didn't understand that I was doing what I wanted to do. That being in the Special Forces was my life. It's what I'd trained for, what I'd gone through hell to achieve."

"So you got a divorce because she wanted you to leave the army and you wouldn't," Cleo said.

"I wasn't quite that simple. It might have been if…if Hope hadn't gotten pregnant."

Cleo felt as though someone had hit her square in the stomach and knocked all the breath out of her. "Pregnant?" Suddenly her lungs filled with air. She gasped. "You have a child?"

Not answering her question, Roarke continued, knowing if he deviated from the linear retelling of his past history, he might not be able to tell her everything. And Cleo had a right to know. Then maybe she'd be able to understand and someday forgive him.

"Even though the relationship was doomed, I stayed married to Hope until Laurie was nearly two years old. Looking back, I've wondered why the hell, if I'd stuck it out that long, I couldn't have just hung in there a few more years. Long enough to realize what was happening with Hope." Roarke rubbed the palms of his hands up and down his thighs, then gripped his knees. "I was gone a lot. Off on assignments around the world. I thought our being apart would make things easier for both of us. It did for me, except I missed Laurie. But it didn't help Hope. As a matter of fact, it made things more difficult for her."

"You have a daughter? She must be nearly grown now." Cleo laid her hand over her tummy, the gesture purely protective maternal instinct. Her child had a half sister, one that she'd never know.

"Dammit, Cleo, will you stop interrupting!" Roarke shot out of the chair, every muscle in his body tense, his back ramrod straight, his big hands clenched. "If I didn't think I owed you this much—this truth about myself— I wouldn't relive the past. I wouldn't reopen all my old wounds. I wouldn't do this for any other reason, for any amount of money."

Cleo slipped off the love seat and walked over to where Roarke stood gazing sightlessly out the windows, his back to her. She raised her hand, holding it over his back, but didn't touch him. Knotting her hand into a fist, she lowered it to her side.

Suddenly she knew, as if the truth had been staring her in the face all along, and someone had just now removed the veil from her eyes. Something terrible had happened to Roarke. Something so unbearable that it had changed his life forever and sealed off his heart, made it impossible for anyone's love to ever reach him again.

Something had happened to Laurie. Roarke's little girl

hadn't grown up. She had died and Roarke had buried all his love along with her.

"Go on, please," Cleo said. "I won't interrupt again."

His wide shoulders lifted and fell as he breathed deeply. "I found out later, from a distant cousin, that Hope had suffered from depression for years. Ever since she was around twelve and her father committed suicide. Hope had found his body. Her mother had a nervous breakdown shortly after that and died in a mental hospital."

"Oh, how awful."

"Anyway, when Laurie was two, Hope and I got a divorce. She even agreed to it. Of course she got custody of Laurie, and I got visitation rights. But I didn't see much of Laurie that next year. I was away most of the time. My career was very important to me."

Cleo longed to put her arms around Roarke and comfort him, but she knew he wouldn't welcome her embrace. Not right now.

"Hope started drinking, but I didn't realize how bad the problem was until it was too late." Roarke fingered the moiré drapes, then shoved aside the sheers and looked down into the yard. "One evening she got in the car with Laurie. According to the police, Hope was so intoxicated—" Roarke paused. His body jerked several times. "It was a one-car wreck. Laurie was thrown through the windshield. When the ambulance arrived, she was dead. Her neck was broken."

Cleo laid her hand on Roarke's back. He flinched. She eased her hand upward and gripped his shoulder. Sobs lodged in her throat. Dear God, what it must have been like for him to have lost his child. And how tragic that it had all been so senseless. So preventable. If Hope hadn't been drinking. If. If. If.

"My drunken, mentally unbalanced ex-wife put my

three-year-old baby girl in her car and I didn't do a thing
to stop her. And you know why?" Roarke's voice rose to
a shout. He spun around, knocking Cleo's hand off his
shoulder. He glared at her with dry, pain-filled eyes. "Because I was halfway around the world playing soldier. I
was in the middle of a jungle with a Special Forces group
doing a dirty little job for Uncle Sam."

"Oh, Simon." Tears distorted her vision so completely
that she could barely make out her husband's face. "You
blame yourself. You think Laurie's death was your fault."

"It was my fault." His tone lowered to a soft, calm
lifelessness. "I was more concerned about my military career than I was about my child. I left Laurie alone with a
woman who couldn't even take care of herself, let alone
a three-year-old."

"You didn't know. You said you had no idea how much
Hope was drinking, and you didn't realize that mental in-
stability ran in her family."

"I didn't take the time to find out. I had more important things to do. My daughter was not my first priority.
She should have been."

"How long ago did Laurie die?" Sniffling, Cleo swallowed her tears.

"Nearly fifteen years ago."

"Where is Hope now?" Running her fingertips under
her eyes, Cleo wiped away the moisture.

"She's in a private sanitarium in Florida. She's been
there over fourteen years, and the doctors say that after
all this time, there's not much chance for a recovery."

"And you take care of her," Cleo said, understanding
her husband more completely now than many women
understood their husbands after years of marriage. "You
pay all her bills, don't you?"

"I let Hope down. She needed help back then and I just didn't see it. Maybe if I had—"

"Don't do this to yourself." With quivering hands, Cleo reached out and cupped Roarke's face. "You've been living with this guilt all these years and it's nearly destroyed you."

"I don't want to hurt you, Cleo." He covered her hands with his, then pulled them away from his face and held them between their bodies. "I should have known I was playing with fire when I agreed to take this job, especially when one of the stipulations of our agreement was that I father your child."

"You must have had a very good reason for agreeing."

"Yeah, I thought they were good reasons. Now I'm not so sure."

"Security for Hope?" Cleo asked, certain of his answer.

"Partly." He held Cleo's hands, encompassing them with his. "I'm nearly forty. I want out of the cloak-and-dagger business. I told you that last year I got shot up on an assignment and nearly died. If something happened to me, there would be no one to pay Hope's expenses."

"So you agreed to marry me, be my bodyguard and father my child so you'd have the money to take care of Hope after you retired from the Dundee agency?"

"I'm going to buy a small farm somewhere." He released Cleo's hands. "The rest of the money is going into a perpetual trust for Hope."

"Thank you for telling me about Hope and about Laurie. I know it must have been painful for you. I'm sorry."

"You had a right to know."

"Yes…well…I—I appreciate your…"

He didn't touch Cleo. He didn't trust what he might do if he touched her now. She looked so small standing there, so forlorn and lost. He'd done this to her. He'd taken the light out of her eyes. She had thought something magical was happening between them, and selfishly, he hadn't been honest with her. He'd let her believe.

"I won't leave until you are no longer in danger. I promise you that." He looked directly into her moss-green eyes and saw the rage inside her. Outwardly she was calm, totally unemotional. Roarke knew she'd already put up a defensive barrier between them. He had hurt her. She wasn't going to allow him close enough to ever hurt her again.

"Thank you." She walked away from him, then paused as she stepped into the bedroom. "I think I'm going to lie down and take a nap. I'm very tired, and I want to make sure I get plenty of rest. I intend to take very good care of *my* baby." She emphasized the word *my*.

Her sedate composure worried him far more than if she'd thrown a temper tantrum. He wished she'd throw something at him. Beat her fists against his chest. Call him names. But that wasn't Cleo's style. She had a temper, but it had a low boiling point and her expression of anger was more subtle than hysterical outbursts.

He followed her out of the sitting room.

"Lock the door behind me. I'm going to Kane's room to discuss a scheme we've been working on to capture our problem maker at McNamara Industries."

"Fine. Go ahead. You can tell me all about it later."

Roarke walked outside. Cleo closed the door and locked it. He leaned back against the door, resting his head for a second. He'd give anything if he could take away Cleo's pain, the pain he'd caused. But he couldn't ease her suffering. Hell, he couldn't even ease his own.

Suddenly, he felt something moist on his face. He touched his cheek, removed his hand and looked down at his fingers. They were damp. Wet with his tears.

But that wasn't possible. He hadn't cried in fifteen years.

CHAPTER FIFTEEN

Cleo insisted that she was well enough to go to work. Nothing Roarke, Beatrice or Pearl said changed her mind. She reminded Roarke that just as he had a job to do, so did she. He thought if he heard her say one more time that people were counting on her, he'd shake her until her teeth rattled.

They'd slept in the same bed last night. The bed they'd shared since the first night of their marriage. The bed in which they'd made love so many times. But he hadn't touched her. He knew that if he had, she would have refused him. He'd been right all along about Cleo. She was the kind of woman who'd get sex and love all mixed up.

"What if your and Kane's little scheme doesn't work?" Cleo placed her empty cup down on the tray. "You don't know for certain that Trey or Hugh is the person we're after, and even if one of them is, he might not step into your trap."

"Ellen Denby has been playing the blond airhead around Trey and Hugh, letting bits of so-called secret information accidentally slip out." Roarke tossed his napkin down on the tray beside his breakfast plate. "She's led them to believe that she's totally incompetent and can be easily manipulated. She's even hinted that for the right amount of money, she'd be willing to look the other way while someone tampered with the computer again or created another accident."

"Do you honestly think Trey or Hugh is gullible enough to believe her?" Cleo asked. "Don't you think they're smart enough to figure out that she's lying? After all, they know Kane is a professional. He'd hardly hire a bimbo to be on his security force."

"You don't know what a talented actress our Ellen is. She's pulled the wool over brighter minds than Trey's or Hugh's. Believe me, she knows what she's doing. She's implied that her intimate relationship with Kane is what got her the job."

"Something my cousin and future cousin-in-law are just the types to believe." Cleo got up and walked into the bedroom. She picked up her black jacket off the bed, put it on and fastened the gold buttons. "If you're right, then tonight we should know who was behind all our problems at the plant."

"Maybe. If we're lucky," Roarke said as he followed her into the bedroom. "Ellen's going to let it slip that she'll be alone on duty tonight inside the plant and there'll be no one else around except for the guard at the front gate." He lifted his holster from the nightstand, removed his Beretta, checked it and replaced it, then strapped on the holster. "We're giving our saboteur a perfect opportunity to wreak havoc at the plant without getting caught. Or so we hope he thinks."

"Hugh and Trey both have security clearance at the back entrance, so they could enter the plant without the guard seeing them."

"Exactly."

"So it's possible that by morning, all my problems will be over and neither I nor McNamara Industries will be in any more danger."

"If we catch our man," Roarke said. "And if he and the

person who's been trying to kill you are one in the same." He lifted his jacket off the back of the chair.

"If he is, then your job will be finished and you can leave. You can get a divorce, collect your payoff and be long gone before I even have a bout of morning sickness."

"Yeah. Sure. That's what we both want, isn't it?" Roarke put on his jacket, walked across the room and opened the door. "Are you ready to leave for the plant, Boss Lady?"

THE DAY HAD seemed endless. Cleo discovered that ignoring Simon Roarke was easier said than done. She found it impossible to pretend he wasn't around when he was at her side constantly. After all, he *was* her bodyguard. And he could hardly guard her if she was one place and he another.

She supposed that if Simon hadn't told her the truth about his past—about Hope and Laurie—she might have gone on thinking that there was a chance he'd change his mind and stay with her. That he might actually want to spend the rest of his life with her. That someday, he would grow to love her.

But there was no hope now. No false dreams to hang on to. No illusions about a marriage of convenience that she now realized could never be anything more.

There was no love in Simon to give. The anger and guilt and remorse he felt over Laurie's death had slowly killed all the love inside him. And no matter how much she loved him, Cleo knew she couldn't bring his deepest emotions back to life. Only Simon could do that. And he never would. Loving someone meant taking a risk on being hurt. He'd been hurt too deeply, had endured an agony that would be a part of him forever. A man who walked around with third-degree burns scarring his emotions would never again take a chance on getting burned.

She glanced over at Roarke. He sat behind the Jacobean desk, while she curled up on the leather sofa. They had agreed to wait downstairs together in the study. Wait for Morgan Kane to call and tell them that they'd caught their man. That either Trey or Hugh had walked into their trap.

Roarke flipped through the pages of a book on farming techniques, which he'd found in Uncle George's library. Cleo held a biography of Amelia Earhart on her lap. The minutes dragged by, making the waiting unbearable.

They'd eaten dinner with the family and tried their best to keep up appearances, but Cleo suspected that they'd failed at presenting the happy newlyweds act they'd finally perfected. But it didn't matter. What difference did it make anymore whether the family believed theirs was a real marriage? They'd all know the truth soon enough, once Simon left. Once they got a divorce.

Both Daphne and Trey had excused themselves from a family night at home, Daphne saying she had a date with Hugh and Trey telling them that he was going to the country club to play cards with a group of his friends. Both explanations were reasonable. Daphne saw Hugh almost every night and Trey did play cards at the country club fairly often.

Cleo glanced down at her watch. "It's ten o'clock. You'd think if something was going to happen, it would have happened by now."

Roarke closed the book and laid it on the desk. "Not necessarily."

"If it has to be Trey or Hugh, I hope it's Hugh," she said.

"You're thinking of your family, aren't you? That it would be easier all the way around if Trey isn't guilty."

"Do you have any idea what it will do to Aunt Oralie

if it is Trey? She dotes on her children. She thinks they can do no wrong."

The telephone rang. Cleo jumped. Roarke picked up the receiver.

"Roarke here. Yes. I see. No, go ahead and call Phil Bacon. Cleo and I will meet you at the sheriff's department." Roarke hung up the telephone.

"That was Kane, wasn't it?"

"Yes. Our simple little trap worked."

"Who?" Cleo asked.

"Trey," Roarke said. "They caught him red-handed. He's trying to talk his way out of it, but there's no question that he got into the computer again and deleted several files. Of course he had no way of knowing that he was destroying useless files, dummy orders that we'd entered today, or that he was being videotaped."

Cleo could tell by the look on Roarke's face that there was more to what had happened than he was telling her. "What else? You're not telling me everything."

"Trey had rigged some explosives that he planned to set off in the main production room of the plant."

"What! How would Trey know the first thing about explosives?"

"Every man and his brother can find that information on the internet or order it through the mail," Roarke told her. "It doesn't take a genius to assemble a simple little bomb."

"Trey." Cleo gritted her teeth. "I didn't want it to be Trey. I can't believe he'd try to kill me. Aunt Oralie raised him to be selfish and greedy, but I never thought he was capable of murder."

"He may not be." Roarke shoved back the chair and stood. "He may be guilty of only sabotage. Kane's calling Phil Bacon, so I imagine by the time we get down to the sheriff's department, they'll have brought in Trey for booking."

"He'll be arrested and put in jail, won't he?"

"Yeah, and if I have anything to do with it, he won't be getting out on bond anytime soon."

ROARKE WISHED HE could have spared Cleo from this ordeal. If the saboteur had been anyone other than a member of her family it would have been easier for her. But then, she'd known all along that it had to be someone with something to gain. Someone who would benefit if she agreed to sell McNamara Industries.

Trey Sutton had called Hugh Winfield, who had shown up at the county jail shortly after Roarke and Cleo had arrived. Cleo had reminded Hugh that as one of McNamara Industries' lawyers, he could hardly represent someone who'd tried to sabotage the plant. Hugh in turn had called Drennan Norcross, an old warhorse of an attorney, who, with his white hair and thick mustache looked the part of a forties-style Southern lawyer. Drennan actually wore white suits in the summertime and carried a gold-tipped black cane, which he said helped him get around better since his rheumatism had gotten so bad.

While Drennan spoke to his client, Cleo and Roarke waited, along with Morgan Kane and Ellen Denby. But Hugh Winfield suddenly disappeared.

"He's gone to the house to tell the family," Cleo said. "They'll all be down here in a little while."

"We'll handle that when it happens," Roarke told her. "I don't want you to worry. You're recovering from a concussion. You just got out of the hospital yesterday. Getting upset isn't good for you. Or for the baby."

She noticed that he hadn't said *your* baby or *our* baby, just *the* baby. Of course he was right. Getting upset and worrying about how she was going to handle Trey's capture and the family's reaction weren't good for her or her baby. And her child had to be her number-one priority. Regardless of the fact that she had conceived this baby to fulfill a stipulation in her uncle's will, she already loved her child and wanted it desperately.

In the future, she might have other children, but they would not be Simon's children. This tiny life growing inside her would soon be all she had of Simon. Their child and her few precious memories of the days and nights they'd shared during their brief marriage.

Drennan's cane tapped along on the hardwood floor as he shuffled down the corridor leading from the jail cells that were located in a separate west wing of the sheriff's department.

"Well, Phil, Trey's ready to sign a statement." Drennan clasped Sheriff Bacon's shoulder. "But he wants to talk to Cleo first."

"What sort of statement is Trey willing to sign?" Phil Bacon asked.

"The boy knows he's been caught red-handed, so to speak." Drennan chuckled, the sound a smirky good-old-boy laugh. "He's willing to own up to playing around with the computer and to rigging up some little old homemade bomb that probably wouldn't have done more than cause a loud sound and create some smoke."

Cleo rolled her eyes heavenward. Drennan Norcross was making Trey sound like a misguided Boy Scout who'd been caught putting a garden snake in the scoutmaster's cot.

"Is he willing to confess to trying to murder his cousin?" Roarke asked.

"Hell, no. Trey Sutton is no murderer, sir. The boy

doesn't have it in him to try to harm Miss Cleo." Drennan smiled at Cleo, his white teeth glistening.

"I want to talk to Trey," Cleo said. "I want him to look me in the eye and tell me that he didn't try to shoot me or poison me or—"

"Cleo will agree to speak to Trey, but not alone," Roarke said.

"Of course," Drennan agreed. "He said you'd want to come along with her."

"Are you sure you want to do this, Cleo?" Phil Bacon asked. "We don't need a signed confession, not with eyewitnesses—" Phil glanced at Kane and Ellen Denby, who waited discreetly just outside his open office door "—who caught Trey in the act." Phil lifted a videotape off his desk. "And even recorded what he did."

"I understand," Cleo said. "I'm glad that we've caught our saboteur, but unless Trey was behind the attempts on my life, then I'm still in danger. And so is my baby."

"Baby?" Phil looked from Cleo to Roarke. "Well, congratulations, folks. Hell, Cleo, this is hardly the place for a pregnant lady. Down here at the jail having to deal with a mess like this."

"I promise that as soon as I talk to Trey and hear what he has to say, I'll go home."

"Come on, then," Phil said. "I'll walk you and Mr. Roarke on back. If you'd like, I'll dismiss my deputy and stay in the room with y'all."

"Could we speak to him privately?" Cleo asked.

"I'm afraid not." Phil shook his head. "Sorry."

"All right. Let's go get this over with." Cleo turned to her husband. "He'd be a fool to confess that he's tried to kill me."

Roarke nodded, then slipped his arm around her. She didn't resist the comforting, protective gesture. They fol-

lowed the sheriff down the hall and into the small, private
inquisition room that also served as a private meeting area
for lawyers and their clients.

Phil dismissed his deputy, who exited the room before
Cleo and Roarke entered. Trey stood up the minute Cleo
entered the room.

"I'm sorry, Cleo," Trey said. "I did what I had to do,
what I thought was best for the whole family. We'd all be
better off if we sold the company while it's still worth
something. The way things are these days, there's no way
for a small plant like ours to survive."

Roarke watched Cleo's face, the tensing of her jaw, the
slight flaring of her nostrils, the narrowing of her pensive
green eyes. She was trying to control her anger, trying to
stay calm.

"Don't apologize to me," Cleo said. "There is no excuse for what you did, for the thousands of dollars you
lost for McNamara's, the lives you put in danger."

"I never meant for anyone to get hurt." Trey came toward Cleo, his hands open in supplication. "You've got to
believe me. When I took that shot at you right after Uncle
George's funeral, I had no intention of harming you. I just
meant to frighten you."

"You were the one! My God, it was you all along." Cleo
curved her fingers into claws and lifted them toward Trey.
"You put spiders in my bathroom and poison in my tea.
You—"

"No, Cleo. No! I didn't. I swear I didn't. All I did was
take a shot at you to try to scare you."

When Trey reached out for Cleo, Roarke stepped between them. Trey gazed into Roarke's stern face and
backed away.

"Do you expect me to believe that you haven't been
behind the other three attempts on my life?" Cleo wanted

to put her hands around Trey's throat and choke the life out of him for what he'd put her through, for what he'd done to her and Aunt Beatrice and all the employees at McNamara's.

"I don't know who's been trying to kill you," Trey said. "But I would never hurt you. Scare you into selling McNamara Industries? Yes. But try to kill you? Never."

"Come on, Cleo, you don't need any more of this. Not tonight." Roarke put his arm around her shoulders. "Don't do this to yourself." Leaning over, he whispered in her ear, "Think of the baby."

She allowed Roarke to lead her out of the interrogation room and back down the hall toward the sheriff's office. When they reached the end of the corridor, Cleo heard her aunt Oralie's voice.

"Oh, God, they're here." Cleo leaned against Roarke.

"You don't have to see them tonight, honey. I can take you out of here the back way. We can check into a motel. You can face them tomorrow."

"No. I'm not running away. It's past time I took charge of this situation." Cleo moved out of Roarke's arms and walked down the hall.

He followed her, but stayed several steps behind, ready to come to her aid only if she needed him.

Daphne caught a glimpse of Cleo and called out loudly, "There she is mother! You tell her to get Trey out of this jail right now."

Oralie rushed toward Cleo, hysterically waving her arms in the air. "What have you done to Trey? How dare you have him locked up in this awful place. I demand that you have him released this very minute."

"How could you allow the sheriff to arrest Trey?" Daphne pursed her lips and glared at Cleo.

Cleo marched past Daphne, past Oralie, and stopped

dead still in front of Perry Sutton. Aunt Beatrice stood
several feet away, her arm around a weeping Marla. Aunt
Beatrice shrugged her slender shoulders and smiled sadly.

"Trey was caught tampering with the computer system at McNamara's as well as placing a small bomb in
the main production room at the plant. He's confessed
to being behind all the sabotage that's taken place since
Uncle George's death."

"That's not possible," Oralie cried out. "You're fram-
ing Trey. You want him out of McNamara's. You never
wanted him working there in the first place."

Cleo ignored her aunt's outburst, keeping her eyes focused on her uncle Perry's somber face. "Trey also admitted to being the one who took a shot at me right after
Uncle George's funeral."

"You're lying!" Daphne shouted.

"Trey has been arrested and is facing some serious
charges, Uncle Perry," Cleo said. "If he's convicted, and
I have no doubt he will be, he's going to be in prison for
years."

"I understand." Bowing his head, Perry looked down
at the floor.

"Well, I don't understand," Oralie said. "This is a family
matter. There was no need to turn Trey over to the sheriff."

Cleo spun around and faced her wild-eyed, angry aunt.
"Trey tried to shoot me, Aunt Oralie, and he put McNamara Industries' employees in danger, as well as cost the
company thousands of dollars. He committed more than
one crime. What do you think I should do—slap him on
the hand and tell him to be a good boy from now on?"

"You—you can't let him go to prison. I won't allow
it! Do you hear me? I won't allow it." Oralie pointed her
finger in Cleo's face.

"Get your finger out of my face right now, Aunt Oralie, or I'm going to bite it off!"

"How dare you threaten me!" Oralie lowered her finger.

"If you think that was a threat, you haven't heard anything yet."

Phil Bacon walked up the hall and stopped by Roarke's side. "What's going on?"

"Shh, I think my wife is just about to set up some new ground rules."

"Trey is going to have to pay for his crimes. He'll go to trial and if he's convicted he'll be sentenced to prison," Cleo told her aunt. "I will not lift a finger to help him."

"You're cold and heartless and—"

"I will not discuss this with you ever again after tonight. I want you and your family to move out of Aunt Beatrice's home. Uncle George left the house to her, you know. After all, it did belong to her mother's family. Aunt Beatrice has been far too generous allowing y'all to make her home yours all these years." Cleo took a deep breath. "I'll give y'all one month to find somewhere else to live."

"You don't mean what you're saying." Oralie stared at Cleo in disbelief.

"Yes, I mean every word I've said. I'm going to have a baby and my child is my first priority. I don't want my son or daughter living in a house with y'all."

Oralie glanced across the room at her cousin, who still had her arm around Marla's trembling shoulders. "Beatrice, you won't let her do this, will you?"

Beatrice looked at Perry, who had his back to her. "Yes, Oralie, I'm afraid I will let her. It's long past time that you left."

Oralie fussed and fumed and cried. Roarke walked

around the edge of the room and watched Cleo as she came toward him.

"I'm tired," she said. "There's nothing else I can do here tonight. I'd like to go home now, Simon."

She looked so pale and delicate, as if the lightest breeze might blow her off her feet. He wanted to lift her in his arms and carry her away from everything and everyone who'd ever hurt her. But he didn't. He knew she needed to walk away on her on two feet, under her own steam. Cleo McNamara Roarke had finally taken complete charge of her life, and he, for one, felt like applauding her.

CHAPTER SIXTEEN

ROARKE LAY IN the darkness, listening to Cleo breathe. She had slept restlessly, tossing and turning most of the night. He'd slept very little and had been awake for quite some time. Dawn light came through the windows and French doors, permeating the room with a muted, rosy glow. He looked at Cleo, her face partially in shadow as she lay on her side, her back to him. She was so lovely, her features so utterly, completely feminine.

The oddest thought went through his mind. He wanted to memorize her face, so that over the years he would never forget exactly how she looked at this precise moment.

Cleo awoke with a start. Gasping for air, she shot straight up in bed. Roarke sat up beside her and pulled her into his arms. Maybe she didn't want his comfort, but he knew she damn well needed it. She was a strong woman, but sometimes the strongest people needed someone to lean on, someone to let them know they weren't all alone. He halfway expected her to resist him, but she didn't. Relaxing against him, she laid her head on his shoulder.

"You're safe, honey." Brushing away an errant red strand of hair that had fallen across her forehead, Roarke kissed her temple.

He hadn't realized how much he'd missed her girlish giggles or her breath-stopping smiles or her warm, enthusiastic loving. He'd become used to Cleo. As the old song went, he'd become accustomed to her. That had been his mistake—his letting himself get emotionally involved. There hadn't been a woman in his life on a steady basis since his divorce from Hope. Women had come in and out of his life over the past fifteen years, but not one of them had put a dent in his defensive armor.

But Cleo had.

"Is it over, Simon? I mean really over?" Lifting her head off his shoulder, she looked at him, her eyes pleading for reassurance. "Now that Trey is in jail, am I safe?"

He wished he could tell her that it *was* over, that she *was* safe. But he couldn't. His gut instincts told him that Trey Sutton was telling the truth, that he had been responsible for shooting at Cleo right after George McNamara's death, but not for any of the other attempts on her life. If Trey had been honest with them, that meant the greater danger to Cleo still existed. Whoever wanted her dead was still free to try again.

Holding her securely in his embrace, Roarke stroked her arm tenderly. "I don't know. I honestly don't know. I'd like to think that we don't have anything else to worry about, but I tend to think Trey was telling us the truth last night."

"If he was, that means Daphne or Hugh or Uncle Perry or maybe even Aunt Oralie or Marla was the one behind the other three attempts on my life." Cleo shuddered, then draped her arms around Roarke's waist and buried her face against his chest. "Don't leave me." She whispered the plea, her lips brushing his collarbone. "I need you. The baby and I need you. Just for a little longer."

He grasped her chin with one hand. She gazed up at him. "I'm not going to leave you, honey. I'm not going anywhere until I know you're safe. You and the baby."

The baby. His baby. God help him, he'd tried so hard

not to think of the child as his, but it was his. Nothing could ever change that fact.

He saw the need in her eyes, felt the hunger in her quivering body, and knew that Cleo could no more resist him than he could her. An overwhelming passion existed between them, a desire so strong that it overrode their common sense.

Lowering his mouth to hers, he consumed her with a kiss that combined tenderness with savagery, a gentle conquest, but a conquest all the same. Cleo pressed her body against his. Placing his hand in the center of her back, he shoved her harder against him, rubbing his chest over her aching nipples. Her satin-covered nipples hardened, jabbing into his chest.

He deepened the kiss, his tongue thrusting, mimicking the most intimate invasion of all. She clung to him, urging him, encouraging him, returning in full measure the fury of his loving attack. When they were both breathless, Roarke slowed the kiss and turned his attention to her neck.

She moaned softly, then whispered his name. He slipped his hand under the cover, up beneath her gown and between her thighs. He sought and found her hot, moist core.

"Let me love you." He murmured the words against her neck.

"Yes." She sighed. "I need you so much."

He tossed the covers aside, eased Cleo's gown over her head and threw it on the floor. Lifting his hips, he eased his briefs down his legs and flung them into the air. He mounted her slowly, forcing himself not to move too quickly, not to rush this sweet, sweet moment.

Roarke tormented her breasts with his lips and tongue, creating an unbearable urgency within her. Grasping his buttocks, Cleo urged him to take her. He cupped her hips, lifting her to meet his forceful plunge. Her body welcomed his entrance, claiming him completely.

They made love in quiet, hurried desperation. Each in such urgent need of the other. Each aware on some level that this might be their last time. Their fulfillment came too quickly. White-hot. Rocking them to the depths of their souls.

She would never know this ecstasy with anyone else. Only with Simon. Only with the man she loved with all her heart. Only with the father of her child.

SEVERAL HOURS LATER when Cleo and Roarke came downstairs for breakfast, they found the house unnaturally quiet. On their way to the dining room, they encountered Pearl pushing a serving cart toward the open French doors leading to the patio.

"Good morning, Pearl," Cleo said. "Are you serving breakfast outside today?"

Pearl continued pushing the cart, laden with a coffeepot and a pitcher of orange juice, toward the patio. "Perry called down an hour ago and said Oralie wanted me to set things up outside. He said the sunshine and fresh air might do her some good."

Cleo tensed at the mention of her aunt and uncle. Last night she had given them their walking papers, ordering them out of the house within the month. But this morning, it was business as usual, Oralie presiding over the household as if she were the queen bee.

"Has anyone come down yet?" Roarke asked.

Pearl stopped in the doorway. "I haven't seen anyone except Daphne. She was asking about you, Mr. Roarke. Wanted me to let her know the minute you and Cleo came down for breakfast. She's on the phone in the study."

"You might as well find out what she wants," Cleo said. "I'll walk on outside with Pearl and pour us both a cup of coffee."

"No," Roarke said. "I'll go on outside with you. Pearl can tell Daphne where we are."

Pearl pushed the cart over the threshold and out onto the patio. "I know the sheriff arrested Trey last night. Hugh Winfield came by and told the family that Mr. Kane had caught Trey up to no good at the plant." She paused momentarily, turned her head around and looked directly at Cleo, who stood in the doorway. "I didn't hear you and Mr. Roarke come in last night, but when the rest of them returned, Oralie was making enough noise to wake the dead. She was crying and screaming and carrying on like you wouldn't believe. I heard her say that you was kicking them all out of the house. Is that true, Cleo Belle—are you getting rid of that bad rubbish once and for all?"

"Yes, Pearl, she is." The feminine voice came from behind Roarke, who had stopped just inside the house, a couple of feet away from Cleo.

They all glanced back at Daphne. She ran the tip of her index finger up Roarke's arm, but she gazed past him at Cleo. "She's given us a month to get out. Generous of her to give us that much time, don't you think?" She looked at Roarke then, her full, red lips curving into a forced smile. "I'd like to ask a favor of you, Mr. Roarke." She emphasized the word *mister* when she spoke. "You're the only one I know who might possibly help me."

Pearl turned back around and went about setting up the coffee and juice for the family's breakfast. Cleo followed Pearl.

"Wait, Cleo," Roarke called after her.

"No. It's all right. Find out what you can do to *help* Daphne. I'll fix us some coffee."

"I'll join you in a minute," Roarke said.

Cleo nodded and waved at him, then headed straight for the silver coffee server that Pearl had just filled. The housekeeper handed Cleo a china cup, then waddled off toward the house.

"I'll be back directly, as soon as I take my apple cinnamon rolls out of the oven," Pearl said, disappearing inside the house.

As Pearl passed them in the dining room, Roarke noticed her disapproving glare aimed directly at Daphne. He grinned at Pearl. Her lips twitched, but she didn't return his smile. She just stared at him briefly, shook her head and headed toward the kitchen.

He glanced outside, watching Cleo as she poured one cup of coffee, set it down on the table, then repeated the process.

"What can I help you with, Daphne?" Roarke asked.

Daphne walked around Roarke and closed the French doors. He glanced outside, checking once again on Cleo, who he knew was deliberately ignoring him and her cousin.

Daphne danced the tips of her long red nails up the front of his shirt. "You can intercede with Cleo for us. You're the only one she seems to listen to these days. The only one who has any influence over her."

"Why would I intercede for your family? I hardly know any of you, and what I do know, I don't like."

Laying her hand flat on Roarke's chest, she rubbed her palm around and around. Roarke grabbed her wrist. They glared at each other.

"If you got to know me, you'd like me. I promise." She licked her moist red lips. "If you'll help us, I'll be very grateful."

"Exactly what do you think I can do?"

"You can persuade Cleo not to kick us out. After all, we are family. And you could ask her to help Trey. He didn't actually try to kill her. He told you himself that he only wanted to frighten her, scare her into selling the damn company."

When Daphne wiggled her fingers, trying to caress Roarke, he tightened his hold on her wrist. "The only person who can help Trey now is Drennan Norcross. A good lawyer might get him a reduced sentence since he has cooperated and confessed."

"Cleo cares more about McNamara Industries than she does her own family." Daphne twisted her arm, trying to pull free of Roarke's tenacious grip. "She'd rather save the jobs of a few hundred people than do what's best for us."

"Cleo has done more for your family than most people would have under similar circumstances. She's had to put up with your jealousy and greed all her life, and since her uncle's death, someone in this family, if not Trey, has attempted to kill her more than once."

Glowering at Roarke, Daphne tugged on her wrist. Releasing his hold on her, he shoved her hand toward her. "I can't help you, *Daffie*. Not you or Trey or your mother or father. For once, y'all are going to have to help yourselves."

CLEO KNEW THAT Roarke wasn't going to fall for any of Daphne's persuasive promises, but years of losing boyfriends and even a fiancé to Daphne made Cleo uneasy. What could Daphne possible want from Roarke? Why had she waylaid him in the dining room? Probably for no other reason than to aggravate her.

Nervous and restless, Cleo shoved back her chair, lifted her cup and saucer and stood. She looked up at the clear, blue sky, at the beautiful morning sun shimmering an orange gold on the eastern horizon. The day was Southern summertime beautiful.

She walked around the pool, careful not to get too close to the edge. She didn't want to accidentally slip in and have to change clothes before she went into the office for a few hours this morning.

Sipping her coffee, occasionally glancing toward the dining room, where she could see Daphne and Roarke, and enjoying the fresh, morning air, Cleo continued her stroll around the pool.

She heard a noise from behind her. Thinking Pearl had returned with warm apple cinnamon rolls, Cleo started to turn around. Something hard and heavy hit her across the side of her head. A hand reached out and shoved her into the pool. Cleo opened her mouth to scream. A thick, heavy darkness surrounded her, silencing her cry for help.

OPENING THE FRENCH DOORS, Roarke looked outside. Cleo wasn't walking around the pool as she'd been doing only minutes ago. He glanced around the patio area. Cleo wasn't there. Where was she? His heartbeat accelerated, the thunderous roar deafening him to any other sound. He ran outside, his gaze searching. Suddenly he saw her—in the pool. God, no!

Fully clothed, Roarke jumped into the pool and lifted Cleo's head out of the water. She lay lifeless and unbreathing in his arms. He swam with her to the pool's edge, hauled her up onto the patio and laid her down on the stone floor. He straddled her hips.

Daphne hovered over him. "What happened? Is she all right?"

"Call 911! Get an ambulance here on the double!" Roarke shouted.

Daphne ran into Pearl when she rushed toward the house. "Call 911," Daphne said. "Something's happened to Cleo. I'll go get Mother and Father and Aunt Beatrice."

Roarke had performed resuscitation techniques before. He knew the drill. But this wasn't just anybody lying beneath him. This was Cleo. His wife. The mother of his child.

Forcing himself not to think, not to feel, only to perform, to do what he had to do, Roarke opened Cleo's mouth and positioned her tongue. Pinching her nose shut, he breathed into her mouth. He removed his mouth, allowing time for her lungs to empty. He repeated the process quickly, again and again.

While he gave Cleo artificial respiration, he concentrated fully on the task at hand. But while his mind focused on what he could do to save her, his heart prayed for divine assistance.

"I called 911." Pearl scurried out onto the patio, halting at Roarke's side. "The ambulance is on its way."

On some level he heard her, but didn't take time to acknowledge her presence.

Beatrice rushed outside, followed by Oralie and Perry. Daphne waited in the doorway.

"Come on, honey," Roarke said, then breathed into Cleo's mouth again.

She choked, then spit up mouthfuls of water. She gasped for air. Relief relaxed Roarke's tense body. He laughed as he ran his hands up and down her arms. She coughed repeatedly. When she tried to sit up, he put his arm around her shoulder and lifted her.

"You scared the hell out of me, honey." He grasped her shoulders, bunching the sleeves of her jacket. The light pressure of his fingers drew droplets of chlorinated water out of the linen material.

Cleo reached out and touched Roarke's cheek. "What— what happened?"

"I found you in the pool, unconscious."

"Someone hit me." She coughed again and again, then breathed deeply. Her lungs ached as the air entered them. "They hit me over the head and—" she coughed once more "—they pushed me into the pool. I tried to call out, but everything went black."

Roarke ran his hand over her head gently, threading his fingers through her wet hair. Lifting his hand, he looked at his palm and saw fresh, bright red blood. Maneuvering himself around without moving Cleo, he inspected her head, and discovered a small tear in the skin an inch or so above her right ear. A thin, water-mixed rivulet of blood seeped down the side of her neck.

"Did you see anything?" Roarke asked. "Do you have any idea who hit you?" Where the hell was that ambulance? Despite the fact that Cleo seemed all right, he couldn't help but wonder if this second blow to her head in such a short period of time might not have done some unseen damage. And what about the baby? Would those few minutes Cleo's body was without oxygen have harmed their child in any way?

"I heard something behind me." Cleo tried to get up. Roarke held her, forcing her to stay seated on the stone floor. "I want to get up. I'm wet and soggy. My head hurts. Take me upstairs and let me change clothes."

"No, no, you must stay still, dear," Beatrice said, moving closer to Cleo. "An ambulance is on the way. You need to go to the hospital and let Dr. Iverson make sure you're really all right."

"I am all right." Cleo crossed her arms over her chest. "Look, I don't want to waste time on an unnecessary trip to the hospital. Someone just tried to kill me." She turned her head, then cried out in pain. When Roarke reached for her, she brushed his hand aside. "One of you—" Cleo pointed to Perry Sutton, then to her aunt Oralie and finally to Daphne "—tried to kill me."

"Nonsense," Oralie said. "You must have slipped, hit your head and fallen into the pool. It had to have been an accident."

"It was no accident!" Cleo grabbed Roarke's hand. "And you were in the dining room with Daphne, so... that leaves only Aunt Oralie or Uncle Perry."

"Honey, I want you to stay calm and take it easy until Dr. Iverson checks you over," Roarke said. "Think about the baby, if not yourself."

"I am thinking about my baby," Cleo told him. "I'm thinking about what would have happened if you hadn't found me so soon."

"Good thing he was close by, like he always is," Pearl said. "You was keeping an eye on her through them doors." Pearl pointed to the open French doors, where Daphne stood. "Didn't you see anybody?"

"Daphne!" Roarke bellowed her name. Releasing Cleo, Roarke stood and glanced at Beatrice. "Aunt Beatrice? Please?"

He nodded toward Cleo, and her aunt immediately understood that he was turning his wife over into her care. Roarke glared at Daphne. "Come here," he said. She took several hesitant steps toward him, then when she looked into his angry eyes, she hurried to him.

"Don't harass my poor baby," Oralie said. "Isn't it enough that you've put one of my children in jail? Must you persecute Daphne?"

"You stopped me from going out on the patio with Cleo. You closed the doors and tried to divert my attention. You knew I wouldn't help you, knew talking to me would be useless," Roarke said.

Daphne turned to flee, but Roarke caught her wrist. "Let me go. I've done nothing wrong."

"Oh, but you have. You helped someone scheming to harm Cleo. You tried to separate me from Cleo just long enough for your partner to make another attempt on Cleo's life."

"I don't know what you're talking about." Daphne's eyes widened. Her chin quivered. She tugged on her wrist, trying to free herself from Roarke's grasp. "All I did was ask you to help Trey and help us. Mother insisted I talk to you as soon as possible this morning. She believed that I could convince you to use your influence with Cleo."

"Your mother?" Roarke jerked Daphne by the wrist, pulling her around to face Oralie. "Is that right Mrs. Sutton? Were you the one who sent Daphne to divert my attention?"

"I most certainly did not!"

"Mother?" Daphne stared questioningly at Oralie.

"Where were you five minutes ago, Mrs. Sutton?" Roarke glanced at Perry Sutton. "Was she with you?"

"No," Beatrice answered for him. "Perry was with me. We had—" she lowered her voice, as if what she was about to say was a secret "—we went for a walk together this morning, as we often do. We had just returned, when we ran into Daphne in the hall."

"When you went upstairs to get your parents and your aunt, did you find them?" Roarke asked Daphne.

"You don't have to answer him!" Oralie backed slowly toward the house, all the while glaring daggers through Roarke.

"Mother?" Daphne asked. "Please, Mother!"

Oralie turned quickly and ran from the patio, brushing past her daughter as she fled inside the house.

"Oralie!" Perry called to his wife as he rushed after her, following her inside the house.

"Your mother wasn't upstairs, was she, Daphne?" Roarke asked. "She was already downstairs somewhere, waiting and hoping for another chance to kill Cleo."

"No!" Daphne cried. "No. She just wanted me to talk to you. She didn't want Cleo to throw us out of the house. Please, try to understand. She didn't...she wouldn't..."

"Simon?" Cleo fought off Beatrice's attempts to keep her seated on the patio floor. Grabbing a chair for support, Cleo rose to her feet.

"Stay here. Wait for the ambulance," he told her. "Let me handle this."

"Do as he asks," Beatrice pleaded.

Cleo sat down in the chair. "You think Aunt Oralie—"

"Hush, sweetheart." Beatrice patted Cleo and hugged her head against her stomach the way a mother would in comforting a child. "Oralie has always been jealous of you, but I never dreamed that she...it isn't in her to murder. I thought she'd gotten over her...but she hasn't. Why didn't I realize that she's been pretending all these years?"

"What are you talking about?" Cleo lifted her head and stared up at Beatrice.

"Oh, my dear, dear girl, it's all my fault." Tears streamed down Beatrice's face. "When your father was killed and your mother deserted you, Daddy and I brought you home to live with us. You were such a tiny little thing. None of us had ever seen you. You were born after James went to Vietnam and Arabelle wasn't on good terms with us."

"Please, Aunt Beatrice, what does all this have to do with Aunt Oralie?"

"Oralie has always been terribly jealous of me, of my relationship with Perry." Beatrice hung her head, avoiding any eye contact. "After I brought you home and made such a fuss over you, and when Oralie saw how Daddy doted on you, she got the ridiculous idea in her head that you were my child, and not really James's little girl."

"What?" Cleo turned around too quickly. Pain shot through her head. She suddenly felt very dizzy.

"You've always resembled me a great deal, Cleo." Beatrice smiled sadly. "We both take after Daddy's mother. She was a petite, green-eyed redhead."

"Oralie assumed that Perry was Cleo's father," Roarke said.

"Yes," Beatrice replied. "For quite some time nothing we said or did could convince her otherwise. She tormented us with her accusations. But finally, she said that she would accept Cleo into the family and forgive Perry, as long as he stayed away from Cleo and never paid any attention to her."

"That's why Uncle Perry—"

"He didn't dare be more than civil to you." Beatrice wept openly, gasping with sobbing breaths. Calming herself, she looked directly at Roarke. "Please, Simon, go on and do what must be done. There's no telling what Oralie will do now that we've found her out."

Roarke shrugged off his wet jacket and tossed it on the table. "Stay put," he told Cleo.

Roarke found Perry Sutton standing in the middle of his and Oralie's sitting room, his arms outstretched to his wife. Oralie had opened the double doors leading outside onto her balcony. She stood facing Perry, her back to the balcony. Daphne sat rigidly on the edge of the bed in her parents' bedroom. Her eyes were dazed, her face deathly pale. Roarke halted a few feet behind Perry. But Perry didn't turn around. With his arms open wide, he kept saying, "Come to me, Oralie," over and over again.

Oralie pointed a finger at Roarke and laughed hysterically. "If she hadn't married *him,* it would all be over now. She'd be dead and my children would be safe. It would all be ours, not hers. Not Bea's."

"Oralie, honey, everything will be all right if you just come on back in here with me." Perry took a tentative step toward her.

She backed all the way onto the balcony until her hips rested against the wooden banister. "Don't! I'm not going to let you trick me. Not any of you."

"No one's trying to trick you," Perry said. "I just want you to come back in here and let's talk this over. We can make everything all right. Cleo's fine. You didn't hurt her."

"I wish I'd killed her. I tried!"

"Hush, honey, you're only upsetting yourself." Perry stood perfectly still.

Roarke placed his hand on Perry's shoulder. "Has she threatened to jump?" Roarke whispered.

Perry nodded affirmatively.

"What's he saying to you?" Oralie screamed. "Don't you believe anything he says. He's Cleo's husband. He'll take her side. But you mustn't take her side. You have to be on my side. Mine and *my* children's."

"I am on your side."

"No, you're on Cleo's side, too. Because she's Beatrice's child. Yours and Beatrice's. You lied to me. All of you. Uncle George. Beatrice. You. But I knew better. I couldn't allow you to love Beatrice's child more than my children. That's why I tried to drown Cleo when she was a little girl. If only I had succeeded then, everything would have been all right."

Marla Sutton gasped loudly. She halted in the doorway of Perry and Oralie's suite. Cleo and Aunt Beatrice stood directly behind her.

"Yes, Oralie, I know," Perry said. "Remember? You promised me then that you'd never try to harm Cleo again."

"Yes, I promised."

"You broke your promise, didn't you?"

"It was easy, you know." Oralie put her hands behind her back and grasped the banister. She tossed back her head and laughed. "I almost got caught getting those spiders out of the science lab at Covenant. I did run into Professor Martindale, but he didn't remember who I was. Wasn't that fortunate? And the poison was so simple. I just got it out of a smelly old sack in your greenhouse. I remembered that one day when I went down to the greenhouse, you said you needed to get rid of some of those old insecticides and a sack of rat poison. But you never did. Wasn't that lucky for me?"

Cleo gripped Beatrice's hand. "Did you know that Aunt Oralie tried to kill me years ago? Did Uncle Perry tell you?"

"No, I had no idea," Beatrice said. "We all assumed that your nearly drowning when you were a child was nothing more than an accident. We were always having to scold you children for playing around the pool unsupervised."

"The little buzzers under the saddle were the most fun." Oralie's voice boomed with a maniacal strength. "I found those in a sack in Trey's dresser. They'd been left over from some party that he'd given a few years ago, before he and Marla married. I had so hoped that when Sweet Justice bucked her off, Cleo would break her neck."

Marla gasped a second time. Cleo tightened her grasp on Beatrice's hand.

Oralie lifted one of her legs and swung it over the banister.

"Don't, Oralie," Perry pleaded. "We can fix things. We can make things right again."

"I tried to make things right and I failed," she said. "I can't let y'all call that silly Phil Bacon to come and get me. He'd put me in jail, just like he did Trey. I'm not going to jail. They'd take away all my jewelry." She fiddled with the rings on her fingers. "And I couldn't wear my nice clothes." She stroked her silk blouse. "And they wouldn't let Pearl bring me breakfast in bed when I'm having one of my bad days."

"You won't have to go to jail." Perry turned around and looked at Cleo and Beatrice. "Please, tell her that she won't have to go to jail. Please."

Cleo closed her eyes momentarily. A part of her didn't care if Oralie jumped to her death. Another part of her wanted desperately to save her aunt.

"Aunt Oralie, please come back inside." Releasing Beatrice's hand, Cleo walked over and stood beside Roarke. "No one is going to take you off to jail."

"You're lying!" Oralie laughed again, the hysteria accelerating, the laughter growing louder and louder.

"Mother." Daphne rose from the bed and walked into the sitting room. "Please, don't do this. Don't. I love you. I—"

"I'm sorry, my darling girl. So sorry." Oralie lifted her other leg over the railing and sat on the narrow banister, her feet dangling over the side.

Perry rushed forward, crying out his wife's name. She turned, looked at him and smiled. "I love you," she said, and jumped off the balcony.

Perry grabbed for Oralie, his fingers brushing her silk blouse as he reached for her. But she was too far away.

He gripped the banister. Helpless to stop her descent, he watched his wife fall to the ground. Daphne dropped to her knees and wept. Marla screamed, then fainted dead away. Beatrice ran onto the balcony; she held out her hand to Perry, but didn't touch him. Roarke draped his arm around Cleo's trembling shoulders. Off in the distance an ambulance siren wailed.

CHAPTER SEVENTEEN

DR. IVERSON HAD assured Roarke and Cleo that their baby apparently hadn't suffered any damage from Cleo's accident. Cleo had cried tears of joy, and Roarke had held her in his arms, grateful that the baby was safe. He wished he could share Cleo's joy. He couldn't. And she seemed to understand. Although they continued making love, Cleo never again told him that she loved him, never again asked him to remain in River Bend permanently.

He did stay for Oralie Sutton's funeral. The family kept it a private affair, which everyone agreed was best, considering the circumstances. In the days following Oralie's suicidal jump from the balcony, Daphne clung to her father instead of Hugh. Perry turned to Beatrice for solace and support. And ever reliable and dependable, Cleo made all the arrangements, sparing no expense. Trey Sutton was released on bond in time for the somber event, and after his preliminary hearing, he and Marla stayed with her parents while awaiting his trial.

Roarke had remained at Cleo's side, still her bodyguard, still her husband, until all the loose ends were tied up. He had fulfilled his obligations to her, above and beyond those required in their legalized agreement.

She was two and a half months pregnant, but still as slender as a reed. She hadn't been bothered much with morning sickness and she glowed with good health and vitality. He didn't dare let himself imagine how she would shine with maternal beauty as her pregnancy progressed.

Roarke placed the last item in his suitcase, then snapped the lid shut. He glanced at Cleo, who sat at the writing desk at the foot of the bed. She ripped out the check from her checkbook, pushed back her chair and stood.

She held the check out to him. "This should buy you that farm you want, and take care of all Hope's needs as long as she lives."

"Thanks." He took the check without even glancing at it. He folded it in two, pulled out his wallet and slipped the check inside.

"I won't go down with you," Cleo said. "I'd rather we said our goodbyes here."

"That's fine with me." He reached out and took her hands.

She didn't move in closer; he didn't bring her toward him. They kept a foot of space between them.

"Take care of yourself," she said.

"Yeah, I will. You take care of yourself, too. And the baby."

"We'll be just fine."

"I'm sure you will. You're a strong woman, honey. A survivor." He released her hands, turned around, lifted his suitcase off the bed and walked toward the door.

"Simon?"

He paused, his hand on the doorknob, and looked back over his shoulder.

"Do you want me to let you know when our baby is born?"

He opened the door and stepped into the hall. "No. I don't want to know."

He closed the door behind him. Cleo slumped onto the bed, curled into a ball and cried. She had hoped and prayed something—anything—would change his mind and he would stay with her. It had taken every ounce of courage she possessed not to beg him to stay. But if he didn't love her, if he could never risk loving another woman and child, then nothing she said or did would have kept him at her side for a lifetime.

Cleo laid her hand over her tummy. "We'll be all right without him, my sweet baby. But I'm afraid your father's never going to be all right without us."

IN THE FIRST week after he left Cleo, Roarke set up a fund that would take care of Hope's bills, now and in the future. He made a trip to Florida to see her, but she didn't recognize him. She seldom did. He took her a box of her favorite candy mints and she smiled that childlike smile that always reminded him of Laurie's.

The second week, he visited with his old buddies at Dundee Private Security in Atlanta and haunted a few nightspots with Gabriel Hawk and Morgan Kane. He got rip-roaring drunk and suffered a hell of a hangover.

The next night, he picked up a bosomy, petite redhead in a bar and took her back to his apartment. Before he got her halfway undressed, he called her "Cleo Belle." He apologized, gave the lady cab fare and sent her packing.

The third week he hired a real estate agent and started searching for a small farm, anywhere in the South. He told himself that time would take care of everything. That given enough time, he'd forget the way Cleo laughed. The way she walked and talked. The way she clung to him, calling out his name when he pleasured her. The way she made him feel when they were together. The fact that she was carrying his child.

Beatrice called him to tell him that Trey had been sentenced to ten years, a split sentence—five years in prison, five on probation. Cleo had testified in his defense.

"Cleo's well," Beatrice said. "She's gained three pounds. But I worry that she's working too hard. She practically lives at the plant since you left."

The fourth week, his agent showed him pictures of six different properties. One in particular caught his eye. It was a forty-acre spread in Franklin County, about twenty-five miles outside River Bend, in a rural community called Laurie Falls. His heart skipped a beat when he read the name. Laurie Falls.

The fifth week, he bought the farm at Laurie Falls, packed his meager belongings and drove straight through to Alabama.

The sixth week, he picked up the newly installed telephone in his den and called his wife.

"I DON'T SEE why you have to move out." Beatrice followed Cleo as she buzzed around the kitchen, preparing herself a sandwich for lunch. "What with Trey in prison and Daphne off in Europe, and Marla back home with her parents, if you leave, whatever will Perry and I do but rattle around all alone in this big house?"

"I'd think you two would enjoy having the house to yourselves and the chance to be alone." Cleo took an enormous bite out of her sandwich. In the past couple of weeks, her appetite had surged out of control. She went to bed hungry and woke up hungry. She wondered sometimes if she was eating for more than two, but Dr. Tanner assured her that she wasn't having twins.

"But buying a house and moving out on your own when you're four months pregnant seems a bit foolhardy to me."

"If Daphne can break her engagement to Hugh and move to Europe in search of a new life, then why can't

I simply move across town and start over again? I want to give my baby and me a fresh start, away from all the memories this house holds. Good memories, and bad."

"I think you should go to Atlanta and tell Simon Roarke that he's damn well going to live up to his responsibilities as your husband and the father of your baby." Beatrice opened the refrigerator door, removed a bottled fruit drink and unscrewed the lid.

"I've been telling her to do just that for weeks now," Pearl said. "But she's too stubborn, too filled with McNamara pride, to go after her man. She reminds me of you sometimes, Bea."

"Are you implying something, Pearl?" Beatrice asked. "I wish you'd just say what you have to say and stop beating around the bush."

"All right." Pearl pointed a meaty finger at Cleo. "Go to Atlanta and get Mr. Roarke. Do whatever you have to do, but convince him that you're not letting him go. I don't think it would take much convincing. After all, he's been gone six weeks and he hasn't done a thing about getting a divorce, has he?"

"Pearl is absolutely right!" Beatrice took a sip of her drink.

"And you—" Pearl pointed at Beatrice "—you stop twiddling your thumbs while Perry Sutton plays the grieving widower. You've waited nearly thirty-five years for that man. Why wait any longer?"

Beatrice gasped. "My heavens, Pearl. Oralie hasn't been gone two months yet."

"What difference does it make how long she's been gone? Dead is dead. She ain't going to be no deader two years from now."

"Oh, hush up. You say the most outrageous things and still call yourself a good Christian woman."

The ringing telephone interrupted any reply Pearl might have made. She wiped her hands on her apron and lifted the receiver from the wall phone.

"McNamara and Sutton residence," Pearl said.

"Hello, Pearl, my love, how are you?" Roarke asked.

"I'm fine. And you?"

"Fine," he said. "Finer than I've ever been in my life."

"Well, I'm glad to hear it. It's about time you were coming to your senses. Did you want to speak to someone other than me?"

"Is Cleo there?"

"She might be."

Cleo and Beatrice stared at Pearl. Cleo mouthed the question "Who is it?"

"Before I let her talk to you, I want to know exactly what you're going to say," Pearl told Roarke.

"I'm going to tell her that I'm not giving her a divorce. Not now. Not ever."

"Hold on just a minute." Pearl held out the telephone toward Cleo. "It's for you. Some man who says he's your husband."

"Simon?" Cleo almost strangled on a piece of bread that had lodged in her throat. She grabbed Beatrice's drink out of her hand and took a hefty swallow.

Walking across the kitchen, she stared at the telephone in Pearl's hand as if it were a live snake. She hesitated when Pearl tried to give her the phone.

"This is the call you've been waiting on, girl. Take it."

Cleo grasped the telephone. "Hello."

"Cleo, I want you to drive out to Laurie Falls today and meet me," Roarke said. "I'll give you the directions. Will you come?"

"Laurie Falls? Over in Franklin County? What are you doing there?"

"I'm living on my farm," he said. "It's not big. Just forty acres, and the house needs some work. But I like the place. I want you to see it."

"You're going to live in Laurie Falls? But—but that's only twenty miles or so from here."

"Yeah, I know. That'll make it convenient for you to visit Aunt Beatrice and Pearl whenever you want, and it won't be too long a drive back and forth to work."

Cleo wondered if she was dreaming, if any minute now her alarm clock would ring and she'd wake alone in her bed. She held the phone with white-knuckled fierceness.

"Are you all right, Cleo Belle?" Pearl asked.

"Is that Simon on the phone?" Beatrice glanced from an unresponsive Cleo to Pearl.

"Cleo, honey, did you hear me? Will you come out to the farm today? We need to talk," Roarke said.

"Yes, you're right. We need to talk." Cleo sucked in her breath. "Give me the directions to your farm."

AN HOUR LATER, Cleo drove her Jaguar up in front of a two-story frame house badly in need of paint. Simon Roarke stood on the wide, wooden porch. He looked wonderful in his faded, worn jeans and cotton shirt. When he walked toward the driveway, the first thing she noticed was that he wasn't wearing a gun. By the time she opened the car door, Roarke was there to meet her.

"Thanks for coming," he said.

"I don't understand." She closed the door and walked away from the car and toward the house. "Why did you buy a farm so close to River Bend, so close to me and... and my baby?"

"Our baby."

She snapped her head around and stared at him. "What did you say?"

"I said *our* baby. That is, if you're willing to stay married to an idiot like me and allow me to help you raise our child." He looked at her with a mixture of hope and pleading in his eyes.

"You've changed your mind? Six weeks away from me and you suddenly change your mind? What happened? Did you get an attack of conscience and decide that you should be a part of your child's life after all?"

"I want to be a part of your life, Cleo." He held out his hand to her. "I want us to stay married and build a life together. Here. On this farm."

She didn't take his hand, didn't even look at it. "Why, Simon? Six weeks ago, you couldn't wait to get away from me and this—" she laid a protective hand over her stomach "—child. What changed your mind?"

"You're not going to make this easy for me, are you?"

"Why should I? You certainly didn't make things easy for me when you left me."

"Will it help if I get down on my knees and beg?" He bent down on both knees and folded his hands together in front of him. "Marry me, Cleo. Marry me for real this time."

Her lips twitched with an almost smile. "It seemed pretty real to me the first time," she said. "Besides, we're still married, as far as I know. Unless you got a divorce and forgot to tell me."

Roarke grabbed her hands. "All right, if the first time was good enough for you, it's good enough for me." Still holding her hands, he rose to his feet. "So when can you move in? Today, I hope."

"I can't just move in here with you." Cleo tugged on her hands, but Roarke held tight. "I have no idea what's happened to you. Why you—"

He silenced her with a kiss. She struggled to get away

from him. The harder she fought his embrace, the harder he kissed her. When he finally let her come up for air, he looked into her moss-green eyes and smiled.

"I love you, Cleo. That's what happened to me these past six weeks. I found out that I love you and that without you, I don't have a life."

"Oh, Simon." Tears gathered in her eyes. "You love me? You really love me?"

"With all my heart and soul." He lifted her into his arms and walked toward the house. "Can you ever forgive me for being such a jerk? I couldn't let go of the past, of all my old hurts. I was afraid to love you, afraid to reach out and grab the happiness you offered. But with every passing week we were apart, I realized that I was more afraid to go on living without you."

"Are you sure?" she asked.

"Yeah, honey, I'm sure," he said. "When the real estate agent gave me pictures of this house, in Laurie Falls, so close to River Bend, I knew we were meant to be together here. You. Me. And our baby."

He carried her into the house, through the empty living room and down the hall. He kicked open the door to the only furnished room in the house. A huge, antique brass bed dominated the room. Roarke laid his wife on the bed and came down beside her.

She draped her arms around his neck. "I love you so much, Simon. And I've missed you."

"Ah, Cleo Belle, I've missed you like crazy."

He started to kiss her again, but Cleo turned her head to one side.

"Simon?"

"Yes?"

"How do you feel about the baby? I have to know."

"I'm scared, honey. I messed up real bad at this father

business the first time around and my little girl died. I don't want to ever fail this child." He laid his hand lovingly on Cleo's stomach. "You're going to have to help me. I won't ever be able to forget Laurie, and I'll never completely forgive myself for what happened to her. But maybe, if I'm a good father to our baby, I can somehow redeem myself."

"I'm giving you a son," she said. "I had the ultrasound done yesterday. He's perfect in every way and—"

Roarke kissed her again, and within minutes they lay naked atop the new beige sheets. They made love with a fast, furious frenzy the first time. But the second time they didn't hurry, as they learned each other all over again, pleasuring each other with slow, tormenting deliberation.

When the sun went down, they raided the refrigerator, the only appliance in the enormous farmhouse kitchen. And after they dined on milk and cereal, they returned to their bedroom and made love again.

At dawn, Roarke woke Cleo, wrapped her in the top sheet and carried her out onto the front porch. He sat down in the wooden rocker and held her in his lap. She laid her head on his shoulder and kissed the side of his neck.

"I wanted us to share the sunrise together on our first morning here at our new home."

"I love you, Simon Roarke."

"And I love you, my darling Cleo Belle."

EPILOGUE

SITTING IN A wooden rocking chair on his front porch, Simon Roarke watched his sons, six-year-old Johnny and three-year-old Jimmy, frolicking in the front yard with the family's Irish setters, Brady and Corey. The sun lay on the western horizon like a scoop of orange sherbet, the edges melting into a pool of luscious colors. The evening breeze cooled the summertime heat, but did little to lessen the humidity.

Cleo walked out onto the porch, carrying two glasses of lemonade. She handed one to her husband, then sat down beside him in a matching chair. Rocking slowly, she sipped the cool, tart liquid.

Roarke leaned over and kissed her. She sighed, deep in her throat. "What was that for?" she asked.

"That's for being the most wonderful woman in the world and making me the happiest man alive," he said.

Cleo smiled broadly, and for one split second Roarke's heart stopped beating. Every time he looked at his wife, she took his breath away. Every time he touched her, he wanted to make love to her. And every time he thought about how much she'd given him, he ached inside with a pleasure almost too great to bear.

In the seven years since their hasty marriage of convenience, Roarke had gone from being a lonely, cynical man who lived his life on the edge, to a contented family man, a gentleman farmer living the good life that had once been only a dream for him.

"Who've you been talking to on the phone for so long?" he asked.

"Aunt Beatrice for a while, and then Pearl."

"What great news did those two have?"

"It seems Daphne got married again. To a European count this time."

"What does this make—husband number four or five?"

"Four, I think," Cleo said. "And Marla is pregnant. Isn't that wonderful? I think she and Trey are making a good life for themselves now that Trey's working at McNamara's again and they're living back at the house with Aunt Beatrice and Uncle Perry."

"I agree, honey. I never thought Trey would change. But I have to admit that he's a different man from the one who tried to sabotage McNamara's."

"I'm glad he accepted Uncle Perry's marriage to Aunt Beatrice. I was afraid he and Daphne would both create problems."

"Daphne can't cause too many problems thousands of miles away, and I don't think you have to worry about Trey anymore."

"Oh, Simon!" Cleo gasped.

"What's wrong?" he asked anxiously, then relaxed when she smiled at him.

Laughing, she took the glass out of his hand and set her glass and his on the small, wooden table at her side. She reached out, grasped his hand and laid it over her protruding belly.

He grinned when he felt his child move inside Cleo. "She's got some kick, hasn't she? She's going to be a feisty little gal, just like her mama."

"Only two more months to wait for Miss Sara Ann

Roarke to make her debut." Sighing contentedly as Simon rubbed her tummy, Cleo looked at her strong, healthy sons, both of them tall and big for their age. She knew they would grow to be large, handsome men like their father.

Johnny, their eldest, named after his paternal grandfather, was the spitting image of Simon, except for his auburn hair. Brown-haired Jimmy, their younger son, named after Cleo's dad, took after the McNamaras, with his fine, delicate features and his striking green eyes. They were perfect children at moments like this, and normal little heathens as a general rule.

Cleo was glad that their first two children had been boys. Simon would have had a more difficult time becoming a father again if they'd had a daughter the first time. Losing Laurie would always be a sorrow in Simon's soul, but realizing what a good father he was to the boys had helped him forgive himself and ease some of the guilt he'd always feel over his daughter's death. Now, after so many painful years of remorse and regret, he was ready to open his heart and love a new daughter. Sara Ann could never replace Laurie, but she would bring her father the joy only a little girl could give him.

Simon and Cleo were happier than either had once thought possible. From their deep and passionate love, they had created three children and shared a marriage that would last a lifetime.

* * * * *

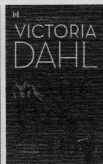

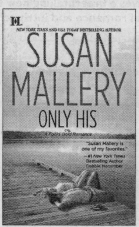

REQUEST YOUR
FREE BOOKS!

2 FREE NOVELS
FROM THE SUSPENSE COLLECTION
PLUS 2 FREE GIFTS!

YES! Please send me 2 FREE novels from the Suspense Collection and my 2 FREE gifts (gifts are worth about $10). After receiving them, if I don't wish to receive any more books, I can return the shipping statement marked "cancel." If I don't cancel, I will receive 4 brand-new novels every month and be billed just $5.99 per book in the U.S. or $6.49 per book in Canada. That's a saving of at least 25% off the cover price. It's quite a bargain! Shipping and handling is just 50¢ per book in the U.S. and 75¢ per book in Canada.* I understand that accepting the 2 free books and gifts places me under no obligation to buy anything. I can always return a shipment and cancel at any time. Even if I never buy another book, the two free books and gifts are mine to keep forever.

191/391 MDN FEME

Name	(PLEASE PRINT)
Address	Apt. #
City	State/Prov.	Zip/Postal Code

Signature (if under 18, a parent or guardian must sign)

Mail to the **Reader Service:**
IN U.S.A.: P.O. Box 1867, Buffalo, NY 14240-1867
IN CANADA: P.O. Box 609, Fort Erie, Ontario L2A 5X3

Not valid for current subscribers to the Suspense Collection
or the Romance/Suspense Collection.

Want to try two free books from another line?
Call 1-800-873-8635 or visit www.ReaderService.com.

* Terms and prices subject to change without notice. Prices do not include applicable taxes. Sales tax applicable in N.Y. Canadian residents will be charged applicable taxes. Offer not valid in Quebec. This offer is limited to one order per household. All orders subject to credit approval. Credit or debit balances in a customer's account(s) may be offset by any other outstanding balance owed by or to the customer. Please allow 4 to 6 weeks for delivery. Offer available while quantities last.

Your Privacy—The Reader Service is committed to protecting your privacy. Our Privacy Policy is available online at www.ReaderService.com or upon request from the Reader Service.

We make a portion of our mailing list available to reputable third parties that offer products we believe may interest you. If you prefer that we not exchange your name with third parties, or if you wish to clarify or modify your communication preferences, please visit us at www.ReaderService.com/consumerschoice or write to us at Reader Service Preference Service, P.O. Box 9062, Buffalo, NY 14269. Include your complete name and address.

BEVERLY BARTON

77503 WITNESS	___ $7.99 U.S.	___ $9.99 CAN.
77447 WORTH DYING FOR	___ $7.99 U.S.	___ $9.99 CAN.

(limited quantities available)

TOTAL AMOUNT $ _____
POSTAGE & HANDLING $ _____
($1.00 FOR 1 BOOK, 50¢ for each additional)
APPLICABLE TAXES* $ _____
TOTAL PAYABLE $ _____

(check or money order—please do not send cash)

To order, complete this form and send it, along with a check or money order for the total above, payable to HQN Books, to: **In the U.S.:** 3010 Walden Avenue, P.O. Box 9077, Buffalo, NY 14269-9077; **In Canada:** P.O. Box 636, Fort Erie, Ontario, L2A 5X3.

Name: _____
Address: _____ City: _____
State/Prov.: _____ Zip/Postal Code: _____
Account Number (if applicable): _____

075 CSAS

*New York residents remit applicable sales taxes.
*Canadian residents remit applicable GST and provincial taxes.

PHBB1011BL